Taking to the Skies

June - August 1941

A Misfit Squadron Novel

Simon Brading

YORKSHIRE

JUNE 1941

1

'Leader, this is Badger Four. Target acquired. Descending and beginning my run.'

Today's target was one of the hardest he'd ever had to hit. Tucked in tight behind a line of trees, with the houses of a village on one side and the buildings of a farm on the other, the only way to hit it properly without putting civilians at risk was to go over the trees. It meant a sharp banking climb, followed immediately by a steep dive to get back down on the deck. It was going to be very tricky, but it was nothing he hadn't trained for. Or done dozens of times before, for that matter.

'Arming payload.'

He reached forward to flick up the trigger guard protecting the switch on the instrument panel, the first in a row of four, but then had to put his hand back on the throttle as the line of trees came racing towards him.

He could see the target on the other side of the trees, ahead of him still but approaching fast, and he kept half an eye on it, judging his moment. When it was almost level he pulled the stick sharply back and to the side, dancing on the rudder pedals to stop himself from sliding straight into the trees. He rolled, going completely inverted over the tops of the trees, the branches reaching out for him less than a foot from the canopy. *Plenty of room.* He completed the roll and dived, cutting back on the throttle to stop himself powering into the ground, but then immediately brought the stick back into his lap. He levelled off smoothly, ten feet from the ground and instantly flicked the switch.

'Bombs away!'

The switch activated the pump and opened the valve on the number one tank under the left wing of his aircraft, forcing the liquid from the nozzles mounted along the boom hanging behind the undercarriage. He kept the aircraft exactly level and exactly ten feet from the ground until the end of the field, then flicked the switch off and pulled up.

'Boom!' he said under his breath.

He leaned out of the open cockpit to look back and watched the mist settling on the crops. It looked like a nice even spread. As always.

'Leader, this is Four. Target destroyed. One down, three to go.'

Tayler smiled and banked sharply around, preparing for another "bombing run".

Rob Sherborne shaded his eyes and watched the aircraft nearing the airfield. A patchy and much repaired green biplane put together from a cheap kit, it was nevertheless the pride and joy of his best friend, Tayler Oakley, who called it "Finch" and had used it to secure the crop spraying contracts for every farm within twenty miles. The aircraft turned onto the downwind leg of the circuit - or was it the upwind leg? He could never remember - and Tay saw him and waved. Rob lifted his hand in answer, but dropped it quickly; he never liked to distract Tay when he was landing or look like he was paying him too much attention, just in case he tried to show off and did something beyond the capabilities of his aircraft. As it was, he received an overly violent wing waggle that caused the aircraft to drop alarmingly and disappear from sight into the trees bordering the airfield. It reappeared after a few seconds, though, and Rob released the breath he'd been holding, realising that it had just been an optical illusion and his friend wasn't going to end up in pieces on his last day as a civilian.

A month ago, Tayler had turned eighteen and Rob, who had turned eighteen a few months before, had gone to the Royal Aviator Corps recruitment office with him the very next day to sign up. The papers had taken a while to go through, but finally they had been told to report to the bus station in Leeds from where they would be taken to RAC training facilities in Wales.

Being a pilot in the RAC had been a dream of Tay's for about a decade and, understandably, he was excited and eager to get going. Rob wasn't. He knew how to fly - Tay had taught him in Finch - but the RAC had never been his dream. However, the two of them had done everything together that two boys from neighbouring families, born within a few months of each other, could do, so signing up with him had seemed like the right thing. There was no reason to believe that they would be posted to the same squadron, of course, or even that they'd be flying the same make or type of aircraft, or that Rob would be flying at all and wouldn't be assigned to ground crew, but at least they would train together. That would take months and by that time the war might even be over and they could just come home.

Finch was on final approach now, so Rob climbed off his springcycle and wandered across the grass to the wooden shed where Tay stored and maintained the aircraft. He watched his friend stick a perfect landing, then swing the aircraft off the field and taxi a little too fast for comfort, in a direct line to the shed, ignoring the marked out taxiways. As he usually did. There was nobody around to bring him up on his poor etiquette, though; there was nobody in the tiny control booth and nobody actually running the airfield. The local flying club that was based there currently only had four members: two of them were currently on active service in the RAC; one had crashed his aircraft a couple of years previously and hadn't bothered to repair it; and the fourth, now eighty, hadn't flown for half a decade. The taxiways were only still marked out because the groundskeeper had been told to do so when he'd started work twenty years ago, when the airfield had seen a fair amount of traffic, and had never been told to stop.

Tayler swung the aircraft around just in front of the shed and shut down the spring before opening the little gate on the side of the cockpit and climbing out onto the wing. He patted the fuselage affectionately, then jumped down and came towards Rob with a big grin on his face.

He halted, stamping his feet comically, then saluted. 'Mission accomplished, sah!'

'Congratulations.' Rob said dryly. 'That'll teach those pesky Prussian pests to mess with our crops!'

Tayler laughed and pointed his thumb over his shoulder. 'Do you want to take her up? There's plenty left in the spring.'

Rob shook his head. 'No, thank you. I'm sure I'll have my fill of flying in Wales.'

'You can never have too much flying! And it's been too long since you took her up. You don't want the instructors thinking you don't know what you're doing.'

Rob shrugged noncommittally.

'Suit yourself,' Tayler said. 'Come on, then, let's get her into hibernation.'

Tayler had asked Rob to help him put Finch in storage and it took them a few hours, not so much because there was a lot to do, but because the tools at their disposal weren't exactly the best and they had to pretty much do everything by hand, including fully easing the spring with a hand key and flushing the sprayer system with buckets filled at the airfield's standpipe. Eventually, though, they were done and Tayler got onto the springcycle behind Rob and they raced the mile and a half down the country lane to the village.

Their families had laid on a goodbye lunch for them down in the village pub's garden and by the time they'd washed and put on their Sunday best everyone was already there waiting for them. They ate their fill, had what, to their parents' knowledge anyway, was their first taste of alcohol, and devoured the cake Rob's mother had made them with real chocolate icing, bought at great cost from a confectioners in Leeds. After that, when the sun was going down and the younger children had been sent home, they moved inside. Tayler's father, who'd been a vaudeville musician before the war and had come home from fighting in the Great War with his musical talents intact but minus one leg, sat at the pub's piano and the real party began.

It was a bittersweet sendoff, as such things always were, with everyone fully aware that it could well be the last time they saw either or both of the boys alive. There was a hint of desperation about the celebrations as well, with everyone trying to seem happy and carefree, but accomplishing quite the opposite. The only ones who seemed remotely themselves were the boys; they had long been resolved to this course of action, knew full well what they were getting into and couldn't wait to be off.

That wasn't to say they didn't take full advantage of the evening.

Tayler, with his wavy light brown hair, blue eyes and ready smile, had always been popular with the girls and certainly had experience, but neither he nor Rob had ever had what could be considered a proper girlfriend. They were, however, two of the most eligible bachelors in the area and a lot of the girls in the village and the surrounding farms were suddenly very sorry to see them go. Rob, who was short and dark and shy and had generally avoided female companionship of any kind, suddenly found himself having his first kiss. And second. And third.

All too soon, though, it was time for last orders and Rob and Tay, who had started the day as boys in the eyes of the village and, to tell the truth, their own as well, staggered home feeling, and having been treated, like men.

They woke at five the next morning, feeling rather worse for wear, and were each fed large breakfasts before catching the bus to the train station in Ilkley, the closest town, to catch the five fifty-seven to Leeds.

2

'Throttle back, lower flaps, lower landing gear...'

The Honourable Benedict Charles Henry Victor Wilberforce frowned in concentration as he turned onto the final leg of his last circuit of the day. To his satisfaction, this one was turning out better than the others he'd attempted that afternoon; he was lined up exactly in the middle of the airfield this time and was at the precise height stipulated in the manual, no more, no less. That didn't mean he could relax yet, though; landing was the most complicated thing you could do in an aircraft - there was a lot to do and think about and a lot could still go wrong.

The airfield came ever closer as he danced on the rudder pedals and flicked the stick back and forth to compensate for the occasional gust of wind, keeping the aircraft aimed directly at a spot twenty yards from the low perimeter fence.

The fence disappeared beneath the nose of the aircraft and then there was just grass in front of him.

'Pull back on the stick, reduce throttle...'

The aircraft slowed and he had to lift its nose above the horizon in order to hold it off the ground, but eventually there was no way it could stay aloft any longer and it sank, touching down exactly where he'd wanted, precisely level with the front door of the mansion. He had misjudged how high he'd been by a foot or two, though, and he winced when the aircraft bounced, but it was only a tiny bounce, a matter of inches, and the aircraft immediately settled back on the ground again.

It was a short taxi to the house and he swung the aircraft around and shut it down before clambering out. He jumped off the wing and jogged up the stone steps that climbed the slight slope to the lawn. A butler was standing at the top of the steps with a glass of champagne on a silver tray and he took it then threw his gloves and helmet down in its place before turning to look back at his aircraft.

A sleek silver monoplane with single a red stripe running down the middle of the fuselage, it was the training version of the Hawking Hound and had two seats, one behind the other, which certainly came in handy when he wanted to impress a girl or take one of his chums up and give them a fright. The Hound was a fighter that had been developed and built in the interwar years and was the immediate predecessor of the Harridan - the fighter that had so successfully defended Britain for the last couple of years. Slightly underpowered when compared to even a Mark I Harridan and not quite as manoeuvrable, it was still the closest thing in performance to a military fighter aircraft that a civilian could buy, which was why he'd insisted his parents buy it, rather than one of the more usual training aircraft on the market; if he wanted to be a fighter pilot and fly Harrys or Spits then this would give him the best chance. His parents hadn't argued and, in all honesty, they probably would have bought him the Hound *and* a trainer if he'd asked, but he hadn't wanted to waste time in something that bore no relation to any of the aircraft he'd be flying on active duty in the Royal Aviator Corps.

He watched the fitters checking it over for a second, then smiled at the man who'd been in the back seat of the aircraft behind him and was only now limping up the last few stairs.

'Well, Johns? That last one was pretty good, what?'

Benedict's instructor, Aviator Lieutenant Arthur Johns RAC (Rtd), was a grizzled man in his late fifties. A Great War veteran, he had been in the RAC at the start of the war and had survived two whole years of intense fighting before being shot down in flames. He had lost his leg in the crash and suffered burns over half of his body, so he walked stiffly with the aid of a cane, but that didn't stop him from doing things in an aircraft that Benedict could only hope to be capable of some day. He had been a good teacher, insofar as Benedict felt confident now that he could handle an aircraft exceedingly well, but he seemed to have run out of things to teach and had begun harping on more and more about wishy-washy stuff like using his intuition and senses and such. Annoyingly, that seemed to be what he was going to say this time as well.

'It was indeed a good landing, Mr Wilberforce, near perfect, in fact, but there is more to flying than that. Even though you have nearly six hundred hours logged, you're still concentrating far too much on the mechanics of what you're doing rather than letting yourself relax into it. Flying is about feelings and instinct, it's about the aircraft being an extension of your body and not something you have to consciously control.' Johns looked for some sign of understanding in the boy's eyes, but, as always, there was none, just impatience and exasperation. He knew he had to try one last time, though, before the boy went off and got himself killed. 'If you want to be a great pilot and not just a good one then you must work on that. And if you want to survive once you get into combat, then you can't just be worrying about when to push what pedals and levers.'

Benedict waved the advice away, as he had so many times before. 'I'm sure all that will come when I have a few hundred more hours logged. Speaking of which...'

'Here you are, sir.' Johns said resignedly, knowing that it was useless to insist. He held out an expensive black leather book, a pilot's logbook, that he'd already filled in with the times of the young lord's flight whilst they were taxiing.

Benedict scanned it quickly, glancing at his chronograph to make sure the times were correct, then signed it without filling in any observations and handed it back.

'Jolly good!' He drained the glass of champagne, handed it off to the butler, then stomped into the house without another word and into his ready room - a converted cloak room next to the door where he could admire his framed pilot's degree certificate and the many trophies he'd won in local flying competitions while he dressed and waited for his fitters to bring his aircraft up from the hangar. He removed his flightsuit, tailored for him personally by Henry Johnson of Johnson's of Bond Street, and tossed it over the back of his armchair. It was a shame he couldn't take it with him; it would certainly help to make him stand out from the riffraff, but, while the RAC had now relaxed their archaic regulations prohibiting personal flightsuits, cadets still had to wear the hideous and almost completely useless uniform flightsuits. His parents would have it sent to him as soon as he graduated and in the meantime the maids would make sure it was taken care of.

He slipped on his dressing gown and trotted up the stairs to his rooms. After a quick wash, he dressed in his best suit, also from Bond

Street, then came back down to find his mother and father waiting for him in the drawing room.

His parents were dressed in their finery, ready to receive the guests who were coming that evening for Benedict's farewell party, her mother in evening wear and jewels, his father in his RAC dress uniform.

Squadron Leader Lord Oscar William Percival Victor Wilberforce, Viscount Harrogate, was a small man, with thinning hair and glasses. He wasn't a pilot, had never flown in an aircraft, in fact, and had no desire to do so, but when his son had expressed his interest in becoming a pilot in the RAC he had done everything he could to further that ambition. That had included not only buying the best aircraft and finding the best instructor available, but also joining the RAC as a volunteer and obtaining a part-time position as an administrator at the nearest airbase as a way of gaining access to high-ranking officers who could accelerate his son's career.

The viscountess, Beatrice, his mother, was a vacuous socialite who had been selected for her looks and breeding rather than for her wit and intelligence and barely a day went by when Benedict didn't count himself fortunate to have received his brains from his father and looks from his mother and not the other way around, like so many in the world's nobility. He had learnt at a very early age not to look for love from her since having him had merely been the fulfilment of her duty to the family, not something that she herself had desired. She spent her time riding, mostly to neighbouring estates in order to socialise with the ladies of those houses, and doing whatever else it was that ladies of her standing did.

They made a rather odd pair, but somehow they worked together and were as supportive of him as he could ask.

Benedict stood in front of them and gave them the merest of bows. 'Father. Mother.'

'I saw your circuits and bumps, Benedict,' his father said. 'Good show.'

'Yes,' his mother added, smiling vacantly.

'Thank you, sir.'

'You are ready, then?' the Viscount asked.

'I believe so.' Benedict smiled. 'I have my bags packed, my RAC-approved haircut and my logbook to prove my proficiency.'

'Jolly good.'

There was an uncomfortable silence wherein all parties searched for something more to say, but it was, as was usually the case when the family were together without any outside influences, a failure.

'Well,' Viscount Harrogate said eventually. 'The guests should be arriving soon. Sky Vice-Marshal Wymark, the commander of the local fighter group, will be here and Sir Douglas Pewtall has promised to fly up if he can get away from Whitehall. Unfortunately, though, the war minister sends his regrets.'

'I suppose that was only to be expected,' said Benedict as graciously as he could under the circumstances.

'Quite; he is a very busy man. But at least this way we can steer the conversation away from politics and more towards the RAC and your prospects.'

The butler entered the room and Viscount Harrogate looked at him over Benedict's shoulder.

'The guests have arrived, my Lord.'

'Thank you, Cuthbert,' he nodded, then smiled at Benedict. 'Come, let us see about your future.'

The dinner was a pleasant affair, with some of his father's best wines brought out for the occasion. The menu comprised of some of Benedict's favourite foods, most of which, he was assured, would not be available until he had got his wings and an acting commission and was dining in the officers' mess. The conversation was equally interesting, with his father, Vice-Marshal Wymark and Sir Douglas Pewtall, when he showed up during the second course, at his end of the table.

His father had tried many times to convince the authorities that Benedict didn't need to go through RAC training, that his piloting skills were sufficiently good for him to go straight into a fighter squadron, but he'd been denied every time. That didn't stop him giving it one last try, but Sir Douglas wouldn't be persuaded and Benedict was delivered at a few minutes before seven the next morning to the bus station in Leeds, where he boarded a bus for the journey to Wales along with the other recruits from the area.

3

'You did *what*?!?' Eleanor's father screamed, his face inches from hers, spraying her with saliva, the stench of cheap beer washing over her.

'I joined up,' she answered defiantly, 'I'm eighteen, I...'

For a man who had been drunk all day every day for the last seven years, he could still move quickly and she didn't see the hand that struck the side of her face coming. Her head was spun around with the force of it and she staggered back a step, but this time, unlike every other time her father had struck her, she didn't tear up or cower from him. Instead, she straightened back up, set her jaw and glared at him defiantly.

Geoff Perkins had worked as a builder for eighteen years until, only one month after his wife, Ellie's mother, had died, an accident, which some said had been caused by his own drunkenness, had put him on an invalid's pension. He was a big man and still an imposing figure even now, a decade later, although the vast majority of his muscles had run to fat. He had a good five inches on her and more than ten stone, but something in her eyes made him lower the hand he'd raised to strike her again and retreat a step.

'Fine,' he said, 'go! Throw away your life! But don't you dare ever come back; you're not welcome here anymore!'

'Don't worry, I won't.'

Eleanor spun on her heel and stomped from the room. She went up the stairs to her bedroom and grabbed her suitcase from under the bed.

She owned very little in the way of clothes and what she did have had been washed so many times they were threadbare and almost transparent and should have been replaced long ago. She assumed the RAC would issue her with uniforms, though, so she took just whatever she couldn't do without and instead filled the case with the things that were important to her. Her mother's jewellery was long gone, sold for the upkeep of the house and to keep her father supplied with alcohol, but she'd managed to hide her mother's combs and brushes from him and there were a few photographs and keepsakes.

Less than five minutes later she came back down and deposited her suitcase at the front door before going to the kitchen. She made herself a doorstep sandwich and wrapped it in a clean tea towel along with a few apples and a paring knife. Then, as an afterthought she made another sandwich and put it on a plate on the table. She wiped the work surface down and made sure the room was spotless before going back down the hall to her suitcase.

On the way, she passed the sitting room. Her father was curled up in his armchair, crying. He saw her and whined. 'Who's going to take care of me?'

She could have said many things, none of them nice, but she opted instead to ignore him and just put on her hat and coat and stepped into her shoes, then picked up her suitcase and went out. She walked on the cracked flagstones of the path through the front garden, past the vegetable garden she'd planted and maintained and the apple tree with her's and her parents' initials carved into it.

She stopped at the gate and looked back at the house. It was in a bad state, with broken tiles on the roof, crumbling bricks and flaking paint, all damage that would have been easy enough to repair for her father if he'd cared enough to do it.

It had been a happy home once. Perhaps, it might be again.

Not for her, though.

Eleanor had planned to walk the ten miles to Leeds, but an army lorry delivering munitions to a base just outside the city stopped for her and gave her a lift most of the way. She got to the bus station just as the sun was going down and sat on a bench to watch the people coming and going as she ate. Her own bus didn't leave until seven the next day so she walked around the city for a while, then, when she got tired, she curled up under a bush in one of the parks with her hand wrapped around the handle of the paring knife and tried to sleep.

She was unable to do more than doze fitfully, though, and at the first sign of the world getting lighter she got up and went back to the bus station where she tidied herself up in the bathroom before joining the other recruits waiting for the bus that would take them to their new lives.

RAC DRUID
BASIC TRAINING

JUNE - JULY 1941

4

The four recruits being picked up from Leeds were met by a surly aviator sergeant, who asked them their names and checked them off a list but refused to answer any questions. He marched them over to a bus waiting on the other side of the station and saw them aboard, where they joined four other recruits who had come from further afield. He gave the driver, an airman who didn't look much older than the recruits, a curt nod, then got off, shut the door, and hurried away, probably for breakfast.

It was more than one hundred miles to the RAC training facilities in Wales and the journey took a miserable four hours. It was an old bus, with bad springs, uncomfortable wooden bench seats and a hydrogen engine so loud that it was impossible to talk at a normal volume, so the eight passengers gave up trying after a shouted exchange of names and the barest of details.

The last hour or so was along winding country roads, going up and down the Welsh hills with rain pouring down outside and the windows steaming up so much that they couldn't be seen through. It was still raining when they arrived and another aviator sergeant, this one in a long rain jacket, got on.

'Off! Everyone off!' he shouted. 'Come on, move it!'

They grabbed their bags and scrambled to get off the bus only to be accosted again as soon as they stepped down, by an airwoman this time.

'Run!' she yelled at each of them, pointing towards the open door of a green-painted stone building about ten yards away, down a gravel path.

Another airwoman was in that doorway and as they ran past her, bent double against the pouring rain, she shouted at them as well. 'Come on, get in here! Find a seat and land on it, recruits!'

Aviator Sergeant Frank Smedley stepped down from the bus and sighed as he watched the last of the recruits who'd be his responsibility for the next couple of weeks stagger towards the door. A bedraggled young woman, she was wearing completely inadequate clothing for the weather and, needless to say, was drenched by the time she got inside.

He shook his head as he strode down the path towards the door; it didn't exactly inspire confidence in the quality of recruits if they didn't have the sense to dress for the Welsh weather and, not for the first time, he wished that the RAC hadn't accelerated the training of new recruits. However, with an invasion fleet across the channel, there wasn't any time to spare and if any of them had the potential to be fighter pilots then they were needed right away. Otherwise they wouldn't be needed at all because they'd all be speaking German before they got their wings.

He stood just outside the doorway and looked in at the young men and women dripping all over the linoleum floor of the briefing room. They occupied only eight of the twenty-four seats, whereas most recruit groups filled the room. A disappointingly small group. He only hoped that at least one of them would be worth the trouble he and his team would be going to for them.

He marched into the room, removing his hat precisely when he crossed the threshold and tucking it under his arm.

'Silence!' he glared at them as he stomped to the front of the room, daring them to make the merest of sounds. There was a small podium there, but he stood in front of it, uncomfortably close to them, rather than allow them to settle in and relax.

'Right, then, you sorry looking lot. The next person through that door is going to be an officer. Aviator Lieutenant Wallington. You will stand when I tell you to and you will stand straight! Otherwise I will have you practising it outside until either the rain stops or you drown! When I tell you, and not before, you will sit back down and you will sit straight and listen to what he has to say.' He looked around the room, meeting the eyes of each of the recruits in turn.

'You will find that life is very simple here. People like me tell people like you what to do and you do it. If you manage to get that through your thick heads then nothing will go wrong. If you don't, then bad things may happen. Especially if you are in the air, because then the only thing left to do will be to write a letter to your parents.' He let that sink in for a moment, then went back to the door. He put his hat back on, then went back outside and stood motionless in the rain, trying to keep the smile off his face; getting to scare recruits was one of his favourite perks of the job.

Eleanor had started shivering and couldn't stop. When the other recruits had seen that it was raining they'd all dug around in their bags and pulled out raincoats and protective hats, but she'd had nothing to pull out. She was already wearing her only coat and her one hat was made of felt and would just disintegrate if she wore it. As a consequence she wasn't just wet after the run to the briefing room, but soaked through, even down to her underwear, and she was sitting in a puddle of water that her body was failing to warm very much. She crossed her arms and hugged them tightly to herself in a desperate attempt to keep warm, but otherwise held as still as she could. She didn't want to show any weakness, not in front of her fellow recruits, who she was sure were already looking at her as if she didn't belong, and especially not in front of the instructors; she didn't want to give them any excuse to throw her out, didn't want to be forced to choose between going home with her tail between her legs or find some way of surviving on her own.

Benedict grimaced and shifted in his seat to ease the pressure on parts of his anatomy that hadn't been so abused since his first years at Eton. He could have been chauffeured up in comfort in the family autocar, or flown his Hound and been here in minutes, but he'd been told that he couldn't. "Secrecy" had been the official reason, but Benedict suspected it was more about the RAC not showing favouritism, or making sure that the other recruits were on an equal footing with him, or some such rot. He *wasn't* on an equal footing, though, and he never would be; he was better prepared than every single one of them and he would soon prove it.

Tayler and Rob had taken seats next to each other at the back of the small group, but, while Rob had his eyes fixed on the sergeant standing in the rain and was nervously biting his lip, Tay slouched slightly in his chair and gazed around at their fellow recruits.

There were four boys and four girls in total, counting him and Rob. Three of the girls were country types, if their rough clothing was anything to go by. Farmer's daughters, most likely. The fourth girl and one of the boys were obviously townies - the boy in a dark suit and the girl with a smart calf length skirt and jacket number. The last boy was obviously a toff, judging by the expensive looking Mackintosh draped over the back of the seat next to him and the permanent sneer on his face, and Tayler took an instant dislike to him.

Most of the others were sitting stiffly, terrified, by the looks of things, unsure what was going on and unused to being shouted at and ordered around. The only ones who weren't were the toff, of course, who looked as if he found everything oh so very amusing, and one of the country girls, who had her arms crossed and a determined look on her face.

Tayler smiled at the sight, glad that at least one of his companions had some backbone, but then frowned. He shifted in his seat, leaning forward to get a better look at her face, not because she was attractive, although she was, with a smooth pale complexion, extremely kissable lips and long dark hair that was shining like silk, but because she was shivering and those lovely lips were rapidly turning blue. He took in her old and much-repaired clothing and the lightweight jacket that had done nothing to protect her from the rain and realised that she was soaked through and wasn't warming up at all. She was in real danger of getting ill and he steeled himself to break the silence and say something, but, before he could, an officer appeared in the doorway and he was surging to his feet with everyone else.

The officer returned the aviator sergeant's salute, then entered the room, stopping to remove his hat just inside, once he was out of the rain.

'At ease,' he said, before turning to go to the podium.

'Sit!' The sergeant bellowed, making Tayler, and most of the other recruits, jump, even as their legs gave way beneath them and their behinds hit the chairs. The sergeant grinned in satisfaction, then closed the door, shutting off much of the noise of the rain.

The officer tossed his sopping wet hat on the podium, then turned to face the room. He was old, in his sixties or maybe seventies, with only a ring of grey hair around the back of his head and liver spots covering his bare scalp. There was no indication in his expression as to whether he liked what he saw or not, but to Tayler he seemed tired, or perhaps resigned.

Aviator Lieutenant Rupert Wallington surveyed his new charges. He always took a moment just to look at them every time a new group came in, seeing if he could spot the ones that would be special. The Gwen Stone or Chastity Arrowsmith among them. He never could. This lot didn't look like much, but, then again, none of the new recruits ever did. Not until they'd gotten the uniform on and come to terms with the fact that they were now part of something much bigger than them.

'Britain needs pilots,' he said, launching into his welcome speech. 'Our factories are turning out aircraft faster than ever before, but we have very few people to fly them, or at least very few that would have a chance of coming back if they went up against the Prussians. Before the war it took us anywhere between eighteen to twenty months to train a fighter pilot, but with an invasion fleet across the channel that might come at any moment we can't afford to take nearly that long. In 1940, when things got bad, we were forced to put people up in the air with only four months of training, but that was far too quick and many fine men and women lost their lives because they just weren't prepared. At the end of September we finally got a bit of breathing room and we began an accelerated training schedule of eight months. It seems to be working, but eight months is still too long, because by the time any of you went through that the Prussians might have moved in and put their feet up on the table. So, it might seem that we're in a bit of a bind, but the RAC, in its wisdom, has come up with something new and a bit different - a two track system whereby those of you that have experience or talent or both are given the chance to prove that you can be ready quicker, while everyone else is given the full eight months of training. That way we get at least a few good pilots earlier than we would normally would.'

He paused to look around the faces turned up towards him. This information tended to provoke a reaction from at least a few of the recruits, giving him a good idea of the ones who did have experience. None of them seemed to be particularly interested, though, except for the boy in the expensive black suit - most likely the Wilberforce scion he'd been told to look out for. That wasn't particularly promising; they probably all wanted to be engineers or something, just when Britain needed pilots.

'That is still in your future, though,' he continued glumly, feeling even more dejected than before, 'because first you have to do basic training. My job is to get you through that as quickly as I damn well can and send you on so that you can get into a cockpit as soon as possible.'

He shared a glance with Sergeant Smedly, who gave him a wry smile. Neither of them liked what the RAC had done with the training schedule, especially because basic training, which they both regarded as just as important as flight training itself, had been reduced to two weeks from the previous two and a half months. However, under the circumstances, it was at least understandable.

He sighed. 'There is no time to waste, ladies and gentlemen. The threat of invasion is greater now than it has ever been and you must expect to be pushed beyond what you think is your limit to make you as ready for it as you can be.'

He looked around the group one more time, his eyes sad. 'Welcome to RAC Druid. Do your best and hold nothing back for later, because there *is* no later. Dismissed.' He nodded at the sergeant, who nodded in turn at the airwoman.

'On your feet!' she bellowed. 'Grab your bags and follow me!'

She opened a door at the back of the room and the recruits filed out.

Once the door had closed behind them, Wallington sighed and leaned heavily on the podium.

'Only eight, Sergeant?'

'Yes, sir.'

'Hardly seems worth it... We will just have to hope that we get more from London and the south next week.'

'Yes, sir.'

Tayler hung back slightly as they trooped out of the room so that he could slot in behind the girl and, as soon as they were through the door and out of sight of the officer and sergeant, he wrapped his coat around her. She looked at him, but her eyes were dead and there was barely any recognition in them of him, or much consciousness of what he'd done. He gently pried her bag from her numb fingers and her hands, now free, came up to wrap the coat more tightly around herself.

They trudged down a corridor with bare white walls, past what looked like classrooms, with chalkboards and desks, then through the thick door at the end. The door led outside and Tayler found himself on a short gravel path leading to the neighbouring building. Thankfully, it was covered, so they were fairly well protected, but his shirt got soaked through when a sudden gust of wind blew the rain almost horizontally onto them. He couldn't see much of the base because of the curtains of water falling on either side of the path from the covering, but he got the impression of a large open space to one side, which could have been the airfield, with a large building next to it that might have been the hangar. He peered into the rain, trying to get a better look and see if he could spot any aircraft, but it was impossible, especially with the airwoman yelling at them to keep up.

The neighbouring building was painted the same green as the first and had the same thick door, but it was much bigger and turned out to be more homely and less like a school, with brown carpet on the floor and wood-panelled walls. There were dozens of photographs on the walls showing what looked like groups of students arranged for the occasion in front of a training aircraft on the parade ground where they'd been dropped off. The all looked very smart, very fit and very happy, a far cry from the current bedraggled bunch. There were also far more of them in each picture than the eight that had come from Leeds.

'Bathrooms are here!' the airwoman called out as they passed them, one each for men and women on either side of the end of the corridor. 'Next to them you have the laundry room and the airing cupboard. Make a note of where these are because you're going to be spending a lot of time in them!' She continued on, passing a few closed doors before stopping near the middle of the corridor. 'And these are your bunk rooms. Men on the left, women on the right, just like the bathrooms. You'll find a footlocker with your name on inside. Put your bags next to it, then come back. Sharpish!'

Tayler put the girl's bag into her unresisting hand and gave her a gentle push in the direction of her bunk room, then trotted into his behind the other boys. There were a dozen beds, six on either side of a central aisle, but only four footlockers, so it was easy enough for them to find theirs, and they dropped their bags and ran back out. Three of the girls joined them quickly, but the last, the one who'd been shivering, took a bit longer and earned a glare from the airwoman.

Tayler glanced at her as they continued down the corridor past more bunk rooms. There was colour in her cheeks now and her lips looked less blue, but her eyes were still worryingly glazed.

'This is the mess,' the airwoman said as they passed through the door at the end of the corridor and entered a large open space filled with long tables. 'While at Druid you get meals only. There is no bar service for recruits during basic. You'll have to wait until you move on for that.'

There were sour faces at that news, but nobody dared voice a protest.

The airwoman marched them through the empty mess and out the other side.

'Kitchen is here,' she said pointing to a door on the left as they went past. 'Recruits help out with cooking and cleaning - you'll find schedules in your footlockers.'

She opened the next door on the right and stepped into the room beyond.

'Dafydd! Here's the new lot.'

An airman was lounging in a padded wooden chair behind a long counter that faced the door. The room behind him was filled with row after row of metal shelves, reaching from floor to ceiling, with tall piles of neatly folded clothing, mostly in RAC blue, stacked on them. He looked up from the newspaper he had been engrossed in and took in the recruits crowding the doorway. He took a deep breath, folded the newspaper carefully, then tossed it on the counter before standing.

'Alright, let's be having them.'

'Get back! Form a line! Along the wall!' the airwoman called out. 'One at a time. You! In!' She pointed at the first of the recruits in the line, one of the girls, and jerked her thumb at the room.

Tayler had manoeuvred himself so that he was behind the girl again and when the airwoman's attention was elsewhere he leaned forward.

'Are you alright, miss?' he whispered.

She turned her head to peer at him over her shoulder. 'Yes... Why wouldn't I be?' she answered slowly, her voice slightly slurred. She didn't seem to realise anything was wrong with her, or that she still had Tayler's coat around her shoulders.

'Oh, nothing. Don't worry.' Tayler said with a smile.

The recruits went in one by one in quick order, coming back out with a kitbag after a minute or so. Soon, it was Eleanor's turn and she went and stood in front of the counter. The airman, Dafydd, looked her up and down.

'What size feet?'

'Thirty-six.'

He grunted and walked to his right, then bent down and chose some boots and plimsolls from the shelves on the wall. He came back and plunked them down on the counter, then turned and walked down the aisle to his left, collecting items as he went. He brought back a long overcoat, two sets of coveralls, a pair of blue shorts and a blue cricket shirt and piled them neatly on the counter, before going down another aisle and grabbing several pairs of socks and items of underwear.

He smirked, not unkindly, when she blushed at the thought of him handling something so intimate.

'Don't you worry,' he said in a lilting, Welsh-accented voice as he bent to grab a small toiletries bag and two towels from under the counter, 'everyone wears pants. Even officers.'

He winked, then walked to his left and took a small cap from one of several piles. 'Try that on for size.'

She took it from him and placed it on her head. He adjusted it and looked at it critically. 'That'll fit nicely when your hair isn't so wet.' He pulled it off her and placed it on top of the pile. 'Right, then.' He picked up a large canvas kitbag in RAC blue from the floor next to him and started packing the clothing neatly inside piece by piece while ticking it off a list on the counter.

'There you go. Sign here.'

Eleanor took the pen he held out to her and signed her name automatically at the bottom of the list.

'You take care of yourself.' He gave her a nod, then looked past her.

'Next!'

Eleanor slung the kitbag over her shoulder, then moved aside for the next recruit, a boy who smiled at her as she went past. She barely noticed, though, and just went and joined the end of the line of recruits who already had their bags. She stood there stiffly for a minute, hugging herself and rubbing her arms, finally starting to relax as warmth slowly returned to her body, but then something occurred to her and she looked down at her arms. Then at her body.

'This isn't my coat.'

'No,' a voice in her ear said softly. 'It's mine.'

She turned to look at the boy standing behind her, the one who'd got his clothes after her. 'Why am I wearing it?'

The boy smiled. 'You looked like you were in a bad way and I thought you needed it more than I did.'

She scowled. 'I am grateful for your concern, but I'm not sure that I did and I would thank you not to interfere in future.' She juggled the kitbag while she shrugged out of the coat. She had a slight feeling of loss as the air started to cool her still wet clothes, but ignored it and handed it to him.

The boy looked slightly hurt and opened his mouth to say something, but she deliberately turned away from him before he could and fixed her gaze on the back of the head of the girl in front of her. She wasn't going to go down that road; once you started letting people help you then you began to rely on them. Then, when they inevitably let you down, the only person that got hurt was you.

She'd learnt the hard way that the only person she could rely on in this world was herself.

Benedict watched the exchange between the two country bumpkins with interest. Rifts were already opening in the group it seemed. Good; that would only make him stand out more.

All in all, everything was going as well as could be expected. His father had warned him that he would have to put up with things he wasn't used to and didn't particularly want to do, like sharing a bedroom with others and wearing the awful clothing recruits were issued with. However, his father had also said that it would only be for a while and that it was a necessary sacrifice in order to get to where he wanted to be.

Benedict certainly hoped it wouldn't be for long, because if just one of his bunkmates started snoring he wouldn't be held accountable for his actions.

'Right! Half an hour to wash and change!' the airwoman barked at them once they'd marched back to their bunk room. 'Put on your coveralls only! No outdoor gear or hats! There's plenty of hot water, so take a shower and get warm. We don't want anyone catching their death on their first day! Dismissed!'

It might have been her imagination, but Eleanor thought the woman's eyes strayed to her while she was telling them to get warm. Even if it had just been her imagination, the last thing she wanted was sympathy or to show weakness, so she hugged her kitbag to her chest to try to stop, or at least hide, the shivering that had returned since she'd given the boy his coat back and went into the bunk room with the others. Hers was the second bed on the right and she put her things on it, then looked around, unsure as to whether she should put her things away first or go to the bathroom.

The other girls immediately started undressing and Eleanor followed suit, albeit much more shyly and making sure she kept her back turned to them. She wrapped the towel she'd been issued around herself - she was relieved to find it was so big it covered her almost completely - then picked up her sodden clothes and looked around wondering where she could hang them to dry.

'Bring them here!' one of the girls, the short-haired one who'd been wearing a smart jacket and skirt, called out from the middle of the room.

Eleanor looked at her uncertainly, not sure she'd been talking to her, but the girl beckoned her over with a smile and pointed to something at her feet.

Eleanor went and peered down at where she was pointing. The room was carpeted with the same thin, hard-wearing carpet as the corridors, but there were a few rectangular spaces cut out of it in a line running down the middle of the room between the rows of bunks, exposing small metal grills surrounded by curious wooden slats.

'Do I just put my clothes on top of it?' Eleanor asked.

'Watch this,' the girl said, grinning.

She bent down and pushed in a couple of panels, one at each end of the grill, then put her hands in and pulled. The slats unfolded, extending upwards and outwards, until they reached waist height, at which point they clicked into place, forming a clothes horse. The girl then bent down again and slid open the grill, releasing warm air to rise through the wooden slats.

'There you go,' the girl said. 'The pipes for the hot water in the bathroom run under the floor. They heat up the rooms in winter and we can open the vents and use the clothes horses to warm towels or dry clothes without having to go to the airing cupboard.'

Eleanor stared at the contraption. 'How do you know all that?'

The girl shrugged. 'I read about it in an engineering book.'

Eleanor blanched. 'Do you need to know about engineering to be a pilot?' She'd had to leave school long before her teachers got around to such advanced subjects.

The girl laughed. 'No! But I don't want to be a pilot.'

'You don't? Then why did you join the RAC?'

'My parents can't afford to send me to university and, unless I want to apprentice in an aircraft factory or something and be stuck working a machine for years, this is the best way to get an education.'

'Oh,' Eleanor said, not quite knowing what to say. She began to arrange her clothes on the clothes horse.

One of the other girls, a tall, heavyset blonde with a deep voice and sun-browned skin, who looked like she been living and working on a farm all her life, came over to hang a pair of stockings on the end of the horse. 'I haven't joined up to be a pilot either,' she said. 'My fiancée joined up six months ago. He's ground crew at Biggin and I want to join him.' The girl was an imposing presence, almost frightening, in the way she towered over the rest of them with arms bigger than their legs, but when she smiled her face lit up. 'The name's Charlotte, by the way. Everyone calls me Lottie, though.'

'I'm Jemima. Jem.' The engineer said, before looking at Eleanor expectantly.

Eleanor hesitated, but it was one thing trying not to make friends so that she wouldn't be hurt when she lost them, quite another to be outright rude and not introduce herself.

'Eleanor,' she said hesitantly, 'but my friends called me, uh, call me Ellie.'

She blushed at the slight fib. Yes, her friends had called her Ellie, but it had been five years since she'd been forced to leave school to look after her father and years since she'd seen any of her friends.

'I'm Sandra.' The last girl said, letting down her long brown hair while she came over to join the group. 'And I *do* want to be a pilot. But I don't have any experience, so they probably won't let me.'

'What about you, Ellie?' Jemima asked. 'Do you want to be a pilot?'

Eleanor shrugged again. 'I don't know. I haven't really thought about it.'

'Then why did you join the RAC?' Lottie asked, puzzled.

Because it was the only way I could get away from my drunken, abusive father. 'Uh... because I wanted to do my bit and they were the only ones recruiting in the village the day I decided to join up.' *True enough, if not the whole truth.*

'Well, that's as good a reason as any, I suppose.' Jemima said, grinning as she turned and walked towards the door. 'Come on, we need to get moving if we don't want to be shouted at again.'

Sandra snorted as she followed her out. 'I'm not sure the NCO's actually *can* do anything except shout.'

The bathroom turned out to be warm and well-appointed, with half a dozen sinks opposite the same amount of cubicles just inside the room and a row of showers behind a dividing wall at the far end.

Eleanor let herself lag behind as the other girls went straight to the showers and immediately shed their towels, again not showing any hint of shyness. They hung them on the hooks on the back of the dividing wall, then turned the spigots. Hot water and steam immediately filled the small area and the girls collectively sighed in relief and delight.

Even though her feet felt like blocks of ice and she could barely feel her fingers, Eleanor held back; she had never been unclothed around anyone else, not that she could remember anyway and didn't exactly feel comfortable. However, when she saw that none of the girls was making a big thing of it, or were looking her way she hurried to the shower at the very end and hung her towel on the hook.

They were there to banish any last vestiges of cold from their bodies, not to wash, so the other girls left after only a few minutes, but Eleanor remained behind. The water heater had long since died at home and she luxuriated in the seemingly unlimited supply of hot water, feeling the tension she'd been holding for years flow out of her.

'Come on, Rob! We only have half an hour, remember?'

Rob blinked, torn from his thoughts, and looked up at Tayler, who was already undressed and halfway through the door. 'I'll be there in a minute!' he called, waving for his friend to go without him.

'Alright!'

Tayler disappeared, leaving Rob alone in the large bunk room.

He went back to staring at the floor between his bare feet, unable to stop thinking about the officer's not particularly welcoming welcome speech.

Rob had never wanted to be a pilot. He had only learned to fly because it had been Tayler teaching him and it had given them something else to do together. He'd never found the same kind of fun in it that Tay had, though, and much preferred riding his springcycle, or just reading a book, to pottering around aimlessly in the sky. He had been considering saying that he just wanted to be ground crew and then, if he was lucky, he could be one of Tay's fitters. But how could he do that after what Aviator Lieutenant Wallington had just told them?

He and Tay had been busy helping with the harvest at the height of the battle in the air last summer and they had only been vaguely aware of what was happening and how it was going, but what they did hear on the radio every evening was always overwhelmingly positive, with many more Prussian aircraft shot down than British ones. There had been rumours that maybe those reports weren't true, that maybe the situation was a lot worse than the news was making it out to be, but then the Prussians were thoroughly thrashed on September 15th and nobody questioned the numbers anymore.

And nobody thought for one moment that pilots could possibly have been sent up before they were ready.

But that was apparently what had happened.

And if the invasion came, or more likely *when* the invasion came, the RAC would undoubtedly do the same again out of sheer desperate necessity.

How, then, could he not become a pilot? No matter how much he didn't want to.

How would he live with himself if he just sat back and let someone with far less experience than him fly in his stead?

Rob huffed; at least if he trained to be a pilot he'd be able to keep an eye on Tay a bit longer and maybe stop him from doing anything stupid. Stop him from doing anything *too* stupid, anyway.

While the other male recruits showered, Benedict stood at the sink. He possessed the best foul-weather gear that money could buy and had been so well-protected from the elements that he hadn't even needed the clockwork heater that was incorporated in the coat for extreme conditions. He had no need of a shower, therefore. However, he did wash his face, comb his hair and clean his teeth; you never knew when you were going to be talking to someone important and would need to be presentable.

5

Exactly half an hour after the airwoman had dismissed them, a corporal arrived outside the doors to their bunk rooms.

'Recruits!' he bellowed at the top of his lungs. 'Fall in!'

Slightly self-conscious in their shapeless and unflattering coveralls, the recruits rushed out into the corridor and lined up, unwittingly slotting into the same order as before.

'Right! Come on, then!'

At the far end of the building, past the kitchen and store room, was the medical centre. The corporal took them into a waiting room with cheap wooden chairs against the walls and told them to sit and wait in silence and not to, under any circumstances, dare touch the periodicals on the low table in the middle of the room.

Two doors led from the room and, before even a minute had passed, a woman in her late thirties or perhaps early forties, with a white coat over an RAC officer's uniform, opened the one on the left.

'Eleanor Perkins?'

'Yes, ma'am!' Eleanor shot to her feet and hurried across the waiting room and into the office.

The doctor closed the door behind them and waved in the direction of two chairs set in front of a small wooden desk on the far side of the room. 'Take a seat.'

Eleanor picked a chair and perched on the edge of it, sitting as upright as she could. The doctor didn't immediately go around the desk to her own chair, but instead moved to a sink at the side of the room and began to wash her hands. Eleanor watched for a moment, but then curiosity got the better of her and she looked around. There wasn't much to see, though, just a high examination table against the wall and a privacy screen in the corner.

The doctor finished and dried her hands before finally sitting behind her desk. 'Eleanor, I'm Doctor Crispin. How are you?'

'Fine thank you, ma'am.'

'I have your medical records.' The doctor opened a buff folder. 'There isn't anything for the last six, no, seven years. Since 1934 when you were... eleven. Is that correct?'

Eleanor nodded. 'It is. I haven't been ill is all.'

'Hmm,' the woman frowned, 'you should still have been having regular checks. Especially when you started your monthly cycles. You have, right?'

'Yes, ma'am.'

'Well, no matter; I have to do a complete physical anyway.' The doctor lifted her left hand and pointed over her shoulder at the wall behind her. 'Can you read the bottom line on the eye chart, please?'

'M F I W G E P T.'

'Good. Follow my finger.' The doctor held up her finger in front of Eleanor and moved it forwards and back and side to side. 'Good.' The folder had a form attached to it and the doctor made a mark, then gestured at the privacy screen. 'Strip down to your underwear, then sit on the bed, please.'

Seeing as she was only wearing coveralls over her underwear, it took less than a minute for Eleanor to do what she was told.

The doctor picked up her stethoscope and a couple of other instruments, then stood and came around the desk. She smiled at Eleanor as she walked across the room, but her step faltered, along with the smile and Eleanor closed her eyes and took a deep breath, knowing what the doctor was looking at.

'Look at the light, please.'

Eleanor opened her eyes to find the doctor standing in front of her, one of the instruments, some kind of torch with magnifying lenses on it, pointing at her.

'Good,' the light moved down. 'Open your mouth.' A wooden spatula pushed her tongue down. 'Say, ah.'

'Ahhhh...'

'Thank you.' The spatula went away and the doctor put her hands under Eleanor's jaw and felt around for a moment, but then she stepped back and looked down Eleanor's body.

'I'm sorry, but this is going to hurt.'

Eleanor nodded mutely. She winced as the doctor began probing her ribs, first on one side, then on the other. It hurt more on the right, where the bruises were only a couple of days old, than on the left; her father had been too drunk to do too much damage that day, a week ago, when she'd been slow to get his dinner, and the bruises there were already faded to a sickly greenish yellow.

'There doesn't seem to be anything broken.' The doctor laid her hands over Eleanor's ribs on each side. 'Take a deep breath for me, please.'

Eleanor complied, filling her lungs.

'And exhale... Does that hurt at all?'

Eleanor shook her head.

'Is there anything else I should know about?'

Eleanor shook her head again.

'Anything more serious in the past?'

Eleanor held up her left hand. 'Two broken fingers.'

The doctor took her hand gently and grimaced. 'These didn't heal straight.'

'I had to splint them myself.'

'How long ago?'

'Four, maybe five years.'

It was the doctor's turn to take a deep breath and she muttered something to herself, then put her hand in Eleanor's. 'Squeeze my fingers.'

Eleanor squeezed gently afraid to hurt her.

'Harder.'

She slowly applied more pressure until she thought she was going to break the doctor's fingers, but the woman showed no discomfort.

'That's good enough.' The doctor looked her in the eye, searchingly, then frowned again and touched the side of her face. 'I don't suppose you're going to tell me how this... how any of this happened?'

Eleanor winced at the touch of the woman's fingers; she'd thought she'd been able to roll with her father's slap enough for it not leave a mark, but apparently it had and she hadn't seen it in the steamed-up mirrors of the bathroom.

'No. Sorry, ma'am,' she said, shaking her head. 'It's in the past now, anyway. It doesn't matter anymore.'

The woman sighed, then nodded her understanding, if not acceptance. 'You can get dressed now.' She returned to her seat at the desk and started scribbling on the form.

Eleanor pulled on her coveralls, then went to stand in front of the desk.

The woman finished writing before looking up. 'I'm clearing you for all duties. You can train with the others and you can fly, if they want to put you in an aircraft.'

'Thank you, ma'am.'

The woman stood and led her to the door. Before she opened it, though, she turned and looked Eleanor in the eyes. 'I'll have some cream sent to you for the bruises, but if you need to talk, I'm here most days.'

'Thank you, ma'am.'

The doctor opened the door and motioned for Eleanor to go out, then raised her voice. 'Jemima Trotter!'

'Yes, ma'am!'

Jemima smiled at Eleanor as she hurried passed her, but Eleanor didn't see. She couldn't see very much at all through the tears that were misting her eyes for some reason.

The recruits were checked one by one, which didn't take very long and then the same corporal took them back down the corridor. He stopped just before going through the door to the mess and turned to face them. 'Tea break! Five minutes!'

He pushed through and moved to the left, where a long table pushed up against the wall held a huge tea urn, easily as big as a man, and pile after pile of tin mugs. Tins of biscuits were stacked next to the urn, along with a smaller urn, with condensation beading on it, filled with fresh milk. He poured himself a tea, grabbed one of the tins of biscuits and a plate, then went over to a table in the middle of the room where a group of men and women were sitting and chatting, hands wrapped around mugs.

The recruits hurried to follow suit, hungry and thirsty after their long journey. In their rush to be finished in the allotted time they jostled each other, getting in each other's way.

'I love how everyone's really getting into this whole military discipline thing.' Tayler whispered to Rob as they watched two of their companions grab for the same biscuits and knock them all over the table. They laughed and stood back to wait for the others to finish, before getting their own.

When they reached the table the other recruits had claimed, they were silent, stuffing biscuits into their mouths as if there was no tomorrow.

Tayler grinned at Rob, who rolled his eyes, but shrugged.

'Morning, everybody,' Tayler said loudly, standing behind the chair at the head of the table and looking down at the other recruits, at least one of whom had spit out tea in surprise. 'My name's Tayler, but my friends call me Tay. I want to be a pilot, preferably a Misfit, but I'm willing to settle for just driving a Harridan.'

Tayler grinned, then pulled the seat out and plunked down in it. He looked up at Rob, looming over the chair next to him. 'Your turn.'

'Thanks. So much.' Rob said, rolling his eyes again before looking around the group. 'I'm Rob,' he said, rather more calmly, 'I want to be a pilot too.'

He sat down hurriedly and started eating his biscuits, his eyes fixed firmly on his tea and his cheeks colouring.

There was silence for a moment and it looked like nobody else was going to join in, but then the big girl leaned forward. She beamed and waved cheerfully as she looked up and down the table at the boys. 'I'm Charlotte. Lottie. Pleased to meet you all.'

That got the ball well and truly rolling and after everyone had introduced themselves, some more openly and warmly than others, a discussion commenced as to which was better, the Spitsteam or the Harridan. It was cut extremely short, though, by the return of the corporal.

'Recruits!' he bellowed, from far too close, his voice resounding almost painfully in the largely empty space. 'I'm assuming you know your way to your bunk room from here. If any of you have personal pilot's log books, then go and get them now!'

The corporal looked at them expectantly, but his face fell when only Benedict moved.

The boy smirked when he saw nobody else was standing up and he strutted away, milking it for all he was worth.

The corporal saw and his face went beetroot. 'Run, recruit!'

The recruits laughed as Benedict broke into a panicked run, but went silent again when the corporal glared at them. 'The rest of you, clear up your mess!'

Benedict came running back through the door as they were putting their dirty mugs and plates in the racks next to the swinging double doors leading to the kitchen. When he saw what they were doing he slowed right down, but the corporal apparently had eyes everywhere.

'Did I tell you to stop running, recruit?'

Benedict ran to the table, but someone had already taken his mug and plate away and Sandra had wiped the table down with a cloth, so there was nothing to do.

'Looks like some kindly soul has already cleared up your mess, recruit.' The corporal said. 'Well, I think you should repay them by cleaning up for everybody for the rest of the day, don't you?'

Benedict gritted his teeth, seething, but there was only one answer he could give. 'Yes, corporal.'

Once things were clean enough for the corporal he took them back to the medical centre, but they were only there to use the waiting room because Aviator Lieutenant Wallington's office was directly opposite.

The corporal left them there and went to the office to report.

As soon as they were on their own, Tayler leaned in to Rob and asked in a stage whisper. 'Do you think I should tell the corporal that I'm a *very* messy eater?'

Benedict glared at him, but the rest of the recruits could barely contain their laughter.

The corporal returned suddenly and must have seen the smiles on everyone's face except for Benedict's, but he said nothing.

'Cleaner Boy,' he said, pointing at Benedict. 'You're up first.'

Benedict smiled to himself as Aviator Lieutenant Wallington flicked through his pilot's log. It was impressive for someone who didn't earn their living flying and he was confident that it would put him at the top of the class.

The officer finally closed the log and looked up at him. 'This is first-class, Mr Wilberforce.'

'Thank you sir, I'd...'

'But it will count for less than nothing if you do not demonstrate the skill to back it up.'

Benedict frowned. 'I assure you I will, sir.'

'Well, you will have your chance.' Wallington bent to sign the file on the table in front of him. 'You're approved for flight training.'

'Any flight experience, Mr Oakley?'

'Yes, sir.'

Wallington looked up from his notes and his eyebrows lifted in surprise. 'Really? Solo or as a passenger?'

'Solo, sir.'

Wallington blinked. 'You can fly?'

'Yes, sir. I have a Dunn Scott TC-62.'

'What on earth is that?'

'A crop sprayer, sir.'

'A crop sprayer?'

'Yes, sir.'

'Then where's your log book?'

'Don't have one, sir. Never needed one.' Tayler grinned. 'The farmers all know when I've sprayed their crops. No need to write it down.'

'Ahem, just so, just so. And how many hours do you have on that?'

'I don't know... Between fertilising and spraying pesticides... Call it thirty hours a week for four weeks, four times a year, for the last six years...'

Wallington's mouth moved as he did the mathematics in his head, then his eyes widened in shock. 'Good lord, that's almost three thousand hours! Solo!'

Tayler shrugged. 'If you say so, sir. But of course that's just when I was working. I was also up most weekends of the year on my time off, at least a few hours a day, teaching Rob, I mean, Recruit Sherborne to fly, giving joy rides to me mates, impressing the local girls...'

'Yes, yes, I get the idea. Thank you, Mr Oakley. I think we can safely approve you for flight training.'

'Mr Sherborne. Mr Oakley says he taught you to fly.'

'He did, sir, yes.'

Wallington waited for Rob to elaborate, but he didn't. 'How long ago was this?'

'Three years ago. When I was fifteen.'

'And have you done many solo flights?'

Rob shrugged. 'Two, maybe three...'

Wallington smiled in relief. 'Ah, so not many.'

'...hundred, sir.'

Wallington stared at him for a moment, then shook his head and made a note in the boy's file. 'What is it with you farm boys...' He muttered under his breath.

'Sir?'

'Nothing...' Wallington said with a sigh. 'And I suppose you don't have a pilot's degree either?'

'I'm afraid not, sir.'

'Never mind.' Wallington sighed again. 'You're approved for flight training.'

'Do you know how to fly, Miss Perkins?'
'No, sir. I've never even been in an aircraft.'
'But you want to be a pilot.'
'Not especially.'
'Ground crew, then? Or aircrew? A navigator? Gunner?'
'I don't know, sir. I guess I never thought about it.'
'Then why did you join the Royal Aviator Corps?'
'I had my reasons, sir.'
Wallington looked at her for a moment, as if searching for something, or puzzled about something, but then he blinked and shook his head.

'Very well, Miss Perkins, this way, please.'
He stood and took Eleanor through a door behind his desk and into an adjoining room that was identical in size to his office. A multitude of filing cabinets lined the walls, along with a couple of bookshelves, but most of the space was taken up by a contraption with pedals, levers and even a seat, all attached to a fairly large dull metal block.

Wallington cranked a lever, then flicked a switch behind the machine and it began to emit a whirring noise.

'This is the latest in pilot aptitude testing machines, we call it "PAT" for short. It simulates controlling an aircraft in a very simplified manner. I'll demonstrate. You come and stand behind the chair so you can see properly.'

He slid into the chair, put his feet up on the pedals in front of it and grabbed hold of the short vertical metal pole sticking up between his legs with his right hand.

With his left hand he flicked a switch on a panel next to the chair and the whirring noise became a dull buzz.

'Alright then, see the red ball and the white ring?' He pointed to the machine, directly in front of him, where there was a slim metal rod with a small red ball, about half an inch in diameter, on the end. A white ring, about four inches across, was mounted on a stand just in front of it. The red ball had been in the centre of the white ring but was now slowly wandering off to one side.

'Yes, sir.'
'This is the stick,' he said, waggling the metal pole between his legs. 'It moves backwards and forwards and makes the ball go up and

down.' He demonstrated, making the red ball go up as he pulled back on the stick and down as he pushed forward again. 'The rudder pedals control lateral movement. Push on the right foot to make the ball go left and vice versa.' Again he demonstrated. 'The idea is to get the red ball into the white ring and keep it there.' A couple of coordinated movements of stick and pedals brought the ball back to where it had started, but it immediately started to wander away again, though. 'The blighter keeps trying to move away, so you need to continually compensate.'

He moved his hands and feet back and forth for a few seconds, keeping the red ball roughly in the middle of the white ring, then flicked the switch next to the seat. The ball stopped moving and the machine went back to whirring quietly.

'Your turn.' Wallington said, standing and motioning to the seat.

Eleanor sat and Wallington adjusted the seat, moving it forward slightly until her feet were comfortably on the pedals, then flicked the switch.

'Give it a go, get the hang of it.'

The ball started to wander down and to the left and Eleanor pushed the stick and kicked the right pedal. Her efforts only made the ball go further away, though, and there was an angry buzzing noise as it went behind the white ring, like a thousand bees in a disturbed hive.

Wallington chuckled. 'The controls are rather counter-intuitive, I know, but that's just how an aircraft is set up, I'm afraid. Don't worry, if you don't get it, there's always ground crew...'

He stopped talking abruptly as Eleanor brought the ball back up to sit squarely in the centre of the ring. It immediately tried to move away again, but she compensated easily.

'I think I'm getting it, sir.'

'I'll say!' Wallington breathed, impressed despite himself. He watched her for a few more seconds, then went to the machine. 'There are five levels of difficulty. That's level one. I think perhaps we should go straight to level three.'

He turned a dial on the side of the machine and the ball immediately leapt sideways. Eleanor kicked the pedal to stop it, but it surged, trying to go the other way. She pursed her lips and compensated again, but was forced to pull back on the stick as it dropped suddenly. She was getting used to its new violent movements, though, and she was ready for it the next time it lurched and brought it back to the middle of the ring before it had gone more than an inch.

'Alright...' Wallington said slowly after more than thirty seconds had elapsed and the ball hadn't even gotten close to the ring. 'Let's try level four, shall we?'

The recruits spoke in low but enthusiastic tones about the interviews, those who'd already had theirs sharing the experience with those who hadn't. Only two people didn't join in the conversation - Benedict, who was looking even more smug than usual and who nobody wanted to engage with, and Eleanor, who was leaning forwards on her elbows and staring at the floor.

She'd been approved for pilot training, but she really didn't want to be a pilot. That game, or test, or whatever it was, had been fun, but she couldn't imagine that flying would be like that. Especially if there were Prussians trying to kill her while she was doing it. She'd be much safer on the ground and she could learn a trade as well, something that she could do after the war to earn money so she wouldn't have to go back home.

'Ellie!'

Eleanor started and flinched back as Sandra plopped down in the chair next to hers.

'I got approved for pilot training!'

Eleanor couldn't help but smile; the girl's enthusiasm was impossible to resist. 'That's wonderful! Congratulations!'

'I got to level two on that stimulator thing! I could only hold the ball in the ring for a few seconds at a time, but the lieutenant said that just being able to do level one was good enough to be approved for pilot training! What about you? How did you do? Did you go on the stimulator?'

Eleanor grinned. 'I think it's called a *sim*ulator. And yes, I had a go.'

'It was a laugh, wasn't it?'

'Yes. It was...'

'Oh,' Sandra said, her smile disappearing. 'Couldn't you do it? Aren't you going to be a pilot?'

'It's not that; I could do it alright and I was approved for pilot training, but...'

'That's wonderful!' Sandra said, bouncing up and down in glee. 'We'll be training together!'

'Yes, I suppose...' Eleanor tried again. 'It's just that...'

'Pff!' Benedict scoffed from behind Sandra, interrupting Eleanor before she had a chance to explain why she wouldn't be training with her.

'Just because you could do that doesn't mean you'll *ever* be a pilot,' the boy said, 'the pilot aptitude test is nothing like *actual* flying. All it does is make sure you're not too clumsy to be able to move your hands and feet at the same time.'

'How would you know?' Tayler said, leaning forward in his seat to look at the boy. 'You can already fly so you didn't have to do it.'

'I had a go on one a year ago, on a visit to the laboratory where they developed it.' Benedict looked at Sandra smugly. 'I got to level three.'

Eleanor considered telling the boy what level she'd gotten to on the machine, just to wipe the smile off his face, but only very briefly. Nobody would believe her. They'd probably think that she was lying just to spite him and while they might well applaud that, she wasn't that kind of person and wasn't going to do that to anyone, even someone as obnoxious as him. Quite apart from that, though, she didn't want to hurt Sandra. The girl was so happy and so proud about being accepted for pilot training and she didn't want to do anything to spoil the moment for her, beyond how it had been spoilt already.

In the end she just gave Sandra the biggest smile she could. 'I'm really happy for you. Ignore Cleaner Boy, I'm sure you'll be a wonderful pilot.'

Benedict's face darkened and he snarled at her, but the rest of the recruits chuckled. Even the stone face of the corporal, standing outside the door to the office across the hall, seemed to crack a little.

They fell silent, though, when the door to the office opened and Charlotte, the last of them to be interviewed, came out. The lieutenant's voice floated out after her.

'Corporal! A moment, please!'

'Yes, sir!'

While the corporal disappeared into the office, Charlotte sat down, a big smile on her face.

'You look pleased, Chas.' Jemima said, nudging the big girl in the ribs with her elbow. 'Did you get the posting you wanted? With your lad?'

The big girl shook her head. 'No. I changed my mind. I was sitting there and I thought to myself: I'll only get this one chance. So I told the lieutenant that I'd like to try to be a pilot and he let me do that test thing.'

'Oh!' Jemima's eyes widened. 'And how did you do?'

Charlotte smiled. 'I...' she began, but cut herself off when the office door opened again.

The corporal appeared, but he immediately moved to the side to make way for Wallington and the recruits surged to their feet when he crossed the corridor and came into the waiting room.

He stood just inside the door and looked around, smiling widely, seeming much happier than he had been when he'd welcomed them that morning.

'Congratulations to the three of you who took the PAT test! Very rarely has every candidate in a group who took it been successful. And not many recruits have come to us with as much experience as Mr Sherborne or Mr Wilberforce, either. At least, not since the war began. It is clear we have a particularly noteworthy group, even though it is so small. I do, however, have to make special mention of Miss Perkins' effort,' he searched out Eleanor and smiled at her. 'I had a little look through the records and only one other person has *ever* successfully sustained level four on PAT, let alone managed level five, if only for a few seconds, like you did.' He paused enigmatically and looked around the group. 'That was a lovely young lady, who I was fortunate enough to have the pleasure of training, by the name of Chastity Arrowsmith.'

He paused to let that information sink in and nodded in satisfaction at the recognition on most of the recruits' faces. 'So, jolly well done, all of you and keep up the good work.' He nodded to the corporal as he turned to go. 'Carry on, corporal.'

The corporal snapped to attention. 'Sah!' He only relaxed again when the officer had gone into his office and the door had closed.

'Lunch time, recruits!' he shouted. 'On your feet! Line up in the corridor!'

As the recruits rushed to get out of the waiting room, Eleanor found herself the focus of quite a bit of attention. She got a couple of slaps on the back from Jemima and Lottie as they went past, the latter of which hurt quite a bit, and a nod of approval from the dark-haired boy, Rob. The boy who had lent her his coat, Tayler, grinned at her, quite attractively actually, and whispered 'Nice one, Perkins!' as she went past him. The obnoxious posh boy, Wilberforce, was upset and shooting daggers at her, though, but she found that she didn't mind that one bit.

Once the recruits were arranged along the wall outside the waiting room, the corporal walked down the line. 'You have one hour to eat and wash up before classes begin! You'll find pens and paper in your footlockers - you will need those, so don't forget them!'

He marched back to the front. 'Come on, then!'

When they trooped into the mess they were surprised to find more than a hundred people there.

They'd been starting to think that it was only them going through basic training and that nothing else happened at the base, but there was apparently another class of recruits and, by the look of the flightsuits and greasy coveralls on a few of the men and women, at least some flight operations.

They joined the end of the queue filing past the serving tables, behind the other class of recruits. There were twenty-five of them and they turned out to be from Scotland. They had completed their basic training, having been there for two weeks already and were moving on that afternoon - twelve of them to flight training and the rest to ground crew.

Eleanor found herself next to Sandra in the line. She fully expected the girl to be upset with her for beating the score she'd been so proud of on the aptitude test, but the girl surprised her by turning and grinning at her as soon as they'd got their trays.

'Level four! That's incredible!'

'You're not upset?'

'Upset?' Sandra asked, puzzled. 'Why would I...?' her eyes widened in understanding, 'Oh! You thought I'd be annoyed because you beat my score?' she shook her head. 'That's so nice of you! But if anything I'm glad; if you hadn't done so well we wouldn't hear the end of it from that bloody Benedict boy.'

She jerked her head in the direction of Benedict, who had made sure he was at the front of their section of the queue.

Eleanor chuckled. 'Glad to be of service.' She dropped her voice and leaned a bit closer to the girl. 'Maybe you can do something for me in return...'

'Of course!'

'You can tell me who Charity Arrowsmith is.'

Sandra stared at her incredulously. 'You don't know?'

Eleanor shook her head.

'First of all, it's *Chastity*, not Charity, and she's one of the Misfits.'

'Oh.'

'You've heard of them, right?'

'Yes, of course.'

'Well, she isn't one of the original Misfits, she joined the squadron before they went to Muscovy at the end of last year. She was chosen by Abigail Lennox herself because she was such a good pilot.'

'How do you know so much about the Misfits?'

Sandra blinked, surprised again. 'Everyone in Britain knows just about everything about the Misfits. There are lots and lots of articles in the newspapers about them.'

'Ah.'

'You don't read newspapers?'

'My father didn't like to get them. He said they were a waste of money.'

'I'll lend you my scrapbook. You can see what you've been missing! Some of the stories about them are amazing! Better than any novel!'

'What are we talking about?' Jemima leaned in from the other side of Eleanor as they shuffled forwards bit by bit.

'The Misfits.' Sandra said. 'Ellie had never heard of Chastity before.'

'Really? I thought everyone in Britain knew all the Misfits!'

'That's what I said!'

It was their turn to get food, so, somewhat to Eleanor's relief, the conversation ended there. However, when she got to the table, she found that everyone else was also talking about the Misfits; it seemed that the mention of Chastity Arrowsmith had sparked off various individual conversations and thoughts, which had coalesced into a discussion between all of the recruits.

When Eleanor hesitated, Jemima nudged her towards a chair with a wink.

'Don't worry, your secret is safe with us.'

Eleanor smiled gratefully, then took a seat, flanked by Sandra and Jemima, as if they were her wingmates prepared to defend her.

'But, seriously,' Benedict was saying. 'The Misfits might have made sense at the start of the war, but now?'

'Now more than ever, surely?' said Tayler. 'Every war has its heroes and generals, from Wellington to Alexander to Achilles. Without them there is nobody to lead, nobody to set an example, nobody to inspire armies to greater things.' He noticed her looking at him and winked. Embarrassed for some reason, she hurriedly looked down at her plate.

'Fine, then, keep the Misfits, but put them in Spitsteams and distribute them throughout the squadrons. They can lead by example there, instead of being put on a pedestal and having their status as heroes shoved in everybody's faces.' Benedict gestured curtly. 'People only see them as heroes because they're being told to, but they haven't done anything remotely heroic since Muscovy. On the contrary, they lost us Malta and now the whole Mediterranean belongs to the Prussians. We'll probably lose Egypt and the whole of North Africa because of that too!'

'That wasn't their fault,' growled another of the boys, the quiet bookish one, Franklin, who had told them only his name when everyone had been introducing themselves. 'Malta was an untenable situation and the support they'd been promised never arrived.'

Eleanor stopped paying attention after that. When they began talking about things that they all seemed to be experts in and have an opinion about, but that she had no knowledge of, or much interest in, to tell the truth, it just served to reinforce the fact that she shouldn't be a pilot, no matter how well she'd done in the test. She should limit herself to learning a trade she could use after the war. One where she didn't have to worry about anything beyond what she'd been ordered to do.

Rob tucked into his food. It was extremely good, almost as good as home cooking, which compensated slightly for the sour taste in his mouth.

He'd fully expected not to like all of his fellow recruits, after all, it was like school and there were always going to be people he would get on better with than others, but he hadn't expected there to be someone he actively did not like. That he couldn't stand, in fact. Looking around, it seemed that he wasn't the only one, but the posh kid, Benedict, seemed oblivious to the disdain, derision and sometimes even animosity of the people around him. Either that or he didn't care.

Rob wondered how anyone could go through life like that and he hoped the boy came from a loving family, otherwise he was going to be very lonely.

That wasn't the only thing spoiling his lunch, though. For the first time in his life that he could remember he found himself genuinely annoyed with Tayler. And it was about a girl of all things. Tayler's relationships, and there had been quite a lot of them, had never bothered him before, so why should the way he was looking at the girl, Eleanor, bother him now?

Benedict finished his pudding, a rather sub-par suet dish that he nonetheless forced down, knowing that he would need to keep his strength up and that the stash of sweets and chocolates he'd brought with him would only last so long. The rest of the recruits were taking their time, having tea and chatting, but he thought he'd get back to the room and have a quick nap before classes. He stood, tucking his logbook under his arm, then took his tray to the racks before heading to the door leading to the bunk rooms.

'And where do you think you're going, recruit?'

Benedict stopped and found the corporal from earlier watching him from his seat at a table full of NCOs.

'To the bunk room, corporal.'

'Have you forgotten that I gave you a job to do?'

'I thought it was a joke, corporal,' he said weakly.

'Do I look like a joker, recruit?'

'Uh...' Benedict hesitated; actually, the man did look a bit funny, with wildly bushy eyebrows and curly hair that was plastered down on top because of having been wearing a hat, but he knew what was expected of him.

'No corporal, you do not!'

The corporal shared a look with his colleagues, who were all trying very hard to keep straight faces.

'Actually, I do like to tell a joke every now and then, but right now I'm not feeling in a very humorous mood. So, hop to it or I might be telling the one about the boy who wanted to be a pilot but ended up washing plates for the whole war!'

'Yes, corporal!'

Benedict hurried back to the recruits' table, teeth gritted against his anger and cheeks colouring at the laughter he heard behind him. They'd all be laughing on the other side of their faces soon enough, though, when he was an officer and helped save the country in his Spitsteam.

'My name is Aviator Sergeant Smedley and I, along with Corporal Lewis, Airwoman Jones, Airwoman Phillips and Airman Davies, will have the pleasure of being your instructors for the next two weeks. Between us we have more than one hundred years' experience making worthless civilians into something that is useful to the Royal Aviator Corps and the Kingdom of Great Britain.'

The Aviator Sergeant who had met them when they arrived glared at them from the front of the classroom, flanked by the corporal and the airmen and women who had shown them around that morning and gotten them settled.

'Here at RAC Druid you will complete what is known as "basic training" or simply "basic" to those of us who know what we're talking about. Which does not include you, by the way. Here you will learn the history of the RAC. You'll find out about the hierarchy of the armed forces and how to act correctly as a member of them. You'll have classes in first aid and get glidewing qualified. You'll also have classes in aircraft recognition, so that if you're ever in a position to shoot at somebody, you shoot at the right people.' He lifted a hand to point upwards to where model aircraft, ranging in size from less than a foot to almost a yard, were hanging. Some of them were orientated at strange angles and, curiously, a few were painted black, rendering them little more than silhouettes. 'There are models of the aircraft most commonly used by the British, Prussian and Italian air forces hanging in every classroom, so when you start daydreaming, at least you'll still be learning something and won't just be staring at the ceiling!'

The recruits laughed, but none of the instructors did, they either just smiled wryly or remained stoically impassive.

'But that doesn't mean that daydreaming is going to be permitted!'

He gave them a stern look and they settled down again.

'In addition to those classes you'll also be spending a lot of time outdoors, come rain or shine. You'll have daily physical jerks, including a lot of running and time on the obstacle course and you'll have basic survival training. You'll learn to care for yourself, your kit and the weapons we use, as well as learning to fire those weapons and you'll also do a fair bit of square bashing, although not as much of that as usual, because we just don't have the time. And, because of that reduced schedule, you will need to do far more book learning on your own time, otherwise you won't be able to pass the written exams at the end of the two weeks.'

He grinned and took note of which of the recruits groaned at that news and which didn't; not because he enjoyed making recruits suffer, well, not *just* because of that, but because it was a good indication of who to keep an eye on to make sure they didn't fall behind.

'Now, I have to agree that things like marching in straight lines and polishing boots until you can see your face in them aren't the most useful skills for pilots and they're not going to impress the Prussians and make them feel like surrendering, but basic training is about more than just giving you skills and knowledge. It's about discipline. About putting your mind to something and doing it. And it's about learning to work as a team. Whether you're in the air or in the ground, flying a bomber or a desk, you will be relying on the people around you and they will rely on you. There is no room for anyone to have an ego in war because that gets people killed. Just look at Hans Gruber!'

This time the instructors joined in with the merriment, shaking their heads and expressing various negative opinions of the leadership, flying ability and also the acting skills of the Prussian's ace pilot. Smedley didn't take his eyes off of the recruits, though, and when his colleagues had finished he continued.

'As Lieutenant Wallington told you when you arrived, there is no time to waste if you are to be of service to your country before it is too late, so the training you will receive this week has been cut down to the bare necessities. There is still a lot to learn, though, and you will be kept very busy. Some of you will cope easily, some of you will not, but this is not a competition, this is a *team* game, and if any of you fall behind, you all fall behind. So, if you see someone struggling, do something about it. Or face the consequences of their failure together.'

He turned to look at the corporal. 'Remember that group we had from Devon a few months back, corporal?'

'How could I forget them, Sergeant? I don't think I've seen anyone wash so many clothes and dishes or do so many laps of the base, all while sleeping so little. I don't know how they survived.'

'I'm not sure they all did, corporal. I didn't count them onto the bus. Did you?'

'No, sarge.'

The sergeant turned back to the recruits. Many of them were smiling, but those smiles faltered somewhat when they became unsure whether he was joking or not.

'Well. That's enough from me. Your first class this afternoon will be "History of the Royal Aviator Corp" with Airman Davies. I know you've had a long day, but every day for the next two weeks is going to be long and there *will* be a test, so make sure you pay attention.'

He gave the class one last long look and his expression softened almost imperceptibly. 'Good luck, ladies and gentlemen.'

He marched out, taking all of the instructors with him except the airman, who waited for the door to close behind them, then perched on the edge of the teacher's desk at the front of the room.

'Alright, let's get started! The Royal Aviator Corps was founded in 1890 by Empress Victoria...'

Airman Davies was an extremely good teacher and his use of humorous anecdotes to tell the history of the RAC and flight in Britain made the hour-long class pass very quickly. The same couldn't be said for the following class, though. Not only did the subject matter of the rules and regulations of the RAC not lend itself to enjoyment in the slightest, but the teacher, Airwoman Phillips, was a rather humourless woman in her mid-thirties whose monotonous droning had everyone shifting uncomfortably in their seats and stifling yawns. The end of the class couldn't come soon enough for any of them, but the following lesson wasn't much better as, after a very brief tea break, they went to one of the empty dorm rooms. There, Dafydd, the airman who looked after stores, showed them how to shine their shoes, press their uniforms, make their bed and fold and put away their kit, all of which they would have to do every day for morning inspection. Once he'd done that they went to their own bunks to practise while Dafydd wandered between the rooms giving pointers. He didn't let them go until he was satisfied, which meant the class lasted more than the hour that it should have done and they arrived at the mess for dinner when it was already well under way.

After dinner they were technically free, but they had so much to do before bed that they weren't really. As well as make sure their clothes were clean and boots shined, they had to write up their notes from their classes and had been assigned some reading from a couple of the books that had been in their footlockers - *Rules and Regulations of the Royal Aviator Corps* and *The General Service Training Manual*.

Lights out was at nine for the recruits and they were expected to be in bed at that time, although they were permitted to keep reading for half an hour if they desired, using the wind-up spot lamps that were attached to their headboards. Most of them were too tired to do that, though, and when the duty NCOs came back at half past nine they were greeted only by snores.

6

The recruits were awakened at five, the boys by Airman Davies and the girls by Airwoman Jones. They were given ten minutes to wash and dress in their cricket shirt, shorts and plimsolls before being hurried out onto the parade ground by Airwoman Jones, the youngest and, by the way she looked in her shirt and shorts, the fittest of their instructors.

The rain had stopped during the night and the sun was just coming up over the lush green Welsh hills and they blinked in the light as they got their first good look at the base. It was a lot bigger than it had seemed when they'd arrived. There were three main buildings grouped around the parade ground, not just the two they'd been in so far, but behind them, on the opposite side from the airfield, there were almost a dozen more, of differing shapes and sizes, all painted the same grass green, rendering them almost invisible in the morning mist. In addition to the buildings there was an assault course and what looked like a firing range, with a wall of sandbags under a small tin room. There was also a tower made of steel girders that was more than fifty yards tall. It looked like a radio tower, but, instead of antennae, it had a protrusion, like a diving board, at the top.

'Recruits!' Jones shouted to catch their attention after giving them a moment to look around and catch their bearings. 'Form up in two lines!'

She stalked up and down in front of them impatiently as they rushed to organise themselves, inevitably getting in each other's way. Eventually they settled down and she came to a halt and faced them.

'Physical fitness is important for everybody,' she said, her Welsh-accented voice carrying easily in the still air without her having to raise it much, 'but it is especially important in the armed forces and not just for the army, with all the running around they do. Pilots need to be fit so that they can withstand high G forces without passing out in the middle of a fight and I'm sure I don't need to tell those of you who want to be technicians how heavy some of the parts and tools you'll be lugging around are. It is a good idea, therefore, and a requirement for recruits, to have a good level of fitness, so, while you are here, you will have a minimum of an hour of exercise before breakfast every morning. But I would strongly recommend you try to keep some kind of exercise as part of your daily routine after you move on, if at all possible.'

She took a few steps back and held her arms out wide. 'Spread out a bit, make sure you won't hit anyone. We'll start with a simple warm-up.'

She ran them through some basic exercises, making them do things like star jumps, running in place, sit-ups and press-ups, all the kinds of things they had done in PE classes at school and which most of them hadn't done for years.

After that they went for a run. She took them along the track that wound its way through the buildings then looped around the entire airfield alongside the perimeter track. The airwoman took it slowly, at a pace that was not much above a fast walking speed, but, even so, Jemima, Franklin and Eleanor started struggling before they were even halfway round the circuit and dropped behind, followed soon by Tayler, Lottie and Benedict. Only Rob and Sandra made it easily, neither of them breaking much of a sweat; Rob because he'd been on the village cricket team since he was fourteen and Sandra because she'd been on the athletics team at school.

Jones finished the lap, then stood on the parade ground where they'd started, watching the recruits staggering in. Her expression was only minimally disapproving, mostly it looked like she was assessing them.

When they had all finally arrived she gave them a moment to catch their breath then told them to fall in again.

'Well, I can't say I'm pleased, but I'm also not surprised and I have seen worse. Go clean up, put on your coveralls and boots and get breakfast. Quickly! Because at six-thirty you have some lovely drill to learn, you lucky so-and-sos! Dismissed!'

'Urgh!' Jemima groaned as she flopped into a chair in the mess hall and stretched her legs out under the table. 'Are we really going to have to do that every morning? I feel like my legs are going to fall off.'

Eleanor sat gingerly next to her and took a careful bite of bread and butter. 'I didn't know running could make you sick like that.' She had vomited behind a tree about three-quarters of the way around the airfield and was still feeling more than a little ill.

Rob took a big bite of his second bacon sandwich and spoke around it. 'Some people do feel like that when they start exercising first thing in the morning. Especially if they do it before eating. You'll get used to it, but, for now, you just need to get some food in you.'

Eleanor looked at him, then looked at the grease smeared around his mouth, then leapt to her feet and ran for the door.

The toilets were close, at the end of the corridor near the mess, and she burst in, ran into the nearest stall and fell to her knees. She heaved repeatedly, but nothing came because she'd already emptied her stomach on the run and eventually she sat back and leaned against the wall of the stall.

'Ellie? Are you alright?'

Eleanor hadn't closed the door of the stall and Sandra appeared around the partition and peered in at her.

'I'm fine,' Eleanor croaked, her throat burning. 'I just felt a bit queasy.'

'Yeah, the way Rob and Tay eat makes me queasy too.' Sandra grinned, but her eyes widened and her hand shot to her mouth when Eleanor retched and rolled onto her knees. 'Sorry! I shouldn't have said anything.'

'It's alright,' Eleanor gasped out once the spasms had stopped again. She wiped her mouth with the back of her hand and struggled to her feet. She staggered out of the stall and was too weak to protest when Sandra took hold of her elbow and helped her to the sinks where she washed her face and rinsed out her mouth.

She propped herself up on the side of the sink and leaned forward to inspect herself in the mirror. There was a waxy sheen to her skin and she was very pale, but apart from that she didn't actually look too bad. The cream she'd found on her pillow had worked wonders and the bruise on her cheek was barely noticeable now. Also, for the first time in she didn't know how long, she looked almost rested, the deep black rings under her eyes faded slightly after only a single good night's sleep with no need to worry that her father might burst in.

'I'm guessing you haven't done much exercise recently.' Sandra said.

Eleanor shook her head. 'I've been at home taking care of my father. For the last half a dozen years I've walked half a mile to the shop and back twice a week and that's it.'

'I could help you get into shape if you'd like. I could read the homework to you while you do some exercises in the room in the evenings. Or we could go for walks if we get enough time.'

'I...' Eleanor shook her head, about to refuse, but something occurred to her and she caught herself.

Seven years ago, when she'd had to leave school to look after her father, there had been people, good people, who'd offered to help her. The mothers of a couple of her closest friends, a couple of her father's colleagues from work, her teacher, they had all done what they could, helping with the shopping, occasionally bringing round food, or just checking in and seeing if everything was alright and if anything was needed. However, over the course of about six months, as her father had become more and more bitter he'd become more and more belligerent and one by one those people had disappeared, never to be seen again. They had left gaps in the care of her father and the house and she had been unable to fill them for quite a while. Things had gotten extremely bad and that was when her father had first started hitting her. When he had gotten into the *habit* of hitting her. Eventually, though, she'd managed to get into a routine that had kept things ticking over and her father at least moderately satisfied, but she'd learnt her lesson and since that day she'd refused any offer of help, knowing that any easement of her burden in the short term would only lead to more hardship in the future.

She'd hadn't fully realised it until that moment, but that wasn't the case anymore. She was on her own now, completely, and her father was no longer a part of her life. He never would be again. There wasn't any reason to push people away anymore. In fact, there was every reason not to.

Ellie smiled. 'That would be wonderful, thank you.'

Her stomach rumbled noisily and she blushed. 'Sorry!'

Sandra laughed. 'Don't worry! Now, come on; you obviously need to try to eat something and we only have twenty minutes left until we have to be on the parade ground.'

'You go ahead,' Ellie said. 'I need to wash my hands.'

Sandra shook her head. 'You don't get rid of me that easily. I'll wait.'

Ellie's smile widened even as she felt her eyes well up and she bent over the sink to splash water on her face before the girl noticed. She washed and dried herself quickly, then turned to Sandra.

The girl surprised her by grabbing her hand and, as she let herself be dragged out of the bathroom, she found herself having to scrub the back of her hand across her eyes again.

Sergeant Smedley watched the new recruits march across the parade ground with a practised eye. He'd gotten all sorts in the thirty years since he'd started teaching drill and he had to say that this lot weren't at all bad. They all seemed to have a good sense of rhythm and were keeping time together quite nicely, they all knew how to stand up straight and they were mostly the same size and shape, although Recruit Smith did stand out a bit, but having her as the right marker was actually quite pleasing to the eye somehow. They'd even quickly gotten the hang of swinging their arms to a forty-five degree angle, more or less, anyway, and that would only get better with practise.

It was a bit early to say anything, but they might actually be the first group in months that weren't going to give him any trouble. Except...

He frowned. Something wasn't right. Something was spoiling the perfect picture he was trying to paint... He groaned; why did he have to do that to himself? Who was he kidding? Of course there was *something*. There was *always* something.

'Flight... halt! Step, step, stamp!' he called out, not trusting them to remember the basic manoeuvre they'd learned only a few minutes before. 'Stand at... ease!'

He marched over to stand by the side of the small group. 'Recruit Orpwood! Fall out!'

He sighed when the girl just looked at him blankly. 'That means take a small step back, then turn, then leave the formation smartly and march over here to me.'

She didn't get flustered, like many recruits would do when singled out, and fell out pretty well, but he winced when she marched over to him.

'Sergeant?' she asked, coming to a sloppy stop in front of him and just standing there as if she were in the queue at the post office. He didn't pull her up on it, though; it was the first day and he'd learnt that going too hard on recruits too soon was almost always counterproductive. Besides, all that would come in time and he had something more important to deal with first.

'Recruit Orpwood. I assume you don't know what you were doing.'

'Marching, Sergeant?'

'Yeeees,' he said, drawing the word out as he fought to keep his voice even and not start either bawling at her or roaring with laughter. 'Not very well, though.' He crooked his finger at her. 'Come here. Stand beside me.'

He waited for her to do so, then raised his voice. 'Recruit Wilberforce! Front and centre!'

Benedict stamped to attention, performed a perfect left turn, then marched out of the formation. He performed another turn to take him parallel to the other recruits, then one final one when he was level with the sergeant. He came to a perfect parade halt three paces away and stood there at attention.

'Recruit Wilberforce here,' the sergeant said, 'is a bit too keen for his own good. He's obviously been drilled before he came here. By your father, recruit?'

Benedict had coloured slightly at the sergeant's comment and it took him a second to respond. 'No, Sergeant! My father asked the drill instructor from his base to do so.'

Smedley cleared his throat. 'Yes, well, anyway... Recruit Wilberforce is going to demonstrate marching for you, Recruit Orpwood, see if you notice something.'

'Yes, Sergeant.'

'Recruit! Left... turn! Quick... march!'

Benedict turned and began marching on command, his steps even and his arms swinging to a practised and precise forty-five degrees.

Smedley watched for a moment, pleased, despite his instinctive dislike for the boy.

'Recruit!' he bellowed in his parade voice, 'about... turn!'

Benedict did a smart about turn, but spoiled the effect somewhat by tripping over his feet slightly when he began marching again. He recovered instantly, but his face was beetroot and his expression was thunderous when the sergeant brought him back to a halt and told him to fall back in with the others.

Once Benedict was at ease, Smedley looked to Sandra. 'Did you notice anything, recruit? Beyond the fact that Recruit Wilberforce is a teenage boy and isn't used to his feet yet? Something that he was doing differently to you?'

Sandra frowned. 'No, Sergeant. I'm sorry, I can't say that I did.'

That wasn't unexpected, people with Recruit Orpwood's "affliction" often didn't know what they were doing until it was pointed out and even then they needed constant reminders to stop them doing it after they'd been shown what to do. 'Alright, then, recruit. Front and centre, please.'

Smedley gestured to the spot in front of him, recently vacated by Benedict and Sandra went and stood there.

'Face left, please.' He waited for her to do so, then raised his voice. 'Recruit, atten....shun!' Again, the manoeuvre was sloppy, but once again he ignored it.

'Recruit! Quick... march!'

He had fully expected some reaction from the other recruits when Orpwood started forward, but he was surprised when it was only Wilberforce who sniggered. He was surprised and pleased; a group that didn't laugh at the misfortunes of one of their own was rare. And very promising.

'Alright! Stop there, turn around and march back!'

She came marching back. He had to hand it to her, even doing it absurdly wrong she still looked confident and quite smart.

He brought her to a halt, then went to stand with her next to the other recruits.

'Recruit Perkins! Can you tell Recruit Orpwood what she's doing wrong?'

'Yes, Sergeant!' Ellie looked at her friend and gave her a sympathetic smile and a shrug. 'You're using the same arm and leg, Sandra. You're supposed to swing the opposite one.'

'I am?' Sandra looked down at her arms, as if she'd be able to tell.

'You are, recruit.' Sergeant Smedley said with a smile. 'But don't worry, even though it does look bloody silly, it is only a temporary affliction and we will all do everything we can to make sure it doesn't last very long. Isn't that right, Perkins?'

'Yes, Sergeant!'

'Good!' Smedley said, then smiled at Sandra kindly. 'Fall back in, recruit.'

'I hope you've all recovered from this morning, recruits, because it's time to do some more exercise!'

As soon as they'd finished with the drill lesson they had gotten changed back into their sports kit and rushed to the obstacle course, where they'd found Airwoman Jones, this time accompanied by the sour-faced Airwoman Phillips.

'For those of you who have not seen one before, this is an obstacle course. It is a test of balance, coordination and strength and is not only good fun and good exercise, but also an excellent lesson in teamwork because some of the obstacles need at least two people to get over. Which is why Airwoman Phillips has joined us for this session. So,' she started walking backwards towards the first obstacle - a large net suspended horizontally about a foot and a half off the floor, 'what we're going to do is take the obstacles one by one. I'm going to demonstrate and then you're going to have a few goes. Once I'm happy you've got the idea we'll move on to the next one. There are twenty obstacles in all and we only have an hour, so you won't run it today, but don't worry; you will work up a very good appetite by the time lunch rolls around!' she laughed, then turned to the obstacle. 'Right, then!' she clapped her hands, then rubbed them together before diving to the ground in front of the net.

Benedict slid into his chair, then looked at his hands in distaste. They were red, chafed by the ropes they'd been climbing up down and over on the assault course and swollen from washing his sports kit. He was sure he could feel a blister or two coming as well, and then what? Calluses? How was he going to fly properly if his hands were destroyed? This was why pilots had batmen; to do all this menial work for them and free them up to fly. And things were only going to get worse, not better.

'What's the matter, Cleaner Boy?' Tayler said as he arrived with his food. 'Are your poor hands feeling sore? You not used to doing an honest day's work? Most of the rest of us have been helping out around our houses and farms since we could walk, but I bet you have an army of servants to do everything you need. Probably have someone to wipe your...'

Benedict snarled, cutting him off. 'Just because I've been using my brains my whole life and not just my hands...'

'Are you calling me thick?' Tayler growled, cutting him off in turn. He dropped his tray on the table, spilling peas from his plate, then put his hands on the table and leaned forwards aggressively, putting his face only a foot or so from Benedict's.

'Well...' Benedict began, leaning back in his chair and smirking up at him.

'Oi!'

They looked up, startled, and found Lottie looming over them from the head of the table. Her voice hadn't been loud - shouting in the half-full mess hall would have brought down the ire of just about every NCO in the place - but it still demanded their attention and she got it in full.

'You! Sit down!' she said, pointing at Tayler, whose legs all but gave way beneath him, 'and you! Shut up!' she added, turning her finger and full attention on Benedict, who went white.

'We're all in the same boat here,' she told Benedict, 'we all have to do the same stuff, whether we like it or not, so you have two choices: either shut up and do it, or go home,' she spun around to face Tayler, who'd begun to grin at Benedict's discomfort but suddenly thought better of it, 'and as for you. I know Benedict is a berk, but he's *our* berk and we pass or fail with him.'

She looked back and forth from one to the other. 'We're all equal here. It doesn't matter where we came from, just where we're going and I don't know about you but I want to end up in a cockpit. So, don't you dare spoil that for me. Or else.'

She glared at them, daring them to say something and when they remained silent she nodded in satisfaction then sat down and started digging hungrily into her food.

The recruits ate in silence for a moment, none of them wanting to risk Lottie's ire by speaking first, but then Sandra put her cutlery down and leaned forward slightly to look up and down the table. 'Lottie's right; we need to put aside our feelings and work together. But I also sympathise with Benedict - I'm really not used to shining shoes and I hate having to do it every day. I don't mind washing clothes, though, so I'd love to swap with someone.'

'We should draw up a rota.' Jemima said, nodding enthusiastically. 'That would free up a few people every day and give us much more time to study.'

Sandra nodded enthusiastically, then turned to Lottie. 'What do you say?'

Lottie looked at her, then looked at Benedict. 'Alright. As long as nobody gets out of doing their fair share.'

Jemima grinned. 'I'll start drawing up a rota tonight.'

'I'll help,' Franklin volunteered, putting his hand up and smiling shyly at her.

Sergeant Smedley grinned into his tea; usually it took a recruit group a lot longer than just a day to unite and organise themselves enough to spread the hefty workload. Some of them never did, even back when basic had lasted months.

Corporal Lewis wasn't happy, though. 'That situation between Oakley and Wilberforce is troubling, Sarge,' he said quietly, 'I thought it was going to come to blows there. We might lose both of them if it came to that. Should we say something?'

Smedley shook his head. 'I don't think it's going to come to that and no, Smith covered everything very nicely. We'll keep an eye on them, but it's best to let them sort their own problems out and only step in if it gets out of hand.'

'I had Smith pegged as the strong silent type.' Airman Davies said thoughtfully. 'I'm not usually that wrong about someone.'

'I had her wrong too,' Smedley agreed. 'I'll make a note in her file. If she doesn't make pilot and is at a loss for what to do, then she'll certainly have a place here.'

The recruits were back in the classroom for the whole of the afternoon, continuing to broaden their knowledge. History with Airman Davies was just as entertaining as it had been the day before, but they had two classes with Airwoman Phillips, not just the one, and the struggle to stay alert and learn in the face of the boring subject matter and her boring voice was complicated further by the addition of sore muscles. Finally, though, they were released for the day and Jemima began to draw up the rota while Franklin went around asking which of the jobs people disliked the most and which they wouldn't mind doing. Between the two of them they got it sorted out quickly and the nightly chores were rapidly and efficiently dealt with.

The easing of their workload did nothing to ease the enmity between Benedict and Tayler, but there was no confrontation at dinner, or afterwards, when everyone met up in the boys' dorm room to study. The trouble didn't start until the day after, on the obstacle course, when Tayler left Benedict hanging, literally, from the ten-foot wall. A few obstacles later, in retaliation, Benedict tripped Tayler and sent him flying headlong into the mud below the balance beam. Airwoman Jones of course saw everything and once they'd finished the course the entire group ended up running an extra lap around the airfield, as well as working in the kitchen and cleaning the communal bathrooms that evening.

The fact that the whole group was being punished for what they were doing did nothing to dissuade the two boys and the situation worsened over the next couple of days as, not only did their behaviour worsen, but Benedict began to rub everyone else up the wrong way as well. He continued to act haughty and superior and when they started doing problem-solving exercises as a group to promote working together as a team - things like getting across a ditch with one of them acting injured or tying their ankles together to form a long chain and then trying to get over the tall cargo net of the obstacle course - he was always trying to tell them what to do, even when someone else had been put in charge for the exercise, or criticising their decisions. It got to the point where nobody wanted to work with him and they refused to carry out his orders or deliberately sabotaged him when he was put in charge. Tayler continued to be antagonistic towards him, but by end of the third day so was everyone else and the atmosphere in the group had soured to the point where it was affecting their ability to learn and progress.

Faced with the possibility of losing the entire group, Sergeant Smedley decided to take extreme measures. He suspended their theory lessons, brought forward their survival training by a whole week and spent a day making sure they could take care of themselves in the wild before putting them in a bus and dropping them in the middle of the Brecon Beacons.

After two days of bad weather and extreme hardship, with nothing to do but talk while they walked and no other choice but to set aside their differences and help each other just to survive, they struggled to the rendezvous point, forty miles from where they'd been dropped.

After that, even if Benedict never quite lost his snobbish attitude or tried very hard to be friendly, his behaviour at least became, on the most part anyway, tolerable. He and Tayler called a temporary truce and the recruits went back to making good progress, which in turn satisfied the instructors and meant that far fewer punishments needed to be handed out.

7

The first week of basic training was largely about getting recruits acclimatised to life in the military: the discipline; the early mornings that some of them weren't used to; the long hours; the physical fitness; the enforced routine. While they continued to work on all of these things in the second week, their classes changed, becoming more practical and more involved in nature, rather than purely theoretical. Now that they had gotten over the initial shock of what, for most, was a huge change in their lives and were no longer so tired all the time, they were able to work on things that were a bit more dangerous. Things where one moment of inattention due to exhaustion or indiscipline could prove fatal.

According to Sergeant Smedley, this was when the real fun began.

Ellie rolled her shoulders and tugged at the straps laid over them, trying to settle the heavy weight of the glidewings on her back more comfortably, but, just like every other time she'd shifted it, she only seemed to make it worse.

For the umpteenth time she tilted her head back and craned her neck, trying to get a glimpse of what was going on above her, but the only thing she could see through the legs and backs of the others waiting for their turn on the stairs above her was the underside of the platform.

She brought her eyes back down, closing them and pulling in a shuddering breath in an attempt to calm herself.

She'd been fine with all the cleaning and washing and folding and making beds and stuff, after all, she'd been doing all that and more for years. She'd also been fine with doing drill; she'd joined the military knowing that was one of the things the military did most. She'd even been fine with all the exercise because, once it had stopped making her physically sick, she had actually started feeling good in herself. The book learning had been a bit harder, but that was only to be expected seeing as her school days were so far behind her and as for the guns, well, she was never going to be completely comfortable with them, but she'd still learned how to clean them and take them apart and could hit a target more than she missed it.

This, though...

She *really* wasn't sure she was fine with jumping from a platform eighty yards off the ground with only a few thin sheets of metal strapped to her back preventing her RAC career from coming to an abrupt end.

When they'd done the preliminary training on the ground, learning how the glidewings worked and practising the safety procedures and such, Corporal Lewis had told them that the ones they'd be using were the same as the ones used by civilians in tall buildings. He'd told them they were self-stabilising and would carry you safely to the ground on their own without you needing to do anything at all. Meaning that all they needed to do was to go to the front of the platform, lean forwards and let themselves fall.

He'd said it as if it were the most normal thing in the world to climb an eighty-yard high tower and then just walk off the edge and she supposed it was to him. She couldn't think of anything less normal, though.

'But what if I *can't* do it?' she whined, opening her eyes again. 'What if I can't jump?'

'Stop it!' Sandra said, insinuating her hand into Ellie's and squeezing it hard. 'You're just making it worse! If you keep worrying like that you *won't* be able to jump when you get up there, whether you're really are scared or not.'

What Sandra was saying made perfect sense. She was all too aware that the more she thought about it the harder it was going to become to make the leap, but she couldn't help herself. She'd been dreading this moment since she'd found out what the tower in the corner of the base was for and now that she was actually climbing it that dread was swiftly becoming terror. She'd made the mistake of looking down past the stairs, through the iron girders once and had had to clutch at the railing to stop herself from falling over because it had made her so dizzy. And she'd been less than half way up at the time. Since then she'd made sure to keep her eyes on the people in front of her and it hadn't been so bad, but what if she froze when she got onto the platform at the top of the tower? Or was so overcome with dizziness that she fainted? What if she was fine, but just couldn't force herself to jump?

It wouldn't be the end of the world; she wouldn't fail basic training and get thrown out of the RAC. However, it would mean that she would no longer have the choice of becoming a pilot or any other kind of aircrew and she didn't want to have her options limited before she had a chance to decide for herself.

The queue moved forwards slowly as each of the recruits took their turn. Benedict, Lottie, Tayler and Franklin had already had their goes and the sight of them plummeting by almost vertically, picking up speed before their wings could bite into the air and create enough lift to start their long glide to the ground, had been rather unnerving, although Lottie's cry of joy as she flew past had made her laugh and done a great deal to dispel her nerves.

Jemima was next, then Rob, and then it was Ellie's turn. Sandra gave her hand a squeeze, then gently pushed her forwards.

Ellie stood on the back of the platform as Corporal Lewis checked the straps of her glidewings before going behind her and pulling the lever to extend the wings to their fullest. He tapped her on the shoulders.

'Checked and ready to jump.'

'Checked and ready, corporal!' she answered, giving the ritual reply they'd rehearsed that morning.

'Step forwards!'

Ellie stared straight ahead, keeping her eyes on the horizon, as she took one tiny, hesitant step, then another, trying not to be too unnerved by how the floor just came to an end a couple of yards in front of her. The edge was coming ever closer, though, and she realised that if she didn't look down soon she might go off it accidentally and potentially disastrously.

Slowly, apprehensively, she lowered her gaze.

Her eyes widened and her jaw dropped as she got her first good look at how the world was spread beneath her. The highest she'd ever been before was up on top of the hill next to her village, but it was barely higher than the rooftops and the view from there was nothing like this. It was beautiful, breathtaking and it felt like she could see forever. She couldn't imagine how much more she'd be able to see from an aircraft, but, as she continued to drink it in, she found herself quite wanting to find out.

'In your own time, Perkins.' Corporal Lewis said with a grin.

Ellie turned her head to grin at him, then launched herself gleefully into the sky.

There was so much to learn and so little time to in which to do so and before they knew it they had taken and passed their exams and it was their final day at RAC Druid. They started it, as always, at five in the morning with their morning exercises. Their fitness had improved to the point where they could now do two laps of the airfield without anyone being in danger of collapsing or vomiting. However, instead of going straight to their bunk rooms to get changed for breakfast, they were formed up on the parade ground in the weak early morning sunlight and Sergeant Smedley appeared.

He stood in front of them and looked up and down their lines.

'Not such a sorry looking lot anymore, are you?' he said with a chuckle. 'So. This is it. This is the end of your basic training and it's almost time for you to move on and start your career in the Royal Aviator Corps. You have no more training or classes this morning, but that doesn't mean you can just sit around and drink tea until the bus arrives!' he said, dampening their growing smiles before they could grow too wide. 'First up, after breakfast, you'll dress in your best kit and then we're coming back out here to do the all-important group photograph. Once that is done, you'll have your final interviews with Lieutenant Wallington, where he will congratulate you for passing, as if there was any doubt, shake your hands and confirm what kind of job you want to train for. If you want to change, or make the biggest mistake of your life and transfer to the navy or the army, then that is your last chance to do so!'

This time he gave the recruits a chance to chuckle and nudge each other before going on.

'After that you have one last thing to do,' he looked to Airwoman Jones and grinned. 'On your last day, in order to show the personnel on the base how good your teachers are and how much you've learned from them, it is traditional for the recruits to race their instructors on the obstacle course.' He held up a warning finger, cutting off any comment. 'Don't think you're going to get an easy win, though! Even though a couple of us may be advancing in years, we make up for that by being very fit for our ages and more far experienced than you will ever be... We also cheat!'

The recruits laughed and he indulged them again, but just for a moment before waving them to silence.

'Then, all that you'll have left to do is clean up, pack and have lunch, before the bus carries you onwards. So, seeing as this is my last chance to address you like this, I'd just like to say that, despite a few hiccoughs, you have been a pleasure to teach and it is a pleasure to see you all set off on your journey in the Royal Aviator Corps on such a good foot. I look forward to following your careers with interest.'

He nodded to them seriously, then smiled again. 'And that's it. See you after breakfast. Dismissed!'

As the recruits hurried away, Airwoman Jones wandered over to Sergeant Smedley.

'Nice speech, as always, Sarge. But I don't remember you ever saying that bit about following their careers before.'

'That's because I haven't, Brenda. It was the first time I've been able to say it and mean it.' He shook his head and began to wander off towards the mess. 'I don't know what it is about them, but that group is special and I have a feeling they'll do big things. If the Prussians give them the chance, that is.'

Ellie found herself lagging behind her friends as they went inside to get changed for breakfast and she dressed in her coveralls in silence while the other girls chatted excitedly, already imagining what it would be like to get into an aircraft or, in the case of Jemima, get to work on one. It wasn't until she'd eaten half her breakfast that Sandra finally noticed her mood and nudged her gently with her elbow.

'What's up? Don't tell me you're sad to be leaving this place?'

Ellie nodded. 'Yes, of course. It's just...'

'Don't tell me you still don't know if you want to be a pilot!'

'Of course you want to be a pilot!' Tayler called out from across the table. 'Flying is the best thing in the world!' he grinned cheekily and winked at her. 'Well, the second best thing, anyway.'

'Tay!' Rob admonished, punching his friend in the arm. He looked at Ellie. 'Why wouldn't you want to be a pilot? Is there something else you'd rather do?'

'Yeah,' Jemima said, leaning forward and grinning. 'Are you going turn traitor and join the navy?'

Ellie laughed and shook her head. 'No, nothing like that! It's just...' she shrugged. 'I think it would be best if I learned something that would be useful after the war. So that I can support myself.'

'There's plenty of things you could do as a pilot,' Rob said. 'You could fly passenger aircraft and see the world.'

'Or do crop dusting like me and spray the world!' Tayler added, recoiling back from Rob in case he decided to hit him again.

Sandra shook her head in exasperation at the two, then looked at Ellie. 'Seriously, though, those clowns are right. There are plenty of jobs on offer for pilots. Maybe not as many as there are for mechanics or engineers, but enough that someone who was trained by the RAC shouldn't have much trouble getting one.'

Ellie looked down at her half-empty plate. She'd put off making the decision as long as she could, waiting to see whether something would make up her mind for her, but in less than an hour she was going to have to tell Aviator Lieutenant Wallington something. But what? Was she really going to pass up the chance of possibly becoming a pilot?

She was caught in two minds. Her head was still telling her that it would be the sensible thing to do to join Jemima and learn something that could be useful anywhere, but her heart... She'd first started falling in love with the idea of becoming a pilot reading about the Misfits in Sandra's scrapbook every night, whenever she could snatch a few moments. And listening to Tayler talking about the freedom of being in the air had just made it sound even more romantic. She had pushed those feelings to the side as soon as she'd felt them, though, thinking that it was just a fleeting infatuation.

But.

Ever since she'd stood on the top of that tower and seen the world from that new perspective. Ever since she'd felt that initial rush when she'd dived off. Ever since she'd felt the peace and wonder of the glide down to the ground. Ever since then her heart had been screaming at her that it needed that feeling in her life, that she should do anything she could to make it happen again. That she should be a pilot if she could be.

The decision wasn't that hard at all, in the end.

'Bugger it!' she said with a laugh. 'Why not?' she grinned at her friends. 'I'm going to be a pilot!'

The rest of that morning went by in a bit of a rush.

When they trooped back out onto the parade ground fifteen minutes later they found an old Harridan already in place and everything set up to take the photograph. They lined up where they were told, smiled, stood still for the few moments it took, then trooped straight back inside and went to Lieutenant Wallington's office. Their final interviews were over almost as quickly as the photograph and then, after another short break, this time for tea, they put their sports kit back on and went out to the obstacle course.

It seemed that the base's personnel in its entirety had turned out for the race - there didn't seem to be very much to do around the base or in the nearby villages, so it was probably one of the highlights of the week. The spectators were entertained by a close race, which the instructors won, as Sergeant Smedley had predicted they would, but only because they'd cheated to within an inch of their lives. It was all in good fun, though, and they had the recruits in stitches with their clowning, even Benedict, who Corporal Lewis "accidentally" knocked into the mud under the balance beam.

It was a first-rate way to bring the gruelling two weeks of training to a close and afterwards they shared a drink with their instructors, with rank put aside for just that little while. It was nearly lunch time, though, and they still hadn't packed, so they washed their clothes for the second time that morning, hung them in the airing cupboard so that they'd be dry before they left, then went to eat.

The clapped-out bus that had brought them two weeks previously had returned that morning. Another, much larger, group of young men and women had come on it and an airman ushered them into the mess hall just as they were finishing eating. They looked just as shell-shocked and lost as they themselves had been and the recruits couldn't help but be aware of how far they'd come in so little time.

Ellie bent down to look under the bed, then peered in the tiny metal wardrobe and the footlocker, checking she hadn't missed anything. It wasn't exactly as if she had much to miss, though; she hadn't brought much with her and she'd thrown half of it away when she'd been issued her uniform. Satisfied, she pulled the drawstring of her kitbag tight, then looked around.

'You ready, Ellie?'

Jemima, Lottie and Sandra were standing by the door, already finished and waiting for her, Lottie and Sandra with suitcases in addition to their kitbags and Jemima with her portmanteau that was almost as big as she was, filled with books and writing paper. Ellie's own suitcase had gone in the bin the very first evening - it hadn't been in a very good state to start off with and it had as good as disintegrated after getting soaked when they'd arrived.

She nodded. 'You know, I *am* going to miss this place,' she said.

'Why?' Jemima asked incredulously.

Ellie picked up her case and walked over to them. She shrugged. 'I don't know. I just will.'

'I think she's gone barmy,' Jemima said to the other girls as they turned to leave.

'Definitely.' Lottie said. 'I think she must have knocked her head when she fell off the rope climb.'

Sandra chuckled. 'It was pretty funny how the instructors had greased up the ropes...'

Their voices faded as they went past the bathroom and out the door, but Ellie didn't immediately follow them. Instead, she held back and took one last look at the room.

It wasn't much to look at and she was sure for the others it was a step down from what they were used to, but for her it was more than just a place where she had laid her head - here, her life had completely changed, becoming so much better.

That was why she would miss it.

She grabbed her kitbag and walked out of the door without looking back.

'Recruits! Aten... shun!'

The recruits stamped to attention at Sergeant Smedley's order. They were still not quite together, even after two weeks of daily practise, and the man winced, but didn't bawl them out, he just turned smartly and saluted Aviator Lieutenant Wallington.

'Recruits ready to depart, sah!'

The officer returned the salute. 'Thank you, Sergeant. Stand them at ease, please.'

'Sah!' The sergeant saluted again, then turned to the recruits.

'Recruits! Standat... ease!'

The recruits stamped again, opening their legs slightly and putting their hands behind their backs, but didn't relax completely.

The officer looked up and down the two neat rows of recruits. 'Well, we've done what we can to prepare you for what's to come in the short time we had, but from now on it'll be purely up to you whether you succeed or not. Things will be just as tough during the next couple of weeks, but if you work as hard as you have here, keep your wits about you and, above all, ask for help when you need it, then I don't doubt that you will.'

He smiled. 'Safe journey and the best of luck to you all.'

He nodded at the sergeant, who snapped to attention and took a deep breath. 'Recruits! Aten... shun! Recruits! Officer on parade! Dis... miss!'

The recruits did a quarter turn, saluted, then marched forward a few steps before breaking ranks. However, before they could completely relax, the sergeant was already shouting at them, ending as he'd begun.

'Onto the bus, recruits! Move it!'

The last thing the recruits saw as they left RAC Druid for good was their instructors smiling and laughing as they stood around watching the bus leave.

It seemed to bode well for their future.

RAC GWYNEDD
ELEMENTARY FLIGHT TRAINING

JULY – AUGUST 1941

8

'Look! Spitsteams!'

Rob's shout barely carried over the sound of the labouring engine of the bus, but it nevertheless caught everyone's attention and they crowded the windows on his side, causing the bus to sway alarmingly on its dreadful suspension. The driver shouted at them to sit back down and they did, but not before they had all gotten a good look at the pair of sleek aircraft tearing past, actually flying below them, in the valley beside the road, which ran along a ridgeline.

RAC Druid had been in relatively flat country, but they were heading up into the more mountainous region of Snowdonia now. The bus was having trouble with the constant ups and downs and was making far more noise than it had when it had brought them from Leeds, but it wasn't raining and the windows weren't steamed up so they could at least watch the picturesque countryside going by. It was just as uncomfortable, though.

Thankfully, the journey was much shorter and, less than two hours after they'd left RAC Druid, they turned off the road and onto a narrow lane lined by trees whose branches met and intertwined overhead, forming a tunnel. After about half a mile they came to metal gates set in a chain-link fence and were waved through by two guards in RAC uniforms with red caps. However, it wasn't until they'd gone another half a mile that they spotted the first buildings. Green-painted and low, just like the ones at RAC Druid, they were almost invisible in the shade of the tall trees until they were right up to them. However, where Druid had seemed almost deserted at times, this was very obviously an active base and they could see dozens of men and women engaged in various activities between the trees, or walking on the paths between the buildings.

The trees opened up after they'd passed a few buildings, revealing a large airfield and they turned onto the perimeter track. A couple of two-seater trainers were taxiing across the field, towards half a dozen hangars, widely spaced on the far side of the field, but they lost sight of them when the bus turned again and drove onto a parade ground between two of the buildings. It came to a stop in front of the steps leading up to the entrance of the largest building they'd seen so far and the door opened.

An aviator sergeant, with the same stern and unforgiving look to him as Sergeant Smedley, mounted the steps and surveyed them from underneath the peak of his cap.

'Let's be having you then!' he growled, before turning and getting back off, leaving them to follow him.

Once they were all out he led them up into the building without a word, then diagonally across a large, marble-tiled atrium so quickly that they didn't have time to do more than glance at the paintings and trophies on the walls and straight through the first door on the right.

A large wooden desk, the only piece of furniture, dominated the moderately-sized rectangular room from the far end, a pair of flags - a union flag and the RAC colours - hanging behind it against the wall, their staffs crossed.

'Stack your bags at the back then fall in in two ranks facing the desk.' The sergeant moved to the middle of the room and showed them where to line up.

Portraits of several stern men and women in RAC uniforms stared down at them from the wall to their left while, from between the flags, the king smiled benignly. The wall to their right was comprised mostly of windows looking out over the airfield. They were closed, but they could still hear the buzz of airscrews cutting the air on the airfield, causing at least a few of them to grin excitedly and glance at each other. A growled order from the sergeant had them looking to the front again, though, and a couple of minutes later he called them to attention as two officers entered the room.

'At ease, recruits.' One of the officers, a group captain, ordered as he went past them.

He turned in front of the desk and looked at them while the other officer, an aviator lieutenant, went behind it and started laying out papers.

'Welcome to RAC Gwynedd - one small part of what is known as the Officer Orientation College,' the group captain said, 'I'm Group Captain Wyvern, the commanding officer, and this is my adjutant, Aviator Lieutenant Pierce. Congratulations on making it through Druid. You've all shown what you're made of and now it's time to take the next step, whatever you have decided that is. However, before you can do that, you all have to go through a little ceremony. As of now you cease to be civilian recruits and become Royal Aviator Corps cadets. As such you are required to officially join the Royal Aviator Corps and His Majesty's armed forces by taking the oath of affirmation, which states that you will be faithful to the king and will obey the orders of him, his heirs and the officers set over you.'

He looked at each of them in turn, cementing the seriousness of the situation.

'A word of warning to you: this is your very last chance to reconsider, to get back on the bus and go back to your life. Once you take the oath there is no going back, you're in the RAC for the rest of the war. And once you sign, disobeying the order of a superior officer won't just get you extra kitchen duty like it did at Druid, it might get you sent to the stockade. Or the gallows.'

He paused to let that sink in before continuing.

'If you are not completely committed then I would advise you to say so now. Nobody will think the worst of you if you decide against continuing; life in the armed forces isn't for everyone and I'm sure that at least a few of you are wondering what you've gotten yourself in for after the tender ministrations of the instructors at Druid.'

He chuckled, letting the recruits know that they could show their amusement if they wished, but only Benedict took him up on the offer, the rest were too awestruck at the importance of the moment to do so.

'Anyone? Speak now or forever and all that.' He waited a moment, then smiled. 'No? Jolly good show! Right, then! The adj will read the oath in full, then he'll call you up one by one to make your mark. Once everyone has signed we'll get you settled. Adj?'

The adjutant cleared his throat noisily, then read rapidly from one of his pieces of paper. 'I do solemnly, and truly declare and affirm that I will be faithful and bear true allegiance to His Majesty King George, the sixth of his name, His Heirs and Successors, and that I will, as in duty bound, honestly and faithfully defend His Majesty, His Heirs and Successors, in Person, Crown and Dignity against all enemies, and will observe and obey all orders of His Majesty, His Heirs and Successors, and of the officers set over me.'

He set the paper to the side then picked up another with a list on it. 'The Honourable Benedict Charles Henry Victor Wilberforce.'

Benedict came to attention and marched to the desk. He picked up the pen and signed his name with a flourish then turned to the commanding officer.

'Congratulations, cadet,' Wyvern said as he shook Benedict's hand. 'I know your father. He's a good man.'

'He has spoken highly of you, too, sir.'

Wyvern nodded, then released Benedict's hand. 'Fall in, Cadet Wilberforce.'

'Sir!' Benedict stamped and turned smartly, then marched back to his place. He gave Tayler a small smile, before turning to face the front and standing at ease.

'Mr Franklin Warren Dunstable,' the adjutant called.

One by one, the recruits were called forwards and they marched, none of them quite as smartly as Benedict, to the desk and signed the oath before shaking the group captain's hand and returning to their places. Once everyone was done, Wyvern took centre stage again.

'There is a lot more that could be said, but I'll leave it to your training officers and instructors to do so in their own way. What I will say is this - if you are having trouble with anything - with the work, with your health, with one of your instructors or colleagues, even - then please, talk to someone. Do not suffer alone. My door is always open, but we also have several medical professionals on the base, any of whom are available for a chat and your instructors are a very understanding bunch, no matter how stern they seem on the surface. The RAC is a family. We will take care of you if you let us. Please do.' He smiled. 'The best of luck to you all.' He nodded at the sergeant.

'Cadets! Cadets... 'shun!'

Once the officers had left the room, they grabbed their bags and made their way back outside to where a couple of airmen waiting for them.

'Right!' called the sergeant. 'It's time to split up! Dunstable and Trotter, you're going back on the bus with Airman Hughes to Technical Support School, a few valleys away. The rest of you will go with Airman King to your bunks in building G. Say your goodbyes now, quickly, because you won't be seeing each other for a while!'

'Pilots! With me!' one of the airmen called out as he started walking away.

Benedict immediately followed him, but the other five men and women who would be training as pilots surrounded Franklin and Jemima. They had known this was coming and had already said all that they had wanted to say, so they just hugged and exchanged a few last words, then ran to catch up with Airman King and Benedict, leaving Jemima and Franklin to get back on the bus.

They fell into step behind Benedict and Tayler and Rob shared a glance. Tayler inclined his head towards Benedict and Rob nodded.

'Right honourable?' Tayler asked over Benedict's shoulder. 'Kept that under your hat didn't you?'

'He's a right something, anyway.' Rob agreed.

Benedict turned and gave them a scathing look. 'Do you wonder why I didn't say anything? Anyway, my title will do little to help me here.'

'Not for want of trying, I reckon,' Tayler said.

Benedict didn't reply, but his cheeks coloured, giving them all the answer they needed.

'So much for teamwork,' Sandra muttered to Ellie as they followed behind the men.

'So much for the truce.' Ellie answered.

The rest of the day went much as their first day at Druid had gone. Their first stop was to stores, to be issued with more kit, including flight gear, a pilot's logbook, about a dozen text books and proper RAC uniforms, and then they were taken to their bunk rooms and given half an hour to unpack, freshen up and change into their new uniforms.

They had been allocated rooms on either side of the corridor in a barracks building shared with the other trainee pilots. They were much nicer than the ones at Druid, sleeping only six instead of twelve and with bigger wardrobes, a few shelves on the walls over the beds and a small sitting area at the far end of the room with worn but comfortable looking armchairs. It didn't take them long to settle in and put all their things away and a different airman came to get them once the half an hour was up to take them on a tour of the base.

Gwynedd was enormous compared to Druid, with almost a thousand cadets housed in eight barracks blocks. While the base was purely a training facility, it was fully functioning and operated as if it were on the front-line, so that cadets who had finished their specialist training, the training that Jemima and Franklin were about to begin, could put what they had learned into practice in an environment that was as realistic as possible. Under the supervision of experienced officers and NCOs, cadets ran everything, from the kitchens and messes to air traffic control and aircraft maintenance. They even did a fair amount of the administration, under the watchful eye of the adjutant and his assistants. The prospective pilots were the only ones, in fact, that were still in the process of learning their trade and they actually left the base when they got to the stage the other cadets were at when they arrived, moving to specialist facilities elsewhere to finish their training.

They didn't see every building, workshop or facility; that would have taken far too long, but they did get shown the ones that directly concerned them, like the cadet's mess and the classrooms where they would have lectures. The highlight of the tour for every one of them, though, was the visit to the hangars, where a variety of aircraft were housed.

Ellie had been listening to the others speaking about how much they were looking forward to flying for the last two weeks. Every single conversation they'd had, it didn't matter whether it was over lunch, breakfast, dinner, or while they were studying, had somehow turned to the subject. Granted, they were on an RAC base and working towards one day being pilots or something else to do with aircraft, but there was much more to life than just that and it had gotten to the point where she would even have preferred a conversation about cricket. Which was saying a lot.

She hadn't understood why they were so obsessed. As far as she was concerned, flying was just a job and aircraft were just the tools with which you did it, like a gun to fight with, or a broom to sweep the house.

But the aircraft in the hangars were more than just tools, more than just machines; they had personality and charisma and somehow seemed almost alive. Something about them called to her, especially the sleek fighters, the Harridans and Spitsteams, that the other cadets were fawning over. They sat there as if they were cats, ready to pounce on a mouse, and she could well imagine them toying with Prussian aircraft in the same way.

And now she understood.

Tayler nudged Rob and waved at the fighters. 'So, which one do you want?'

When Rob didn't immediately reply, Tayler looked at him. When he saw that Rob was gazing at the Spitsteam as if he were in love he laughed. 'I guess that answers that question.'

'Sorry? What?' Rob asked, frowning.

'I asked - which one do you want to fly, but it's pretty obvious,' he nodded in the direction of the Spit. It was a MK1 and consequently about a year or two out of date, the same as the Harridans, but beggars couldn't be choosers and when they got to a squadron they'd undoubtedly be given later models.

Rob nodded. 'Don't you?'

'Of course, but I wouldn't mind flying a Harridan either; Harrys get more ground attack duties. Spits are always up against fighters, or on escort duty.'

'Really?' Rob asked. 'You joined the RAC to spray crops with a Harridan?'

Benedict ran his hand along the leading edge of the wing of a Spitsteam and grinned.

Mine, he thought greedily.

After the tour they had a brief break for tea, but then at five they made their way to a briefing room in the main building to meet Wing Commander Trevillian, who was in charge of elementary flight training.

They didn't have to wait long until the wing commander entered and they stood to attention.

'Good afternoon, ladies and gentlemen. Sit down, please.' He took a seat himself on the edge of the table at the front of the room and looked down at them, his legs crossed and his elbow propped on his knee, his relaxed attitude in sharp contrast to the stiffness of the officers and NCO's they'd met until then. 'Right, now that you've been to Druid and done all the boring but necessary stuff, it's time to have some fun. Yes, I know we're at war and, yes, war is serious business, but the best pilots are the ones who enjoy flying. And if you doubt that statement then I'd direct your attention to the Misfits.'

He grinned at them.

'I assume Lieutenant Wallington gave you the "Britain needs pilots" speech?' He looked around and when they nodded he smiled. 'Well, I'm fairly confident that all of you *will* be pilots, because there's no great mystery to it. What we don't know, though, is how long it's going to take you to become one and what kind you're going to be.

Right now, the RAC has four basic types of pilots: you've got your Spit pilots, who are mostly dealing with enemy fighters; your Harry pilots who are mostly going after enemy bombers or carrying out ground attacks; your bomber pilots, whose work is fairly self-explanatory; and your transport pilots, who ferry new aircraft from the factories to squadrons or fly cargo aircraft around. Now, I'm sure that most, if not all of you, have some idea of what kind of pilot you'd like to be and what you'd like to fly, but we don't need to worry ourselves with that right now. What we have to worry about is how long it's going to take you to get your wings so you can graduate and go to a squadron.'

He put his hands on his knees and leaned forwards, gazing at them earnestly.

'It usually takes about a year and a half to train a pilot from nothing, during which time they get anywhere between two hundred and fifty and five hundred hours of flight time. However, a few months ago we instigated a new accelerated program for cadet pilots which is designed to take into consideration previous experience and talent instead of merely treating everyone the same. Elementary flight training has been reduced to just two weeks, during which time you will learn every aspect of how to control an aircraft, including advance manoeuvres such as aerobatics and what to do in an emergency. You will be spending six to eight hours in the air each day, including weekends, starting at dawn and only stopping when the sun goes down. The day doesn't finish there, though, because after dinner you will spend another two hours in the classroom, doing your officer training and taking classes in mathematics, aeronautics, ballistics and all the other lovely things you will need floating around in your head when a Prussian is shooting at you.'

He got a few laughs at that, but continued quickly. 'After one week, as long as we haven't lost too much time for bad weather, you should have more than forty hours logged and you'll be assessed on your progress in the air. There is no pass or failure at that point, though, just an honest review in front of a panel of instructors and a kick up the arse if you need it. The real test comes at the end of the two weeks, when those we deem to be ready will take their wings test. Don't worry if you're not ready; less than one in four cadets come even close to being ready, and of those, around half pass.'

He looked around as the cadets did some quick maths and nodded. 'That's right, only one in eight cadets pass the accelerated program. But it's not the end of the world if you're not considered for the wings test at that point or if you fail, because in that case you will shift from the accelerated program into the regular program and complete the full eight-month course. You'll take your wings test in your own time, then move on to a specialist course in the aircraft type of your choice, at the end of which you will graduate as officers and pilots.'

Trevillian paused again, watching the cadets as the realisation that, whatever happened, they were going to be pilots, sank in. He smiled; he loved seeing their young faces light up like that as they saw how close they were to realising their dreams.

'So, what happens if you manage to pass the wings test, you may ask. Well, in that case you will leave Gwynedd and go to RAC Galath for what some bright spark named "Dogfight and Risk Training". This is a two-week course that has only recently been added to the pilot training process in response to our losses in the summer of last year. When the RAC realised that it wasn't enough for their pilots just to know how to control their planes, but that they needed to know how to fight in them as well. There, you'll be taught to deal with high-risk situations by extremely experienced pilots who will also let you in on all their little dogfighting tricks and secrets so that you'll be able to go up against enemy fighters and not have it go disastrously at the first attempt. When they're satisfied with you, they'll send you on your way again, this time up to Scotland to join an Operational Training Unit for the final stage of your training. During your two weeks there you'll fly combat sorties and do things like polish off your formation flying and coordinated attack skills before being assigned to an active squadron.' He nodded, smiling grimly at them. 'That's right. If you do well enough here and show us that you have the skill, the talent and the determination that we're looking for, you might be flying in combat only six weeks from now.'

He gave them a moment to take in that information, then sat up straight and slapped his thighs. 'Well! As you can see, there's a lot to do. I really hope you weren't expecting to get any rest!' He chuckled as he gestured to the aviator sergeant who had entered with him and she stepped forward and handed him a buff folder.

'Right, then. Here's how we'll be proceeding.' He opened the folder and scanned the top piece of paper rapidly, just to make sure that he had the information correct, then closed it again and looked up. 'Cadet Wilberforce is the only one of you with his pilot's degree already, so he will go straight into advanced elementary training tomorrow. The rest of you will work towards the degree, which is extremely rudimentary and really only a formality, and will take it as soon as you are ready. In the case of Cadets Oakley and Sherborne that should only be a day or two if you really have as much experience as you claim.' He gave the boys a stern look. 'Cadets Orpwood, Perkins and Smith, in the meantime, will be starting from scratch, but you should be in a position to take the degree test after a week of hard work.' He smiled apologetically. 'Sorry, but you are going to have to work bloody hard if you're going to catch up with the others and have any hope of getting your wings in two weeks.'

He frowned suddenly as something occurred to him and he opened the folder again and looked down at the page.

'How curious. I hadn't noticed until now.' He looked up and grinned again. 'The line between those who have experience and those who don't isn't usually so clearly defined by gender.' He looked at the aviator sergeant. 'That should spice things up a little!'

The sergeant nodded. 'There has been a fair amount of interest in this particular group of cadets among the staff already, sir.'

'Really?'

'Yes, sir. They seem to think they are special for some reason.' She glanced at the cadets briefly. 'Don't see it myself, sir.'

Trevillian gazed at her thoughtfully, lips pursed. 'Who's running the book, then?' he asked after a moment.

The aviator sergeant's ramrod straight back straightened even more as she bristled at his question. 'Sir! Are you suggesting that someone is taking bets on the performance of the cadets, something that is not technically illegal or against regulations, but frowned upon by the powers that be?'

'It's you, isn't it, sergeant?'

'Yes, sir.'

'Put a fiver on the ladies for me, please! Points across the board.'

'Right you are, sir.'

Trevillian turned to the cadets and took in their mixture of expressions, ranging from amusement to puzzlement. He laughed. 'Find your fun where you can, ladies and gentlemen! Life is too short. Especially for a fighter pilot.'

He snapped the folder shut loudly, making Sandra and Rob, who were sitting in the front row, jump. 'Flying begins tomorrow at oh seven hundred hours. You'll be woken at oh five thirty and will have a quarter of an hour of physical training, just enough to keep you in shape, but not enough to tire you out. Inspection is at six, then you'll have half an hour for breakfast. Report to the elementary flight

training ready room at oh six forty five for briefing and assignments -
for those of you who were too busy daydreaming about Spits to pay
much attention during the tour, that's the first of the small buildings
on the airfield before the hangars.'

He jumped off the desk and stood in front of them with the
folder tucked under his arm. 'This evening your time is your own.
Enjoy it, because you won't be getting much more for the next few
weeks. I would recommend you go and introduce yourself to the
cadet's mess and have a well-earned drink. Only one or two, mind
you - enough to help you sleep, but not to get you drunk; you don't
want to be fuzzy tomorrow morning.' He gave them one last look,
then nodded. 'See you tomorrow, bright and early.'

'Ahhh! That's good!' Tayler said, smacking his lips as he lowered
his half-empty pint. His third. 'No wonder the beer back home is so
awful - the RAC gets all the good stuff!'

The cadets were shoulder to shoulder around a small table in the
cadet's mess. They'd had to scavenge chairs from all over to have one
each and the table wasn't nearly big enough for them, but it was the
only one that had been available.

The mess was a large, pleasant room in the same building as the
main mess where the enlisted men and cadets had their meals and
was filled to capacity with men and women, the vast majority of
whom looked like they were about their age, including the ones
working behind the bar and roaming around collecting empties.
There was a long brass bar along one side of the room, which they'd
quickly found was stocked with snacks and sandwiches as well as very
basic alcohol. A piano with a group of youths surrounding it, belting
out one bawdy song after another, was set against the wall in a small
empty space to one side, but the rest of the room was filled with
circular wooden tables of various sizes.

It was actually quite cosy, with a fireplace for the winter, a
hardwood floor and wood-panelled walls, and looked more like a pub
than a mess on a military base, although the photographs of previous
cadet classes and the two extremely old two-bladed wooden airscrews
hanging over the bar did give the game away somewhat.

'That's enough, now, Tay!' Rob insisted. 'You need to make a
good impression tomorrow.'

'Pshaw!' Tayler waved away Rob's concern. 'As if I haven't flown
with a hangover before!' he frowned. 'Or drunk, for that matter.'

'Rob's right, Tay,' Ellie said, leaning in to be heard over a particularly popular chorus. 'Besides, there'll be plenty of time for drinking when we've gotten through these first two weeks.'

Tayler turned to answer her, but when he found his face only inches from hers, he completely forgot what he was going to say. Their eyes met and he smiled, but she looked away and blushed before he could come up with something clever. Suddenly, he didn't think that drinking any more was such a good idea after all, so he put his glass back on the table.

'Good boy, *Tay*.' Benedict said with a sneer. 'Listen to mummy and daddy.'

'It's my decision, so shut up, *Cleaner Boy*,' Tayler countered, 'or should we call you *Lord* Cleaner Boy now?'

'His lordship is my father.' Benedict answered, looking down his nose at Tayler. 'Not me.'

Tayler hunched over, ducking his head and mimed pulling his forelock. 'Oh, I do so humbly beg your pardon, sir. Sorry, sir. Won't happen again, sir.' Tayler picked up his drink and downed the rest of it in one go. He slammed the glass back on the table, then wiped his mouth on the back of his hand and stared at Benedict. 'Why are you here drinking with us, anyway? You were never part of the team. You only started playing along so you wouldn't die on the Beacons alone or get kicked out. Why don't you go and write to your father to ask for more money or to have a word with the officers on your behalf?'

Benedict gritted his teeth, but he bit back his reply and instead just pushed back his chair and stood up. 'You're right. There is no need for me to be here or to be civil to you anymore.' He turned and pushed his way through the people in the mess, causing more than one person to frown in irritation at him in his wake.

Sandra glared at Tayler, then slipped out of her chair and hurried after him.

'Where's she going?' Tayler asked.

'Are you oblivious to everything that doesn't directly concern you?' Lottie asked, rolling her eyes. 'Sandra is sweet on him.'

'What?' Tayler laughed mockingly. 'You must be joking! How can anyone be sweet on someone like that?'

Ellie shook her head. 'I have no idea.'

'There's no accounting for taste, I suppose.' Tayler shrugged, then grinned. 'So! Who wants another drink?'

Lottie got up. 'Not me. I'm not going to drink away my chances at flying a Spitsteam.' She looked at Ellie. 'You coming, Ellie?'

Ellie took one last long look at Tayler. 'Yes. I'm coming.'

Rob stood as the two women started to weave through the people towards the door. He looked down at Tayler, but in the end realised that there was nothing he could say that hadn't been already, so he just hurried after his friends.

Tayler huffed. 'Bloody sod them,' he muttered as he toyed with his empty glass.

The words didn't feel good, though, and neither did the fact that he was on his own, so, after waiting a few more seconds, just to prove to himself that he wasn't lonely and really wasn't going after the others, he stood and sauntered to the door.

He only started jogging to catch up once the door had closed behind him and nobody could see him in the darkness.

Rob had left the mess only a few seconds after Ellie and Lottie, but they hadn't seen him and had rushed off after Sandra. He could have caught up with them easily, but he found that he really didn't want to. Instead, he felt like taking the opportunity to be on his own for the first time since he'd left home, so he went down the short road to the airfield, crossed the perimeter track and sat down on the edge of the grass, leaning back on his elbows to look up at the stars.

He heard quick footsteps on the gravel path leading from the cadet's mess and he looked over his shoulder. It was Tayler, he'd know that silhouette anywhere, and he gritted his teeth, steeling himself for what was to come, but Tay either didn't see him or didn't recognise him in the pitch dark and just went past at a run.

Good. He really didn't feel like putting up with Tayler anymore that evening.

At Druid, there had hardly been any time for socialising and not much chance for conversation, beyond a few snatched words while they gulped some food down between classes. There had been no opportunity for him to tell Eleanor that he admired her and couldn't stop thinking about her. It didn't sound like there was going to be much time for courtship here at Gwynedd either, but he'd wanted to at least make his intentions known.

He still hadn't been able say anything, though. Not because there hadn't been the chance, but because it seemed that she only had eyes for Tay.

9

'Good morning, cadets, and welcome to your first day of flight training.'

The ready room for the cadets doing elementary flight training was the first and smallest of the row of four single-storey buildings set in a row next to the hangars, alongside the airfield. It was akin to a village hall, with a single large room filled with half a dozen tables and chairs where cadets could work or write up their logs and three small rooms at the back containing separate bathrooms for men and women and a small kitchen area with a large tea urn. It had been built to accommodate up to thirty cadets at a time, but, due to the two-week turnaround of the accelerated program, they had the place to themselves.

Wing Commander Trevillian, dressed in a blue, standard issue RAC flightsuit and clutching a helmet and a pair of goggles, stood in front of the windows overlooking the airfield. Five instructors, in the same kind of flightsuits, were lined up behind him. Not one of the instructors, including Trevillian, looked under forty years of age and a couple looked like they might actually have been too old to fight in the First Great War.

'These men and women behind me are among the most experienced pilots Britain has ever seen. Every single one of them has been teaching people how to fly for more than a decade and if they can't do something in an aircraft, then it probably can't be done. It doesn't matter how much experience you have or think you have,' he looked at Benedict, Tayler and Rob in turn, 'there will still be plenty you can learn from them. Make sure that you do.' He turned to the women. 'As for you, you couldn't hope for a better start to your careers as pilots.' He smiled at all of them. 'So, take advantage of these two weeks. Learn as much as you damn well can. Above all, though, have fun.' He looked at Ellie and tilted his head towards the door. 'Perkins, you're with me. Let's go.'

He gave his fellow instructors a nod, then walked out. Ellie smiled at Lottie and Sandra, mouthed "good luck" at them, then hurried after him.

When they'd arrived that morning, ten minutes early and raring to get started, dressed in their simple and awfully shapeless cadet's flightsuits, there had already been aircraft moving around the airfield and they'd stopped to watch a pair of Harridans being pushed towards the last building in the row, the one for fighter training. There were now a dozen or so aircraft on the airfield. A few of them were already in movement - preparing for takeoff, she supposed - but there were six lined up in front of the ready rooms on the other side of the perimeter track, their noses pointed away from her. Five of them had two wings, one above the other - biplanes - while the other had just the one wing, making it a monoplane. Trevillian was going towards the biplane on the far left and, after a moment to appreciate the sight, she ran to catch up.

'Right, then, Perkins,' he said, stopping by the tail of the biplane and turning to look at her. 'This is the Sapworth Sprite. We've been using these for elementary training for about fifteen years now, ever since we started putting springs in aircraft. It's outdated and slow, but it's also responsive and very forgiving, which makes it perfect for even the most ham-fisted of cadets to take to the sky in.' He patted the aircraft with a fond smile. 'Now, I take it you've studied the parts of an aircraft and could tell me the name of anything I point at?'

She frowned. 'Yes, sir, I believe so, sir.'

He smiled. 'Don't worry if you haven't got it all down pat yet. It's a lot different learning from a book than from experience. A few days around these beauties and you will.' He rubbed his gloved hands together. 'So, first things first. Every time you get in an aircraft, Fleas permitting, of course, you should carry out a full check. Essentially, you walk around the aircraft, waggling things that should waggle and making sure things that shouldn't waggle don't waggle. Oh, and that there aren't gaping bloody holes in anything.' He began walking around the aircraft demonstrating by pulling the elevators gently up and down, then turning the rudder back and forth. 'Most of the time, though, we don't bother with a complete check.' He nodded in the direction of the team of four fitters standing nearby, watching and waiting. 'Our ground crew chaps take pride in their job and are superb at it. However, for the sake of your pilot's degree you're going to have to demonstrate how to do a complete preflight check and we like you to get into the habit, so you're going to have to do it before every single flight while you're in training.'

He kept moving around the aircraft, looking at the flaps and ailerons before moving around the wings. He bent down to check the spring was firmly fastened, then went to the front of the aircraft and moved his hand up and down the airscrew, checking the blades. He kept up a running commentary as he went, saying exactly what he was doing and why, as if he were checking each part of the aircraft off a checklist in his mind, which, she thought, was probably precisely what he was doing.

Finally, they were back at the tail of the aircraft.

'Easy enough so far, right?'

'Yes, sir.'

'There's a few more checks to do in the cockpit, so, I'm going to get in. You stand on the wing next to me and I'll talk you through it.'

Trevillian put on a set of glidewings that one of the fitters held out for him, then climbed into the rear of the two cockpits in the fuselage of the biplane. He continued his monologue as he performed the remaining checks. There wasn't very much to do in such a simple aircraft, though, so he finished quickly and looked up at her.

'Got it?'

'I think so, sir.'

'Good. Because you'll be doing it for this afternoon's flight!' He grinned. 'Oh, don't worry, it's a doddle. Now, hop in and let's go up.'

Ellie put on her own set of glidewings, then went to the front cockpit and climbed over the lip of the fuselage, just as she'd seen Trevillian do. She sat and a fitter appeared beside her. He helped her to strap in and showed her where to plug in the wires leading to her helmet so that she could hear over the radio.

'Are you with me, Perkins?' Trevillian's voice came crackling in her ears.

'Yes, sir.' Ellie said.

'Jolly good! The comms between the two of us are always open in this aircraft, but when we want to transmit to control or another aircraft on our frequency, then there is a white button on the top of the stick. Don't press it unless I tell you to. Understand?'

'Understood, sir.'

'Righty-ho! Signal for the fitters to release the safety on the spring, please. Lift your right hand and twirl your index finger in the air.'

Ellie lifted her hand and rather self-consciously met the eyes of the chief fitter, who was standing in front of the aircraft to her right, watching her and Trevillian. She twirled her finger and the fitter smiled and nodded, then bawled an order to someone she couldn't see. A couple of light thuds resounded through the airframe of the aircraft and the woman gave her a thumbs up.

'Good. Now we can crack open the spring a touch. Put your left hand very gently on the throttle lever and feel what I do.'

Ellie laid her hand on the lever and felt it move forward very slightly until it notched.

'Feel that?'

'Yes, sir.'

'That's idle throttle. It means the airscrew is turning under the power of the spring, but not producing any thrust. Next step is to get the chocks taken away from the wheels. Lift your hand, open it with the flat to the side, then motion with it as if you were moving a curtain aside.'

'Yes, sir.'

Ellie did as she was told again,

'Well done!' Trevillian said. 'If you don't make it as a pilot, you might have a career as a mime!'

Ellie laughed, feeling tension she hadn't even been aware of flowing from her body.

'Before we can do anything else we have to get permission, so we call control. The callsign for the base is Arthur.'

There was a click and a hissing and scratching noise began in Ellie's ear and she realised that Trevillian had pressed the white button on the stick.

'Arthur Control, this is Charlie One, requesting permission to taxi.'

'Charlie One from Arthur Control. Cleared for taxi.'

'Thank you, Arthur Control.' There was another click and the hissing disappeared as the channel was closed. 'We can move now. You're going to follow along with what I'm doing from now on and for the whole flight, which means putting your right hand very loosely on the stick, your feet very gently on the rudder pedals and your left hand on the throttle like before. Before all that, though, give Aviator

Sergeant Skipworth a thumbs up, please, so she knows we're off and can get her people out of the way.'

Ellie gave the woman a thumbs up and the aviator sergeant backed away and looked around in an exaggerated fashion before returning the gesture.

'All clear,' Trevillian said jollily, 'let's go!'

Ellie put her hands and feet on the controls and felt them begin to move, first the throttle, then, as they began to move forwards, the pedals, making the nose swing. Curiously, the stick didn't move. She'd thought that was the main method of control of an aircraft, but it appeared that, on the ground at least, it wasn't.

The aircraft bumped and rattled over the grass, heading towards the hangars, seemingly going very quickly, and for a moment Ellie thought they were going to either take off or collide with the large buildings, but then the throttle moved under her hand, coming backwards, and the aircraft slowed. Before it came to a halt, the pedals moved sharply under her feet and the nose of the aircraft swung round until it was pointing across the field.

'Lesson number one. When taking off and landing, always do so into the wind. Even if it means a bloody great taxi to the other side of the airfield or some trees being in the way!'

There was a crackling noise in her ears again. 'Arthur Control. This is Charlie One. Ready for takeoff.'

'Roger, Charlie One. You are cleared for takeoff.'

'Thank you, Control,' *click*. 'Hold on to your hat, Perkins!'

The throttle moved smoothly forwards under Ellie's left hand and she was thrust back into the seat as the aircraft leapt forwards.

She'd thought they'd been going fast before, but it was nothing compared to the speed with which the biplane was suddenly going. It raced across the grass with the wind whistling past, there were a couple of small bounces and then, just like that, for the first time ever, Ellie was no longer on the ground, although it felt a bit like her stomach still was. The buildings and trees disappeared beneath the wings and then all that was left was sky.

'Still with me, Perkins?'

'Oh, yes, sir!' Ellie answered, looking around in wonder.

There was a laugh. 'Looks like she likes it! Good show!'

Trevillian took the aircraft up to four thousand feet, pointing out the local landmarks on the way, before levelling off, which gave Ellie plenty of time to get used to the sensation of not having anything solid beneath her and for the novelty of the situation to wear off just a little.

'Let's get started with the basics, shall we? Follow along with me.'

Trevillian began carrying out various simple manoeuvres like climbing, diving and turning, talking through each of them and pointing out what the instruments were showing. He pulled the aircraft through a few tight turns and rolled from one wing to the other, demonstrating what it felt like and the stresses it put on the body. Once he was done he levelled out again.

'Alright, I think it's time you gave it a go. Now, I'm going to say "you have control" and, when you're ready, you say "I have control, sir". When I want it back I say "I have control" And you say "you have control, sir". Got that?'

'Yes, sir.'

'Good. You have control.'

Ellie bit her suddenly dry lip and made sure her hands and feet were firmly on the controls, then took a deep breath. 'I have control, sir.'

She tensed when she felt the sudden loosening of the controls as Trevillian's hands left them, but when the aircraft didn't suddenly plunge from the sky or burst into flames she relaxed. Only slightly, though.

'Let's bank gently round to port. Do you remember how to do that?'

'Yes, sir.'

'Jolly good. Off you go, then.'

Ellie moved the stick to the left, slowly rolling the biplane until its wings were about thirty degrees from horizontal, remembering to pull up slightly so that the nose wouldn't drop. She watched the little air bubble on the attitude indicator, making sure that it was centred by applying a touch of opposite rudder so that the aircraft wouldn't start to slide.

'Now level out.'

The stick went back the other way, rolling the aircraft level again, and she let the rudder pedals come neutral. She forgot to push the nose down, though, so the aircraft started climbing slightly. She panicked and overcompensated, putting the aircraft into a bit of a dive, then had to pull up again. The biplane bobbed up and down like a boat for a few seconds and she blushed as Trevillian laughed, but he wasn't being cruel and his next words more than made up for the embarrassment.

'That was really well done! Are you sure you haven't flown before?'

'I haven't, sir.'

'Not even once?'

'No, sir.'

'Well, you're a natural, then! And don't worry about the bumps, you'll get the feel of things soon enough, I'd wager!'

'I thought you already had wagered on it, sir?' Ellie asked, cheekily.

'Ha! Quite! Well, if I want to win my bet, we'd better keep at it!'

'Put us into a maximum rate turn to starboard, please.'

'Yes, ma'am.' Benedict started the manoeuvre while running through the procedure in his mind. *Stick hard over. Apply rudder steadily. Centre stick and pull back...*

It wasn't a hard manoeuvre to perform. Nothing in an aircraft was very hard, in fact. However, there were some things that were tricky to get right, like making sure the nose was directly on the horizon and the rudder perfectly countered the aircraft's tendency to slide towards the lower wing.

'Transition into a split S and level off at two thousand five hundred feet, please.'

'Roger.'

Roll inverted. Reduce throttle. Pull back on stick.

Benedict smiled when he completed the manoeuvre and saw that the altimeter was showing exactly two thousand five hundred feet. He had done everything he was asked to by the instructor as promptly and precisely as he could and was sure that she would find no fault in his abilities.

Tayler threw the aircraft around the sky, trying hard to keep a straight face and not laugh in delight or provide a running commentary of what he was doing in his imagined role as Badger Four of the Misfits. The machine was incredible! He could do things in it that he'd never dream of doing in his TC-62. And it was only a bloody, biplane trainer! He couldn't wait to get into a Harry...

Rob had no idea what half the things the instructor was asking him to do were; all the manoeuvres had names he'd never heard before. However, just because he didn't know what they were called, it didn't mean he didn't know how to do them. He just had to go through the embarrassing process of admitting his ignorance every time and having the instructor explain what they entailed to him.

Tayler probably wasn't having any trouble. He read everything he could find about flying, not only articles in newspapers and magazines like the *Misfit Monthly*, but also the trashy novels they'd started printing recently, some of them highly romanticised and fanciful stories about the adventures of Misfit Squadron. Rob had never been interested in any of that; he'd always wanted to build and race springcycles someday. Maybe he should have borrowed some of the books after he'd made the decision to join up with him, though...

Rob smiled when the instructor asked him to do a loop; at last, one he knew!

10

After the day's flying was done and cadets had finished writing their logs under the watchful eyes of the instructors and left, the instructors went to their ready room in the much larger building next door. Unlike the elementary flight training ready room, which was rather stark, the instructors' ready room was furnished comfortably with sofas and armchairs and had a heater and, most importantly, an honour bar.

Given the fact that some of the instructors were not officers and therefore weren't allowed in the officers' mess, it was the natural place for the various groups of instructors to meet after the day's flying to discuss their students.

There were half a dozen teams of instructors currently on the base, each responsible for a different stage of a cadet's evolution from a purely ground-based entity to a creature of the air, and they each had their area of the room that they had claimed for themselves for their daily reviews. For Trevillian's team it was a round table in the middle of the room around which six chairs could fit comfortably and they each grabbed their tipple of choice and sat down to jot down their notes from the final flight of the day while it was still fresh in their minds.

Trevillian waited until they were all finished before starting off the meeting. He looked to the aviator sergeant sitting to his right. 'Jocelyn, would you mind starting us off?'

Aviator Sergeant Jocelyn Green straightened up and looked around the group. 'Cadet Wilberforce has an extremely good grasp of the technical aspects of flying, but at the moment he has no real feel for it. He is a mathematician when we're looking for artists. I followed through on the controls a few times and it was like he had them in a death grasp the whole time, like he was imposing his will on the aircraft instead of working with it. I've been trying to get him to loosen up, but without much success.' She shrugged. 'He might need a different instructor because, at the moment, I am at a loss for what to do, aside from getting him drunk before going up.'

The other instructors chuckled and Trevillian smiled. 'We'll leave that as a last resort, shall we? I will consider switching assignments, though, but we have to be prepared for him to never fully relax. His instructor is an old friend of ours - Arthur Johns - and he wrote to me a week ago and essentially confirmed what you just said. For now, just keep plugging away, please; you never know, something might nudge him in the right direction unexpectedly.' He turned to the next instructor. 'George?'

The grey-haired aviator sergeant sitting next to Jocelyn Green shook his head. 'I've had a bit of a day. Cadet Oakley has got a good feel for it and he certainly has experience, but he's self-taught and that means he's got rather a lot of bad habits, which he's reinforced over hundreds or maybe thousands of hours. He's slap-dash and imprecise, charging at everything full tilt with a great deal of wasted effort. Having said that, his instincts are superb and he can throw that aircraft round the sky like nobody's business. However, if he doesn't tighten up and refine his technique he'll get picked apart by the Fleas, instincts or not.'

'Is he good enough to take his degree?'

'Oh, certainly. He might be rough around the edges, but he's more than good enough for that.'

'Right, then, he can take it first thing tomorrow and then we'll see about knocking him into shape.' Trevillian made a note on a piece of paper, then looked up again. 'Auntie?'

Squadron Leader Olivia "Auntie" Austin was the oldest of the group and had been like a mother to the instructors of RAC Gwynedd for almost two decades. Pushing sixty, she was the only one of them who'd flown in not one, but two other wars. 'Cadet Robert Sherborne also has a good feel for flying, but his knowledge is rudimentary. What he can do, he does well, without any bad habits, which is remarkable, considering that Cadet Oakley taught him. The gaps in his education aren't what concern me, though; they can be filled easily enough, rather it is his apparent lack of interest in what he is doing. He only joined up to be with Cadet Oakley and I get the impression he doesn't care whether he becomes a pilot or not. Which is a shame, because, in my opinion, he has the potential to become a very good pilot indeed, even a great one, if only he rustles up enough motivation to apply himself. He is also ready to take his pilot's degree tomorrow morning.'

'Hmm,' Trevillian said thoughtfully as he made another note. 'Let's see if getting his degree motivates him at all.' He capped his pen and frowned as he tapped the table with it. 'On paper, the boys looked much more promising than this, but I suppose it is still early days.' He looked up at the next instructor. 'What about yours, Merry?'

Aviator Lieutenant Elizabeth "Merry" Marlott scanned her notes briefly, before looking up. 'Cadet Sandra Orpwood has not made a very promising start, I'm afraid. She has no experience and has found it difficult to coordinate between her hands and feet, getting so frustrated at one point that she broke down and cried. She has shown a little improvement over the afternoon, but not to the point at which I could begin to evaluate her real aptitude.'

'Is she a slow learner, do you think? Or is there some other impediment? Something medical causing a lack of balance, perhaps?'

'I don't think there is any physical impediment; she moves too well when out of the cockpit to have any kind of inner ear problem or the like and that would have been picked up on by now.' Marlott shrugged. 'I'm hoping things are just going to click for her, but if they don't then she might have to be moved to ground crew. For her own good.'

'That would be disappointing. Do everything you can to prevent that, please.' Trevillian said. 'Lieutenant Hyland?'

The fifth instructor, Aviator Lieutenant Harold Hyland was a stiffly upright man in his fifties with the posture and mannerisms more usually found in a drill sergeant, not a pilot, and a meticulously cared-for moustache to match. 'Cadet Smith *is* a slow learner, but she's keen and she is stubborn and she's steadily plugging away at it. I'm confident she'll be a capable pilot soon enough and will be able to get her degree before the week is up, but I doubt she'll catch up with the others in the allotted two weeks. She might surprise me, though, with how hard she is working.'

'Push her, then, please.' Trevillian said. 'We all know that talent can be hidden beneath a lack of knowledge. Let's see what you can find when you take that lack away.'

Hyland nodded formally. 'Yes, sir.'

Trevillian looked around the group. 'So, we have one definite, two probables and two possibles.' He smiled. 'It's not looking good for the girls to beat the odds that have been laid on them.' There were smiles from most of the instructors around the table and quite a few from the other groups scattered around the room who had been doing a poor job of pretending not to listen. There were also some frowns, betraying those who had favoured the underdog with their wagers, but these were in the minority. Those instructors who genuinely hadn't been listening now realised that something was going on and started to do so; it wasn't usual that a group of cadets garnered such interest, but something about this one had caught the imagination of most of the instructors and service personnel on the base. After all, it wasn't every group which included a viscount's son with his own Hound, a girl who'd gotten as far on the PAT simulator as Chastity Arrowsmith and a boy who claimed he had more hours under his belt than most front-line fighter pilots.

'At least it *wouldn't* be looking good,' Trevillian continued nonchalantly, 'if it weren't for Cadet Perkins.'

He made a note on the piece of paper, then began to fold it as he spoke. 'I have never met anyone with such aptitude or proficiency after only a few hours in an aircraft. She has marvellous hand-eye coordination, absorbs everything I tell her like a sponge and if she keeps going like she's started, I will have no qualms in putting her forward for her wings test in two weeks.' He finished folding and held up a paper aircraft. He took aim, then threw it across the room. It landed in the lap of Aviator Lieutenant Crawford, one of the advanced flight instructors. The pilot's degree was a civilian qualification, so it required government approved examiners, not RAC ones, and Peter Crawford was the squadron's only certified examiner.

'Three little birdies for you to take a look at tomorrow morning, Peter, if you wouldn't mind?'

Sandra threw herself on her bed and groaned. 'What a bloody awful day! I could hear the disappointment in my instructor's voice every time she spoke to me. I couldn't do anything right!'

'I'm sure it wasn't that bad!' Ellie said, placing her helmet and goggles carefully on her own bed before stretching some of the kinks out of her back.

Sandra lifted her head to look at her with eyes that were shiny with moisture. 'Every time I tried to do a turn I had to think which rudder pedal I was supposed to be pressing to stop the aircraft slipping. And even then I got it wrong more often than not!'

Lottie stood next to Sandra's bed. 'It took me a while to work it out too. You just need to practice.' She looked at Ellie. 'We'll help you, won't we, Ellie?'

'Of course!' Ellie said, smiling. 'We'll work on it tonight. For as long as it takes. First, though, I don't know about you, but I stink after being in this flightsuit all day and I want to have a shower before dinner.'

Ellie began to peel off her flightsuit, grimacing as it stuck to her in places, especially where straps had gone over her shoulders and around her waist.

'How did you do, Ellie?' Lottie asked as she went to her own bunk and started undressing.

'Pretty well, I think, but I'm not sure; Trevillian didn't really tell me how I was doing, he just kept giving me more and more to do. It was fun, though, I really enjoyed myself.'

She grinned. It had been a lot more than just fun, in fact; it had felt *right*, like it was what she'd been meant to do all her life, and from the first moment the wheels had left the ground, any lingering doubts she might have had about being a pilot had completely disappeared.

Lottie nodded enthusiastically. 'Yes, it was hard work and a bit confusing sometimes, but it *was* fun.'

Sandra groaned and collapsed back on the bed. 'I'm the only one who can't do it!' she complained. 'Everyone's going to be a pilot except me!'

Ellie and Lottie looked at each other then laughed.

Ellie went back to Sandra and shook her by the shoulder. 'Come on, it's only the first day! Don't give up!' She grinned mischievously. 'And speaking of fun... How did it go with Benedict? Did you catch up with him? I fell asleep so quickly that I didn't hear you come back.'

'I didn't either,' Lottie said.

Sandra groaned again. 'Yes, I did catch him. But he didn't want to talk. We just ended up walking all the way around the perimeter track.'

'Ooh! A romantic walk by moonlight!' Ellie said, rolling her eyes at Lottie, who sniggered - neither of them had a very high opinion of Benedict and neither of them could imagine him having any capacity for romance whatsoever.

Sandra sat up and put her head in her hands. 'He's so obsessed with flying that he barely even knows I exist!' She rolled to her feet and started tugging at her flightsuit. 'And before you tell me not to give up - I'm not going to. Now, speaking of romance...' she smiled for the first time, 'what about you and Tay? I've seen the way you look at each other.'

Ellie shook her head. 'There's nothing going on there. I don't want a boy. Not now. Maybe not ever. I have too much to do.'

'But you do find him attractive?' Lottie asked.

'Well... he is, isn't he?' Ellie said, avoiding her gaze.

It was Sandra and Lottie's turn to exchange knowing glances, but, by unspoken agreement, they didn't push Ellie further and just joined her in washing and getting ready for supper.

'So? Are you convinced yet?'

'Convinced about what?' Rob asked, pausing in undressing and looking at Tayler. The boy was lying on his bed, propped up on his elbows, still fully dressed.

'About being a pilot?'

'Why wouldn't I be?'

'I know you've never been in love with flying like I have. I was surprised you joined up with me, to be honest.'

Rob didn't answer for a moment. He hadn't actually thought about it, hadn't noticed, but something had changed in him. Flying Finch, Tay's TC-62, had been fun for a little while, but each time, after less than half an hour, the novelty had worn off and then he'd just wanted to get back on the ground to ride and work on his springcycle. Today, though, he'd found himself enjoying himself more and more as the day had gone on, partly because of the challenge of learning new things, but mostly, he thought, because of the trainer being so much more powerful and manoeuvrable than the crop sprayer. It had been a vastly different experience to flying Tay's aircraft - more like riding his springcycle, in fact. Maybe better. And, somehow, unexpectedly, he found he couldn't wait to go back up in the air again.

He smiled. 'Let's just say I'm a bit more willing to give it a go than I was. And yes, I really would like a chance to fly one of those Spitsteams.'

'Good! Because I was worried you wouldn't give it your all tomorrow. I need you to pass the pilot's degree with me;' he jerked his chin in the vague direction of Benedict, who had chosen the bed furthest away from them, at the far end of the room, 'his bloody lordship can't be the only one of us with one. We need to show him that he's not better than us and that the only reason we haven't got the degree is because we couldn't be bothered to take the test! If either of us fails that all falls down.'

'Don't worry,' Rob said, 'Squadron Leader Austin says I've got it in the bag. There's nothing in the test that I haven't done a hundred times before.'

'That's the spirit!' Tayler looked up at Benedict as he walked between them, a towel wrapped around his waist. 'Hear that, Cleaner!' he called out. 'We'll be getting our degrees tomorrow! That calls for a celebration! Fancy a drink?'

11

'Are you sure I'm ready for this, sir?'

Ellie shaded her eyes and watched Rob turn the biplane onto the downwind leg of his solo flight. It was the last part of his pilot's degree test and once he landed it would be her turn. She hadn't yet developed an eye for how high someone was flying or how fast, but he looked good and, as long as he didn't mess up the landing, it looked like he would be joining Tay in earning his degree.

While going third had given her some time to go up with Trevillian and run through the syllabus a couple more times, it also put a lot of pressure on her and she couldn't believe how nervous she was or how important it suddenly was to her to pass this test and prove that she could be a pilot.

'Unless you've forgotten everything you've learned in the last five minutes, then yes.'

'But what if I get scared and freeze up?'

Trevillian turned to her. 'First off, why would you get scared? You didn't get scared once yesterday, even when I was throwing us around the sky, doing everything I could to make you.'

He grinned at her and she glared at him, but said nothing.

'Secondly, even if your brain does switch off for some reason, your body knows what to do now and has done it enough times for it to be as good as automatic. And third, you're far too stubborn to ever get scared. So, just go up, have fun, do what you already know what to do and pass, then we can go on to more difficult stuff and I'll get to try to scare you some more.'

Ellie laughed. 'Yes, sir!'

They turned as Rob brought the biplane in over the trees and descended towards the grass field. He touched down with the barest of bounces.

'Nicely done,' Trevillian said, nodding in appreciation before looking at her. 'I expect you to do just as well. If not better.'

'I'll do my best, sir.'

They watched as Rob brought the biplane over to where the examiner was standing and swung it round neatly. He shut down and handed the aircraft over to the fitters, then jumped out and bounced over to the examiner, who immediately stuck out his hand.

'And that's two for two.' Trevillian said. 'Go on, then. Make it three.' He waved her towards the examiner, who had already turned and was coming in their direction. 'Time for tea, I think. See you in an hour.'

He shoved his hands deep in his pockets and sauntered away towards the ready rooms, whistling a jaunty tune.

Ellie was still nervous as the examiner followed her around the biplane, watching her carry out the checks. Her legs were unsteady beneath her and she stumbled over her commentary a couple of times, calling the elevators "ailerons" before correcting herself and almost mixing up the order of things. However, by the time she'd finished and he had given her the order to release the spring and taxi, any fears she'd had had been completely obliterated by her excitement at being at the controls of an aircraft again and the prospect of getting back into the air.

She turned the aircraft to point across the airfield, the nose as closely into the wind as she could get it, and when the examiner gave the order she opened the throttle. Trevillian had kept on and on at her about not relying on the instruments to tell her what was happening with the aircraft, but to feel it, even going so far as to make her close her eyes to rid herself of distractions. Consequently, she barely needed to glance at the airspeed indicator to know when the biplane reached the speed at which she could push down the nose and lift the rear wheel. Likewise, a second glance a few seconds later only confirmed what she could already sense - that the biplane would very much like to leave the ground.

She took the aircraft up to four thousand feet and the examiner had her go through the basics. They were things she'd covered in her first couple of flights before Trevillian had taken her on to harder manoeuvres, so she found them extremely easy. It was very close to being boring, in fact.

'Thank you.' Lieutenant Crawford said after she'd brought the aircraft back to straight and level for the umpteenth time. 'Have you done a loop with Wing Commander Trevillian?'

'Yes, sir.'

'Go ahead, then, please.'

Ellie frowned, slightly puzzled, but said nothing and just put the aircraft into a shallow dive to gain speed. Once she had enough she pulled the stick back and brought the nose of the responsive biplane up sharply. There wasn't much to a loop; it was one of the more basic aerobatic manoeuvres, and after only a few seconds she had completed it and brought the aircraft back to level flight.

'Lovely.'

'Was that on the syllabus, sir?' she asked, daring to do so only now that she'd done what he'd requested of her.

'Oh, no. I was just curious. Sorry about that, Perkins.'

'No problem, sir. Would you like me to do anything else?'

The examiner laughed. 'Not for today, thank you! Do you know where the airfield is?'

'Behind us on the right... I mean, starboard, sir. At four o'clock.'

The examiner chuckled. 'Almost had to deduct a point there. Take us home and land, please.'

'Yes, sir.'

Ellie banked around smoothly and put the biplane on course for the airfield. Control put her in a holding pattern a mile or so out for a few minutes, though, because a flight of Harridans were just taking off, but eventually she was able to put the aircraft down.

'Taxi us to the ready room, please.'

Ellie slowed the biplane down enough to turn towards the small building, then blinked in surprise.

'Bloody hell! It's like Piccadilly Circus round here!' the examiner exclaimed.

Ellie had no idea why he thought it looked like the circus was in town - she thought it looked more like there was a garden party going on. Dozens of men and women were milling around on the grass verge in front of the ready room, drinking tea and munching on sandwiches and cake, while a dozen more were lounging in the long row of red and white striped deck chairs that had been set up on the very edge of the airfield. For a moment she thought it was just all the cadets and instructors on their break together at the same time, but then she saw that many of them were wearing uniforms and coveralls and she recognised the base commander, Group Commander Wyvern in one of the deck chairs. Strangely, a lot of them had goggles or helmets in their hands or on their heads and her cheeks heated when she realised that they must have been using the lenses to watch her do the exam. As she taxied over, many of them stopped their conversations and looked towards her.

'Your class has really sparked a lot of interest,' the examiner said, 'but it's not fair that they're watching you like this; it's added pressure that you don't need.'

There was quiet for a moment, then the man chuckled. 'How would you like to have a bit of fun at their expense?'

The crowd fell silent gradually as they turned expectantly to the approaching aircraft. Would Cadet Perkins have passed her degree after only one day in the cockpit? Was it even possible? Most people there didn't think it was and they had been more than happy to wager on the outcome with those few who did.

As one, they searched the faces of the man and woman in the cockpit, looking for some indication of success or failure, but there was nothing to be gleaned from their expressions. It was of no matter, though; things would become more than evident in the next minute. If successful, only the examiner would get out and the cadet would go for their solo flight - a mere formality with no way to fail except to actually crash the aircraft. If unsuccessful, then both would alight.

The aircraft swung around and the group held its collective breath, then let out a collective sigh as the airscrew stopped spinning and both occupants stood up and got out of the cockpit. The instructor jumped down to the ground then turned to address the student as she climbed down behind him. After a few seconds she nodded and hung her head.

'Well, that's that, then.' Aviator Lieutenant Pierce, the adjutant, said with a sad smile, fishing in his pocket for his money clip. He had no flight experience of his own on which to base a decision whether to bet for or against Perkins and had had to ask the opinion of those who did. Without exception everyone had told him that it was impossible, that she couldn't pass her degree and that he'd be throwing his money away if he bet on her. He was a romantic, though, he'd recognised a good story when he saw one and had disregarded their advice. However, it seemed that they had been right - not all stories had happy endings.

'It's not the end. Not by a long shot!' Trevillian said from the chair next to him. 'We all knew it would be hard.' He frowned and shook his head. 'I really thought she would have no problem passing. But these things happen, I suppose, and she'll can have another go in a few days.'

He turned to Group Captain Wyvern and smiled. 'A fiver, wasn't it, sir?'

Wyvern laughed. 'You know damn well it was a tenner, you rotter!'

'What are they doing?' Crawford asked.

Without lifting her head from its defeatedly bowed position, Ellie craned her neck slightly to look over the examiner's shoulder at the men and women milling around in front of the ready rooms.

'They seem to be exchanging money, sir.'

The examiner smiled. 'That's long enough, then. Get back in and give me a circuit. In return, when you get back, I'll give you a lovely certificate with His Majesty's signature on it.'

The sound of the airscrew powering up reclaimed the attention of the group of onlookers and they stopped whatever they were doing to watch as the biplane bounced away.

All eyes went to the examiner, but he just grinned, stuck his tongue out, then pointedly turned his back on them so that he could fully appreciate the sight of the best cadet he'd ever had the pleasure of examining take her first ever solo flight.

Nothing had really changed. Aside from the first couple of flights yesterday morning, she'd been in control of the aircraft herself for most of the day, so she wasn't doing anything she hadn't done dozens of times before, but it was amazing how different it felt when there was just an empty seat behind her. There was nobody to stop her if she did something wrong, or to take the controls from her if she made a mistake and she found herself extremely conscious of every little thing she was doing, even up to the point where she was second-guessing herself.

It was only a single circuit, though, and she'd done enough of them the previous evening, including three in a row without Trevillian once touching the controls, that she'd felt she could do them in her sleep, but the five minutes it took seemed to last an eternity and by the time she landed she was sweating in her flightsuit, far more than the sunny weather warranted.

Crawford was waiting for her, standing exactly where she'd left him, and, after she'd carried out the whole procedure of shutting down the aircraft and handing it over to the fitters, she marched over to him.

He stuck out his hand with a wide smile. 'Congratulations. A very fine showing.'

'Thank you, sir,' she answered, grasping his hand.

'And thank you for playing along,' he said with a wink, tilting his head back towards the ready room where an even bigger group of people were now clustered. 'They were having their fun, so I thought we should have some too.'

'You don't have any bets on us, sir?'

'Not on today's activities, no,' the man said. 'That wouldn't exactly be ethical. Don't worry,' he grinned, 'I'm not missing out; I've had a little flutter on a few other things.' He tapped his nose. 'Nothing for you to concern yourself with. You just keep doing what you're doing and make sure you become the best pilot you can.' He gestured towards the waiting crowd. 'Now come on, time to let everyone know you're a pilot now and not a novice anymore.'

The "pilot's degree" had been given its name in the 1890's, when flying was much more complicated. Back then, aircraft had been steam powered, very heavy, a lot harder to handle, a lot rarer and hadn't been able to stay in the air for very long. Flying had required far more skill, patience and study than it did with the far more advanced and forgiving spring-powered aircraft that were available currently and, while the degree hadn't taken various years to acquire, like a normal university degree, a holder was considered to be just as much an expert in his field as, say, the holder of a degree in natural science, or constructive engineering. However, while it had been the pinnacle of knowledge fifty years ago, it was now considered almost obsolete and didn't even include aerobatics, simply because they hadn't been possible in any real form when the test was first drawn up. There had been talk, just after the First Great War, of updating the degree test, but the decision was made to keep it as it was and instead encourage those who wished to pursue careers as pilots to obtain further training afterwards. Advanced qualifications had since become available from the British Aviation Council and from many universities around the county and most organisations that used aircraft in any capacity required one or more of those qualifications from its pilots, just as the RAC required pilots to pass its own, far more exacting, test before awarding them the coveted "wings". The degree was still, however, seen as being the first, necessary step on the road to becoming an expert pilot and it was the minimum requirement by the British Aviation Council for anyone wanting to fly in British airspace. You couldn't be a pilot in Britain without holding it. Not officially, anyway.

A small ceremony was held for pilots who gained their degree at RAC Gwynedd. It consisted simply of the examiner handing the pilot their certificate in the presence of their instructor and the base commander, if he was available. Considering that most cadets came to the base without any flight experience and had to take their degree before they moved on to more advanced work, then it wasn't a particularly rare occurrence and didn't garner much interest from the rest of the personnel on the base. The ceremony wasn't usually, therefore, attended by anyone except the cadet's classmates, however, between the officers and men who were already there, the ones who came running when word spread that all three cadets had passed their degree and the fitters who wandered over from the hangars, all apparently on their tea break at the same time, there were more than a hundred and fifty people there to witness that day's ceremony. They stayed around afterwards to have an impromptu tea party and the three pilots were thumped on the back, figuratively and literally, by all and sundry. Very soon, though, the fitters were chivvied back to work by their section commanders, the officers wandered back to their jobs, and the students from the other classes were taken away by their instructors, leaving just the six cadets standing in front of the ready room, holding empty mugs. Their instructors had disappeared at some point as well and they were a little bit at a loss for something to do without any orders.

Benedict looked at them, then rolled his eyes and went inside without saying anything.

'Come on, then,' Lottie said, beckoning to the three newly qualified pilots, 'let's see them!'

Ellie, Tayler and Rob held out their degree certificates and opened them for inspection.

The degrees weren't simple pieces of paper, like a degree certificate from a university, instead they were black leather booklets, about the size of a pocket notebook. Inside were pasted the certificates themselves, which simply stated that they were qualified pilots and had been awarded their degrees by a qualified examiner in the name of the monarch. They had each been pre-prepared with the seal and signature of King George and bore their names, written in a fair hand by the adjutant. Actual certificates that could be framed and hung on a wall were available on request from the BAC, of course, but no serious pilot would ever consider ordering, let alone displaying one.

'I'm so jealous!' Sandra said. 'I can't wait to get mine!'

'How's it going this morning, Sandra?' Ellie asked.

Sandra gave her a wry smile and shrugged. 'A bit better. I still don't feel comfortable, but I haven't been getting as mixed up this morning.'

'That's great!' Lottie said.

Lottie and Ellie had spent about an hour with Sandra the night before, one of them sitting in front of her, pushing her feet back and forth, acting as rudder pedals, while the other "banked" her chair by tilting it from side to side. As an exercise in coordination it probably wasn't the best and if anyone had walked in on them they would have undoubtedly been mocked, but it was all they'd been able to come up with and anything was better than nothing when Sandra had been so miserable.

Rob chuckled and shook his head. 'I wish I could have seen that!'

The girls had told Tayler and Rob what they'd done over breakfast. They had laughed about it, but they all knew what was at stake and what would happen if Sandra couldn't get her head around such basic concepts.

'What about you Lottie?' Sandra asked.

Lottie grinned. 'You know me. I'm getting it. Slowly, but I'm getting it. Lieutenant Hyland says I might be ready to take the test in a couple of days if the weather holds.'

'Keep plugging away at it,' Tayler said, 'and if you need help, I'm sure you girls can come up with something silly to do.'

'It's not silly if it works.' Sandra retorted.

'And I really hope it does work.' Tayler said, putting his arm around her shoulders and shaking her gently. 'I know how much you want to fly.'

'How much we all do.' Rob added, wrapping an arm around Tayler and beckoning to Lottie and Sandra to join them.

'I hope Jem and Franklin are doing alright.' Sandra said softly once they were all together in a ring.

The recruits had become very close during basic training at Druid. When they had been cold, wet and tired out on the obstacle course, or in danger of being swept away during a storm on the Brecon Beacons, when someone had been close to giving up and were feeling that they couldn't go on, when it had felt like it was all going to be too much for them, at those times the only thing that had gotten them through was each other.

Things were very different now, though. When they had been at their lowest, sharing an embrace in this way had been how those who were coping better could bring up the spirits of those who weren't. Now, it was a way for them to share their elation and satisfaction with each other.

There was silence as each of them, in their own way, took advantage of this rare moment of calm and peace.

'I can't wait to get back in the air,' Tayler said softly, making everyone smile and nod in agreement. 'But first,' he added, looking at each of them in turn, 'I need to pee.'

He disengaged from the group and ran into the building and the others laughed and followed him.

Lieutenant Crawford sat at the large table in the middle of the room, sipping at a mug of tea, fully aware of the men and women clustered around him. He ignored them, though, and just picked up another biscuit. He dunked it, then popped it whole into his mouth and chewed. Only when he'd swallowed it and washed it down with the rest of the tea did he look up at Trevillian.

'Something I can do for you, Magnus?'

Trevillian laughed. He pulled out the chair next to him and sat. 'Come on, Peter, stop playing coy; you know you're dying to tell us about it.'

The examiner reached out to take another biscuit from his plate. 'They all passed very satisfactorily.'

Trevillian didn't take the bait and just smiled at him.

'Oh, alright,' the examiner said, tossing the biscuit back down. 'If you insist.' He looked around the instructors. 'Sit down, then.' He pushed his empty mug towards Trevillian. 'You know how I like it.'

Trevillian chuckled and went to fill the mug from the tea urn, putting milk and three sugars. He placed it in front of Crawford, then sat down and looked at him expectantly. The man ignored him, though, and just picked up his tea and took a sip. Trevillian rolled his eyes, but most of the instructors just laughed; Peter Crawford had always been a bit of a comedian but he was well-liked and he was also an extremely experienced pilot, hiding a false leg under his trousers that had been earned over Britain in the big battle of the afternoon of 15th September 1940, during which he'd shot down three MU9s. He was also one of the best judges of talent on the base. Even more so than Trevillian.

Eventually, the examiner put down the mug. 'As always, the cadets were much as you had described them.' He looked at Aviator Sergeant Barton. 'Cadet Tayler Oakley. He can fly well enough for something as forgiving as his crop duster or our Sprite trainers, but he needs to learn more control if he's going to fly a Spitsteam and not have it spin out of control every five minutes. Under normal circumstances I wouldn't see him gaining that in the short time he has and I would think that the most he could aspire to is a Harridan. However, if he buckles down he might surprise me.'

Barton nodded. 'That is consistent with my own assessment.'

'Cadet Robert Sherborne.' The examiner looked at "Auntie" Austin. 'He has good technique and has a good feel for the aircraft. However, aside from brief moments, his flying is largely joyless and, in my opinion, that will hold him back from becoming an excellent pilot.'

Squadron Leader Austin frowned. 'Brief moments?' she muttered before catching herself and nodding. 'Thank you, Peter.'

'What about Perkins?' Trevillian asked. 'We all saw you do that loop. That's not on the degree syllabus.'

'And last, but not least, Cadet Eleanor Perkins.' The man said pointedly, looking at Trevillian. He paused, then picked up his mug and took a slow sip, slurping noisily. He smiled into his tea as groans sounded from around the table, but he didn't keep them waiting for long; he knew they were eager to get back to their students. Just as eager as he was to share his views with them. 'She is one of the most natural pilots I've ever seen. She doesn't do something because it's the way she's been taught to do it, but because it feels right to her.' He shook his head in admiration. 'She is remarkable. I have the feeling that if you just put her in an aircraft and told her to go up and play she'd come back after a few days knowing everything that we could teach her about flying and doing it better than us. And as for the loop,' he shrugged, 'I felt like seeing if she could do it. And I rather wanted to see the expression on her face while she did.'

12

'Perkins! Let's go!'

Ellie looked up as Trevillian popped his head into the door of the ready room and beckoned for her to come. She leapt to her feet and gave her friends a wave before hurrying after him.

The sight of four monoplanes parked on the airfield across the perimeter track from the ready room brought her to a halt, but only briefly and she grinned and ran to catch up with Trevillian.

He smiled. 'Congratulations, Perkins, how does it feel to be a proper pilot?'

Ellie blinked at him, expecting him to be joking, or at least making fun of her, after all, the pilot's degree wasn't exactly the RAC's measure of a good pilot, but he was looking at her seriously. Curiously, even. 'Um,' she frowned. 'I don't really feel any different, sir. Excited to be progressing and glad that I didn't fail, but not really any different.'

'Good,' Trevillian nodded in satisfaction. 'I'd be worried if you did feel any different.' They arrived at the tail of one of the monoplanes and he turned to face her. 'Once they get that little booklet, some of the more arrogant cadets start to think they don't have to work as hard anymore. Some even think that they know everything they need to. We instructors try to disavow them of that belief, but this is the stage at which we lose the most pilots, either through accidents or because they do something stupid and we have to cut them. I wouldn't expect that of you, of course, but better safe than sorry.'

He patted the aircraft. 'Right then. This little beauty is the Hawking Huntress. She's a big step up from the Sprite in terms of performance, with a top speed of just over three hundred miles per hour, but she's nothing you can't handle. Checks are essentially the same, just ignore the fact that there's only one wing; the other one hasn't fallen off, they just forgot to put it on.' He grinned, then walked away. 'Join me in the cockpit when you're done!' he called over his shoulder as he climbed up onto the back of the wing.

Ellie watched him get into the rear cockpit, taking note of how he unlatched a tiny door in the side of the fuselage to make the process easier and stepped onto the seat before lowering himself, but then applied herself to the job at hand.

The Huntress might have had a vastly different design to the Sprite, but that only served to reinforce how similar they were where it was important and the fact that they worked in exactly the same way. It was a beautiful aircraft, but she was too eager to get into the air to hang around and admire it, so she finished her checks as quickly and efficiently as she could, gave the chief fitter a nod, then clambered up onto the wing. She fumbled with the catch on the little door on the fuselage for a couple of seconds before she found the trick to it, but in short order she was sitting and a fitter was leaning in to help her strap in. She plugged herself into the radio, nodded her thanks to the fitter and only then looked around the cockpit.

The first thing she noticed was the stick between her legs. The one in the Sprite had been a simple pole with a grip on the end while this one had a great big ring on the top of it. The next thing she noticed was just how many more dials and indicators were on the dashboard.

'Don't panic yet, Perkins, it's all very straight forward.'

Trevillian ran her through the cockpit checks, which turned out to be a bit more involved than those for the Sprite, but not too complicated, then had her release the spring.

'Alright, gently does it. Just crack the throttle open a tad.'

Ellie gingerly pushed the throttle forward a touch.

The noise coming from the airscrew changed pitch and intensity, but the aircraft didn't move and Trevillian laughed.

'You can crack it a little wider than that!'

Ellie blushed and pushed a bit harder. The airscrew changed tone completely as it bit into the air and the aircraft lurched forward as it overcame its inertia.

The wind had veered while they had been inside and was coming more from the north, which meant she had to taxi around the edge of the field to the other side. It was a fairly long trip, but that meant she had more time to get used to the cockpit layout. She moved her hands back and forth between all the switches and levers, starting the process of making the gestures instinctive, and took a good hard look at the gauges and instruments on the panel in front of her, making sure she knew where they were so that she wouldn't have to search for them, something that was extremely important particularly during taking off and landing when it was a really bad idea to take her eyes off where she was going for too long. She also tried to find a comfortable grip on the round thing on top of the stick that Trevillian had called a "spade grip". He'd explained that they weren't that usual, in fact only Harridans and Spitsteams had them, but that they'd installed them in their Huntresses so that new pilots could get used to them "before it counted". It felt strange, to say the least, and she wondered how much of a difference it would make to her precision and control in the air.

They reached the far side of the field and Ellie turned the Huntress into the wind and brought it to a halt. Trevillian said nothing, which meant he was leaving it up to her to contact control and gain permission to take off. It was given immediately and, after a short pause to give Trevillian another chance to give her instructions or take control, Ellie opened the throttle wide.

She was pushed back into her seat, but not nearly as hard as she had been in the Sprite and she was surprised when the aircraft gained speed much slower. She'd thought that the aircraft would have accelerate harder if it was faster and more powerful, but that wasn't the case apparently. Maybe because the aircraft was bigger and heavier. However, it wasn't long before she felt the stick come alive in her hand as the control surfaces started to bite into the air and the nose came down with barely any encouragement from her, raising the rear wheel off the ground. The aircraft all but lifted itself into the air a couple of seconds after that and all of a sudden the lumbering beast had become a bird of prey.

'Heading two nine zero. Take us up to eight thousand feet, please.'

Ellie moved the stick to bank the aircraft and frowned when her hand slipped. She adjusted her grip and completed the turn, blushing again as she realised how ragged the manoeuvre had been. Again, there was no comment from the back seat. Trevillian didn't speak again until she had levelled out at eight thousand feet in fact.

'Alright. The Huntress is fully aerobatic. She'll essentially do anything you can think off, except fly backwards, although I can't say I've ever tried, so I don't know for sure. We've got an hour before we have to head home. Stay above four thousand feet and below ten and don't take us out to sea, but apart from that she's yours to do with as you please.'

'Sir?' Ellie asked, not quite sure what she was supposed to do.

There was no answer from Trevillian, though, and when she heard rustling in her ears she craned her neck around to look at him.

She couldn't see him, though; her view was blocked by a newspaper, of all things, and as she stared he flipped through it and started reading.

She settled back into her seat and stared out of the front windscreen.

What should I do? She thought, but then smiled slowly. *What do I want to do? What is it they say? The sky's the limit?*

'I want to have a quick word with the chief. You run along and write up your log and I'll be along in a moment to sign it.'

Trevillian made a show of folding his rather rumpled newspaper as Ellie secured the aircraft and climbed out. He watched as she jumped athletically off the back of the wing, had a quick word with the chief fitter, then strode off towards the ready rooms. He shook his head at the bounce in her step. 'Was I ever that young?'

'Sorry, sir?'

The chief fitter appeared beside him, blocking his view of the young woman and he squinted up at him.

'Oh, nothing, Bill.'

'Right you are, sir.' The fitter noticed the newspaper and frowned, puzzled, but didn't mention it. 'Everything alright, sir?' he asked. 'The young lass said you wanted to have a word.'

'Yes, yes, everything is fine, thank you. I just need a minute.'

'Alright, sir.' The fitter gave him another look, but then went about his business and began securing the forward cockpit.

Trevillian pulled out a pencil and notebook from his pocket and pretended to make a few notes, but in reality he had nothing to make a note of; the flight was burned into his memory and there was no way he was ever going to forget any of it. The truth of the matter was that his legs were shaking and he didn't think he could quite stand up yet. Not without falling on his arse anyway.

It had been one of the most remarkable experiences of his life. At first Perkins had been hesitant, feeling her way, doing the same things she'd learnt in the Sprite. He'd almost felt like he could read her mind, so clear had her intentions been, so logical her process. That was why it had been such a shock when she had suddenly started throwing the aircraft around the sky, testing its limits. She had continued to do that for a good fifteen minutes, trying one manoeuvre after another. She hadn't gotten many of them right the first time and he hadn't expected her to, but she seemed to understand instinctively what she was doing wrong each time and it never took her more than three attempts to be able to do them, if not perfectly, then good enough for them to work. And that was more than good enough, because he knew from experience that it would only take a few notes from him for her to start doing them properly.

She had worked her way through just about every possible aerobatic manoeuvre, including a couple that weren't even on the syllabus until the cadets had moved onto advanced training, and then...

Oh, and then...

Dogfights didn't last nearly as long as she'd played for and they weren't nearly as strenuous.

He'd given up the pretence of reading the paper after only a few seconds because it had become impossible to hold his arms up, but she'd probably not noticed. In fact she'd probably forgotten he was there after the first few minutes and hadn't remembered until he'd told her it was time to go home.

'She's going to make a hell of a pilot.' He chuckled, but then shook his head as he started to unbuckle his straps with shaky hands. 'Actually, she already *is* a hell of a pilot.'

Something was different. The flying was good, it had always been good, but there was a different quality to it today. The change was almost imperceptible, but it was there. It was definitely there...

Remembering what Peter Crawford had said and suspecting something, Auntie Austin craned her head, straining to look in the mirror mounted to the front of the cockpit.

There was a smile on Cadet Robert Sherborne's face.

Finally, she thought, and settled back to enjoy the ride.

Benedict snarled as the Huntress touched down for another perfect landing and he turned it towards the ready room.

What more could he do? What more could they *expect* him to do?

He was doing everything he was asked to do and doing it well. Demonstrating how good he was each and every flight. And yet everyone was making a fuss over Perkins and the others instead of him. Treating them as if they were now on the same level as him, despite his years of hard work. Just because they'd passed their pilot's degree. Which he'd done two months after his thirteenth birthday.

He'd been listening in to some of the conversations during the party after their ceremony and couldn't believe it when he'd overheard that the odds of him finishing elementary training with the highest marks were plummeting. Worse, if things continued as they were, it would be bloody *Perkins* who was the favourite, not him.

If only they would let him take the wings test early, instead of insisting he waited the entire two weeks. He'd easily pass that, then race through advanced training as well and be able to leave all this nonsense behind and go to an operational unit to start doing some real flying.

'Alright, Wilberforce,' the instructor, Aviator Sergeant Green said over the radio. 'Leave her with me. You run along and write up your log.'

'Yes, sergeant.'

And that was another thing, Benedict thought as he undid his straps. They'd stuck him with a non-com, of all things! Him! He should have Trevillian training him, or an officer, at least. Not someone who couldn't even gain a commission.

He jumped down from the wing and stomped off towards the ready rooms.

He didn't see the instructor shaking her head, nor hear her muttered comment that he was "worse than ever".

Tayler laughed as he threw the aircraft around the sky, revelling in the increased speed and capabilities of the monoplane over the biplane. He jerked the stick to the side, slamming the aircraft into the maximum rate turn Barton had asked him to do, kicking at the pedals as the nose started to fall.

He'd passed! Nothing was going to stop him now! He was going to fly a fighter!

CHAPTER 13

Lottie took and passed her pilot's degree two days later and Sandra scraped through hers by the skin of her teeth the day after that, but then the weather closed in and flying was suspended. This unfortunately meant that the cadets spent the entirety of the next three days in the classroom, cramming in as much technical and scientific knowledge as they could and only being let out for meals and exercise. Tempers flared as a result and, while even the most mild-mannered of them found themselves irritable and snappish, things between Tayler and Benedict, where there had already been a fair amount of animosity, got much worse.

Ever since he'd gotten his degree Tayler hadn't been able to resist rubbing it in Benedict's nose whenever he could that they were now on an equal footing and things came to a head on the evening of the third day without flying. A full-on shouting match began on the walk back to their barracks from the classrooms and they were only prevented from coming to blows by the intervention of the others. Thankfully, the foul weather meant that there weren't many people around and the noise of the rain covered their altercation, so no officers or military guard came to see what was happening and there weren't any consequences. However, there was no way the two men were going to be able to share the bunk room that night, so Benedict swapped beds with Lottie and everybody crossed their fingers and hoped there wouldn't be a surprise inspection.

It was a relief, therefore, when the weather broke that night around midnight and the day dawned clear enough for flying to resume, however, that day also marked a week since they'd started training and that meant they had their mid-training assessments. So, after a full day of flying, which came to a close only when it was almost too dark to find the airfield, they hurried back to their bunk rooms to clean up and put on their uniforms before being collected by an aviator sergeant and marched to the main building.

He took them to a corridor on the first floor and pointed at a row of chairs outside a meeting room. 'Sit down and shut up!' he ordered in a low but stern voice before knocking on the door and disappearing inside.

The cadets looked at each other nervously, then did as they were told. Carefully, so as not to crease the trousers and skirts they had pressed the night before. They had hardly taken their seats before the sergeant came back out, closing the door after himself.

'Cadet Oakley! You're first up!'

Tayler stood and sauntered towards the meeting room door, too slowly, it seemed, for the sergeant, who glared a promise of future trouble at him. Unperturbed, Tayler winked at Benedict, who had made sure to be in the chair closest the door, then knocked and went in.

He wasn't smiling when he came out five minutes later, though, and the sergeant smirked when he called Sandra's name.

The rest of the cadets went in one by one. Most came out, if not smiling, then at least thoughtful, but Benedict came out wide-eyed and white as a sheet. When they'd all taken their turns the sergeant told them they had the rest of the evening off and dismissed them.

'Dinner?' Rob asked, after they'd made their way out of the building. Sandra, Lottie and Ellie agreed readily, but neither Tayler nor Benedict replied and Rob took his friend around the shoulders and guided him towards the mess hall.

Sandra gave Benedict a concerned look as she went with the others, but he followed them automatically, so she just left him alone. She had tried to engage him in conversation a few times since that first night when he had stormed out of the mess, but he always seemed to have something else to do and after one too many rejections she had stopped. That didn't mean she'd completely given up hope, but, after a late night conversation with Ellie and Lottie, they had helped her come to the conclusion that she needed to give him time and not try to force things when he had so many other things on his mind.

It wasn't quite time for most of the airmen and women to come off duty, so the main mess was almost empty and they found a table to themselves in the corner where they wouldn't be overheard.

Ellie had no real desire to tell the others what had been said about her, so she turned to Lottie as soon as they sat down.

'You look happy,' she said, smiling herself. 'Come on, then, spill it!'

Lottie grinned. 'Lieutenant Hyland said I'm making "steady progress" and if I keep it up I might get to take the wings test. He said it was going to be extremely hard, but that it was in my hands.'

'That's great news! I'm sure you'll make it!' Sandra said, patting her on the shoulder before looking around the group. 'My review wasn't quite as positive, I'm afraid - Wing Commander Trevillian essentially told me that if I didn't stop getting the controls mixed up then I wouldn't be allowed to be a pilot at all, let alone take my wings test early.'

Lottie shrugged as she stuffed a piece of bread into her mouth then spoke around it. 'Well, we're going to have to keep working with you every night to make sure that doesn't happen, then, aren't we?'

Ellie nodded emphatically and Sandra reached out to take their hands, smiling her thanks before looking across the table. 'What about you, Rob?'

Rob skewered a roast potato then looked up and smiled. 'I...'

He got no further, though, because there was a growl from the seat next to him and a clatter as Tayler threw down his cutlery. He surged to his feet, making his chair squeal painfully against the wooden floor and stormed off.

They stared after him in shock and for a moment none of them moved, but then Rob shoved his own chair back and stood. 'Can someone deal with our trays please?' he asked nobody in particular, before hurrying after his friend.

Ellie shared a look with Sandra and Lottie. If before she had been reluctant to speak about her own glowing review, she was even more so now and was relieved when they just shrugged and applied themselves to their food.

'I will have no choice but to recommend that Cadet Wilberforce not take his wings test without first completing the full advanced training course.'
Benedict stared at his plate, his food untouched and unseen, as the words went round and round in his mind.

'He has good technique and will undoubtedly obtain his wings eventually, but unless he learns to relax and not treat an aircraft like an unruly horse that needs to be controlled with a firm hand, he will never be up to the standards of a fighter pilot and I could not in all conscience allow him to be sent up against the Fliegertruppe *as one.'*

When he'd heard his instructor's assessment, his first instinct had been to protest and request a second opinion, but he'd realised immediately that Aviator Sergeant Green's opinion *was* a second one - he'd been hearing the same thing from Johns for months, but in his arrogance he hadn't listened.

And now it was too late to change.

There was nothing he could do. He wasn't going to be a fighter pilot.

Rob was delayed leaving the mess for a few seconds because he had to stand aside to let a group of a dozen or more NCO's to enter and when he got outside it took him a moment to spot Tayler. His friend was stomping rapidly along the path through the trees towards their barracks, head down and hands in pockets and Rob winced as he went straight by a couple of officers without saluting or acknowledging them in any way. Thankfully, the two were deep in conversation and didn't notice him, otherwise it could well have meant a black mark on his record, or something far worse if his temper hadn't improved and he gave them any mouth.

He stuffed his hat onto his head and jogged after him, slowing down to salute the officers, then accelerating once he was past.

'Tay! Wait for me! Tay!'

He couldn't call out too loudly for fear of bringing down the wrath of some NCO or MG, but he didn't think that was the reason Tayler didn't acknowledge him.

He fell into step beside his friend, intending to just walk in silence for a while and give him a chance to speak, but when they'd been going for more than a couple of minutes and Tayler still hadn't even looked at him he began to lose his patience.

'Tay, what's wrong?'

'What's wrong? What's wrong?!?' Tayler snarled, rounding on him. 'I've got more flight time than the rest of you put together, more than most front-line RAC pilots, but I've just been told that I'm probably not ever going to get my wings. That's what's wrong.'

Rob blinked at him in shock. 'I thought everything was going well.'

'So did I.' Tayler growled.

'Did they say why?'

Tayler's lip curled. 'Barton said I'm sloppy and erratic. That I lack discipline and my technique isn't clean enough.'

'And this is news to you *why?*' Rob asked, suddenly feeling more than a little fed up with his friend.

'What?' Tayler asked, his eyes widening in surprise.

'Oh, wake up, Tay!' Rob shouted. 'How could you not see this coming? You've *never* had any kind of discipline or self-control - you work when you want and how you want and you do what you want without thought for anyone else. So why did you ever think you'd do well in the armed forces? And it's not like you've made an effort to change since we got here. You drink every night, barely study and you've obviously not been listening to your instructor. So, this really shouldn't be a surprise to you.'

Rob shook his head dismissively and started to walk away, but then spun around and returned. He thrust a finger in Tayler's face, making him cringe back. 'I'm here because of you. You know that, right? This was never *my* dream. I never wanted to be a pilot and I certainly didn't want to be in the RAC. But I didn't want you doing this on your own. Because I knew something like this would happen. And now it looks like it might be *me* who'll be a pilot, not you, and that is pissing me off no end. So, I'm going to say this one time and one time only and then you are on your own - stop feeling sorry for yourself and do something about this. Or don't and give up. I'm beyond caring for you.'

This time Rob did leave, stomping back the way he'd come. Even in his angry state, he was still aware of his surroundings, though, and he snapped off what must have been the angriest salute of all time to a passing aerial officer, making her flinch back even as she returned the gesture.

The three women finished their meals in silence, none of them feeling much like talking after Tayler's outburst. It wasn't as if Benedict's increasingly dour presence was doing much to inspire conversation either. Conversation would have been difficult anyway, because a lot of people were coming off duty now and the mess hall was rapidly and loudly filling up.

Ellie and Lottie stood up, collecting their trays and distributing Rob's and Tayler's between them, but Sandra remained seated.

'I'm going to stay,' she said, smiling up at them.

Ellie frowned at Benedict, who was aimlessly pushing his food around his plate without eating, before giving her a concerned look. 'Be careful, Sandra.'

'Don't worry, I will.'

'Alright, then. See you later.'

'Good luck!' Lottie called as the two walked away.

Their places were immediately taken by a group of airmen and women and Sandra nodded a greeting at them, before turning her attention back to Benedict. She had a bit of pudding left so she toyed with that, pretending that was the reason she was still there in case he glanced up and noticed her lingering behind.

It wasn't him looking at her the next time she lifted her head, though, it was everyone else at the table and she frowned as something in the back of her head told her that one of them had said something to her.

'Sorry?'

The woman next to her, an airwoman not much older than her, smiled. 'I asked if you were one of the new group of cadet pilots.'

'Yes, I am,' Sandra nodded, smiling. 'Sorry, we had our one week assessments today and we're all a bit distracted.'

The people around her laughed and the woman glanced across the table at Benedict. Sandra frowned when she saw that he had given up any pretence at eating and was just staring at the table with his head in his hands, his elbows either side of his plate.

'How did it go?' a corporal asked.

'Well...' Sandra started, but faltered when she saw how the dozen or so people at the table, as well as quite a few at the neighbouring tables, were leaning in to listen. There was far more interest in their expressions than should really be there, which puzzled her for a moment until she remembered that there was a lot of money riding on the outcome of her group's training for some reason. 'I...' she said hesitantly.

At that moment, Benedict stood. He picked up his tray and wandered away, moving as if he were sleepwalking.

'I'm sorry, will you excuse me?' Sandra said, putting on her best smile, even though butterflies seemed to be churning butter in her stomach. She stood up and nodded to the corporal, the only NCO present, before hurrying after her classmate. She caught up with him at the clean-up area, but instead of scraping his plates and putting the tray in the rack he just slid it onto the table distractedly and continued towards the door.

Sandra rolled her eyes and grabbed it before anyone could call him back. She dealt with both trays as quickly as she could then rushed after him.

It was now dark out and it took a moment for her eyes to adjust. It then took a few moments more to find him in the dim moonlight because he wasn't walking along the path towards the barracks, but in the other direction, down the short road to the airfield.

'Where are you...?' she muttered as she started after him, then rolled her eyes again, this time at herself, when she realised that he wasn't really going anywhere, he was just going. She started after him, walking steadily, waiting to see which way he would turn when he got to the airfield so that she could cut him off, but he didn't turn, he just kept going across the perimeter track and onto the grass of the airfield.

There were no flight operations at night, but that didn't mean that people could just wander across the airfield if they felt like it. Thankfully, their blue uniforms didn't particularly stand out in the dark, but it wouldn't be long before an MG came to investigate, which would mean trouble, so she broke into a run, hoping to bring Benedict back, or at least adjust his course towards the nearest part of the perimeter track, before they did.

'Benedict!' she said as she caught up to him. 'We're not allowed on the airfield at night, remember?'

Benedict stumbled to a halt and gazed around, as if seeing where he was for the first time. 'Right... Of course,' he said, but made no effort to move.

'Honestly!' Sandra breathed, rolling her eyes for a third time. She took his arm and guided him towards the nearest part of the perimeter track, which was thankfully only a couple of dozen yards away. Once they were there she pulled him to a halt and turned him to face her.

'Benedict, what's the...' she cut herself off suddenly when she saw that there were tears streaming down his cheeks. 'What's wrong?'

She reached out to him, but hesitated, remembering how much it had hurt when he had brushed her off before. The pain she saw in his face overcame any thought of herself, though, and she completed the manoeuvre, stepping in close and putting her hand on the back of his head to guide it down to her shoulder.

For a moment he resisted and she thought he was going to pull away, but then all the tension seemed to flow out of him and his arms went around her as sobs wracked his body.

After what seemed like an age, but was undoubtedly only a couple of minutes or so, he lifted his head.

'I...' he said, but then stopped as their eyes met.

Afterwards, Sandra wasn't sure which of them moved first, or whether they had moved at the same time, but suddenly, somehow, *magically*, they were kissing.

CHAPTER 14

Tayler walked around the aircraft, doing his preflight checks under the watchful and disapproving eye of Aviator Sergeant Barton. He sighed as he ran his hand over the blades of the airscrew and shook his head; he wasn't making this any easier for him. He finished his circuit of the aircraft, but instead of climbing up to the cockpit he went to stand in front of Barton.

'Cadet?'

When Rob had shouted at him he'd been so angry that he'd very nearly gone after him and knocked him down - it was what he would have done back home if someone had mouthed off at him like that. Something had stopped him, though. Something at the back of his brain that was still rational, even as he lost himself to rage, had screamed at him that if he did that he would lose his friend forever. So, he'd stood in the shadows under the trees beside the path, clenching and unclenching his fists and glaring into the night, suppressing the violent urges that were threatening to take him over. When he'd finally calmed down enough to think he'd quickly come to the conclusion that his friend was right - he'd been acting like a fool and throwing away his chance without realising it. Worse, while he'd thought he'd been the life and soul of the party, in reality he'd been acting just as badly as Benedict.

He'd trudged back to the bunk room and found Rob already in bed. He'd tried to apologise, but his friend hadn't wanted to listen, he'd just turned his back on him and told him to buck his ideas up.

He'd lain awake for ages, unable to fall asleep, but while he'd been staring up at the moonlight reflected on the ceiling, he'd come up with the beginnings of a plan.

'Sergeant, I'd like to make a request for today's flights.'

'Go ahead.'

'Could we please go back to basics? I'd, uh, I'd like to...' he gritted his teeth. 'I'd like to learn to fly properly and get my wings.'

Barton regarded him coldly and Tayler thought for a moment the man had already given up on him and was going to refuse his request, but then the thin lips under the moustache twitched in a tiny, almost imperceptible smile.

'That's a good start. But good intention alone aren't enough.' Barton nodded in the direction of the cockpit. 'Let's go. Time's a-wasting.'

'Yes, Sergeant!' Tayler threw him one of his best grins, then ran and jumped up onto the wing.

It had taken almost losing his best friend to wake him up out of his stupidity and it might already be too late to fulfil his dreams, but he was damned if he was going to give up without a fight.

Benedict carried out the aerobatic manoeuvres as they were requested of him, but for the life of him he couldn't seem to make himself care whether he did them perfectly or not. His mind just wasn't on it that morning; it was elsewhere - back on the airfield the night before. Back with Sandra.

He smiled absently, only half aware that the horizon was rotating around the nose of the aircraft as he felt the ghost of the touch of her lips against his, felt her soft strength in his arms, felt how her hands had slid over his back.

He wasn't going to convince Sergeant Green that he belonged in a fighter flying like this, but would that be the end of the world? It was a bit early to think about such things, but Sandra wasn't too hopeful of her chances of passing the wings test in a week either, so they'd stay in training together, maybe get assigned to the same squadron afterwards and then who knew what might happen.

He found it wasn't a completely unpleasant thought.

The rest of the flight flew by, figuratively as well as literally, and before he knew it they were getting out of the aircraft and handing it over to the fitters.

'Sergeant.' Benedict nodded his thanks to Sergeant Green and started towards the ready room. Usually she stayed behind to have a word with the fitters before going to the instructors' ready room, but today she surprised him by walking beside him.

'Excellent work, Cadet Wilberforce. Looks like yesterday was a bit of a wake-up call for you.'

'Excuse me?' Benedict frowned. How did she...?

'The assessment.'

'Ah, yes. The assessment.' He sighed in relief. 'Of course. That was it.'

Sergeant Green's brow furrowed slightly as she looked at him, puzzled at his behaviour. 'Anyway, keep it up. You still have plenty of time to turn things around.'

Benedict watched her wander off towards the neighbouring building, but didn't go inside right away, instead he turned and looked back at the aircraft he'd just been flying and, perplexed, tried to work out what he'd done differently and how he could do it again.

The cadets didn't normally get to have lunch at the same time. There weren't any set schedules for the instructors, they could fly whenever they wanted, for as long as they wanted, so the cadets just hurried to the mess whenever they had some free time around midday to grab a quick bite. That day, though, it seemed that the instructors had conspired to be on the ground at the same time and the cadets found themselves around a table all together for once.

It was a vastly different group from the previous night and Lottie looked a question at Ellie, who could only shrug. They were the only ones who'd gone straight to their bunk rooms after dinner and had been in bed and asleep before any of the others had gotten back. What with the morning exercises, having to get their rooms and kit ready for inspection and snatching a quick breakfast, all while making sure to get to the ready room before the instructors arrived, there wasn't much chance to talk in the mornings and they had no idea what had happened or where everybody had been. There was no doubt that something had happened between that meal and this, though, because there were smiles where before there had been scowls on the faces of Benedict and Tayler and a scowl on Rob's face where before there had been a smile. Surprisingly of all, however, was the fact that Benedict and Sandra were sitting exceedingly close and couldn't keep their eyes off each other.

Annoyingly, nobody seemed to want to speak to them and explain the change, so all the two of them could do was eat and watch and wait until the evening, when they resolved that they would press the others for answers and wouldn't let them go until they'd given them. Even if Lottie had to sit on them to prevent them from leaving.

'Rob! Wait!'

Tayler ran to catch up with Rob, wanting to talk to him on his own before they got to the ready room, but his friend didn't slow down or even look at him.

'Rob!'

'What?' Rob snarled without looking at him.

'Look,' he fell into step with him, 'I'm sorry. I really am. About everything. And you're right about me.'

'I know I am.'

Tayler laughed, but Rob didn't even smile, he just kept walking, his eyes fixed forward.

'I'm going to change, though. I promise. I've already started actually... But I'm going to need some help, you know, with all the book stuff I should have been doing.'

Rob still didn't look at him, but his expression softened ever so slightly.

'Please, Rob.' Tayler said softly. 'Please help me.'

Rob glanced at him, but only for a moment. 'No more drinking, no more staying up late and the first time you complain then we're done. Got that?'

'Yes. I've got it.'

'Good.' Rob grunted. He still didn't look at Tayler, though, he just accelerated his pace, leaving him behind.

'I can't figure out what I did this morning.' Benedict said, frowning at a Spitsteam taxiing across the airfield. 'I got distracted during the flight and started thinking about... *things*...' he glanced sideways at Sandra and smiled shyly, 'I wasn't thinking about what I was doing and my technique must have been sloppy, but then, when we land, she acts like I've made some huge step forward.'

'And she didn't tell you why?'

Benedict shook his head.

Sandra considered a moment. 'I'm guessing you enjoyed thinking about... things,' she grinned as he blushed and looked away from her, confirming her suspicions, 'but did you enjoy the flight itself?'

It was Benedict's turn to think. 'Maybe.' He shrugged. 'I don't know. Does it matter?'

Sandra looked at him in surprise. 'Of course it matters!' she blinked at him. 'Don't you usually enjoy flying?'

'No. But what's that got to do with anything?'

'Everything!' she pulled him to a stop and turned him to face her. 'I mean, I can understand you not really enjoying what we're doing right now because we're just working on the same techniques over and over, but flying is supposed to be fun!'

'Is it?'

'You mean to tell me you don't ever have fun when you're flying?'

Benedict shook his head. 'No.'

'Why not?'

'Because flying is very important to me and I have to use every opportunity I can to work on doing everything perfectly.'

'But why does everything have to be perfect?'

'Because the slightest mistake might mean disaster in an aircraft and, besides, I need to be better than the enemy.'

'Alright...' Sandra said slowly, trying to understand his thinking. 'Let me ask you this, then - the Misfits are better than most enemy pilots, right?'

'I suppose.'

'And is that because their technique is "perfect"?'

Benedict chuckled. 'The Misfits aren't exactly known for their perfect technique, quite the opposite in fact...' he trailed off and frowned again. 'I guess they're better because they're... more experienced?' he blinked, unsure of himself.

'And the Prussians aren't experienced?' She smiled. '*You* have as much experience in the air as Chastity Arrowsmith. More, probably, because I think I remember reading somewhere that she didn't start flying until she was eighteen. Does that make you better than her?'

'No, but...'

'And Ellie,' she asked. 'The instructors are saying she's a better pilot than any of us. Is that because her technique is better? Or is it because she's got more experience than you and Tay?'

'No, but...'

'So,' she went on ruthlessly, 'there's something you're missing, something you haven't taken into consideration.'

Benedict thought briefly. 'Talent?'

'Alright,' Sandra conceded, 'yes. She's definitely got talent and so do Chastity and the other Misfits, but not all fighter pilots have talent. Most of them have had to work hard to get where they are. And their technique is far from perfect. *But they've still got their wings and they're still flying spits.*'

'So, what is it I'm missing, then?'

'Nothing.'

'What?' Benedict stopped walking and stared at her.

'You're not missing anything. You've got everything you need to be an incredible pilot. You're talented, you're experienced and after flying for however long it is you've been flying...'

'Nine years.' Benedict interjected.

'*However* long you've been flying...' Sandra said again, giving him a scathing look, 'your technique isn't going to get any better. The trouble is that you're *only* worried about your technique and that doesn't make you a pilot, that just makes you a man operating a machine. And if that's the case you might as well be working in a factory.' She lifted a hand to touch the side of his face, but quickly stopped herself and looked around, very conscious of the men and women going past them on the path. 'Your hands and feet know what they're doing without you constantly trying to tell them, so just let them do it and use your mind for other things.' She rolled her eyes when he grinned. '*Not* daydreaming about me! Just try enjoying the flight, maybe?'

'I don't know if I can do that.'

'Well, you're going to have to if you want to fly Spits; you can't be thinking about your hands and feet when there is a dogfight going on around you to keep track of.' Sandra saw his continued scepticism and sighed, theatrically. 'Oh, alright. You can think about me if you want to. But only until you find another way to relax.'

Trevillian stood at the ready room window, looking out over the airfield as he sipped from a mug of tea that he'd felt the need to sweeten with an extra spoonful of sugar. He had let Perkins continue with her experimentation that morning and was feeling a little worse for wear again. It had been his last chance to do so, though, because, now the assessments were out of the way, they would be starting work on the second-week syllabus.

He huffed and shook his head, smiling wryly; the one week assessments were a nice gentle way to get cadets up in front of a review board for the first time so that they would know what to expect when it mattered, like right before their wings test. They weren't supposed to contain any surprises for them because the cadets were supposed to already *know* exactly how they were doing because their instructors were supposed to make sure to *tell* them exactly how they were doing at every stage of their training.

This group, though...

While most cadets progressed in a very linear fashion and it was usually obvious within a day or two of arriving whether they would be going for their wings test after two weeks or continuing with the full course, this group, quite frankly, baffled him and his team.

Perkins was actually the most predictable of the lot. She had come with no experience but an incredible amount of talent and from the first minute of the first flight he had seen she'd have no problem completing the course in record time.

Wilberforce, Oakley and Sherborne, on the other hand, had not lived up to the expectations that had been heaped on them. Not even close. They were each enormously experienced, but all three had shown that they were flawed in some way or other and as the week had gone on they'd just gotten worse. To the extent that he'd started to have serious concerns as to whether any of them would be good enough to become fighter pilots, let alone be able to stay on the fast track. Sherborne had somehow broken out of that downward spiral and was now making excellent progress, but the other two were still in jeopardy of failing completely and, by the look on their faces when they'd left their assessments, they hadn't been expecting that at all.

And then there were Orpwood and Smith. He had never seen two more unlikely pilots and if he'd encountered them in other groups he would have had no hesitation in advising them to consider other career paths. In the first few days he'd been close to doing so several times, but, somehow, they had pulled the proverbial rabbit out of a hat and were now looking very promising indeed. His team couldn't take the credit for that, though, well, not all of it, anyway. No, their unexpected improvement was almost entirely due to the fact that the cadets, the women anyway, had become such a close-knit group. He'd heard about how Perkins and Smith had worked with Orpwood - they'd had a surprise inspection one evening and been spotted conducting a rather bizarre exercise. The exercise might have been comical and caused quite a few laughs around the instructors' ready room the next day, but it effectiveness couldn't be denied - he'd never seen Merry so surprised, or admit how wrong she'd been about a pilot in her initial assessment.

He had hoped that the group would do something similar to help Wilberforce and Oakley, but neither of them had shown any change for the better. At least not until that morning, when Wilberforce had apparently shown some improvement and Oakley had finally seemed to be making an effort.

Had the others had some hand in that? He thought it more than likely, and that was why he'd made sure they all had their lunch breaks at the same time today; to give the group a chance to continue doing, well, whatever it was that it was doing.

Movement in the corner of his eye caught his attention and he leaned in closer to the window to peer along the perimeter track. He chuckled.

'Jocelyn!' he called out over his shoulder. 'I think I may have an answer for you.'

Aviator Sergeant Green stood from the armchair where she'd been engrossed in the enjoyment of one of her only vices - romance novels - and strode over to stand with him.

'Well, that would do it,' she said, chuckling at the sight of Benedict and Sandra walking together. They probably thought they were being discreet, but it was patently obvious that something was happening between the two of them.

Trevillian looked down at the dregs of his tea and swirled them thoughtfully.

'Honest opinion, Jocelyn. Do we push him hard in the hope that he'll continue to improve enough to take the wings test? Or do you think it's too late for that now and we should inform him now that he won't be taking it, so it won't come as so much of a shock later?'

Green looked out the window, contemplating the fitters readying the aircraft for the afternoon's flights, taking her time. 'If we push him he might have a chance, but the pressure might just as easily make him revert to how he was before. However, we might just as easily destroy his confidence altogether if we tell him he won't be taking the test.'

'And a pilot without confidence...' Trevillian said with a sigh.

'There might be a third option, though.'

'Oh, yes?' Trevillian asked, looking at her with a small smile. 'Have you had one of your ideas?'

Green smiled. 'I might just have. I know you like to jump straight into all the scary stuff, but can I have the afternoon?'

'If you think it will do some good, yes.'

'Thank you.' She turned and searched the room. 'Merry, could I have a word, please?'

Fifteen minutes later, Trevillian stood on the edge of the airfield with Aviator Sergeant Green and Aviator Lieutenant Marlott and they watched as the trainer accelerated over the airfield, then pulled smoothly into the air and began to climb. They chuckled as it wobbled slightly, but then it was gone, disappearing over the treetops.

'Are you sure about this?' he asked. 'He was looking anything but relaxed.'

'I don't want him relaxed,' Green replied, grinning, 'I want him distracted.'

'Well, he's certainly going to be that!' Trevillan laughed. 'She looked fairly keen about the idea, though. What did you tell her?'

'Not much, just to tell him what to do and keep him talking while he did it.'

Merry pursed her lips. 'Well, it's not a teaching technique I've ever come across, but I'm willing to give anything a chance at least once.' She turned to Green who, like her, was now left without anything to do for an hour or so. 'Fancy a game of chess, Jocelyn?'

'Why not,' Green said. 'I could go for another cup of tea as well.'

Trevillian nodded to them as they left, then looked back up at the sky. 'Good luck, you two.'

He smiled wryly and shook his head as he trudged back across the perimeter track to the elementary flight training ready room. He didn't go in, though, but instead put his hands on the door frame and poked his head in.

'Perkins!' he bellowed. 'It's time to fly! Stop dawdling!'

Benedict was feeling rather confused.

First, his assessment had plunged him into the depths of despair. Then the kiss with Sandra had lifted him to the heights of ecstasy. And then, this morning, he'd been floating around somewhere in limbo when he'd daydreamed his way through the first flight of the day.

Now this.

'Alright, we've been assigned to zone three for this flight, so come to a heading of two-seven-zero degrees, please, Cadet Wilberforce.'

'Yes, ma'am!' he said, not sure whether to be resentful at the situation he'd been thrust into, or laugh. The fact that when he craned his head around to look at the "instructor" in the back seat he found Sandra grinning at him sent him careening towards the latter of those two options, though.

He didn't know what the instructors were trying to do, or what they were thinking, but this seemed like a very pleasant way to spend an hour or so.

However, he changed his mind extremely rapidly when they got to their training area and, as soon as he'd started into the first set of manoeuvres she'd asked for, her sweet voice came back over the internal communications.

'So... Was that your first ever kiss last night?'

15

'The first week of elementary flight training is all about learning to control an aircraft and how to push its limits, and yours, *safely*,' Trevillian said to the group of cadets standing on the airfield in front of their aircraft, 'but this week you're going to use that knowledge in a manner that is all but safe. This week we are going to push you. We are going to take you to the edge of your endurance and the limit of your capabilities. This week is when we find out whether you'll only ever be just a pilot - someone who can fly an aircraft from one place to another without crashing it - or whether you have the mental fortitude to be a fighter pilot.'

He looked at each of them in turn as he spoke, meeting their eyes. 'Today we're tossing you straight into the deep end with spins, which so far you've only encountered in the classroom. They're some of the hardest things to deal with in an aircraft, so don't worry if you can't handle them right away because less than half of the cadets who come through here can.' He grinned at them. 'We've had cadets pass out, uncountable cadets throwing up, a few who had to be carried to their bunks at the end of the day, a couple who wet themselves and one who panicked and tried to open the canopy and climb out.' He held up a finger and looked at them sternly. 'Be warned: if you make a mess in the cockpit you *will* be cleaning it up yourself. Oh, and if you do decide you want to go for a walk at ten thousand feet, make sure you know your way home because nobody's coming to get you if you land in the middle of nowhere!'

He laughed at their worried faces. 'But, as I said, don't worry too much; even if you do have trouble at first, you'll get used to them eventually, just like you have everything else you've done so far.'

He chuckled as their expressions didn't lighten. 'Get through today, though, and it becomes a bit easier because after we're finished doing our best to scare the heck out of you we'll be spending the rest of the week working on advanced aerobatics, which you'll need for dogfighting, and we'll be making a start on how to handle emergencies. After all, there's no point training you and sending you up in an extremely expensive and desperately needed aircraft if you just prang it the first time something goes wrong. And, believe me, there are any number of things that can go wrong in an aircraft, even during a normal flight, like a bird strike or a mechanical failure, but if you've got some Prussian actively trying to shoot you down, then that number increases exponentially. Not to mention the fact that there is often limited time and even more limited resources to make repairs between sorties and, even though our fitters can work miracles, they can only do so much and your aircraft may well be falling apart before you even get into the air.'

He glanced over their shoulders to where fitters were waiting by the aircraft, listening in, and saw many of them nod in agreement and whisper comments at their fellows. He smiled and looked back at the cadets. 'There's a lot to learn and very little time to learn it if you want to take your wings test at the end of the week. So, it's time to buckle down, ladies and gentlemen. Show us what you're made of.' He nodded. 'Good luck.'

Benedict found that he was more than a little disappointed to be back with Sergeant Green and not with his new favourite instructor, Sandra, but he'd known that it wasn't going to last. He'd thought that they'd be called down at any moment and separated during their first flight, actually, but it hadn't happened and they'd even gotten in a second flight before the end of the day.

'Alright, Wilberforce, take us up, please.'

'Yes, ma'am.'

The wind was convenient today for taking off from right in front of the ready room so Benedict called control and got permission, then pushed the throttle forwards. The sun had been shining brightly for the last few days and it hadn't rained, not even overnight, so the ground was nice and hard - it was making a wonderful cricket pitch for break times between flights - and it did nothing to slow the

Huntress. The needle of the air speed indicator rose swiftly and he pushed the nose down at precisely forty-five miles per hour, then waited for the needle to rise to precisely eighty before pulling back on the spade grip and lifting her smoothly into the air. The treetops sped by underneath as he was bringing up the gear and his hands and feet danced on the controls as he fought against the swirls of air that were above them when there was even the faintest of wind, making sure the aircraft stayed perfectly straight and level.

'Sandra!'

Sergeant Green's voice was loud in his ears as she called out the name, but even as he frowned, wondering why the hell she was calling - he wasn't quite sure if she qualified after only a day, but hopefully soon he could call her - his girlfriend's name, he found himself relaxing, his death grip on the control's easing.

He chuckled. 'Message received loud and clear, ma'am.'

'Alright, then, Perkins, we're going to do some spins now. Do you remember how they told you to deal with them in class?'

'Yes, sir.'

'Good. Let's see how you do, then. I have control.'

'You have control, sir.'

Trevillian reduced the throttle to idle and pulled the nose up slightly, slowing the aircraft down. When the buffeting began, warning of an approaching stall, he pulled back on the stick and pushed his right foot fully forwards. The nose of the aircraft lurched to the side as she stalled completely and began a sickening rotation.

'There we go. You have control.'

'I have control, sir.'

'Alright, see if you can...'

Trevillian trailed off as Ellie smoothly brought the aircraft out of the spin before it could even really get going and brought it back to level flight.

He laughed; she hadn't discovered spins while he'd been letting her play and he'd thought she would have problems with them.

He should have known better.

'Not too shabby, Perkins! Let's do it again, this time after we've been spinning for a while. See how you deal with the disorientation.' He put his hands back on the controls. 'I have control.'

'You have control, sir.'

Ellie's head was spinning and her body was vibrating gently when she staggered into the ready room. She hadn't felt like that since the very first days of flying, when the unusual forces that a body was put under during even normal manoeuvres were still unfamiliar to her, but spins were completely different from anything else they'd done over the last week. They were far more violent and far more stressful than just about anything else that you would normally do in an aircraft, which, she supposed, was why they were being left to this late stage.

She stumbled to the table and flopped down in a chair. Rob and Benedict didn't appeared to be as shaky as her, but Rob was staring at the table and Benedict was leaning back in his chair with his eyes closed, so they weren't unaffected. Sandra looked like she'd suffered much more, though, she was pale and her hands were shaking gently as she held a, thankfully almost empty, mug of tea. Typically, Tay was grinning and seemed to be thoroughly enjoying everybody else's discomfort.

'Where's Lottie?' she asked him. 'Bathroom?'

Tayler shook his head. 'Hasn't come back yet.'

However, even as he spoke, they could hear the sound of an aircraft taxiing towards them.

Ellie struggled back to her feet. 'I need tea. Anyone else?'

Nobody wanted one and Ellie went to pour two mugs. She grabbed a plate of biscuits while she was there and was just bringing it all back when she heard Lottie crunching up the gravel path to the door.

'Lottie, I've got you a...' Ellie began to say as the big woman appeared in the doorway, but the words caught in her throat when she saw her friend's face and she dumped the teas on the table, heedless of the hot liquid spilling down the side and over her fingers, then rushed over to her.

'What's wrong?'

She grabbed Lottie's arm and guided her to a chair, but then had to help her into it. She knelt beside her while Tayler wiped one of the teas with a napkin and put it in front of her.

'Thanks.' The big woman said softly, smiling weakly. She carried the mug carefully to her mouth in both hands and slurped up a mouthful noisily. She didn't put it back down, though, but held it cradled in her hands, as if she were cold, her head bowed over it.

The others watched her, waiting patiently for her to recover enough to want to talk to them, their own troubles forgotten, at least for the moment.

After a long minute she lifted the mug up again, took a longer, thankfully quieter, drink, put it on the table, then sighed and lifted her head.

She looked around the concerned faces and huffed. 'You lot look as bad as I feel.'

Sandra reached out and put a hand on hers. 'What happened?'

'Spins,' she said. 'Spins happened.'

'To us too,' Rob said, 'but Squadron Leader Austin told me it's usual for people to be shaken up by them; they're frightening and about the most violent thing you can experience in an aircraft that won't tear off the wings. So, you don't have to...'

'So you all screamed and covered your eyes every time you went into one?' Lottie said, cutting him off angrily. Her anger was short lived, though, and tears began to stream down her face.

It was almost inconceivable that the big woman, who looked so strong, who'd been imperturbable even when things weren't going very well for her, and who had been the rock on which they'd stood during much of their basic training, should break down like that, so it took the others a moment to react, but then Sandra and Ellie both moved to wrap their arms around her while Rob and Tayler reached across the table to hold her hands. Benedict refrained from joining in, but he at least didn't sneer at them or make any snide comments, which he would have done only a day or two before.

Lottie quickly became self-conscious and stopped crying. She pulled her hands away and wiped her tears on the sleeve of her flightsuit, then wrapped her arms around Sandra and Ellie and crushed them to her.

'Thank you.'

She smiled and released the two women, who struggled to their feet and into chairs.

Ellie rubbed her ribs and exchanged a pained but amused glance with Sandra before looking back at Lottie, who was tipping the base of the mug to the ceiling as she drained it.

The big woman put the mug down, none too gently, smacked her lips, wiped her mouth with the back of her hand, then chuckled wryly before peering up at the group from under heavy eyelids.

'I'm done.'

'What do you mean?' Sandra asked, frowning.

'I mean that the only person I'm fooling is myself. Everyone else knows I'm not cut out to be a fighter pilot. I mean, just look at me! I can barely fit in a cockpit!' She grabbed a biscuit and stuffed it into her mouth whole, then spoke around it as she chewed. 'I don't have the instincts either. I'm having to work twice as hard as anyone else just to barely make the cut and then today...' Tears started to well up in her eyes again, but she snarled and wiped them away aggressively. 'I've never been so terrified in my life. All I could do the first few times Lieutenant Hyland put us into a spin was scream.'

'But you got over it, right?' Ellie asked.

Lottie shrugged. 'Not entirely. By the fifth or sixth I wasn't screaming anymore, at least, but I was still in no state to recover the aircraft. All I wanted to do was curl up and wait for it to end.'

'You were the last one down, though,' Ellie pressed. 'You obviously didn't run from it.'

Lottie shook her head. 'No. I told Hyland that I wanted to keep trying as long as we could. It was no use, though. I couldn't stand it and I couldn't recover the aircraft.'

'So, what are you saying?' Sandra asked hesitantly. 'Are you leaving?'

'Oh, no!' Lottie said, smiling at her. 'I've come too far to give it all up now, but Hyland will go back to working on the basics with me and I won't be trying to get my wings at the end of the week.' She grinned. 'I'm gonna apply for bomber training! There's a bit more space in one of those and I'll be able to stretch my legs.'

'Are you sure?' Sandra asked.

Lottie nodded. 'I never thought I'd be a pilot and being a bomber pilot will still be far beyond even my wildest dreams, so, yes, I'm sure.' She looked around the table. 'How did everyone else do with the spins? No trouble, right?'

Ellie, Sandra, Rob and even Benedict laughed at that.

As Trevillian had said they would, they did begin to handle the spins a bit better and at the end of the day they were each able to keep their heads enough to recover from them. That didn't mean they didn't still put an incredible strain on their bodies, though, and they were relieved when he told them they had finished with them and would start working on advanced aerobatics and emergency procedures in the morning.

What he didn't tell them was that that was going to be put them under an entirely different kind of strain.

'Right, start off with a maximum rate turn to port for 360°, then roll into a split S and back into a maximum rate turn to starboard, please.'

'Yes, sir.' Ellie answered. The manoeuvre was a tad basic compared to what they'd been doing for the last half an hour, but she could see how it would be useful in a fight.

She stood the aircraft on its wing and pulled the spade grip back into her lap, at the same time applying opposite rudder to keep it from sliding out of the sky. Suddenly, though, the pedals went slack under her feet and she lost all feeling from the rudder. The nose of the aircraft dropped sharply from the horizon and the aircraft started to accelerate, losing height rapidly.

'Oh dear, Perkins,' Trevillian drawled slowly from the back seat, 'it looks like your rudder cable just broke. Better take us home.'

Ellie was already rolling the aircraft upright again and she completed the manoeuvre, bringing the aircraft back to straight and level. She tested the rudder pedals, but they just moved freely without doing anything.

'I didn't know you could do that, sir.' She said, craning her head to look at him in the mirror over her head.

'Oh, yes.' He grinned. 'I can disconnect any and all of your controls from back here. It's a nice safety measure in case I get a real berk in the front seat. Now, let's see how you do getting us home.'

'Yes, sir.'

Ellie sighed. It looked like the fun was over for the morning; nursing the aircraft home would just be a basic glide with gentle turns and there wasn't enough tension left in the spring to make it worth coming back up again afterwards.

'And do make sure to use the pretend emergency codeword when you call it in, please; we don't want people to start thinking they're going to lose all the money they've placed on you and get in a panic.'

Ellie laughed. 'No, sir, we wouldn't want that!' She clicked the button on the grip. 'Arthur Control, this is Charlie One. Jackrabbit, I repeat, Jackrabbit. Five miles out. Over.'

Alright, it's 9:04, that's close enough, Merry Marlott thought to herself, *time to shake things up a bit.*

Orpwood had been doing very well that morning, carrying out the advanced aerobatic manoeuvres in an acceptable fashion without once mixing anything up. It had been a very pleasant surprise.

'Come out of the turn and pull us up into a loop, please.'

Merry waited until Orpwood had pulled the aircraft up and was almost inverted before springing her surprise.

'You've taken a hit in your left arm!' she called out suddenly, 'put it in your lap, please, and get us home as best you can.'

Merry felt the stick go slack under her hand and sighed. 'The other left arm, Orpwood.'

Rob grinned as he pulled the trainer out of the latest of loops, rolls and turns and brought it onto a heading for home.

'How far away do you reckon the airfield is, Mr Sherborne?' Auntie Austin asked him from the back seat.

Rob quickly scanned the landmarks, triangulating his position, making sure they really were where he thought he was.

'About two miles, ma'am.'

'I concur.'

Rob's eyes widened as the aircraft suddenly lost power and the airspeed started to drop alarmingly. He put his hand on the throttle and found it in the middle, where he'd left it. He pushed it forwards to no result, then tried pulling it all the way before pushing it forward again, but nothing happened.

'Ma'am, there seems to be a problem with the spring.'

'Is that so?'

'Permission to switch to the auxiliary spring.'

'I don't think that will be necessary. Just call in a fake emergency, please, and try not to crash on the way home, would you?'

'A fake...? Oh.' Rob laughed. 'Roger that, ma'am.'

He grinned as he pushed the nose down slightly so that the aircraft wouldn't lose any more speed before he was ready to do anything - this flying lark was turning out to be a heck of a lot of fun in the end.

Ellie handed the aircraft over to the fitters after the second flight of the day and trudged over to the ready room. Sandra was in the doorway, waiting for her with a mug of tea and she accepted it gratefully and accompanied her friend inside. Lottie was already at a table and there was the usual plate of sandwiches and biscuits there. It was already more than half empty, meaning either the big woman was hungry today, or that one or more of the boys had already passed through.

Lottie looked up as they approached and frowned. 'I think this is the first time I've ever seen you come back from a flight without a smile on your face. What happened?'

Ellie threw her helmet and gloves on the table and flopped into a chair. 'What happened was that it wasn't a bloody flight! We did six emergencies in a row and didn't get above two thousand feet the whole time! It was like doing circuits and bumps for a whole hour!'

'Six?' Sandra asked, gaping at her incredulously. 'I've only done one each time I've gone up and I don't think the boys have done any more than that.'

'Really?' Ellie asked, raising her eyebrows. 'I thought everyone...' She scowled. 'I understand the importance of knowing what to do in different emergencies, but I would have thought knowing how to fly properly would take priority.'

Sandra shrugged. 'Maybe Trevillian thinks you can already fly properly and wants to make sure you have the best chance of surviving.'

Ellie shook her head. 'I don't know. But I hope that's it with the emergencies now.' She selected a cheese sandwich from the plate before looking at Lottie. 'What about you? How are you doing?'

'Really well.' Lottie said around a biscuit, nodding enthusiastically. She swallowed then grinned. 'Lieutenant Hyland says I'm flying better than ever. I guess it's because there's no pressure now.'

'Are you going to rejoin the fast track?'

The big woman laughed. 'Not a chance! It's a huge weight off me. Besides,' she punched Ellie gently on the arm, 'now I can sit back and enjoy watching you lot,' she winked, 'and tonight I'm going to try to lay a bet of my own.'

Ellie winced and rubbed her arm. 'I'm not sure they'll let you do that.'

'Well, if they don't, I'm sure I can allow myself to be plied with drinks to gain access to my inside information.'

Sandra laughed. 'Don't let Tay hear you say that, he'll be jealous!'

After the tea break, which was as short as it could be while still giving the fitters enough time to rewind the aircraft, Trevillian came and fetched Ellie.

Sandra and Lottie wished her luck as she stood and rushed after him and she flashed a grin at them as she went, convinced that he wouldn't keep going with the emergency procedures and that she would get some proper flying in before lunch.

She was soon disabused of that notion as Trevillian called out an emergency before she had even taken off, while they were still accelerating. That set a precedent for the entire flight as he called two more in quick succession. Once, he got her to take them up to ten thousand feet and she thought they were finally going to do some proper flying, but all he did when they got there was open the canopy because it had been "peppered with bullets" and made her land with the wind buffeting her.

At the end of the flight, during which she hadn't even done a single loop or roll, Ellie handed the aircraft over to the fitters and gave Trevillian a nod. She had only gone a couple of steps towards the ready room before he called out to her, though, and she turned back.

He looked her up and down. 'How are you feeling, Perkins?'

Ellie was seething inside, but she forced herself not to show it. 'Fine, thank you, sir.'

'You aren't, maybe, feeling, oh, I don't know, a little frustrated, maybe?' he asked casually.

Ellie gritted her teeth, but somehow managed to answer. 'No, sir.'

Trevillian laughed. 'Well done! You pass!'

'Sorry, sir?' Ellie asked, her irritation slowly being replaced by puzzlement.

'Well, when I saw yesterday how spins were doing absolutely nothing to shake you up I was fairly sure that you wouldn't be at all bothered by emergency procedures. In fact, the more I push you, the more you seem to enjoy yourself. So, unfortunately, that left me with only one option - the only way to test your mental fortitude and push you to the limit of your rather impressive endurance, was to attempt to frustrate and bore you to death.' He laughed again. 'And by look of that jaw of yours it almost worked.'

Ellie made a conscious effort to relax

'Does that mean we've finished with the emergencies, sir?'

'Well, I'm still going to have to surprise you every so often, but yes. This afternoon we'll get back to something that we can both enjoy.'

16

'That was so much fun!' Tayler said as he dumped his tray on the table and flopped into the seat. 'Real flying!'

'Yeah,' Rob said, rolling his eyes at Ellie. '*Fun.*'

'*Real flying.*' Ellie grinned at him. Lottie and Sandra had already filled the others in on what Trevillian had done to her that morning and that she had had anything but "fun".

'I know, right?' Tayler continued, not noticing in his excitement that they were making fun of him. 'I mean, anyone can fly an aircraft when it's working perfectly, but it's when everything goes wrong that you can tell if someone is a good pilot or not.'

'I know,' Rob said, barely able to keep a straight face, 'why don't you ask Barton if you can go up with a blindfold on next time? You could pretend that you'd gotten glass in your eyes or something. That would be a real challenge.'

'A blindfold,' Taylor mused. 'Maybe...' his eyes narrowed suddenly as he finally caught on to what they were doing. 'Hey!'

Ellie, Rob and Lottie laughed. Benedict didn't, which wasn't surprising, but Sandra didn't either, which was. She was just poking at her food without much enthusiasm.

Ellie prodded her. 'You're quiet.'

Sandra blinked and looked up at her. 'What? Oh. Yes.' She turned to look at Benedict. 'I need to speak to you.'

She put her fork down and stood without waiting for an answer.

Benedict looked up at her for a moment, unsure what to do, but then stood as well and together they wended their way through the tables towards the door.

'Do you think she's pregnant?' Tayler asked quietly.

The others looked at him for a moment, waiting for a punchline or something, but then burst out laughing when they saw he was serious.

'How do you not know how that kind of thing works?' Ellie asked, 'You live in the country.'

He shrugged. 'I fly over farms, I don't live on them.'

Benedict followed Sandra out of the door. She didn't stop there, though, but kept going across the path and onto the grass and only came to a halt when she was a few steps into the trees. Even then she didn't look at him, but stared down at the ground with her arms crossed over her chest.

He stood behind her, waiting for her to turn around and speak to him, but as time passed and she just stood there he wasn't sure what he should do. This whole relationship thing was very new to him. Yes, he'd kissed a few girls and fumbled around with a couple of them, but they hadn't meant anything, they'd just been as bored as he was.

He thought perhaps that he should put an arm around her shoulder or hug her; that was what Lottie or Ellie would do. First, though, he should probably say something.

'Um...' he started, stepping closer to her, but she spun around suddenly and he staggered back again.

'Look,' she said, her words coming out in a rush. 'I know we've just started seeing each other and that we haven't done anything yet and I know you must have had lots of girlfriends, so you probably don't care, but I wanted you to know before I tell anyone else that I'm going to join Lottie and leave the fast track.'

'Uh...' he blinked trying to process what she'd said.

'Yes, well,' she said, her head dropping again when he failed to answer. 'That's all I wanted to say. We can go back to dinner now and I'll tell everyone else.'

She started to walk past him.

'Stop! Wait!' when she ignored him and kept walking he went after her and grabbed her arm and gently pulled her to a halt.

'What?' she asked, without looking at him.

'I'm sorry, I was... It was a lot... You surprised me.' He turned her around and looked her in the eyes, urging her to see how sincere he was. 'I had no idea that was how you felt. Are you sure?'

Sandra nodded. 'Yes. I thought I was doing alright and was sorting out my problems, but today, as soon as Lieutenant Marlott started pushing me, I got more confused and started making more mistakes than ever.' She stepped back out of reach of him and half turned away again. 'I'm sorry, but this means I won't be going with you when you move on at the end of the week.'

Benedict shrugged. 'I might not pass.'

'Of course you will! You're doing so much better now. Every time I see Sergeant Green she's smiling,' she grinned. 'And she doesn't strike me as the kind of person who smiles very often.'

Benedict smiled. 'I guess.' The smile disappeared quickly, though, and it was his turn to look down at his feet.

'Are you upset with me?' Sandra asked quietly.

He shook his head. 'No. Not with you. With the situation, with the war, with everything else. But not you.' He lifted his head and smiled at her weakly. 'We have a few days left. Let's enjoy them as best we can.'

Sandra nodded. 'And eight months aren't too long. You can come and see me when you get leave. Or I can come see you.'

'And we can try to get posted together after you get your wings.'

'Yes! I still want to fly Spitsteams, but even if I fly something else we might still go to the same base.'

Benedict tilted his head towards the mess. 'Do you want to tell them now?'

Sandra looked towards the door, then grabbed his hand and started pulling him further into the trees. 'Not quite yet.'

After two more days of cramming as many advanced techniques and emergency procedures into their flights as they could, the four recruits that were still hopeful of getting their wings were starting to run out of time before their test. However, even though there was still so much to learn about flying, the tests weren't just about flying. As well as the written part of it, there was also the small matter of bring glidewing qualified. The jump they had done at Druid was only the most basic of tests that they had to pass in order to pass basic training, but as pilots they needed to be able to do a lot more than just glide to the ground.

They showed up at the ready room after breakfast as usual, but found a canvas covered troop transport waiting outside instead of their aircraft and were unceremoniously bundled into it by an aviator sergeant.

Half an hour's uncomfortable ride late, they were deposited in a large field that was literally in the middle of nowhere, about ten miles from Gwynedd. There they found a tall glidewing tower, a small hangar, an aviator sergeant, two corporals, Wing Commander Trevillian and a pile of glidewings.

Trevillian leaned against the wall of the green painted hangar and sipped from an enamel mug as the NCOs divided the six recruits between them and quickly ran them through the basics of glidewing care and usage that they had already done at Druid. They pointed out the differences between the very basic ones they'd used before and these, which were the ones issued to RAC pilots that they'd been wearing since they started flight training. That took less than an hour and then they put on the glidewings and trudged over to the tower that stood slap bang in the middle of the field.

They had to carry out four jumps to be certified, three of them from the tower. The first was the simple glide, starting with the wings fully extended, that they'd done at Druid. The second was slightly more interesting: a white cross, made of canvas, was laid out on the field, a hundred yards away at ninety degrees to the jumping platform and they had to use the manoeuvring straps to guide themselves as close to it as possible. It was easy enough, but Sandra and Tayler made a complete hash of it and didn't land anywhere near, so they were given a second try while the others watched from below cheering them on.

Throughout the first couple of jumps, Trevillian had watched the proceedings from his place beside the hangar, occasionally disappearing inside, probably for more tea, but he wandered over and joined them at the base of the tower while one of the corporals was explaining the third exercise to them. This flight would still be fairly easy, but the toughest so far. They had to jump with only two of the four panels of the glidewing open, extend the wings once they were falling, then pull up from the dive and direct themselves to the white cross. When the corporal was finished she ordered them to start climbing, but Trevillian stopped them before they could.

'I thought we could make this more interesting.' He looked at the aviator sergeant leading the team of glidewing instructors. 'If you don't mind, of course?'

'Of course not, sir,' the aviator sergeant replied before sharing a grin with her team; they'd already been eager to give this group their training and any good anecdotes they got from it would go a long way in the NCO's mess.

'Thank you.' Trevillian nodded to her, then looked at the cadets. 'For those of you that are finding things a little easy, I'd like to suggest a challenge. For this last jump from the tower, instead of heading directly to the target, why not take a little detour *around* the tower first. Closest to the cross wins a prize, but please, try not to hit the tower as you go round; it's a lot of paperwork for me if one of you kills yourself,' he grinned, 'not to mention glidewings are expensive to replace.' He nodded to the sergeant, then sauntered away towards the canvas cross with his hands in his pockets, whistling as he went.

'Right, then, you lot! Up you go!' the aviator sergeant bellowed.

Thanks to the daily exercise over the last three and a bit weeks, the cadets were a lot fitter than they had been when they'd arrived, but this was their third time climbing the tower, or in the case of Sandra and Tayler, their fourth, and it was starting to get a bit much, especially with the weight of the glidewings on their backs. They were out of breath when they got to the top, but had a chance to recover slightly when the aviator sergeant leaned on the rail at the back of the platform and shouted down at them.

'Listen up! There is no need to take the wing commander up on his challenge unless you feel very confident that you can do it. Thankfully, the wind isn't strong today and it isn't gusting, but it will still be extremely dangerous. Make sure you leave plenty of room between you and the tower because if you do hit it, or even just touch it, you risk serious injury at the very least.' She paused to let that sink in, looking down at them with a serious expression, but then suddenly grinned. 'Having said all that, I know how bloody mad most pilots are and I don't suspect you're much different, are you? So, good luck and take care if you do try it. Wilberforce! You're first.'

Benedict climbed the last few steps up to the platform and went through the final safety checks with the sergeant, then extended two panels of his wings and walked to the front of the platform. Without any hesitation or ceremony he dived off.

The cadets excitedly watched through the girders of the tower as he fell past them, extending his glidewings smoothly as he went. However, they were disappointed when he turned directly towards the cross and glided easily down to land on it.

Tayler blew a raspberry, prompting laughter among cadets and NCOs alike, then bounced up the stairs to take his turn. After the checks he strode to the front of the platform, turned to wink at them, then leapt off with a whoop. His wings extended and he immediately turned away from the cross.

The cadets shouted encouragement as he went around them and he turned his head to grin at them, but that threw his balance off slightly and he veered towards the tower. His eyes widened in alarm and he managed to turn away before he came even close to hitting the girders, but he had overcompensated and was now heading in completely the wrong direction. He turned towards the cross as soon as he could, but he had run out of height now and landed almost directly behind the tower, a long way from the target. He closed his wings, then waved up at them when they jeered him.

It was Rob's turn next and right from the start the remaining cadets could tell that he was taking it much more seriously than his friend. He carried out his final checks then went to the edge of the platform and took a deep breath before leaning forwards and dropping straight down without jumping outwards. Unlike the others he took a moment to fall before opening his wings and, as a consequence, he was going quite fast when he deigned to pull up. He whizzed around the tower in a roughly circular flight path and, even though he was nearing the ground, he still had quite a lot of airspeed to play. He pulled up gently and flew parallel to the ground, getting closer and closer to the cross until finally, when he was twenty yards or so short, he was forced to flare and put his feet down if he didn't want to slide face first along the ground. Trevillian called something out to him that they couldn't hear and he nodded and retracted his wings, then turned and waved at them before sitting where he was and leaning back on his hands.

Ellie laughed and waved back at Rob. He'd done really well and it was going to be really hard to beat him. That didn't mean she wasn't going to try, though.

The only question was how to go about it? Should she go with Rob's strategy and gain speed or extend the wings immediately and try to conserve height?

She watched Sandra climb the stairs and check her equipment and then called out encouragement along with Lottie as the girl went to the front of the platform. She climbed down a few steps to where they were closest to the support struts, wanting to get a good look at what Sandra did, hoping it would give her an indication as to what the best strategy would be, but her friend didn't take Trevillian up on his challenge and instead followed Benedict's example and flew straight to the target.

'Perkins!' The aviator sergeant called. 'You're up!'

'Good luck, Ellie!' Lottie whispered.

Ellie turned to smile at her, then climbed the last few steps up to the top where the aviator sergeant met her and tugged on her straps one by one.

She patted her on the shoulders. 'Checked and ready to jump.'

'Checked and ready, Sergeant!' she answered.

'Step forwards!'

Ellie extended the first two panels of her glidewings, then stepped carefully forwards, but then stopped and smiled. She put her foot back, then used it to push off into a run. It was only three steps to the edge of the platform and she leapt out as high and far as she could, as if she were diving into the lake near the village where she'd learnt to swim as a child. The wings, even only open a couple of panels, extended her dive, but she didn't want to get too far from the tower, so she immediately banked around, extending the wings to their fullest as she went. This tactic meant she was going far slower than Rob had gone and it would take her longer to get around the tower, but as a consequence she was able to cut the corners a lot closer without any danger, so close, in fact, that she felt that she could almost reach out and touch it, or shake hands with Lottie as she went past. She was still quite high when she completed the turn and was able to glide serenely towards the cross. She passed over Rob's head with about six feet to spare and set down more than five yards beyond him.

'Good show, Perkins!' Trevillian called out.

'Well done, Ellie!' Sandra shouted from the cross, clapping, while Tay cheered.

Rob stood and came over to her as she retracted her wings. 'Well done! The prize is yours.'

'Sit down! Both of you!'

Trevillian's order took them by surprise and they stared at him. He pointed over their heads and they turned and immediately hit the deck as Lottie passed over them, her dangling feet inches away from taking off their heads. She landed beyond them and staggered a couple of steps, narrowly avoiding falling flat on her face as her feet caught on the edge of the canvas cross.

'And we have a winner!' Trevillian shouted with a laugh as the cadets surrounded the big woman. 'Bravo, Cadet Smith!' he looked at the three instructors as they landed nearby in quick succession. 'I think that was a performance worthy of a prize, don't you?'

'I'm fairly sure none of us could have done any better, sir.'

'Quite! Quite!' Trevillian looked at Lottie. 'So you have a choice to make, Smith. I have two models from Dunne of Hamleys. The first is of Abby Lennox's *Dragonfly*, from the start of the war, which I have already assembled and painted and is therefore ready for display. The second is a model of Gwen Stone's *Excalibur*, which I was saving for a rainy day to put together. It is still in the box and comes with all the necessary paints and glues. Which would you like?'

Lottie frowned. 'Models, sir?'

Tayler, who'd been staring at Trevillian and was quite obviously boiling over with envy, couldn't help himself. 'Model *aircraft*, Lottie.' He held his hands up, around three feet apart. 'They're about this big and the ones that John Dunne makes for Hamleys are the best in the world. You can even get little springs for them and have them fly around the room on wires! They're *so* expensive!'

'Oh,' Lottie still looked doubtful. 'And are they hard to put together? Because Excalibur has to be my favourite aircraft ever, but if I wouldn't be able to put it together...'

Trevillian laughed. 'Smith. You have seven or eight months of training ahead of you at Gwynedd. If you can't work out how to put it together in that time then come and see me and I will happily help you!'

Lottie brightened. 'Thank you, sir! Excalibur, then, please!'

'With pleasure, Smith! Now, time for a tea break, isn't it Sergeant?'

'Yes, sir!' the aviator sergeant said, beaming; they'd gotten their anecdote. And then some.

As well as a tea urn, the small hangar contained bathrooms, a few battered chairs, tools to repair glidewings and a small transport aircraft. While the cadets rested and had their tea, the instructors went over the aircraft, doing preflight checks, before pushing it out onto the apron in front of the hangar. Afterwards, they grabbed themselves a mug each, but gathered the cadets around the aircraft while they drank it.

'You have one last flight to do before you earn your qualification,' the sergeant said in between sips. 'In a minute we're going to take you up to ten thousand feet and you're going to jump,' she grinned. 'Land without killing yourselves and you pass. Land on the airfield and you won't have to walk back. Any questions?'

She looked around the cadets. There was usually one inane question from a nervous cadet, but she didn't expect any from this group. She was surprised, therefore, when a hand went up, and even more surprised to see who it was.

'Yes, sir?' she asked.

'My qualification is about to go out of date.' Trevillian said. 'Would you mind if I joined you?'

'Not at all, sir. Please do.'

'Thank you.' Trevillian nodded, then wandered away, tipping the base of his mug to the sky to drain it.

The aviator sergeant watched him go for a second, mystified, but then looked at the cadets. 'Takeoff is in five minutes. It'll take this bird a while to get up to ten thousand feet and there are no bathrooms on board, so make sure you go now if you need to!'

Five minutes later, the cadets clambered into the back of the aircraft with their glidewings on their backs and were directed to sit on the hard wooden benches against the side bulkheads. Trevillian followed them in and he lounged on the end of one of the benches, down at the tail, with his arms crossed and his eyes closed.

The two corporals sat with the cadets while the sergeant went to the cockpit. They heard his voice checking in with Arthur Control at Gwynedd and then moments later they slid sideways along the benches as the aircraft accelerated.

It took a long time for the aircraft to take off and even longer to climb and the sergeant had to fly a square pattern around the airfield otherwise they might have been over Birmingham by the time they'd reached ten thousand feet. Eventually, though, they were almost high enough and the corporals unstrapped themselves and stood to perform final checks on everyone's glidewings.

Trevillian opened his eyes and unstrapped himself as well. He stood and stretched as much as he could within the confines of the aircraft then bent to look out through the window. He grunted in satisfaction, then walked up to join the cadets and, while one of the corporals checked his glidewings, he smiled at them.

'This last jump, out of a perfectly good aircraft at a nice safe altitude will get you your glidewing certification, which you need to fly combat operations. However, if you ever have to get out of an aircraft for real, then it's not going to be flying straight and level and it probably won't be up this high either. That doesn't mean that I'm going to ask the sergeant to start doing aerobatics or put us into a spin to make this more realistic, but you could at least not just go through the door as if you were heading out for a stroll.'

He nodded to the corporal standing beside the side door and she slid it open.

Trevillian grinned at them. 'See you on the floor.' With two running steps he reached the side of the aircraft and, without slowing down, he tucked forwards, as if he were doing a somersault off the high dive and went spinning away.

The cadets stared speechlessly at the now empty sky through the door for a moment before Tayler laughed.

'Well?' he asked. 'What are you waiting for?'

He swaggered across the aircraft to the door then looked back at them. 'Last one out's a wet blanket!' He shouted, before diving out with a whoop, throwing his arms around so that he spun sideways like a drill bit.

Ellie strode to the door. She paused on the lip a second, wondering what silliness she could do, but she'd never been one for cartwheels or tumbling so in the end she just turned her back on the sky, waved to her friends, and let herself fall backwards.

The aircraft fell away from her surprisingly rapidly, but then she lost sight of it as her head dropped towards the ground and the ground came into view again. For a moment she thought she would continue to turn and end up with her head pointing completely downwards, but then the air caught her and brought her back to horizontal. She laughed as she lay there on her back and actually put her hands behind her head, as if she were laying on the bed.

The aircraft was now just a dark cross against the sky, far above her, and a dot detached itself from it as she watched, followed a few seconds later by another, then another soon after.

It was really quite peaceful, falling like this, as if she were in a prolonged dive with the throttle all the way back, and she enjoyed the sensation for a second or two, but it wasn't long before she started to get nervous; she couldn't see the ground like this and had no idea how close it was getting. The instructors had said they had about forty-five seconds before they absolutely had to deploy their glidewings from ten thousand feet, but she had completely lost track of how long she'd been falling - it could have been anything between fifteen and thirty seconds already.

She tried to turn over, but found that, no matter how much she swung her arms around or kicked her legs, the pressure of the air against the wide glidewing pack just kept her in place. Panic was just about to set in when she realised that she was being stupid. Quickly, she found the lever on her side and turned it, deploying the first panel of her glidewings. Immediately, her centre of balance shifted, coming up, and she grabbed the strap on her right and pulled it as hard as she could. She flipped and went almost completely round before the wings caught the air and held her. Her eyes widened as she saw the ground rushing up towards her and she quickly deployed another panel, then a third, before tugging on both control straps and pulling up from the dive. Her airspeed dropped rapidly until she was going slowly enough for her to deploy the last panel without buckling the wings and she put herself into a gentle banking glide. Only then did she draw in a deep breath and take stock of her situation and she laughed when she saw she was still at least three thousand feet up.

She continued to bank, quartered the sky around her, searching for her friends and found them, all rather a lot higher than she was. Trevillian was the closest to her and he dived towards her and formed up on her wing.

'Don't tell me,' he shouted. 'You came out backwards.'

'Yes, sir.'

'Trust you to pick the one way that could get you killed!' He laughed then pointed down and slightly to their left, where the tiny white cross was just about visible. 'Race? Loser makes the tea?'

'You're on, sir!'

'Doesn't count if you don't land on the cross, though!' he called, just before he pulled the lever to completely retract his wings and dropped like a stone.

Ellie laughed, then pulled her own lever and fell after him.

In the end, Trevillian pipped her to the post, alighting on the cross about five seconds before she did, but, considering that was about the head start he'd had on her, Ellie didn't consider that she'd done too badly.

'Close one, Perkins.'

'Well done, sir.'

They looked up into the sky to see the others floating down, still thousands of feet above them.

'We have some time. Walk with me.'

Trevillian set off towards the hangar, pulling his hat and goggles off as he went and Ellie fell into step with him.

'Well, that's that out of the way,' he said, 'and now we can get back to work.' He looked sideways at her. 'Not that you actually need to keep working towards your wings test; you'd pass it with ease even if you took it right now. The practical part anyway. How's the theory coming along?'

'I've had some problems with the mathematics side of things, sir, but Sandra has been helping me and I think I'm about up to scratch.'

'Good, good.' Trevillian walked in silence for a moment, but then sighed. He came to a halt and stared down at his feet. 'A word of warning, Eleanor. Everyone is saying you're an excellent pilot, *I'm* saying you're an excellent pilot and everyone will continue to say that you're an excellent pilot because it's true. I know you're handling the praise well right now, but you mustn't ever let it go to your head, because if you go into a fight thinking you're better than everyone else then you're likely to be proven wrong. There is *always* going to be someone better than you or who has a better aircraft, which gives them an edge over you and that *may* end up killing you, but complacency *will* kill you every time. Go up against the enemy afraid. Keep that fear close, always. Don't let it rule you, but never let go of it because it will keep you sharp and it will keep you alive.' He lifted his head and turned to look at her. 'And for Victoria's sake, *never* stop learning because, just as there will always be someone better than you, there will always be people with more experience than you, even if they're not as good as you, and they will more than likely have something you can take on board.'

He stayed there, looking into her eyes and she wondered if she should say anything, but, before she could, he grinned and continued towards the hangar.

'Well, Perkins, that's all I wanted to say. Now, come on,' he said, looking sideways at her, 'you owe me a cup of tea!'

17

Over the next day and a half, Ellie, Tayler, Rob and Benedict repeated everything they'd learnt, seeking to polish off their flying enough to satisfy the examiners for their wings test. However, at the end of the second day, the penultimate day of the two week course, their time was up and they marched over to the main building, to the same meeting room they had visited a week previously, for their final assessments. Lottie and Sandra were given permission to skip the last flight of the day to go with them for moral support and they all sat in the chairs in the corridor and waited to be called.

They were waiting for almost ten minutes this time, getting more and more nervous, until the aviator sergeant who'd brought them came out and ordered Benedict to the door.

Benedict marched in under the aviator sergeant's orders and came to a halt in front of the long table. When they'd had their one week assessments the huge table had been almost empty, with only the six instructors behind it, but today there was a veritable crowd, including the base commander, Group Captain Wyvern, the adjutant and a few other officers he didn't recognise taking up the majority of the chairs.

'At ease, Cadet Wilberforce.' Wyvern said, without looking up from the papers spread on the table in front of him. 'You had a bit of a shaky start, I see, but it looks like you've pulled your finger out. Is that correct, Sergeant Green?'

The other instructors were gathered around the end of the table and Benedict's instructor stood and moved to join him.

'Yes, sir. That's right, sir,' she said, standing at ease next to Benedict. 'Cadet Wilberforce has always been technically very proficient, but came to us very inflexible and lacking in the necessary ability to adapt to a changing situation. In the past few days he has largely overcome this obstacle and, while he still has work to do, as long as he doesn't forget himself during the test he should have no problem passing.' She looked down at Benedict. 'However, I believe his interests would be best served if he were to be granted special dispensation to remain another two weeks and take the test with the next class when he has had a chance to better assimilate this new philosophy. But, I also believe that the choice as to whether or not to do so should lay with him.'

'Hmm,' Wyvern said thoughtfully, tapping the file in front of him with his pen. 'We've never done that before, but then again we've also never had someone who didn't just fit neatly into the yea or nay categories.' He looked at Benedict. 'Well, Wilberforce? What do you say? Would you like to take the test tomorrow and risk a failure going on your record, or train with Wing Commander Trevillian's team for another couple of weeks and ensure success?'

'I...' Benedict began, but was surprised when he realised that it was no longer an easy choice. A few days ago he would have chosen to take the test in a heartbeat, but that was back when he had been alone in the world and had only himself to think of. Now, there were *feelings*, of all things, to take into consideration. Both his and Sandra's.

The brief conversation they'd had outside the mess hall about her decision to remain behind at Gwynedd hadn't been the only time they'd spoken about being separated at the end of the week. They hadn't wanted to bring it up, but it had been inevitable and Sandra had continued to insist that he leave her behind, that they could visit when they were on leave and so on and so forth. He knew she would be very happy if he chose to stay, though, even if it was only for a couple more weeks. And, frankly, another two weeks with Sandra would be wonderful. Despite their wildly different backgrounds they had so much in common and he really felt connected to her. And when they managed to snatch a few moments alone together... He wouldn't even be giving up on his dream, he would get his wings after the two weeks and...

A sudden surge of anger and self-loathing all but overwhelmed him as he realised how close he was to ruining everything; if he gave up now he'd only be setting himself back two weeks, yes, but that would mean he would never be recognised as a great pilot. He'd be seen as being inferior to the others and, while he could just about accept being looked at as inferior to Perkins, who was a once or twice in a generation talent - even he could see that - there was no way he would accept being compared that way to the bumpkins.

He met Wyvern's eyes with all the confidence he could muster. 'I'll take the test, sir.'

Tayler marched into the room and performed a parade halt in front of the table, trying to make a good impression in front of the board. He'd thought he'd done a good job, until he heard the aviator sergeant sigh almost inaudibly next to him. None of the men and women around the table seemed to be paying much attention to him at that moment anyway, though, so he turned his head slightly and winked at her before composing his face into what Rob had called the "upper-class twit trying to hold it while being presented to the king" look, which was supposed to convey respectful attentiveness.

'Well, if we completely disregard the first eight or nine days of your time here, then you've done very well, Cadet Oakley,' Wyvern said, closing the folder on his desk.

There were muted chuckles from around the room and Tayler grinned. 'Thank you, sir.'

'And the less said about your academic results the better, although, you have managed to bring them up considerably over the last few days.' He leaned forward to peer down to the end of the table. 'Sergeant Barton. Anything to say?'

Barton stood and let out a deep sigh. 'I feel like I've aged more in the last two weeks than the whole of the last war...' He smiled wryly as the men and women around him chuckled. 'Cadet Oakley did indeed have a rough start to his time here, but, if he doesn't get excited and start playing silly buggers, he'll pass without any problem. And God help his instructors at Galath.'

'Are you saying he's erratic?' Wyvern asked with a frown.

'Yes, sir.'

Wyvern blinked at him. 'Then *should* we be sending him on? Even if he does pass.'

'Yes, sir.'

'You don't think we should hold on to him and sort him out first?'

'No, sir,' Barton said, shaking his head emphatically. 'One man's erratic is another man's brilliance and, if he passes, I believe we should leave it to the experts at Galath to figure out which is the case.'

'I see.' Wyvern looked at Barton thoughtfully for a moment, then turned to Tayler. 'Well, Cadet Oakley? Do you fancy your chances?'

'You bet, sir!'

Wyvern laughed. 'Yes, actually, I have bet on it!'

'Well, there's really nothing much to be said about your flying, Cadet Perkins,' Wyvern began, 'I've never seen such a glowing report, especially from Wing Commander Trevillian. However,' he turned over the page in the file open on the desk in front of him, 'your academic scores could be better.' He scanned them quickly. 'I do not see anything here to indicate you'll have any problems passing, though.' He leaned back in his seat and looked at Trevillian. 'I don't suppose you'd consider keeping her back for a couple of weeks would you?'

Trevillian laughed. 'Not a chance, Bill! I did tell you not to bet against her.'

'Damn,' he closed the folder and sighed exaggeratedly, 'well, I guess I'm just going to have to approve you to take the test, then, Perkins. Good luck! Dismissed!'

'...but that was just a slight hiccough.' Squadron Leader Austin was saying. 'After he'd gotten it into his head he did actually want to be a pilot he made excellent progress and I have no doubt he'll make an excellent one.'

Wyvern looked at Rob. 'You didn't want to be a pilot?' He looked sideways at Trevillian and his instructors. 'I'm not surprised; they're all daft.'

Trevillian blew a raspberry and there was laughter and catcalls until Wyvern held up his hand with a grin.

'So, Cadet Sherborne. Do you wish to go beyond being merely daft and join the ranks of the truly daft?'

'Yes, sir, I reckon I do.'

'Victoria help you, then!' he signed the paper in front of him. 'Approved!'

After dinner that night they gathered in the girls' bunk room to revise for the written portion of the wings test.

Sandra and Lottie had continued to go to classes with them and they did as much as they could to help everyone. Even Benedict, whose father had provided him with the entire syllabus four years previously and had tested him almost constantly since, helped out occasionally, but not without making sure they knew how superior he was to them.

It was impossible to cover everything the exams covered in one night, though, and being rested was just as important as knowledge, so, subscribing to the believe that "if they didn't know it by then, they never would", no matter how erroneous it might be, they went to bed.

18

Just because they were taking their wings test that day, didn't mean that the cadets didn't have to go through their normal routines, and they were woken at the same time as they had been every other morning to exercise and tidy up for their daily inspection before going to breakfast. During the meal they were approached by all and sundry, who wished them well even as they eyed them in what they probably thought was an unobtrusive fashion, most likely looking for some indication of where to lay last-minute wagers.

The day had dawned bright and clear with a wind that was steady, but not too strong - a perfect flying day - but the four cadets wouldn't be doing any of that until after lunch; first they had their written exam to worry about and after they'd eaten they put on their uniforms and were taken to one of the classrooms.

They had to take two written exams for their wings, each lasting two hours, with an hour to rest in between. The first exam comprised of purely theoretical things such as mathematics and physics, while the second dealt with aircraft and flight specific subjects like navigation, aeronautics and aerodynamics.

They were completely drained by the time the second exam finished, even Benedict, and were rather glad they had a break for lunch and didn't have to fly straight away. Sandra and Lottie joined them and they stumbled to the mess. They grabbed trays of food before flopping into chairs at one of the tables against the wall, as far away as they could get from everyone else, not wanting to be pestered during their break. Nobody bothered them, though; either their expressions were forbidding enough to frighten people away, or the other mess users were displaying a consideration they hadn't until then.

'How did you do?' Sandra asked softly.

'Not bad.' Tayler said around a mouthful of food. 'Should've passed,' he added as an afterthought whilst stuffing another forkful of mash potato and sausage in after the first.

Rob winced at his friend's table manners but nodded. 'There was nothing too complicated. Even for Tay.'

'Hey!' Tayler protested, spraying the table with half-chewed food.

The others were well used to this kind of behaviour from Tayler and had learnt not to sit in front of him, but they still expressed their disgust in their own way and Rob threw a napkin at him.

'Ellie?' Sandra asked looking at her in concern.

Ellie was poking at her food in silence. She had passed a restless night, worried about the written exams and had just seen her fears realised. 'I don't know,' she muttered, 'I really don't. I answered all the questions, but I don't know if I got them right or not.'

Lottie put her arm around her shoulders and shook her gently, for her anyway. 'I'm sure you've done fine! All you need is a pass, anyway. What's that? Fifty percent?'

'Seventy.' Benedict said smugly.

The flight portion of the wings test was also in two parts, the first of which involved going up with an instructor in the back seat, the second of going up solo, while the examiner flew nearby, observing.

Unlike the pilot's degree, for which Lieutenant Crawford was the only qualified examiner on the base, there were several instructors at Gwynedd that could administer the wings test, which meant that all four of them could go up at the same time. That was just as well because each part of the test lasted about an hour and there wouldn't have been enough hours in the day to do them one by one.

Unlike the written test, there could be and were no surprises. The examiners couldn't spring something on them as a surprise because there literally wasn't anything they could come up with that they hadn't done.

For Ellie it was a relief to get back into the cockpit. The fact that she had an examiner watching her every move didn't bother her in the slightest and she was able to enjoy herself to the extent that she could forget the mess she'd made of the written tests. All too soon, though, she was landing after the second flight and the worry returned.

The trouble was, it didn't matter if she got full marks on the practical examination; if she failed the written part then that was it, she failed everything.

The four candidates landed within minutes of each other and Trevillian gathered them to him once their examiners had let them go.

'Right. That's it. The test is over. The marks will take an hour or two to be published, so if I were you I'd take yourselves off to the cadet's mess. I'll tell Smith and Orpwood where you've gone and get their instructors to let them off early so they can go wait with you. Have a drink, play a game of darts or clockwork conkers, maybe even have a sing. Just do *something* to pass the time and take your mind off it for a while, because there's nothing more you can do and there's no point in worrying.' He waved them away. 'Now, go on. Shoo!'

By the time they'd washed and changed out of their sweaty flightsuits, Lottie and Sandra had arrived and they waited for them to get ready before making a beeline to the mess together.

It was early evening and most people were still on duty so the mess wasn't crowded, but there were still a fair few people there.

They had become used to rooms going quiet when they entered them and being watched whenever they went anywhere, but nobody even glanced their way. They were too busy clamouring around a woman standing on the piano stool in front of a chalkboard propped up on the piano lid.

Benedict scowled and stalked straight to the bar, taking Sandra with him, but the rest of the cadets stood where they were, just inside the door and peered at the commotion, wondering what was going on. They were especially puzzled by the fact that the woman was an aviator sergeant and shouldn't be in the cadet's mess at all.

'Are they in trouble or something?' Ellie asked.

'No,' Tayler said with a laugh. 'That's the aviator sergeant who's running the book on us. Look at the chalkboard.'

'My name's not up there.' Ellie said. 'There's just yours and Rob's.'

'Who do you think "The Lady" is?' Tayler asked. 'It's not Benedict, although it would suit him. Just as well as "The Lord" does.'

'Oh!' Ellie exclaimed, blushing and putting her hand to her mouth. 'Why would they call me...?' she trailed off as she realised that the activity around the piano had stopped suddenly and everyone was looking their way.

Tayler laughed into the silence. 'Don't mind us, sergeant! Carry on!'

The aviator sergeant grinned and gave him a mock salute. 'Thank you, sah!'

There was another moment of silence, but then the noise redoubled as everyone resumed their shouting at the same time.

The cadets wandered over to join Sandra and Benedict and Tayler leaned against the bar, unhappily eyeing the selection of soft drinks. Since he'd promised Tayler that he would stop drinking and would work harder he had stopped coming to the mess altogether. Not only because there hadn't been time, but also because he hadn't wanted to be tempted. However, before he could make up his mind, Rob appeared and bumped shoulders with him.

'Test is over and our deal no longer applies. Have a drink if you want.'

Tayler looked at him in surprise, then a slow smile lit up his face.

'Thanks, Rob.' He looked at the barman, then at the beer taps. 'Evening!' he winked at Rob before turning back to the barman. 'I'll have a ginger beer, please!'

Rob laughed. 'Make that two, please.'

After they'd all gotten drinks, they claimed one of the empty tables and settled in to wait. Shortly after they'd sat down, the aviator sergeant came over and smiled down at them.

'I'm off to the officer's mess now, but before I go, I just wanted to say that I hope you've all done well, no matter if it costs me money, and thanks for being so understanding.'

She nodded and began to go, but Tayler called out after her. 'Sergeant!'

'Yes?' she asked, turning back.

'Who was the favourite in the end?'

'Well,' the sergeant said, grinning, 'the boys have been hands down favourites throughout to take the overall prize.'

Tayler laughed. 'Tell us something we don't know!'

The sergeant winked at him. 'As for the individual winner - the odds have been heavily in favour of Cadet Wilberforce since I opened the book. However,' she looked from Benedict to Ellie, milking the moment, 'last minute wagers placed over the last few days have shifted the odds and now they are completely even between him and Cadet Perkins to take top marks. It's anybody's game.'

She checked her chronograph and her eyes widened. 'Oops, sorry! Got to dash!'

'And what about our commission!' Tayler shouted after her as she hurried away.

She flashed him a grin over her shoulder. 'The wings are their own reward, aren't they?'

The mess began to fill up soon after that, but the noise level didn't rise very much. There was no full-on party as there was most evenings, with the cadets drinking as if there was no tomorrow and getting louder and louder, instead there was a kind of hushed expectancy, with quiet conversations taking place in small groups huddled around the tables.

After half an hour they went back to the bar for more drinks. As they wended their way through the tables they were followed by sneaked glances and hissed whispers, so they decided to get double rations so that they didn't have to go back again for a good while.

Finally, after what seemed like an age but was in reality only an hour more, an airman burst into the mess, the noise of the door slamming against the wall rendering the room silent in an instant.

'The adj has the marks! He's on his way to the ready rooms!'

He stood there panting for breath, but received no reply. Instead, every eye went to the table at the side of the room.

For a moment the cadets didn't move, so firmly were they caught in the spotlight, but then Tayler heaved a huge sigh and pushed his chair back.

'Well,' he said slowly, 'we might as well wander over and take a gander, I suppose…'

He stood, taking his time to push his chair under the table, then walked slowly towards the entrance, watched by everyone. The door had closed after rebounding from the wall and he opened it. He turned in the doorway, placed his hat carefully on his head, straightened it, the winked at them and broke into a run.

Rob, Lottie and Ellie laughed, then leapt to their feet and raced after him. Benedict and Sandra stood up more slowly, smiling at each other, and, hand in hand, they joined the general rush for the door.

Tayler sprinted ahead of the crowd, taking a short cut through the trees to the perimeter track before turning and racing along it towards the ready rooms. There was a covered corkboard next to the elementary flight training ready room that notices and flyers were pinned to for the pilots to peruse and they'd been told the marks would be pinned there when ready.

As he was nearing the buildings he met the adjutant coming the other way and he saluted with a grin, but didn't slow.

The adjutant laughed. 'Congratulations, young man!' he called out to Tayler's back, before turning and stepping smartly out of the way of the other cadets and the mob following closely behind. He laughed again as they tripped over themselves trying to salute him and in the end just turned his back so that they wouldn't have to.

Tayler arrived at the board twenty or more yards before any of the others and they saw him scan it. Unexpectedly, he threw his head back and roared with laughter.

'What?' Rob asked as he, Lottie and Ellie ran up. 'What's so funny?'

Tayler's only answer was to wave his hand at the board as he staggered away.

'What's Tay laughing at?' Sandra asked as she and Benedict arrived, let through by the crowd.

It took Ellie a moment to understand the numbers on the piece of paper pinned to the board; the marks for the practical and written exams were shown separately and a third mark, the combined one was shown afterwards. Her heart leapt when she saw that she had passed both parts of the exam and therefore had gained her wings, but she doubted that was what Tayler had been laughing at, neither was he laughing at Benedict failing because the toff had passed. With slightly lower combined marks than hers, she saw with not a little satisfaction. No, what Tayler had been laughing at was that neither she nor Benedict had gained the highest overall marks. That honour had actually gone to Rob.

'Congratulations, Acting Aerial Officer Perkins,' Group Commander Wyvern said, pinning a set of brass wings to the chest of the brand new officer's uniform jacket she'd found waiting for her on her bunk the evening before. He shook her hand, then lowered his voice and winked. 'Jolly good show!'

'Thank you, sir!' Ellie smiled and stepped back as soon as he released her hand. She saluted him, then turned as smartly as she could and marched back to join the end of the line with the three other newly-promoted officers.

'Whoever said good things come in small packages must have been thinking of this group.' Wyvern said, looking around at the hundreds of men and women who had gathered that morning to witness the ceremony and send the four youngsters off. 'Never, I believe, have we been so proud of a group. Or so entertained by one,' he smiled as laughter rang out and he waited for it to die down before continuing, 'but now we send them on their way, safe in the knowledge that we have done our best by them and in the hope that one day soon they will do their best for the Kingdom of Great Britain. Congratulations, pilots, and happy hunting. Dismissed!'

Wyvern led the thunderous applause as the four pilots fell out and were swamped by all and sundry. He felt the presence of the adjutant at his side and leaned in to him, knowing that his friend would have some comment to make - usually he could come up with something negative about a group, even if they had done well. He didn't disappoint this time, either.

'You owe me a fiver, sir.'

Wyvern laughed. 'Best five pounds I've ever spent!'

Ellie had been pounded on the back so many times that her teeth seemed to be rattling in her head and her hand was throbbing so much from being shaken that she didn't think she'd be able to hold a stick for days. She was relieved, therefore, when the dozens of people crowding around her suddenly stepped back, giving her some much needed breathing room, and she turned to find Squadron Leader Trevillian smiling at her.

'Congratulations, Perkins.'

'Thank you, sir,' she said, 'I hope you didn't lose too much money on me and the girls.'

Trevillian grinned. 'Well remembered! I did bet on the girls, yes, but I didn't lose money on you; I bet on you to take top marks in the flight test, not overall, and my winnings for that more than made up for my losses.'

He stepped in close to her and lowered his voice so that only she could hear him. 'It's been an absolute pleasure, Perkins. Thank you.'

He smiled at her again, then turned and disappeared into the crowd before she could reply.

If the men and women of Gwynedd had been given their way they would have converted what was supposed to be a simple ceremony into a full-blown party, but there were duties to attend to and a bus waiting to take the four new pilots on to their next home. So, after a hug and a few last words with Sandra and Lottie, they boarded the bus and, waved off by their friends and the huge crowd, left RAC Gwynedd behind for good.

Benedict peered out of the window as the bus pulled away.

He'd managed to snatch a few minutes to say goodbye to Sandra, sneaking off around the side of the building to get some privacy, but it hadn't nearly been enough. Everything that had needed to be said had been said the night before, so they'd just held each other until their time ran out.

When they'd parted, they'd agreed not to look for each other when the bus left, in case it made them cry, but he couldn't keep his promise, he needed to see her one last time. Just in case.

He eventually found her, at the back of the crowd near the corner of the building, right where he'd left her. She was looking directly at him and he huffed; so much for their promises. He lifted his hand, but right at that moment the bus turned the corner and she was gone.

RAC GALATH
DOGFIGHT AND RISK TRAINING

AUGUST 1941

19

The bus was a different one from the one that had ferried them around Wales previously. It was far newer, had comfortable seats and was a lot faster and they sped along narrow, deserted roads further into the hills, heading north-west. They'd thought they'd been in the middle of nowhere before - there were only a few towns and villages around Gwynedd, the nearest almost five miles away - but in the hour they were driving they passed nobody on the road and only went through one single village with only half a dozen houses.

After wending their way through increasingly mountainous country they finally came to the gates of an RAC base perched on the side of a hill. There were a couple of military guards on the gates and they waved the bus through, smiling and shouting something out to the driver that was lost in the wind and the noise of the engine.

RAC Galath turned out to be a small base, comprising only a dozen smallish buildings and half a dozen hangars built in an L-shape around a lush green field. There was no huge parade ground, just a small gravel-covered space between two of the buildings, and no large building of the type that contained endless offices and meeting rooms, such as there had been at Gwynedd. None of the training facilities that they'd become used to seemed to be present, in fact, and, if that didn't tell them they were stepping onto an operational base, then the line of eight Spitsteams in front of the hangars certainly did.

'They're all single-seaters!' Tayler exclaimed as they crowded the windows on the airfield side of the bus, 'not a trainer among them!'

The bus turned into the small parade ground and came to a halt next to the flagpole and they hurried back to their seats to wait for someone to come and order them off the bus. When seconds passed and nobody came they peered out of the windows and saw a man, an officer, leaning against the doorway of the closest building, his arms folded, watching them from the shadows.

'Well?' The driver asked, turning around in his seat to look at them. 'What are you waiting for?' He gestured impatiently at the open door. 'You're officers now, aintcha?'

They looked at him, then at each other. It felt strange doing something for themselves after a month of having been told what to do every moment of the day that they weren't off duty, but he was right and after a moment's more hesitation they stood and started uncertainly towards the front of the bus. They got off and went around to the storage compartment at the back of the bus to get their bags, but three airmen and one airwoman appeared out of nowhere and grabbed them before they could do so and hurried off with them towards one of the smaller buildings, which was recognisably a barracks.

Slightly at a loss for what to do, they looked at each other again, then turned to face the officer, who was still watching them, a broad grin on his face, obviously enjoying their discomfort. By unspoken agreement they walked towards him.

The man stepped out of the doorway into the sunlight and came to meet them.

'Bloody hell, that's one of the Misfits...' Tayler swore under his breath even as they stopped to salute.

The officer laughed as he returned their salutes, obviously having heard him. 'It seems that at least one of you knows who I am. For those of you that don't, I'm Squadron Leader Drake, and yes, I was a pilot in Misfit Squadron until we were deemed no longer necessary for the war effort. I'm the one who's in charge of your training here at Galath.'

He shook their hands one by one. 'Welcome. Welcome.' He smiled. 'Want to go and see some Spits?'

Shoving his hands deep into his pockets he sauntered away across the airfield without waiting for a reply.

The four new pilots grinned at each other, then eagerly hurried to catch up.

'Galath started off as a private airfield serving a nearby coal mine.' Drake explained as he walked. 'The owner was an aviation enthusiast and he and his family used to fly to and from London depending on where he needed to be. The mine closed twenty years ago and the airfield with it, but the RAC reopened it a few months ago when it decided it needed somewhere to run advanced training from, sparing no expense to put up some of the most uncomfortable facilities known to humankind.' He glanced sideways at them. 'Don't worry, we've blocked the worst of the drafts and we now have reliable hot water, but we've only got the one mess for everyone and I'm afraid there's a very limited selection of drinks. There's plenty of fresh lamb, though, and we've got cabbages and leeks coming out of our ears, so I hope you like those!'

When they got to the Spitsteams, Drake turned to face them. 'While you're here you'll have a few classes to fill in the gaps in your knowledge and you'll also have to take your officer exams to confirm your ranks, but all that kind of stuff will be kept to a bare minimum. What matters here, the only thing that matters, in fact, is how you fly. The thing that will define your success or failure here at Galath is what you do in the air. In one of these.' He patted the wing of the first of the aircraft, which they saw had his name stencilled under the cockpit. There was also a cartoon version of him on the nose, wielding a spade to dig a hole. He saw the direction of their gazes and laughed. 'Maybe I'll tell you about that one day. If you impress me enough.' He gestured for them to follow him and started to walk back the way they'd come. 'Time to continue our tour. Don't worry,' he called out over his shoulder when they dragged their feet and kept glancing back, 'you'll get a much closer look at them soon enough.'

Drake took them to the combined briefing and ready room next to the hangars, showed them their bunk rooms - they had individual rooms that were tiny, but nevertheless a welcome bit of privacy - pointed out the mess and the building with the only two classrooms on the base as they went past, before ending their tour in stores.

'Once you've got your kit, go back to your rooms, get changed into your flightsuits, then come meet me in the mess. We'll have a cup of tea and a chat then get straight to work.' He nodded to them, waved to the woman in charge of stores and then left them to it.

'Morning, sirs and madam,' the woman said, 'I've got your gear ready for you over here. Just need you to sign for it.'

She took them over to a table against to the wall on which were lined up four smart brown leather travelling bags, embossed with the

RAC crest and their names. Each of them had several items arranged in front of it, as well as a typed inventory form and a pen.

She picked up a clipboard and began to read from it.

'Perkins. Oakley. Sherborne. Flightsuit, one. Helmet, one. Flying boots, one. Goggles, one. Chronograph, one. Compass, one. Thermal undersuit, one. Dress uniform, one. Dress shoes, one pair. Sign, please.'

She watched them sign, then collected their papers before looking back down at the clipboard.

'Wilberforce. Dress uniform, one. Dress shoes, one pair. Personal package, one. Sign, please.'

The others peered at the tightly wrapped brown paper package inquisitively, but Benedict just smirked at them. He put it in the bag, signed the form with a flourish, then walked out.

The woman put his form with the rest of them and gave them a sympathetic look before wandering off into the seemingly endless rows of shelves filling the small building.

Ellie smoothed down the front of her new flightsuit and inspected herself in the mirror attached to the back of the door in her room. Unlike her cadet's flightsuit it fit well, although a little tightly for her liking, accentuating bits of her she had never really acknowledged were there. She could put up with that, though, because the one thing it did, and did extremely well, was make her look like a pilot and she smiled as she ran her fingers lightly over the embroidered wings patch on her chest. The flightsuit was also refreshingly clean and fresh, unmarked and unstained, whereas her cadet's flightsuit had been used by countless people before her and had had two small tears, worn knees and suspiciously thin material around the crotch where it had been scrubbed a bit too hard.

There was a knock at her door and Tay's voice floated through it. 'We're off to the mess, Ellie! See you there!'

'I won't be long!' she called out in reply.

She heard his and Rob's footsteps retreating down the hallway and considered hurrying after them so that she wouldn't have to walk to the mess on her own, but didn't; there was something she wanted to do, that she *had* to do first.

On her bed were the leather helmet and goggles that had come with the flightsuit. Tayler had said they were a new type of goggles that they were only now issuing to pilots, more robust and with a better array of lenses than the older version, which had been fiddly and only incorporated a couple of lenses. However new or impressive they were, it had taken her several minutes of extremely careful trial and error to get the lenses fixed to the helmet, but she still had no real idea how to operate them and didn't want to play with them in case she broke or bent something. That didn't mean she couldn't put the helmet on, though, and she bend over almost double to pull the helmet onto the top of her head, making sure the chin straps were fastened before straightening up again and turning to face the mirror.

She grinned. She'd thought she'd looked like a pilot before, but now...

She just wished that her mother could have seen her like this.

Despite there being only one mess hall for everyone, there was a quite clear separation between where the lower ranks and NCOs had their meals and where the officers dined. The side of the room closest the door was rather bare and filled to capacity with the long, cheaply-made tables and chairs they were used to in the messes of Druid and Gwynedd. The far side of the room, in sharp contrast, was furnished comfortably, with a carpet on the wooden floor and round dining tables of different sizes, between which moved a trio of white-jacketed and white-gloved men and women. The tables didn't occupy the whole space, though, because up against the far wall was a small bar, surrounded by armchairs. All in all, it looked like a comfortable place to eat and drink, even if the officers did seem to be rather on display to the men and women eating in the other section.

When Ellie arrived, she found Tayler and Rob already sitting in the officer's section at one of the larger tables with Squadron Leader Drake and a woman in a dark grey leather flightsuit. Uncharacteristically, Tay looked thoroughly daunted by the situation and he kept darting glances at the woman as he awkwardly drank tea from a delicate china cup for maybe the first time in his life. Rob, however, seemed to be enjoying himself immensely and was deep in conversation with Drake. There was no sign of Benedict and she briefly wondered if he had gotten lost before deciding that she didn't particularly care if he had.

She self-consciously walked around the outside of the room towards them, feeling more than a few eyes on her. Far fewer than there had been every time she or her fellow cadets had appeared in the common areas of Gwynedd, though, and she could tell it was just natural curiosity on their part - there wasn't any undertone of sizing her up for the likelihood she would make them money, which had made her feel so uncomfortable before.

'Ah, Perkins! Take a seat!' Drake said as she approached, standing and motioning to a chair.

'Thank you, sir,' she said, blushing as one of the white uniformed stewards appeared and pulled it out for her.

'Tea, ma'am?' he asked as she sat.

'I can get it...' she began, looking around, but then she felt her cheeks heat further when she realised that the only tea urn in sight was in the other section across the room. It seemed like she wasn't going to be allowed to serve herself anymore, at least in the mess. She smiled at the waiting man. 'Yes, please.'

He nodded and walked away, somehow appearing unhurried even when moving at high speed.

'We're just waiting for Wilberforce, then,' Drake said, checking his chronograph. 'There's no hurry, though.'

The waiter arrived with tea for Ellie and a plate with sandwiches and biscuits and she smiled up at him. 'Thank you.'

'Ma'am,' he replied, nodding solemnly before retreating as quickly as he had before.

She picked up one of the sandwiches, cucumber, she saw, without crusts for some reason, and took a small bite. It was a bit bland, but she was hungry, so she took another larger one, then looked around the table. Drake was telling an anecdote of some kind and she listened in eagerly, hoping to hear something about his time as a Misfit. Disappointingly, though, it quickly became apparent he was talking about cricket and, from what little she knew about the game, she was just about able to work out that he was telling Rob about a famous game he'd watched years before, featuring some famous batsman doing something famous. Even though she found cricket incredibly boring, she still listened; it was Lord Drake telling a story, after all. It was just as well he seemed to be reaching the climax of the story, though, because she didn't know how long she'd be able to feign interest.

'So, with only one over left to play,' Drake was saying, 'Yorkshire are nine wickets down and need seven to win. Oxfordshire bring Watkins back for some pace, but everyone can see he is tired and he marks out a shorter run up. He lobs the first one down, but it's completely lacking any real sting and Bertram gets hold of it nicely and drives it past cover. It's cut off before it can go for four, though, and even though Bertram could have gotten three, he stops at two so as to keep the strike. Watkins puts a bit more onto the next one, forcing Bertram to defend. He has a go at the next one, though, but only manages to drive it to mid-off who plays at fumbling it, tempting him to go for a single and put the eleventh man on strike, but Bertram doesn't bite and we're down to three balls left with six needed.'

As Drake paused to sip his tea, Ellie started, realising that she'd actually become caught up with his story. Not that she was finding cricket any more interesting than she had before, but the way he was speaking about it so passionately was enthralling. The woman next to him obviously wasn't impressed, though, and she raised an eyebrow and rolled her eyes at Ellie, making her smile.

'The next ball, I don't know what happened, but Watkins' leg seemed to give out beneath him a little. Some people say his foot slipped slightly, but I reckon it was just tired muscles. Whatever the case, he tosses down a long-hop and Bertram wallops it past square leg. For a moment it looked like it was going to go the distance, but it dropped just short and bounced just inside the boundary rope for four. Just a couple of feet more and that would have been it. Two balls to go, two needed and Watkins rallies and sends down the perfect ball. Bertram sees it and uses a forward defence, but it sneaks past his bat, only just misses the stumps and goes straight into the keeper's gloves. The fielders go up, asking for it, saying they'd heard it nick the edge, but the umpire doesn't give it and Watkins isn't interested either; he knows Bertram didn't get his bat on it and if the fielders heard something it was probably his bat against his pads.'

Drake licked his lips and stared off past Rob's shoulder, reliving the experience. 'Last ball and Bertram comes thundering in, giving it his all. He goes up and... and...' Drake faltered, frowning at something on the other side of the room.

Tay turned to look and started sniggering. This made everyone else look.

It was Benedict. He had finally arrived and it was plain to see why he'd been delayed as he waddled towards them - his flightsuit, meant to be tight fitting to aid the retention of blood where it was supposed to be when carrying out strenuous manoeuvres, was a little *too* tight fitting.

The woman snorted. 'He looks like a sausage,' she said around a mouthful of cake. 'A British one. Not a decent Muscovite one.'

Drake watched Benedict come, but didn't say anything until he was standing at the table. 'Excellent flightsuit, Wilberforce,' he said with a welcoming smile, 'but it seems that you've gone through a few changes over the last month. Will you be able to fly in that?'

Benedict nodded. 'I think so, sir.'

Drake looked dubious, but still smiled amiably. 'Sit down then and we'll see if your legs go to sleep while we're talking.'

Benedict blushed and moved to the nearest chair. A steward moved in smoothly and pulled it out for him and he sat gingerly. 'Tea, please, and sandwiches.'

'Very good, sir.'

He shifted uncomfortably, cursing his own stupidity. Of course his body was going to have changed after a month of hard physical exercise. Of course his flightsuit was going to need adjusting. He should have gotten someone to measure him at Gwynedd and asked his father to have it taken to Bond Street before sending it. Hopefully he'd be able to still use it; he really didn't want to have to use one of the RAC ones. In the meantime he'd have measurements sent off for a new one.

He looked up and started when he saw that Lord Drake was still frowning at him.

The woman next to Drake shook her head and tutted, then said something incomprehensible in a foreign language that sounded like swearing. She leaned forward and gestured for him to stand up.

'Get up, Sausage Boy,' she ordered in impeccable English.

'Sausage Boy?' he asked. 'Get up? I'm sorry, but...'

'Stand!' she commanded again, raising her voice.

Benedict hurried to do as he was told, moving awkwardly around the chair.

She twirled her finger. 'Turn!'

Blushing, feeling the eyes of not just everyone around the table, but the entire mess, including the lower ranks, now on him, he did as he was told. He recoiled back when he completed the turn and found her standing right next to him. He hadn't heard or sensed her moving. So much for his fighter pilot's instincts...

'Hold still,' she warned him.

'What...?' he began, then finished with a squeak when a wicked looking knife appeared from nowhere in her hand.

She grinned menacingly, then brought the knife arcing down towards him.

He closed his eyes, not quite believing that Lord Drake wasn't intervening to stop the obviously mad woman, at the same time as he hoped that whatever she did to him wouldn't hurt too much.

'There!' the woman said, slapping him on the shoulder painfully and making him jump and open his eyes. 'Get the suit to me this evening and I'll finish the job properly.'

Benedict looked down at his body and found himself intact. The same couldn't be said for his extremely expensive flightsuit, though; the woman had sliced holes in it.

'What have you...?' he asked angrily, but then stopped himself when he realised that the uncomfortable pressure had completely disappeared. He moved his arms and lifted a leg and found himself to be completely unencumbered, as if the suit had been tailored to fit his current measurements. 'How did you...?'

The woman flopped back down into her seat and grinned at him. 'I was a seamstress before the war.'

She gave Drake a sideways look and he barked with laughter.

'Thank you,' he said, sitting back down, marvelling at the change in his suit. His tea had appeared while he'd been otherwise occupied and he sipped at it. He reached for a sandwich, but before he could pick one up Drake spoke up.

'Do you like cricket, Wilberforce?'

'Yes, sir,' he answered, frowning slightly in puzzlement at what cricket had to do with anything.

'Well, while we were waiting I was regaling your companions with a tale of the final county championship game from '31.'

Benedict thought for a moment. ''31? That was Oxfordshire against Yorkshire. Yorkshire won in the final over.'

'Indeed, yes! Well done!'

'My father is a member of the MCC, sir, and served as chairman of the Yorkshire Cricket Association for a few years. I was there, sir.'

Drake laughed. 'Of course you were! And, as for the result, well, saying that Yorkshire won is a rather oversimplified way of putting it!' He leaned back in his chair and looked at Rob. 'Where was I?'

'Last ball, sir.' Rob answered, relieved that the interruption hadn't made Squadron Leader Drake forget to finish his story.

'Ah, yes! So, Bertram comes thundering in and puts everything he had behind the final ball. It's as fast as any of the balls he'd bowled earlier on in the day and it's a good line and length, despite the amount of effort he's had to put into it. It bounces just forward of the crease and outside the off stump and Watkins steps to it and plays one of the most perfect cover drives I've ever seen, before or since. You could hear the home crowd hold its breath, thinking that that was it, that Oxfordshire had lost, but the captain, good old Rachel Calthorpe, who'd captained England the year before, had told Bertram to put the ball down the offside and overloaded that side with fielders. It went past cover, but there was a deep extra cover that hadn't been there before and he raced across to grab it before it got anywhere near the boundary. By this time Bertram and the eleventh batter, I can't remember their name...'

'Fallow, sir.' Benedict chimed in.

'Oh, yes,' Drake said, pointing at him. 'Jane Fallow, the leg spinner, that's right. Well, they'd already run one by the time the ball had been fielded and they came racing back for the second they needed to win the game. The man on deep cover had a good arm and he chucked it at the stumps where Smith was running and, by some miracle it hit them directly. Oxfordshire all thought they'd got her and won the game, but the umpire thought about it for a few seconds and gave her not out and the game to Yorkshire.'

Drake shook his head. 'Nobody could believe it, not the crowd, not the Oxfordshire players and I'm fairly sure Smith herself couldn't quite believe it either, but the umpire had been in prime position to see and he was certain, so that was it. Match and championship to Yorkshire and a story that everyone who'd witnessed it could tell their children, grandchildren and novice pilots!'

'Wow, I wish I could have seen that,' Rob said wistfully. He'd never gotten to go to a proper cricket game, not one at county level anyway, just a few village ones that were usually so one-sided to be laughable, or over in a few hours because everyone was in a hurry to get to the pub. He wondered idly if the RAC had proper cricket teams and whether he could get on one, or if they just knocked a ball around every so often for fun, like the personnel had at Druid and Gwynedd.

'It was certainly something special, that's for sure.' Drake said, then clapped his hands. 'Right, then, before we get to it, I have a couple of things to say.

'First off, introductions.' He put his hand on the woman's shoulder. 'This is Aviator Lieutenant Tatiana Guseva.'

The woman lifted her hand to them without taking her eyes off her plate, which had miraculously sprouted another slice of cake while nobody was looking.

'At the table behind me is Squadron Leader Niven,' Drake said, half turning in his seat to address the officers there, 'as well as Aviator Lieutenants Evans and Brunel.'

The two men and one woman held a hand up in greeting, but didn't pause in their discussion or even look up from the papers spread on the table in front of them.

'Squadron Leader Niven and Lieutenant Guseva you may recognise as being former Misfits, like myself, but Lieutenants Evans and Brunel are no less worthy of your trust and admiration. They are veterans of France and the battle over Britain of last summer and have almost fifty kills between them. Between the five of us we comprise the entirety of the instructing staff here at Galath.'

He lifted a hand to indicate a group of about a dozen men and women a few tables away. They were hungrily putting away sandwiches and didn't look like very much older than the four of them. 'The RAC has been taking advantage of the relative quiet recently to rotate a few of its newer pilots through to get some advanced training, but they've been recalled and are leaving this afternoon, so it looks like you'll have the place to yourselves for the next two weeks.'

He popped the remains of a biscuit into his mouth and washed it down with some tea before continuing. 'Next. If you hadn't noticed, you are no longer cadets, but officers, well, acting officers anyway, until you take your exam, which, to be frank, is a bit of a formality, especially for bright chaps like you. That means you now get a day off every week. Here at Galath, everyone has their day off on Sunday, except, that is, for the few unlucky souls who've drawn the short straw and are on the rota that week to stay on duty. I'm afraid there isn't very much to do; we're about as far away from civilisation as you can be in the British Isles without heading out to the Shetlands or something and there's probably more to do there. We run a bus into the nearest large-ish town for those people who fancy some food or drink that isn't available on the base, but the town's not much to look at and is more than an hour away and there aren't usually many takers. If you don't fancy that then I don't blame you and you can stay here; there's plenty of activities on offer. Weather permitting there is always an informal cricket match to watch or play in, or there are a few clubs like chess, bridge, tiddlywinks and even hopscotch, unless that closed down...?'

He looked at Guseva, who shook her head and spoke around her latest mouthful of cake.

'Still going.'

'Good for them!' Drake said with a grin. 'I can't see how they can spend hours playing that, but there you are; you can play hopscotch, if that's your thing! If it's not, and you don't fancy any of the other sporting options, there are also a few classes. Squadron Leader Niven, for example, teaches ornithology and takes a group out birdwatching every second Sunday of the month.' He glanced over his shoulder to make sure his fellow instructor wasn't listening, then bent forward and lowered his voice to speak conspiratorially. 'I don't see the attraction myself, but I can't deny that the study of birds does aid somewhat with the design of aircraft, if any of you have any interest in that?'

He didn't seem surprised when everyone shook their heads and he leaned back in his chair again.

'Your time is your own, of course, and you don't have to do anything in particular with it if you don't want. You can stay in bed and only come out for meals, or you could read - we have a small library of donated books and you can order anything you can't find there through stores. At a pinch, you could even get drunk if you want and quite a few men and women do opt for that. The only thing you can't do, actually, is fly; we don't want you burning yourselves out before you go on active duty and the fitters are just as deserving of a rest as you are. If not more so.'

He turned serious suddenly, sitting up and looking around the table, meeting each of their eyes in turn. 'Is that understood?'

'Yes, sir,' they chorused.

'Good,' he smiled again. 'That's that, then - that's all I wanted to say. Now we can get down to business.' He finished his tea and pushed the cup to one side where it was instantly collected by one of the stewards. 'When the war minister ordered the Misfits disbanded, the king informed Sir Douglas Pewtall that he would be silly to miss out on the opportunity that was being presented to him to take advantage of our experience while we didn't have anything better to do. RAC Galath was hastily converted and the three of us were tasked with putting together an advanced training course. We came up with something in short order and handed in a proposal, which Pewtall approved immediately, almost without looking at it. The pencil pushers in Whitehall couldn't just leave it as the "Advanced Training Course", though, and one or more of them, who undoubtedly spend too much time in the pub, came up with the name "Dogfight and Risk Training School", or DARTS as it is more commonly known. It's a painfully convoluted name, but rather apt, because that's exactly what you're going to do - you're going to be dogfighting the instructors and willingly putting yourselves into risky situations - fun stuff like flying through the mountains far lower than is really sensible.' He wiped his hands on a napkin, then relaxed back in his chair again. 'By passing the wings test in two weeks you've shown you have the talent and skill to handle an aircraft and handle it well. In the next two weeks we will see whether you have the instincts, the determination and the daring to fight effectively in one.' He grinned. 'In other words, we're going to find out exactly how crazy you all are.'

Perfectly on cue, chimes rang out from a large grandfather clock across the room as it struck the half hour and people began to stand up and move towards the exit.

Drake pushed himself back from the table and stood and the four pilots hurried to do the same. Ellie picked up her plate and cup, but a steward appeared at her elbow and indicated that he would take them.

'Please, allow me, ma'am.'

'Oh, right. Of course. Thank you.'

She allowed him to take them, then blushed when she realised that everyone was looking at her.

Drake smiled. 'Don't worry, Perkins, not everybody is comfortable having everything done for them all the time, but you'll get used to it.'

He led the way across the room, following the tide of men and women moving to the door out to the airfield. 'I bet you can't wait to get started.' He said over his shoulder. 'One question first, though - do you all know how to ride a bike?'

20

During their short tour of the base they'd only gotten as far as the first of the line of hangars, but Drake now took them to the end of it, where they found a moderately sized shed. It looked nothing more than a storage space for spares or tools, but turned out to be anything but when the half a dozen fitters waiting for them swung back the large doors, opening up the entire front of the building to reveal a fully equipped springcycle workshop.

Rob gasped and ran forwards, eager to inspect the row of machines within, but stumbled to a halt in confusion after only a few steps.

'They... You... You put *wings* on them?!?' he asked incredulously.

'Indeed!' Drake said, grinning widely. 'Lady and gentlemen, I present to you the very latest word in DARTS training aids.'

He opened wide his arms as the fitters wheeled out four of the dozen or so springcycles from the shed and set them on their side stands in a row on the grassy field next to the shed.

Drake beckoned to the pilots. 'Come and have a look at your new aircraft.'

They gathered round the springcycles. As Rob had already noted, they had wings attached to them, just behind the seats. Or rather, they had long, thin pieces of metal of differing lengths, from a couple of yards, to almost four, shaped to a very rough approximation of wings attached to them. The cycles had been painted to resemble aircraft - two of them in British camouflage pattern complete with roundels and one in the standard grey Prussian camouflage, but the fourth, amusingly, had been painted a bright red and had "blood sausage" scrawled on the side of the spring box.

'These wonderful machines have been lovingly cobbled together by our excellent crew of fitters to exact specifications provided by the mastermind behind this aspect of your training - me.' Drake said to the chuckles of the fitters. 'I'm not going to say anything about them or what this is all about, though, I'm just going to let you ride them for a while. Afterwards you're going to tell me what you think is the point of the exercise and what you've learned.' He gestured to the cycles, 'Choose your machine and let's get started!'

Benedict went straight for the machine with long, elliptically-shaped wings. It was a crude representation of an aircraft, as were they all, but was obviously supposed to be a Spitsteam.

Lord Drake was being very mysterious about it, but it was obvious what was going to happen - just as in real life, the Spitsteam was going to prove superior to the others and the moral was going to be something like they should all be trying their hardest to make sure they got into squadrons that flew them. The only doubt he'd had was whether he should choose the Blutsauger instead; confrontations between the Crimson Barons' machines and Spitsteams had been few and far between and never just one on one, so nobody really knew which one was superior. In the end, though, he'd reasoned that Lord Drake's message to them would never be that the enemy had better machines, so the Spitsteam it was.

Ellie hesitated, not just because she didn't know which of the three remaining machines to choose, but also because she wasn't really sure she would be able to ride one. She'd had a bike when she was younger, but, like most of her nice things, after her mother died it had been sold. She hadn't ridden a bike for six or seven years as a consequence, but they said you never forgot, right?

Making up her mind, she decided to take the bike painted in drab grey Prussian colours, but she was beaten to it as Tay and Rob rushed forwards, laughing, to claim it and the red one. That left her with the other British one, the one made up to look like a Harridan, and she went to take possession of it.

The fitter took it off its stand and held it for her as she swung her leg over.

'This is the throttle, ma'am,' he said, pointing out a switch on the right handlebar.

She waited for him to go on, but he didn't and she looked up at him. 'And the brakes?'

'No brakes, ma'am!' he answered with a grin before stepping back. 'But...'

'Alright then!' Drake called out, preventing her from asking what kind of bike didn't have brakes, 'off you go and have a bit of a play for a few minutes.'

The other three pilots immediately whizzed off with no sign of hesitation and not a single wobble, but Gwen took a moment to make sure she had the cycle perfectly upright, with equal weight on each of her feet, before gingerly flicking the switch with her thumb. She had to paddle with her feet for a few moments to stop the machine from toppling to the side, but eventually it was going fast enough for it to stay upright on its own and she could lift them, fumbling for a second before she found the pedals and settled them in place. She knew she must have looked clumsy and probably not a little silly, but she'd rather that than have had the cycle accelerate out from underneath her and topple her off the back, or to lose control and have it slew sideways - probably knocking over a few fitters, knowing her luck.

The cycle reached what seemed to be its top speed after only a few seconds. It wasn't much more than a quick running speed, but the sensation of the air rushing past her face made it feel like it was going much faster and she swallowed nervously. It was a whole different feeling than being in an aircraft and the way the machine bumped over the slightly uneven ground was unnerving. She would have liked to continue going straight for a while to get used to the cycle, but she assumed that whatever Drake wanted them to learn would involve more than that and, besides, she was going to run out of room fairly quickly if she didn't turn soon.

The first couple of times she leaned the cycle over she threw too much weight into it and it bounced off a pair of castors that had been fixed to the end of the wings and she ended up almost upright again. However, once she got the hang of shifting her weight smoothly she learned that she could put the castors onto the floor and keep them there for a "maximum rate turn" as the drag of the small wheels actually helped the cycle turn quicker. She continued to experiment, swerving the cycle back and forth, testing its limits just as she had the Huntress, and after a minute or so she found her apprehension had completely disappeared and she was actually starting to enjoy herself. It was nothing like flying, obviously, but it was easy to see why Rob was so enthusiastic about springcycle riding, especially if his went faster than this. It seemed that the others were having fun as well and she winced when she saw that Tay was laughing his head off as he bounced his cycle from one wing to another, making it leap six inches or so into the air each time. Thankfully, the wings seemed to be firmly attached and sturdy and didn't look like they were going to break any time soon, but even so, she didn't think that was the way he should really be behaving on his first day at Galath.

A quick glance at Squadron Leader Drake told her that he didn't seem to mind, though; in fact it rather looked like he was enjoying the show.

Rudy Drake watched his latest charges zooming around. He could always tell a lot about them, about the individuals and the group as a whole, from the first few moments of this particular exercise. Far more than he could in the air, when he couldn't see their expressions, far more than on the ground, where they were guarding themselves in the presence of a senior officer, and certainly far more than from the files that had been couriered over from Gwynedd yesterday evening.

Oakley was no surprise. It had been obvious from the off that the report from George Barton would be spot on and he was charging around the field with wild abandon, throwing the cycle about just as he'd apparently done his aircraft during the first week of elementary flight training.

Sherborne was accompanying him and was whooping and laughing just as loudly as Oakley, but he was far more reserved in his control of the cycle. Unlike his friend, his wings weren't bouncing off the ground every time he turned and there was a preciseness to his movements that spoke to a control and coordination that was well above average.

Wilberforce's control of the cycle was smooth and competent, but there was no flair, no attempt to push the limits of the machine and not much in the way of apparent enjoyment. In fact, he looked like he'd gone back to how he'd been described in his initial reports, perhaps because of the unfamiliar circumstances, or more likely because he was scared of making a mistake under the gaze of a Misfit. That was disappointing, but no reason for him to be discarded as ordinary quite yet. After all, many excellent pilots had started out the same way.

As for Perkins... His assessment of the others had taken only moments; they were open books, clear for all to see, but she was different. At first glance her riding had been hesitant, but on closer inspection it had quickly become apparent that she was analysing, not just the cycle, but the situation itself as well, watching the others, even as she was working out how best to operate a machine she was obviously unfamiliar with. He kept his eyes on her, not wanting to miss the moment; he'd seen behaviour like this once before and heard about it just one other time and if she was anything like those two people - like Gwen or Chastity - she'd finish analysing and start playing right... about... He laughed delightedly as the woman gripped the handlebars of the cycle tightly, took a deep breath, then threw the machine into a blistering series of turns.

Drake called them back with a whistle after a couple of minutes and they raced back and coasted awkwardly to a halt in a ragged line in front of him.

'That's enough time to get used to your mounts,' Drake said, grinning widely, 'now it's time to joust. Fleas against RAC. Wilberforce against Sherborne and Perkins against Oakley. Get onto your opponent's six and you get two points and the game starts over. Find a glancing shot and you get one point, but the round continues until someone gets behind their opponent.' He gestured to one side of the field, 'Fleas start at that end, RAC at the other. You'll go head to head, passing down the right side. Make sure you leave enough room for each other or the cost of repairs will come out of your pay and don't start to turn until your wings have passed each other otherwise you'll be docked a point.' He gestured to four fitters waiting to the side astride a couple of unmodified springcycles. 'These ladies and gentlemen are the referees. Whatever they say, goes. The game ends after five minutes or when someone reaches five points. Whichever comes first.' He looked along the extended line of cycles. 'Questions? No? To your places then and start on my whistle.'

Ellie swung the cycle around and powered to where one of the referees was already waiting for her. The woman pointed to a spot for her to stop and wait and she turned to point across the field, then cut her spring and came to a halt. A hundred feet away, on the other side of the cleared area, Tay did the same with his red cycle and came to a rather ungainly halt, paddling with his feet and swaying from side to side until he managed to regain control. He grinned at her and waved and she lifted a hand in salute, but had to hurriedly put it back on the handlebars when Drake blew his whistle.

She switched the spring back to unwind and the cycle rolled forwards. Tay was heading slightly to her left and she aimed to pass him on his right as they'd been instructed. His wings were a lot longer than hers and she had to make a small adjustment in her calculations when she worked out that they were going to pass far too close. Tay, of course, hadn't noticed or didn't care and just kept going in a straight line.

His cycle was much faster than hers and they went past each other well on Ellie's side of the field. She immediately put the cycle on its side, laying it over as far as it would go, but taking care not to bounce off the castors as she did so. She used the slight drag from the castors to make the turn a tiny bit tighter, but, when she looked up, she found that it wasn't going to be necessary to strive for such a small advantage; unexpectedly, Tay was trying to do the same as she was, even though his turning circle was so much larger than hers because wings were so much longer and his machine was going so much faster. Within seconds she had brought her cycle around within his turn and was able to straighten up and close the distance rapidly.

When he finally realised that he wasn't going to out turn her he straightened up and tried to turn away from her, but it was far too late.

'Ratatatata!' she crowed triumphantly as she came up behind him.

'Two points to Perkins!' the referee called out. 'Back to starting positions!'

'Get you next time, Ellie!' Tayler shouted as he turned away.

'Bet you won't!' she replied with a laugh.

As she bounced back to her starting position, she glanced over to where Rob and Benedict were circling each other. It looked like the dogfight was going much the same way as hers had, with Rob harassing Benedict, who was trying desperately to get away. She grinned when she saw that Benedict's expression was almost as dark as his flashy flightsuit, but then had to bring her attention back to what she was doing as she turned and lined up for another bout.

'Well?' Drake asked as the four pilots shut down their cycles and handed them over to fitters. 'What did we learn?'

'That the Spitsteam isn't necessarily the best aircraft in the air?' Benedict said sulkily.

Drake inclined his head. 'Well, it isn't necessarily, but that's not the point of the exercise.' He looked around the group. 'Anyone?'

Tayler shrugged. 'That victory or defeat depends on the pilot?'

Drake laughed. 'Well, that's a given and it shouldn't have taken playing silly buggers on springcycles to tell you that!'

Ellie glanced down the line at her friends, wondering why they were messing around and not answering the question properly. It was obvious...

'Perkins?' Drake asked. 'Something to say?'

'Yes, sir,' Ellie said, straightening and looking at him. 'In both dogfights, the aircraft that had the tighter turning circle won, despite being slower.'

Drake grinned. 'And? Are you saying that we should all be flying biplanes?'

'No, sir!'

'Then what's going on?'

'Well, sir.' Ellie blushed. 'The faster aircraft were not being flown in a way that played to their strengths.'

'Just so! Just so!' Drake looked along the line of pilots. 'Oakley! What should you have done if you had half a brain?'

'Join the navy, sir!' Tayler replied without hesitation.

There was a moment of shocked silence, but then Drake and the entire watching group of RAC personnel, which had grown considerably in the time they'd been racing around the field, burst into laughter.

When it had died down, Drake shook his head. 'From what I've seen so far you would do well in the Royal Nave, Oakley, but just pretend for the moment that the RAC is willing to put you in the cockpit of a very expensive fighter aircraft and you are up against a slower but more agile opponent. What would you do?'

Tayler thought for a moment, then replied. 'Open up some distance, then turn. Or better still gain height and come in from above.'

'Wonderful!' Drake said, 'I knew someone would eventually get to the conclusion that Perkins arrived at before she even had her first bout.'

Ellie's cheeks heated up even further as he gave her a knowing look and she felt the eyes of every single one of the spectators settle on her. To her surprise he winked at her, before addressing the pilots again.

'Obviously, you can't gain height with the cycles, but there is plenty enough room to open up some space, so go try it again. And try not to get shot down this time, Oakley, otherwise I might well pack you off to the Biscuit Bangers.'

Over the next hour and a half, with a ten minute break in the middle for more tea, the four pilots rode a dozen more times, swapping aircraft and opponents, covering all possible combinations. After each bout Drake called them back and gave them pointers on how they could do better and equated what they were doing to what happened in real dogfights. Little by little it began to sink in that they weren't just learning to fly anymore - they were learning to kill their enemies.

Once they'd somewhat reluctantly, especially on Rob's part, handed the cycles back to the fitters, they strolled with Drake back towards the main buildings.

The man shoved his hands deep into his pockets and smiled at them. 'Time for a spot of lunch and then I think it's about time you all had your first go in a Spit, don't you?'

Waiting for them in the mess was a stew that was composed primarily of, as Drake had predicted, lamb, leek and cabbage. It was wonderfully cooked and extremely tasty, though, accompanied by freshly baked bread and followed by a sponge pudding that melted in the mouth. Not that any of the four really noticed what they were eating.

Humiliating, that's what it had been, humiliating. Being shown up like that on those, those, *toys*, by everyone. In front of Lord Drake and so many of the squadron. And why had they been doing it in the first place? Whatever they'd learned from it they could just as easily have learned in a classroom, without wasting so much time on frivolous tomfoolery.

It had just been one thing after another since they'd arrived at this awful place. The flightsuit not fitting him had been bad enough without adding insult to injury with the springcycles, but then there was the letter from his father...

As well as a few sneakily concealed provisions, there had also been two letters wrapped up in the parcel with his flightsuit. The one from his mother was perfumed and the subject matter would probably turn out to be as inane and inconsequential as she was and he would save that for if he were ever bored, but the one from his father had been blunt and to the point. Far from the praise he'd been expecting for gaining his wings in such a short time, he'd found only disappointment and a rebuke for allowing himself to be surpassed by a bumpkin and a girl with no experience.

Benedict looked out of the large windows through which could be seen the line of Spitsteams in front of the hangars, one of which would be his very soon.

His father didn't understand that everything they'd done up until this moment didn't matter in the slightest, that all that mattered was what he did from now on. He didn't understand that because he couldn't; he'd never been a pilot, had never flown.

He'd show him, though, he'd *make* him proud.

Tayler watched Ellie surreptitiously as she picked at her food distractedly, her eyes drifting constantly towards the windows and the Spitsteams being swarmed over by fitters. Being prepared for *them*. While, admittedly, it was an incredible sight, and he could have sat and contemplated it himself during the whole meal, it paled in comparison with the sight of her.

They hadn't had much time for socialising up till that point, what with training all hours and studying the rest of them, but it looked like that was going to change. In fact it already had, as the atmosphere at Galath was far more relaxed and they had even had their bags unpacked and uniforms pressed for them. He was looking forward to finally getting to act on that first impression Ellie had made on him.

He grinned; this was the longest he'd ever taken to ask out a girl he'd liked, but he bet she would be worth it.

He was so distracted by his imaginations of how the courtship would go that he almost missed it when Ellie glanced his way and he only just managed to look past her and out the window before their eyes met.

He couldn't have her seeing him mooning over her. Not until he'd made a proper move and she'd agreed to step out with him, anyway. After that he could go all Romeo to her Juliet or whatever.

Rob gritted his teeth and stabbed at his food.

He'd thought Tay had forgotten about Ellie, that he'd decided not to pursue her. He'd thought that his interest in her that first day when she was freezing was partly because she was a damsel in distress but mostly because she was female. It wasn't as if she was his usual type. She wasn't one of the lithe, strong girls that he usually rolled around in the hay with, or whatever it was that Tay did with them; she was shorter, plainer, shyer, more reserved and definitely more intelligent - all the things he himself had found so attractive about her. Tay had been chatting up girls at the mess at Gwynedd before he'd got his act together and stopped drinking, but apparently that was just Tay being Tay and he'd just been biding his time.

Unfortunately, that was just what he himself had been doing.

He stuffed the forkful of food in his mouth and lifted his eyes to the window. The Spitsteams were there, being given their final checks, but he just stared past them as his mind raced.

How could he make sure that it was him who asked her out first, before Tay found the chance? Just as importantly, how could he gather the courage to do so?

Ellie stared out of the window in wonder at the Spitsteams on the edge of the field - the "apron", Drake had called it. Were they really going to let her fly one of those in her own? What if she made a mistake? What if she damaged it? Surely it would be better to have it in the hands of an experienced pilot somewhere, actively fighting the Prussians; they were always saying there weren't enough Spitsteams on the front line, how could they afford to have so many here?

Not that she was going to complain.

Ellie smiled to herself. It was like a dream she never realised she'd had was coming true.

She tore her eyes away from the airfield, wondering if the others felt the same way she did and chuckled when she found that they were all gazing outside as well.

21

After they'd eaten and had a chance to freshen up, the pilots met up with Drake at the ready room next to the hangars. He was ready to fly, in a black leather flightsuit similar to Benedict's that looked fairly new. However, instead of taking them straight to the aircraft, he led them to the back of the large space, which was set up as a briefing room, with a small raised platform in front of two rows of chairs. He waved them to seats in the front row while he perched on the edge of the table on the platform.

'I know you're eager to get in the air and I know that up till now you've been hopping up into the sky with your instructors whenever they felt like it and then just making a few notes in your logbooks afterwards, but this is your introduction into the real RAC and, unless you're being scrambled, things don't work like that. We spend a lot of time in rooms like these and do a lot of talking beforehand about what we're going to be doing during the flight and what we should be expecting in the way of weather and opposition. We then do a lot of talking afterwards about what happened and what we should have done differently. Then we put most of that into writing and file it with the Adj.' He grinned at the dismay that was plain to see on their faces. 'We won't start showing you how to do all that paperwork until tomorrow, though, because neither you or I want to delay things more than we have to, but we still need to have a little chat about what we're going to be doing this flight because it wouldn't be safe otherwise.'

He flipped open a small black leather notebook that he had propped on his knee and scanned it quickly.

'Callsign for today is "Table". I will be Table One or Table Lead, with Sherborne as Table Two, Perkins as Table Three, Wilberforce as Four and Oakley as Five. We will take off in loose formation and head due west on two seven zero for ten miles, climbing to six thousand feet as we go. Once we're on station at our assigned training area we'll fly a few figure eights to get you used to the aircraft, but then I'll climb a few hundred feet above you and you'll form up into a finger four formation with Table Two as the initial leader. You'll keep flying the figure eights and we'll swap leads and change the formation every few minutes so that you all get a chance to be in every place and feel what it's like. If we have some time after that we'll head north and I'll show you the mountains before returning to base.'

He looked around the group. 'Any questions?'

When there were none he folded his notebook and stowed it in the thigh pocked of his flightsuit. 'One last thing - while you are here you will have an aircraft assigned to you, just as you will when you're in a squadron. It will be up to you to liaise with your chief fitter before and after his flight and to sign off on the aircraft's readiness. Which is also what you will have to when you join a squadron.' He grinned. 'I recommend you keep on the good side of your fitters; you never know when you might need them to "find" a part or two to keep you in the air and you don't ever want to find a mysterious smell has taken over your cockpit. Believe me.'

He jumped off the table and walked down the aisle between them.

'Come on, then. Time to meet your birds.'

Drake stopped the pilots just before they got to the aircraft and pulled out his notebook again. 'Sherborne, you have G,' he pointed towards a Spitsteam with the letters "DA" and "G" painted on the tail, either side of the roundel, then pointed to the others in turn. 'Oakley, you have K, Wilberforce, L and Perkins, yours is S.' He smiled at them as he stowed the notebook again. 'Off you go and introduce yourselves.'

Ellie walked towards her aircraft, DA-S. The fitters had lined up beside their aircraft as the pilots had appeared from the ready room and the leader of her group, a middle-aged aviator sergeant, called them to attention and saluted her as she neared them.

Ellie's right arm began to swing up by itself, but she managed to stop it before it got more than a few inches - pilots in flight gear were excused saluting because of possible damage to their lenses. The woman noticed, though, and smirked.

Ellie shrugged and gave her a wry smile. 'I'm here because I'm still learning, Aviator.' She stuck out her hand. 'Eleanor Perkins.'

The woman took it and squeezed firmly. 'Maeve McIlroy,' she introduced herself with a faint Sottish accent.

'Pleased to meet you.'

'Same,' the woman released Ellie's hand and half-turned away. 'Would ya like to meet the team, or would ya be wanting to get to Susie first?'

'Susie?' Ellie asked, confused.

'Aye, Susie, yer aircraft.'

'Ah!' Ellie chuckled. 'No, I think you can introduce me to Susie after I've met your team, thank you.'

Sergeant McIlroy nodded, her eyes crinkling slightly in an expression that Ellie thought might signal her approval, then quickly introduced the three women that made up the rest of her team - a corporal who looked to be in her fifties and two airwomen who couldn't have been any different physically; one of them was over six feet tall and stick thin, while the other was five feet at the most and rather corpulent. They made a rather strange looking bunch, but Ellie couldn't have cared less what they looked like as long as they got her in the air and the grease liberally smeared on their coveralls and the determination on their equally dirty faces made her far more confident that they would than if they'd been the ideal image of immaculate RAC personnel that you saw in the recruitment posters.

Once she had shaken hands with them all, Ellie finally allowed herself to look at her Spitsteam. She glanced towards the other pilots and found them already walking around their Spits, carrying out their preflight checks, and moved towards the aircraft to do the same. 'What can you tell me about her, Aviator?'

Sergeant McIlroy sucked air between her teeth and sighed. 'Well, she's been in the wars a bit. And, uh, some people, well, some people say she's bad luck.'

Ellie blinked. 'Really?'

McIlroy nodded. 'The transport pilot who was bringing her here got bounced by an MU10 near Wrexham. The Flea had no reason to be anywhere near there - it was probably part of a raid on Manchester or Birmingham and gotten lost afterwards - and was never seen again, but that was little comfort to the pilot who was fired on by it for about ten minutes. He was in contact with the ground the whole time, trying to call in help and Squadron Leader Drake scrambled with Lieutenant Guseva to intercept him, but the Fleas broke off before they could arrive. Their shooting was as bad as their navigation and they only managed to hit him twice in all that time, but one of the cannon rounds nipped the pilot and, even though the poor man managed to land, he died before they could get him out of the cockpit.'

Ellie blanched and glanced at her, halting in her inspection of the wing.

'Don't worry,' McIlroy said. 'We patched up what little damage there was and gave the cockpit a thorough clean to get the, well, you know, off of everything, but...'

'But?' Ellie asked, continuing her checks.

'But,' McIlroy looked back at her team, who were all listening anxiously, 'the very next flight the pilot reported problems and had to turn back.'

'What problems?'

McIlroy shrugged. 'We couldn't find anything wrong and when the pilot went back up she didn't find anything wrong either. But then two flights later she came down so hard she bent the undercarriage and almost collapsed it. She said the aircraft dived for the ground by itself.'

Ellie frowned at her from under the nose of the aircraft. 'Did you find anything that might explain what happened?'

McIlroy shook her head. 'While we were waiting for parts to fix the undercarriage we took her apart, but we couldn't find anything.'

Ellie finished and came round the back of the aircraft to meet the fitter. She grinned. 'So, the only logical explanation is that she's bad luck?'

McIlroy shrugged again, but didn't say anything else.

Ellie patted the tail of the Spit. 'Well, Aviator, I'm happy with her - she looks wonderful.'

'Thank you, ma'am.'

The sergeant held out a clipboard and Ellie signed for the aircraft. McIlroy saluted and handed the returned clipboard off to the corporal, then clambered up after Ellie onto the wing.

Ellie swung her leg over and stepped into the cockpit. She settled gingerly into the seat, feeling slightly squeamish knowing that it had been covered in blood at some point. Looking around, she could see no sign of it, though, everything was spotless and shining, as if it were brand new, which it almost was, she supposed, if the aircraft had only had two flights. She took a deep breath, then put her hands and feet on the controls and continued with her checks as McIlroy leant over her. The fitter plugged the cord running from her helmet into the radio, ran the tube from the heater into the socket in the side of the flightsuit, then strapped her into the glidewings and the seat. She tugged on the straps, then gave Ellie a thumbs up and disappeared.

As if on cue, there was a crackle and Drake's voice sounded in her ears.

'Table flight, check in.'

'Table Two, uh, Roger,' Rob's voice sounded after a brief delay.

'Table Three, Roger,' Ellie said. She was still familiarising herself with the controls and hadn't adjusted the seat to the correct position yet, but she didn't want to delay anything for that.

Benedict and Tayler checked in and then Drake came back on. 'Alright, let's go. Make sure you maintain your spacing, we don't want any accidents before we even get off the ground.'

They followed Drake diagonally across the airfield, then formed up either side of him when he turned to face into the wind. It took only seconds to obtain permission to take off and then Drake's Spitsteam surged ahead.

Ellie gave him a couple of seconds to get far enough ahead for safety then pushed the throttle through the stops.

The back of her head banged against the head rest as the aircraft leapt forwards and she couldn't help but laugh in delight. Susie was the latest model Spit, equipped with the latest model Rentley-Joyce Ozymandias spring and an advanced hydromatic airscrew, she was so much more powerful than the Huntress she'd flown at Gwynedd and accelerated very nearly as quickly as the Sprite.

The nose of the Spitsteam came down almost by itself as the wings bit into the air and then, only seconds after she'd started rolling, she was in the air. Ellie marvelled as the ground just vanished as the aircraft powered skywards and she craned her head out of the open cockpit to peer down. The airfield was gone already, out of sight behind the tail and now it was just lush green fields and rugged grey rock beneath her, with flocks of white sheep, which had already been reduced just to dots, scattered here and there.

'Form up, Table flight.'

Drake's voice was filled with humour and it called her back from her daydreaming with a vision of his grinning face. She looked around the sky and chuckled when she located the rest of the aircraft; they were scattered around the sky in a haphazard fashion, two of them well below her in formation, one almost directly above her and another about half a mile off her wing and moving away. It was just as well they had left plenty of room between them on takeoff because it seemed that a couple of the others had been paying as much attention as she had to what they'd been doing and they could very easily have wandered straight into each other.

She quickly identified Drake's aircraft as being one of the ones below her and throttled back like she should have done just after takeoff. She let Susie sink slowly, adjusting course carefully to fall in behind Drake's right wing, about ten yards distance from him. Out of the corner of her eye she saw Tayler pulling up outside of her, while Rob arrived a few seconds later on the other side of Drake, joining Benedict, whose Spitsteam it had been in formation with the leader already.

'Nice of you all to join us!' Drake called out. 'I'm going to start our turn to the west now. Nice and easy does it.'

Drake started a comically slow turn and Gwen laughed as she followed him, holding station easily. Eventually, they were pointing due west and they reached six thousand feet in a very short time and levelled off.

'Right, that should do it,' Drake called after a minute or so. 'I'm going to start with the figure eights. Just concentrate on holding station for now.'

Drake kept an eye on his geese, gauging their reaction to being in formation.

It wasn't exactly exciting, but it was a very good, very easy and very safe way of allowing them to get the hang of their new aircraft before he asked them to do anything more strenuous. It was also another very useful tool to see what kind of temperament they had. He'd seen skittish pilots continually edging away from their nearest neighbour, overconfident ones trying to tuck in too close before they were ready, sloppy ones who were too busy daydreaming to hold formation and stiff ones who tried to micromanage their aircraft through every gust of wind in order to keep a perfect station. What he liked to see, and what he was seeing from all four of these young pilots, was a relaxed hand on the stick, although Wilberforce looked a little bit twitchy, as if he wanted to wrestle his aircraft into position and was just holding himself back.

This was looking like a very interesting group indeed.

An hour of switching and swapping formations should have been mind-numbingly boring, but the novelty of being in the Spitsteams had kept them interested for most of the time and they were only just becoming tired of it when Drake descended from his position above them and told them to form back up on him. Once they'd all checked in and reported on how much spring tension they had left he banked them northwards and took them up to ten thousand feet.

'We don't often get days as clear as this, so take a good look.' Drake said, 'In front of us are the range of mountains we use for low level flight training. There's a clear course through its valleys that you'll fly several times while you're here, weather permitting. The first time you go through it will just be you and an instructor and you'll feel your way through at only a couple of hundred miles an hour and a safe height. However, by the time you leave Gwynedd, you'll have the confidence and expertise to fly it at near to top speed and much much lower.'

Drake took them into a shallow dive and Ellie did as he'd said and slotted one of her new RAC issue lenses into place over her goggles to scan the predominantly grey and green landscape ahead of them. The hills and mountains passing below them at that moment were almost as high, but they were fairly flat, the valleys between them wide, however, the ones she could see through the windscreen were much craggier with sharply cut lines between them.

She grinned. If playing around in an aircraft in an open sky was fun, what would it be like to race through valleys below the tops of the mountains? She was sure it would be exhilarating and couldn't wait, but at the same time she was apprehensive; one mistake, one error in judgement, one momentary lack of skill, or even one unexplained loss of control in her "unlucky" aircraft, could cost her or her friends everything. This was part of the "risk" in the name of the course, though, and if she wasn't willing to take her chances among mountains that didn't move or fire bullets at her, then what business would she have going up in a squadron to face the Prussians in a sky that was crowded with possibly hundreds of aircraft?

They flew to the edge of the mountains and then Drake turned them west, giving them a chance to look out over their wings as they went by, but spring tension was starting to get low by them so he soon turned them towards home.

The fitters needed half an hour to rewind the Spitsteams and check the aircraft over, so the pilots retired to the ready room for tea and a chat.

Once they had all visited the bathrooms and had a drink and a plate of biscuits in front of them Drake sat down with them at the large round table in the centre of the room.

'Anyone have any comments or questions from this morning's flight?' he asked, looking around the group. There weren't any and he smiled. 'I agree, there isn't exactly very much to comment on and I'm sure you'll be glad to hear we won't be repeating this morning's training experience. Formation flying is something you need to be able to do, because every time you transit to and from the mountains or a training area you'll be flying in formation, but it's something you'll be working on a lot more when you move on to Operational Training in Scotland and we're not going to waste any more of your valuable time on it.'

He leaned back in his chair and pulled his notepad out of his thigh pocket, but barely glanced at it before speaking to them again.

'Now that you've got the feel for the Spit, it's time to expand your knowledge of its capabilities and yours. For your next flight you'll pair up with an instructor and, under their supervision, you'll have an hour or so to play. Throw the aircraft around the sky, pull any aerobatics you feel like. I want you to push yourselves and your machine and discover its limits. If you can.' he grinned. 'This will be your final flight of the day so no need to hold anything in reserve for later. Just stay above six thousand feet and if your instructor tells you to stop then level off immediately and listen to what they have to say.'

He looked up as the door to the ready room opened and three pilots came in.

'Ah, here they are now.'

The instructors lifted a hand or nodded in their direction, but didn't come over, they just went straight to the table with the tea urn and began helping themselves.

Drake chuckled and shook his head. 'Well, when they deign to join us I'll let everyone know who they're going to be partnered with.' He closed his notebook and put it on the table, then applied himself to dunking a biscuit.

The novice pilots watched the three officers at the sideboard. The Muscovite woman, Aviator Lieutenant Guseva, had filled a handkerchief with biscuits and was trying to fit it in one of the side pockets of her flightsuit. Aviator Lieutenant Brunel had her own extra-large tin mug, which she had filled to the brim and was dropping in lumps of sugar - at least a dozen so far. Squadron Leader Niven was the only one of the three whose behaviour was anything approaching normal, but even he wasn't exactly the picture of a refined RAC officer, instead he seemed more like a squirrel, or a bird, fussing around the table, his tall form bent over as he peered closely at the array of cups and tins of biscuits before selecting the ones he wanted.

Ellie wondered which of the four would be her instructor. She half hoped it would be Drake, but that wasn't so much because of his teaching abilities, but because he was a long-time friend of Gwen Stone and she wanted to hear about the woman who she had read so much about. In the end, though, it wouldn't matter who it was; if they were here then they knew what they were doing and would have something to teach her. Three of them were Misfits after all.

However, she thought, whether they were Misfits or not, Wing Commander Trevillian would be a hard act to follow.

It didn't take long for the three instructors to grab what they wanted and make their way to spare places at the table.

'Thank you for joining us.' Drake said, looking up at them.

In reply he received a grunt from the Muscovite woman, who sat next to him and promptly stole one of his biscuits, even though she had her own plateful, a mute nod from Lieutenant Brunel and a dismissive wave from Squadron Leader Niven, who was sorting his biscuits out into neat piles on his plate and barely looked his way.

'Anyway,' Drake said, picking up his notebook while simultaneously slapping at the Muscovite's hand as she reached for his plate again while she thought he was distracted, 'Oakley, you'll be with Lieutenant Brunel,' he gestured at the woman, who surfaced from behind her huge mug just long enough to nod at Tayler. 'Perkins, you'll be with Lieutenant Guseva. Wilberforce, you're with Squadron Leader Niven. And Sherborne, you're with me.'

He tucked his notebook away and reached for a biscuit that wasn't there anymore. He laughed. 'I'll leave you in the capable, and in some cases far too light-fingered, hands of your instructors. Ready, Officer Sherborne?'

'Yes, sir!' Rob said, eagerly jumping to his feet and hurrying to take his plate and mug to the cleanup area.

Drake watched him for a moment, a faint smile on his face, then stood up. He pushed his plate towards Tanya with a grin. 'Here. You ate them all, you can clean the plate.'

He walked away without giving her a chance to answer.

As he followed his new instructor to their aircraft, Benedict glanced over to the far end of the line of Spitsteams, where Lord Drake was speaking to Rob, still not able to believe it. Derek Niven? He'd been assigned Derek Niven? Yes, he was a Misfit, yes, he had distinguished himself with the squadron, but he had only been one because he'd had his own aircraft, which had quickly become laughably outdated. He looked like a fool, with his mannerisms and his blue and white flightsuit.

None of the instructors was particularly inspiring, not even Lord Drake himself, but someone of his standing would have to be paired with someone of equal status, there could be no question of it. He would have to...

His thoughts were cut off as Niven stopped suddenly and turned to face him and he found himself almost standing at attention as the man drew himself up to his full height and looked down at him.

'I've read your records, Mr Wilberforce, and had a nice chat with Sergeant Green. She assures me that you are competent and have gotten over the problems you were having initially. I certainly hope that that is true because if you can't demonstrate to me that you deserve to be here you'll be on the next bus back to Gwynedd. Do you understand?'

'Yes, sir.'

'Good.' The man nodded, then his face cracked with a smile. 'I'm glad we understand each other. Now, let's see if you can show me something I've never seen before.'

Ellie followed Lieutenant Guseva across the grass towards their Spitsteams. The Muscovite woman hadn't said anything to her, she had just gestured for her to follow, then walked away, still munching on biscuits. She didn't say anything when they arrived at the aircraft either, she just waved for her to go to Susie before turning to hers.

Sergeant McIlroy greeted her with a nod. 'She's ready for you, ma'am.'

'Thank you, Aviator.'

Ellie immersed herself in her checks, performing them rapidly but thoroughly, not wanting to have the enigmatic Muscovite waiting for her. Somehow, though, Guseva was already climbing into her cockpit by the time she rounded Susie's nose and she rushed through the rest of them, doing them far more lackadaisically than she was really comfortable with. She trusted her fitters to have caught any problems, though, and when she was finished she scribbled her name hurriedly on the release form, then leaped up onto the wing and into the cockpit. McIlroy plugged her into the radio as soon as she was settled and strapped in and she turned to the assigned frequency as she hurried through the rest of her checks, just in case the woman started issuing instructions.

At first she thought she was picking up a local radio station, transmitting some Welsh folk music or something, but when she looked across to the other aircraft, intending to give a hand signal that she was having radio problems, she saw that Guseva was singing to herself. The woman noticed her looking and gave her a thumbs up and a quizzical look without pausing in her song or losing the rhythm.

Ellie gave her a thumbs up in return and the woman nodded. She ended her song on a wavering, but beautifully sustained high note, then there was a click as she opened a channel to control.

'India Lead ready for takeoff.'

'India Lead, this is Control, you are cleared for takeoff.'

'Thank you.' There was another click, then the Muscovite woman looked at Ellie and grinned widely. 'Off we go. Follow me.'

Without any further ado, the Muscovite woman's aircraft surged forward and Ellie started, thinking that she was just going to take off straight away, but then the Spitsteam swerved and accelerated across the airfield and she realised that she was actually taxiing, just much *much* faster than you were supposed to.

She wasn't left with any choice but to follow and, with a thumbs up to a shrugging McIlroy, she pushed the throttle forward as far as she dared, swinging Susie around to follow as soon as her rudder could bite the air and before she was going so fast that the Spit would topple over - that would certainly feed the rumours that DA-S was an unlucky bird, despite the fact that the morning's flight had gone without a hitch.

Luckily, they didn't have far to taxi and Lieutenant Guseva soon slowed her Spit and swung around into the wind. Ellie throttled right back and gently applied the brakes to slow down. She adjusted her course slightly so that she could come up onto the woman's wing to take off in formation, but before she had even started to turn, the Muscovite's aircraft was leaping forward. Ellie laughed incredulously and pushed hard on the rudder pedal, applying throttle gently at the same time, shoving the lever all the way forwards as soon as her nose was pointed in vaguely the right direction. There was a heart-stopping moment when the Spitsteam slewed slightly, the torque of the airscrew that was suddenly at full power trying to keep the aircraft turning at the same time as she was trying to stop it, and the right wing dipped as the aircraft went onto one wheel, but a judicious use of reverse rudder quickly corrected that and Ellie was thrust back into her seat as she accelerated after her instructor.

They reached takeoff speed in seconds and the Muscovite's aircraft lifted off the ground, but it didn't climb, instead it remained level while the undercarriage retracted, the powerful airscrew sending up slews of dust and grass. Ellie had naturally started to climb, but she quickly pushed the nose back down and drifted lower. Whether it was because Susie was slightly faster than the other machine or Guseva had throttled back a crack she didn't know, but she quickly caught up and slotted in behind her wing. She didn't get too close, though, in case the Muscovite decided to do something else unpredictable.

The line of Spitsteams flashed past her port-side wing and she caught a glimpse of shocked faces out of the corner of her eye, but she had no time to take note of anything, except for the fact that none of them had even begun to taxi, because even that momentary distraction was enough for the Spitsteam to sink a foot or two nearer to the ground. She flinched and eased the Spitsteam back up a touch, but it was all she could do to stop herself from panicking and yanking the stick back into her lap to claw for empty sky.

Flying like this was nerve-wracking in the extreme, but she found she was actually getting quite used to the idea of disaster being so close, especially because she was fairly sure that, as long as she didn't get distracted again, she'd be able to react in time if a sudden gust of wind threatened to force her down.

However, she was just beginning to realise that the danger wasn't only beneath her, it was also directly ahead - the perimeter fence and the trees behind it were only about a hundred yards away and she was now racing towards them at almost three hundred miles per hour.

'Sharp climb to the right on my mark.' Guseva's voice rang in her ears. 'Three...'

The perimeter fence wasn't particularly high, but the trees just beyond it were and they seemed to be looming higher every moment.

'Two...'

Ellie shot an incredulous glance across at the Muscovite, unable to believe how slowly she was counting and how relaxed she sounded.

'One...'

The fence seemed to be right in front of the airscrew now, the trees filling the whole of her vision, and Ellie's hand twitched on the spade grip, aching to pull on it.

'Mark!'

Ellie yanked back on the stick, only just resisting the temptation to just point the aircraft's nose at the sky, but instead try to match what Guseva was doing and stay on her wing. She found she was erring on the side of safety a bit and slowly drifting away from the other Spit as a result, but it didn't matter too much because, as soon as they were above the treetops, Guseva pushed her nose down again and levelled off, giving her the chance to adjust her position.

As soon as she was back on the Muscovite's wing she glanced across and found the woman grinning back at her, but she didn't know whether that was because she was excited by what they had just done or pleased that her student had been able to keep up and the woman said nothing over the radio to give her any indication either way.

Ellie gave the woman a nod, then turned her mind to the business of flying. She hadn't had a chance to trim anything, or do any of the numerous checks that you were supposed to do just after takeoff. She barely even knew which way they were heading and that wasn't particularly advisable seeing as Guseva hadn't told her where their designated training area was and she didn't know the local landmarks yet - if they got separated it would be up to her to find her way back and, with the way the base was tucked in amongst hills, it would be impossible to find it if she didn't have a good idea where it was first.

Finally, almost a minute into the flight, she had a chance to take a deep breath, relax the muscles she'd been holding in tension and think about what she'd just done. A cold sweat prickled under her flightsuit, sticking it to her back, as she realised just how close she'd come to at least crashing, if not dying. And why? What had the Muscovite been trying to teach her? Was there a lesson in it? Or was the woman just reckless and often put new students in mortal danger like that?

She would probably never know, because she couldn't see herself ever working up the nerve to confront her about it

'Here we are. Time for you to play. Have fun!'

The Muscovite peeled off, banking away hard, before Ellie had a chance to even process what the Muscovite had said to her. The Spitsteam quickly vanished from sight, disappearing below her wing and she realised that, even if Guseva was no longer there, she still needed to reply, so she rather belatedly pressed the button on the spade grip. 'Uh... Roger that, India Lead.'

There was no answer, but Ellie hadn't really expected one and she quickly put the Muscovite out of her mind and turned it to the task at hand.

She started with some simple aerobatics, linking them up with some maximum rate turn. She stalled the machine a few different ways and put it into spins to see whether it was as easy to recover as it had been with the Huntress. She tried every single manoeuvre she knew, getting used to the incredible performance of the Spitsteam and, while she thought she was beginning to get to grips with the machine, she had a feeling that she was only just scratching the surface of what it was truly capable of.

It was hard work and her back wasn't the only part of her sticking to the flightsuit when she levelled off to take a break and assess. She barely had time to catch her breath, though, because Guseva suddenly appeared on her wing.

'This is boring. It looks like you've got the hang of things enough, so let's have some fun. Try and stay on my six. If you can for a whole minute I'll buy you a biscuit, if I get on your six you owe me one.'

Ellie chuckled. 'That does sound like fun, Leader.'

She grinned at the Muscovite, then pulled Susie up into a quick barrel roll that put her onto Guseva's tail without sacrificing any of her speed.

'Nicely done,' Guseva said. 'Ready?'

'Yes, ma'am!'

There was no warning and no countdown this time, the Muscovite's Spitsteam just snap rolled onto its back and dived. Ellie was ready for something like that and immediately followed suit, but, even so, she found that she was twenty yards further back than she had been.

Guseva's aircraft was rolling as it fell from the sky and Ellie wondered why the woman was doing that because it must have been putting an incredible strain on her when she could have just been diving relatively calmly. The answer came to her in a few moments, though - manoeuvring like that meant Ellie couldn't predict which direction Guseva would go when she pulled up and would have to waste time rolling first before she could follow. And if Guseva timed it right and pulled up directly beneath her, which she was undoubtedly good enough to do, she would almost certainly lose her.

How to counter the tactic, though?

She smiled and put the stick hard over, starting her own roll. Much of the time she would lose pursuing Guseva would be due to having to overcome the inertia of the Spitsteam and get it turning. Already being in a roll would cut her response time enormously. As long as her body could handle it, of course.

The ground rotated sickeningly in front of her, the sheer violence of the manoeuvre flinging her sideways in her seat and threatening to tear her head from her neck. She fought against it, gritting her teeth and tightening her muscles and watched closely for any indication that her opponent was going to pull up.

They were screaming down out of the sky, already going more than four hundred miles per hour and a quick glance at the instruments told her that they were fast approaching four thousand feet, which Drake had set as the lowest they could go whilst training. Guseva would have to do something soon.

The other Spitsteam suddenly snapped out of the roll and began to pull up out of the dive. Ellie slammed the stick across to the other side of the cockpit, stopping her own roll, but she misjudged it slightly and had to readjust her course once she started to pull up. Even so, she was only forty or so yards behind, well within easy kill range.

'Well done,' the Muscovite called out almost immediately, 'but I was taking it easy on you that time. We'll climb back up to ten thousand feet and let's see how you do if I really try.'

'That was her taking it easy on me?' Ellie muttered to herself as she climbed after the other Spitsteam, feeling flushed with triumph and supremely confident. 'It looked like she was trying her hardest to me!'

It soon became extremely obvious that the Muscovite had *not* been trying her hardest, and over the next half an hour Guseva did things that Ellie didn't know an aircraft was *capable* of, let alone know how to do them herself.

Flying like that used a lot of spring tension and once the Muscovite had trounced Ellie for the sixth time, she called a stop and flew them back to Galath. Thankfully, there were no high jinks while they were landing because Ellie was absolutely exhausted and didn't think she would have been up to them.

Once she'd parked she climbed slowly out of the cockpit and slid down the wing, landing heavily and clutching at the aircraft for support.

'Are you alright ma'am?' McIlroy asked urgently, running up to her along with the other fitters. 'Did Susie...?'

Ellie held up a hand to cut her off. 'Susie performed wonderfully. I'm just...'

She stopped when she caught sight of a grinning Guseva stalking towards them and groaned. 'I'll be right back, Aviator.'

She stood up as straight as she could and went round the wing to meet the Muscovite.

'Perkins!' The Muscovite called out loudly when she was still yards away, spreading her arms wide.

Ellie cringed, thinking that the woman was going to hug her, but she just clapped her on her shoulders companionably, which Ellie wasn't sure was much better, seeing as the woman wasn't exactly gentle and it almost made her legs buckle beneath her.

'I like you, Perkins. You are a good pilot.' The woman bent to fish in her thigh pocket, keeping one hand on Ellie's shoulder and almost pulling her over again. 'Here! Have a biscuit!' She produced the handkerchief they'd seen her wrap biscuits in and unfolded it to reveal a slightly crushed ginger biscuit. 'Don't forget - you owe me six!'

Guseva smiled as Ellie took it and patted her on the shoulder again. 'We will see what Rudy comes up with for us tomorrow, but today was fun. I enjoyed it!'

The Muscovite winked, then turned and stomped towards the ready room. She stopped after a few steps, though, and shouted back. 'Remind Sausage Boy to have his flightsuit delivered to my quarters!'

Ellie nodded. 'Yes, ma'am!'

Guseva resumed walking, but called over her shoulder. 'Tanya! Call me Tanya!'

Ellie took a bite of the biscuit as she watched her go, slightly bemused by just about everything the woman said and did. She was right about one thing, though; the flight had been a lot of fun.

She popped the last of her hard-earned biscuit in her mouth, then turned and went to hand her aircraft back to her fitters.

22

Ellie had come down so early from her flight that she had time to fill out her log book, go back to her room, wash her flight suit, shower, change and settle into one of the armchairs in the tiny sitting room at the end of the barracks hut with one of her new theory books by the time any of the others arrived.

She put the thick book down as Rob and Tay stomped through the door and looked up at them.

Rob's eyes widened in surprise. 'We saw your aircraft when we landed and thought you'd only just come down. You look like you've been down for ages, though.'

'What happened?' a decidedly surly Tayler asked. 'Did you get called down after that stunt your instructor pulled?'

Rob grimaced and turned decidedly white. 'We thought for sure you were going to crash when you swooped down onto her wing. Your airscrew must have been less than a yard from the ground at one point!'

Ellie shrugged and grinned at their worried expressions. 'That was just a bit of fun.' She laughed as their mouths dropped open, then shook her head. 'No, we did the whole flight, but I spent most of it at full unwind so we had to come down early.'

'What on earth were you doing at full unwind so long?' Rob asked. 'Were you doing aerobatics at full throttle or something?' He blinked at her and asked quietly. 'Can a Spitsteam do that?'

Tay frowned at him. 'I didn't do them at full throttle and I could barely stand some of the turns I was doing. She *can't* have been.'

Ellie shook her head again. 'I wasn't, but I was dogfighting.'

'You were...?' Tay gaped at her, then snarled. He turned on his heel and stalked away down the corridor towards his room, muttering to himself angrily. '*She* had fun. Why couldn't *I* have fun? It was bad enough that Brunel had me...'

His voice was cut off by his door slamming behind him and Ellie looked at Rob questioningly.

He grimaced. 'Every time he did something, Lieutenant Brunel had him repeat it over and over until he'd gotten it perfect.'

Ellie winced, then spoke in a soft voice. 'Poor Tay. I can see how he wouldn't like that, but it was probably the best thing for him.'

Rob lowered his voice to match. 'I know! But I'm not going to tell him. Are you?'

'Absolutely not!'

'Didn't think so!' Rob gave her a half smile. 'I'm going to get changed. Will you wait for us so that we can walk to the mess together?'

'Of course!'

He nodded, then strode up the corridor. He paused outside Tayler's door and lifted his hand to knock, but in the end thought better of it and just went into his own.

A few seconds later Benedict came in, his face thunderous. There was a slight hitch in his step when he saw her, but he didn't stop, he just gave her the barest of nods and kept going.

'Lieutenant Guseva wanted me to remind you about your flightsuit!' she called after him. She was sure he heard, but he gave no reply and just went into his room and closed the door firmly behind him.

'Uh huh,' Ellie said to herself as she lifted the heavy book and found her place. 'Looks like everybody had a *lot* of fun.'

She looked up every time one of the boys came out of their room to go to the shower or wash their clothes, but none of them said anything to her and after fifteen minutes she decided to go and get ready for the mess.

She'd only been in her room for a minute or so before there was a knock.

'Come in!'

Tayler opened the door, but just stood on the threshold, shifting nervously from foot to foot and wringing his hands. 'Hey, uh, Ellie...'

Ellie frowned at his unusual behaviour. 'Tay? Is something wrong?'

'Uh, no! No... I just, uh... I just wondered... how about a drink?'

'Ooh! That would be nice! And we can have it with our dinner, now we're officers. Maybe we can try one of the wines or something.'

'No, I meant, how about having one with me. Later. Uh, on our own. You know?'

Oh! Ah!' Ellie blushed, momentarily lost for words. 'I...'

Tayler's face fell, but then he grinned widely. 'Doesn't matter! Maybe another time.'

He turned away and began to shut the door.

'Tay! Wait!'

He turned back, a hopeful and rather shy smile replacing the false confidence of before. This was the Tayler that she had only seen a few times, in moments when he thought he was alone, or when he forgot himself, or that time things had gotten very tough during survival training. *This* was the Tayler she liked, not the overconfident and, frankly, arrogant one that he tried to pretend he was.

There was no doubt there was attraction on both their sides, although what he could possibly see in her she didn't know, but they'd had no time, or energy, really, to act on it. Now that things were so different, maybe it was high time that they did.

'I'd love to.'

'Really?'

She nodded. 'Yes.'

The confident grin was instantly back and she had to stop herself from rolling her eyes.

'That's great. I'll grab my cap.'

Rob had had a fantastic flight with Squadron Leader Drake and had been planning to use that tailwind of confidence as impetus and try to catch Ellie on her own that evening and ask her out, but when he'd come out of his room and seen Tayler leaving hers his heart had fallen.

It was too late. She was caught and he knew all too well that she wouldn't get away until Tay had gotten what he wanted from her.

'You coming, Rob?'

Rob looked up at Ellie's voice. He'd been staring at the wall, lost in thought and hadn't seen her come out of her room.

'Coming!' He forced a smile and went to join her. He held out his elbow. 'May I escort you, Aerial Officer Perkins?'

'Why, yes, you may, Aerial Officer Sherborne.'

She took his arm and he walked her out of the door, making sure to hold her close so that she wouldn't see that he couldn't keep his smile in place.

Tayler caught up with them before they'd gone very far along the path to the mess and he took Ellie's other arm. She laughed, but soon pulled away from them both so that they wouldn't appear foolish.

Dinner was well under way by the time they arrived and plenty of airmen and women were already sitting at the large tables in the brightly lit room with their food while a couple of dozen more were queueing. A curtain had been drawn across the entire width of the room dividing the officer's section from the rest of the room and they went along the wall to where a hole, the size and shape of a door, had been cut in it.

They stepped through and it was like they had passed into a different world.

The noise of the hundreds of people in the main mess had all but gone, absorbed by the thick curtain, and there were no bright lamps overhead to banish all shadow, instead there were thousands of tiny pinpricks of light hanging down from the roof, like constellations of stars, casting a soft glow over everything. The dining tables were covered with white tablecloths and small clockwork lamps made of wrought iron with bulbs fabricated to look like candles sat on each of them, making them look like islands of sanctuary in the night sky.

It was stunningly beautiful and entirely appropriate for an air base.

'So this is how the toffs live.' Tay said, grinning. 'I think I'm going to like being an officer.'

'Evening, madam, sirs,' a white-jacketed steward with sergeant's stripes on his arm greeted them. 'I'm afraid you are improperly dressed.'

The three of them stared at him, not sure what he was getting at. It was only when Benedict arrived, resplendent in his new dress uniform with his gold pilot's wings pinned to his breast, that they understood. He smirked at them as he brushed past and was quickly ushered to an empty table by a second steward.

'I'm sorry,' Ellie said, turning back to the steward, 'we didn't know.'

'Evening, chaps,' Drake said, entering behind them with Guseva on his arm, 'what's...? Oh!' he sighed and shook his head as he realised what was happening. 'My fault entirely, I'm afraid, Sergeant Hughes. In all the excitement I neglected to inform our new arrivals of the dress code in the evenings. Do you think you could make an exception for them, just for tonight?'

The steward looked at Drake, then considered the three pilots. 'Perhaps just for tonight, sir.'

'Thank you, Sergeant.' Drake nodded and turned to the pilots.

'Would you allow me to apologise by inviting you to dine with me?'

There was no need for them to even think about whether to accept the offer of dinner with two Misfits or not and no need to reply because Drake got all the answer he needed from their eager faces.

'Table for five then please, Sergeant.'

'Very good, sir, this way please.'

The man led them across the room through the tables. Their path took them past Benedict and Drake nodded to him.

'Evening, Wilberforce.'

'My Lord.'

Benedict nodded back expectantly, but Drake just walked past without slowing and didn't invite him to join them as he'd obviously been expecting. Benedict hid his face behind his wine glass in an attempt to hide his disappointment, but it was plain to see. Tay snorted unkindly and opened his mouth, undoubtedly going to rub it in, but Ellie elbowed him in the ribs to stop him; Benedict was being humiliated enough already, having to sit on his own while they enjoyed Drake's company.

Stewards appeared out of nowhere and held out chairs for everyone, then immediately disappeared again, leaving them in the hands of the sergeant, who hovered by Drake.

'What do we have tonight, Owen?'

'Tonight we have *Vichyssoise* followed by a *Navarin d'agneau*,' he stated, pronouncing the names of the dishes with a surprisingly good French accent, 'and for dessert the chef has prepared your favourite, sir.'

'*Le Spotted Dick*.' Drake said in an equally passable accent. He winked at his guests then looked back at the sergeant. 'So, we have potatoes, leeks and lamb.'

'Quite so, sir.'

'Then I think this calls for white wine. Crack open a couple of bottles of my private stock, please. The good stuff,' he smiled at them again, 'we have decent company tonight.'

'Very good, sir,' the sergeant said, 'anything else?'

'No, I think that's all... oh, yes, do make sure that Squadron Leader Niven gets a glass, otherwise he'll have the hump all week.'

'Of course, sir.'

The sergeant gave Drake a nod, a smaller one to Guseva, who was too busy buttering a bread roll to notice, then inclined his head minimally to the three pilots. There was the barest of sniffs of disapproval and then he stalked away.

Drake leaned over the table to speak to them in hushed tones. 'Aviator Sergeant Hughes is a bit of a tyrant, but he runs the mess extremely well. Make sure you keep on his good side, though, or you might find him pouring the dregs of a bottle for you or claiming there's nothing left but the table wine.'

He leaned back in his chair and contemplated them.

'How did you enjoy your first day?' he grinned. 'Was it what you were expecting?'

'Steamcycles with wings?' Tay began. 'How could we *not* have expected that, sir?'

Rob nodded. 'Saw that coming a mile off, sir.'

Drake laughed, but said nothing and just waited.

Rob and Tay looked at each other. Tay shrugged, then turned back to Drake. 'I have to say I was a bit frustrated by Aviator Lieutenant Brunel's teaching methods, sir.'

'I can imagine! That's why I put you with her.'

'Sir?'

'You need a steady hand right now to stop you from slipping back into your old ways and that is Lieutenant Brunel. That doesn't mean she's holding you back deliberately, or that you can't learn anything from her. So, make sure you don't dismiss her guidance before you've given her a chance.'

Tayler grimaced, but nodded his understanding. 'Yes, sir.'

'What about you Sherborne? Anything to say about *my* methods so far?'

'No, sir. I'm perfectly happy and I'm looking forward to working with you more.'

'Well said!' Drake said with a laugh. 'It's never a bad idea to suck up to the boss. At least a little bit.'

Tay nudged Rob, who blushed, but was unrepentant.

Drake laughed again at the interaction, then looked at Ellie. 'Wilberforce made it very clear by his behaviour before and after his flight what he thought, so that just leaves you, Perkins.'

'Well, sir,' Ellie said hesitantly, glancing at Guseva, who had looked up from her bread and was watching her with interest. 'I wasn't expecting to be challenged so thoroughly so soon.'

'I suppose not.' Drake said, looking at her with just as much interest. 'You seemed to manage well and keep your nerve. Tanya hasn't scared you off, then?'

No, sir, not at all.' She gave Tanya a crooked smile, which the Muscovite returned. 'In fact I'm quite looking forward to seeing what else she can cook up for me.'

Drake groaned and rolled his eyes. 'Don't say that. She'll take it as a challenge and do something even crazier than whatever that was she did on takeoff this afternoon.'

'It looked good, didn't it?' Guseva asked, without taking her eyes from Ellie or losing her smile.

Drake sighed. 'Yes, it did look extremely impressive... But that doesn't mean I ever want you doing it again.'

Guseva patted him on the hand. 'Anything you say, Rudy.'

Drake gave them a long-suffering smile, but then looked up in relief as Sergeant Hughes and another steward stepped into the pool of light around the table with a bottle of wine and a silver bucket on a stand, providing a welcome distraction. The other steward placed the bucket and stand next to Drake then retreated while Hughes showed Drake the bottle.

'That's the one.' Drake said after a glance at the label. 'Do the honours, would you, sergeant?'

'Certainly, sir.'

The man popped the cork quickly and efficiently, then poured a little for Drake, who tasted it and nodded. He then poured a decent amount for everyone, starting with Guseva and Ellie and finishing with Drake, Rob and Tayler.

Drake lifted his glass. 'To a very promising group of pilots and, hopefully, a very enjoyable fortnight.'

It was an extremely entertaining evening, with Lord Drake being the perfect host and both he and Guseva regaling them with anecdotes of their time with the Misfits, when they weren't good-naturedly arguing over who had saved whose life the most.

It was almost a shame that it had to end, but Drake had administrative work to do before bed and Guseva wanted to get Benedict's flightsuit sewn up so that he could use it tomorrow, so they bade them goodnight and wandered out of the mess arm in arm.

Rob stood up as soon as they'd gone and looked down at them. 'I'll leave you two to it, then, shall I?' He wiped his mouth with a napkin then threw it on the table before stomping away.

Tay stared after him, puzzled. 'What's up with him?'

Ellie frowned. 'I have no idea.' She watched Rob brush past the curtain irritably and disappear from view, but then turned back and smiled. 'Don't worry about him; we can talk to him tomorrow.' She reached over the table and put her hand on Tay's. 'I thought we were going to have a drink?'

Tay looked down at her hand, then up at her. He grinned. 'Yes, we were, weren't we?'

They stood and made their way through the tables towards the bar at the far end of the room. Benedict had eaten quickly and left earlier in the night, as had most of the other officers, and the mess was almost empty, so they found a couple of empty armchairs away from anyone else and Ellie sat while Tayler went to the bar.

'Evening, sir. What can I get you?' the steward behind the bar asked, putting aside the glass she'd been polishing.

'Evening! Two pints of Best, please.'

'Coming right up, sir.'

The woman poured two pints, fairly expertly in Tay's opinion, and placed them on the bar in front of him.

'There you go, sir, anything else?'

'No, thank you. Uh, so, can you put that on my tab? Is that right? Are we supposed to do that? It's just I didn't bring any money and...'

'That's correct, sir. Bar and mess tabs are settled up once a week on Sundays, but if your bill doesn't exceed your pay then there's no need to do anything except sign your account to say you accept it. Your name, sir?'

'Tayler.' He cringed inwardly when she gave him a blank look. 'Oh, uh, sorry, I mean Oakley, Acting Aerial Officer Tayler Oakley, uh, Corporal...?'

'Morgan, sir.'

Tayler smiled at her, thinking back to Drake's words about keeping the stewards happy and also thinking that it really would not hurt to keep the people behind the bar happy either. 'Pleased to meet you, Corporal Morgan.'

'Sir.'

He was disappointed when she gave him a formal nod, not looking at all impressed or even particularly affected by his attempts at amiability, but he supposed it was only to be expected; there was probably some silly rule in the armed forces that she wasn't allowed to smile while on duty in the mess. She probably wasn't allowed to socialise with officers either, which was unfortunate, because she was rather good looking...

Tayler nipped the thought in the bud before it could fully take root. That was something the old Tayler would think, this Tayler didn't want to do or even think something that would mess things up with Ellie. She was special. She wasn't like the other girls.

He settled for giving Corporal Morgan a last smile, then picked up the drinks and took them over to Ellie.

She was staring down at the table, deep in thought and he worried for a moment that she was regretting her decision to come out with him, but as soon as he got there she looked up and gave him one of those smiles that turned her admittedly quite plain face into one of the loveliest he'd ever seen.

'What were you thinking about?' he asked, setting one of the pints in front of her.

'I was thinking about how much things have changed for me in such a short time.'

'For all of us.'

Ellie nodded. 'I suppose. Well, except for Benedict, that is.'

Tay laughed. 'Yes. While we're all going up in the world he seems to be going down.'

She chuckled. 'He really wasn't pleased when Lord Drake snubbed him like that.'

'Serves him right! He saw you in your day uniform and saw us changing into it but didn't say anything.'

'I hope he'd not going to go back to how he was, now that Sandra isn't around.'

Tay shrugged. 'It looks like he already has. But maybe after this evening he'll wake up.'

Ellie nodded. 'I suppose he might. Especially if he stops to think about what Tanya is doing for him with his flightsuit.'

'Oh, *Tanya*, is it?' Tay said, smirking. 'Since when are you on first name terms with Aviator Lieutenant Tatiana Guseva?'

'Since she told me I was a good pilot and told me to call her Tanya,' Ellie said casually, as if it were nothing. She leaned forward to pick up her glass and lifted it to him. 'Cheers.' She took a long swig and smacked her lips, then grinned; he hadn't moved, he was just staring at her with his mouth open. 'You know, that gormless look isn't exactly attractive.'

'The what?' he blinked at her, then slowly smiled. 'You think I'm attractive?'

'Not right now I don't!'

He laughed, then took a big swig of his drink. 'Ah! That's nice! Seems like the officers get the good stuff.'

'Then you'd better work and make sure you stay one.'

'Don't worry, I've learned my lesson.'

'Have you?' she asked. 'Because you were in a bit of a mood when you came down this evening.'

'Yes, I was. But I'm over it now. It's funny what a bucketful of wine and dinner with two Misfits can do.'

Ellie chuckled again. 'Seriously, though, did you notice how, when we were talking about how we were doing, he *asked* you to give Brunel a chance? Not just *tell* you to suck it up and like it.'

Tay blinked. 'Actually, I hadn't noticed that.'

Ellie nodded. 'As your superior officer and the one in command he could just do what he wants and give you no choice, but he didn't. Things really changed for us when we came here. We're no longer the bottom of the pile and it looks like we're not going to be shouted at by the sergeants anymore.'

Tay shrugged. 'It's not such a big deal. I've been my own boss for years.'

'Well *I* haven't.' Ellie said, fighting back tears. 'This is the first time in my life that I'm being asked for my opinion or given a say in what I think is best for me.'

Her voice caught as her emotions got the better of her and she coughed and took a drink to cover.

Tayler didn't notice, though, he was too busy with his own pint of bitter. He grinned at her again. 'I wonder if Squadron Leader Drake will give Benedict the same courtesy.'

'I expect so. Even if he is behaving badly, he made it here. He's still proved himself as a pilot.'

Raised voices and laughter came from the far side of the seating area and they glanced over to find Squadron Leader Niven sitting with three officers they didn't recognise. They were drinking wine while playing some kind of board game that covered almost the entire rather large coffee table they were gathered around.

'I wonder what Squadron Leader Niven did to make Benedict so angry.' Ellie mused.

'Who knows,' Tay said. 'Knowing Benedict, though, he's probably more upset that he didn't get *Lord* Drake as an instructor than he is at Niven's training methods.'

'Hmm,' Ellie nodded. 'Drake certainly doesn't act all stuck up like a toff, though, not like Benedict.'

'No, he doesn't.' Tay agreed before tipping the bottom of his glass up and finishing his pint. 'Another?'

Ellie shook her head. 'I need to get plenty of sleep if I'm going to have a chance of surviving whatever Lieutenant Guseva has planned for me. And you,' she smiled sweetly at him, 'you have a lot of books you should be reading.'

He groaned. 'Don't remind me.'

Ellie drained her glass and put it on the table, where it was immediately snapped up, along with Tayler's, by a steward. She stood and looked down at him. 'Come on, you can walk me home.'

They strolled back towards their barracks building in silence, taking a scenic route along the gravel paths through the trees, enjoying the night and the weather, which would undoubtedly not last much longer. Even this far from any enemy activity blackout regulations were in full force and there were no lights anywhere, but the sky was perfectly clear, the moon almost full and they could see well enough to navigate. They could even make out the looming shape of the surrounding hills and mountains and the faint white glow here and there on them where flocks of sheep had gathered for the night.

Galath was a very small base and it didn't take long to get to their barracks, even going the long way round, but Ellie grabbed Tay's hand and stopped him before he could open the door.

'You know, I barely remember the day we arrived at Druid because I was feeling so bad and I only vaguely remember someone giving me their coat. We didn't know each other at the time and I didn't get a good look at whoever it was, but it was you wasn't it?'

'Yes. You looked like you needed help, so...' he shrugged.

'Thank you.'

She reached up and pulled his head down towards her. There was an awkward moment as the stiff brims of their caps bumped each other, but they soon sorted themselves out and then suddenly their lips were touching.

When Ellie had stopped to think about it in the past, the notion of two people touching their lips together had seemed absolutely ridiculous to her. There was no reason that it should mean anything more than a handshake or the exchange of a thimble, and she had no idea why people insisted on doing it so much.

She understood why in the first instant.

All of her attention shot to that single, wonderful point of contract, concentrating her mind, like it had never concentrated before, but then there was this incredible expansion of awareness that encompassed him, linked them and did things to her insides that she had no words for and would have been mortified if someone had asked her to explain.

She thought it would never stop, that the feeling would go on forever, and she didn't realise it already had until she opened eyes that she didn't remember closing and found Tay smiling one of *those* crooked smiles at her.

'First kiss?' he asked.

'Yes,' she breathed.

He chuckled, thinking she was joking, but then his eyes widened when he realised she wasn't. 'Really?'

'Yes,' she said, shifting shyly from foot to food. 'And maybe I could have a second, please?'

'Yes, ma'am!'

This time there was no awkwardness. This time it just felt right.

23

After the splendid day and clear night they'd had, it was a bit of a surprise to everyone, except most of the Welsh servicemen and women, when there was a thin layer of mist covering the base the next morning. As a result, flying operations were postponed and the four pilots went to a classroom with Lieutenant Evans until visibility had improved to hear about his experiences of air combat.

The classic idea that most people had of combat in the air was the romantic one that had been pictured so many times in the flyvies and novels of two pilots battling it out and the best one winning. The reality, Evans explained, was far different. One on one combat was actually rather rare. More common was a kind of melee, with a dozen or more aircraft involved, where nobody focussed on a single target but rather took whatever chances they could to fire at whoever they could. Focusing on a single target in that kind of fight meant flying predictably and would more often than not get you killed rather than get you a kill and the rule of the day was to keep being unpredictable and continually turn. Preferably with a wingman sticking with you to do the job of watching behind while you did the shooting.

That wasn't to say that dogfighting wasn't important, though, it just wasn't the be all and end all of the war in the sky.

Evans talked them through some of the battles he'd been in, describing the ones during the height of the battle over Britain of September of the year before when there had been a hundred, two hundred or even, on a couple of notable occasions, three hundred machines sharing the sky. So many that it seemed they were all you could see. Those kinds of massed battles were very much the exception, though; more usually he'd been in a single squadron or flight of Spitsteams on patrol who had encountered a usually larger number of MU9s.

While his stories didn't do much to inform the new pilots of *how* to fly their aircraft in combat, it did do a lot to prepare them for *what* to expect - knowledge that was just as valuable.

The mist was soon thinning as the sun burnt it off and they were called to the ready room by Squadron Leader Drake to be briefed for the first flight of the day over a cup of tea.

'Dogfighting!' Drake announced. 'You've learned all the basic tactics. You've practised all the moves you need - both in your aircraft and on springcycles.' He grinned at them. 'Now it's time for you to use all of it in a situation that is as real as we can make it without inviting the Fleas over for tea.' He lifted his cup in salute to them and drained it before going on. 'You're not going to be good at it straight away, but don't worry, we're not expecting you to be. At this stage we just want you to get a feel for the new dynamic of sharing a sky with someone who wants to knock you out of it. Don't be afraid to try new things, but endeavour not to do anything truly stupid or get too caught up in the moment. Above all, though, listen to your instructors - if they tell you to do something or stop doing something, then just do it and ask questions later.'

He looked around and smiled. 'Having said all that, as long as you keep your wits about you then you'll have no problem. So, go, have fun and come back better pilots than you were when you took off.' He looked at Rob. 'Ready?'

'Yes, sir!'

As the pilots and instructors stood and began to wander away, Ellie looked around. Lieutenant Guseva hadn't appeared before the briefing started and it didn't look like she'd arrived since. Not that it mattered too much. It wasn't as if the instructors actually listened to what Drake had to say - they generally just drank tea, ate biscuits and read the morning papers or caught up on paperwork. She wouldn't sit around waiting for her, though, she'd go and get a head start on her preflight checks.

She made a quick stop at the side table, then followed the other pilots out of the building and across the grass towards the aircraft.

'Good morning, Ellie!'

Ellie barely managed not to scream at the voice coming from right by her ear and she spun around, almost tripping over her own feet, to find Guseva standing directly behind her.

'Good morning, ma'am,' she said when she'd caught her breath.

'Tanya.'

Ellie smiled and nodded. 'Tanya.' She handed over the small packet that she'd just wrapped up. 'Consider my debts paid.'

Tanya's eyes lit up. She took the packet and unwrapped it, then popped one of the shortbread biscuits into her mouth whole. She smiled contentedly as she chewed. 'Mmm... Thank you!' She swallowed, then immediately put another one in before waving in the direction of the aircraft. 'Checks!' she mumbled with her mouth full, then pointed at the sky. 'Up!'

Ellie grinned. 'Sounds good to me.'

Tayler was grinning as he walked beside Aviator Lieutenant Brunel towards their aircraft.

'I hope you're smiling like that because you're happy that you're going to be flying soon.' Brunel said, giving him a withering look.

'Of course, ma'am!' Tayler said. His grin widening further.

Brunel grunted, shaking her head as she separated from him and went to her aircraft.

Tayler ran his hand over the rudder of his Spitsteam, but he wasn't checking it, instead he was gazing past it to where Ellie was inspecting her own aircraft. Their eyes met for a moment and he winked, then chucked as she blushed and looked away.

They had only had time for three kisses before someone had come along and they'd had to go inside, but they had to have been the three best kisses he'd ever had. Or at least the three kisses that had meant the most to him.

Kissing other girls had been nice and all. More than nice actually. But there had been something missing, something that he hadn't even known had been missing until now.

Those kisses had only ever been a prelude - an almost obligatory step towards something else. And there had always been an understanding that he and the girl were there just for their physical gratification, that they had an itch they both needed to scratch. There hadn't been anything beyond that and once they were done they had gone their own separate ways, perhaps to repeat the experience at a later date, perhaps not.

With Ellie there was more, though. Something that went beyond just the physical. But he had no idea what.

Perhaps it was love?

It was too soon to tell, but he was looking forward to finding out.

Ellie blushed and hid behind the Spitsteam, trying desperately to concentrate on the job at hand and not to keep thinking about the night before...

'Drat!' she muttered to herself; there she went again.

'Is there a problem, ma'am?' Sergeant McIlroy asked, worriedly peering at Susie.

'Oh, no, nothing!' Ellie said, blushing again. 'I just have a few things on my mind this morning. Sorry.'

She pushed Tay and all thoughts of kissing out of her mind and continued with her checks. She couldn't afford any distractions at the moment. Not if Guseva picked up from where she'd left off the day before.

Not surprisingly, the woman was once again already in her cockpit and strapped in when Ellie climbed into hers and she looked over and waved, then pointed at her mouth and gave a thumbs up. It was also not particularly surprising that she was eating biscuits in the cockpit.

Once again, they were first pair ready, but there were no surprises, shocks or tests from Guseva that day, and they took off normally.

'So,' Guseva's voice sounded in Ellie's ears once they were climbing towards their training area. 'Oakley is rather good looking isn't he?'

'What?' Ellie exclaimed, looking over towards the other Spitsteam, which had dropped back level with her. 'What makes you say that?'

'I saw the way you were looking at each other just now. You two are stepping out, yes?'

Ellie gaped across at the Muscovite woman, not quite believing that she was going to have such a personal conversation at a distance of twenty yards, with someone she had only just met, who was not only her instructor and superior officer but also a Misfit and a living legend. It was surreal. But then again, so was the fact that she was flying in a Spitsteam just a month after it had seemed that her entire life was going to be spent as a spinster, taking care of her father.

She shook her head and smiled wryly across the gap. 'Yes, we are. Since last night.'

'Congratulations! Have you kissed yet?'

'Um...' Ellie said hesitantly, still not sure she was entirely comfortable discussing her love life with Tanya, but then blinked when she realised that she actually quite wanted to. When she had gone to her room last night she had sat on her bunk for quite a while, wishing that Sandra and Lottie were there for her to discuss the matter with and, despite the difference in age, experience and, yes, rank, at that moment the Muscovite was the closest thing she had to a female friend. 'Yes,' she said eventually. 'We did.'

'Good! You should do more. After all, who knows when we will die?'

Ellie didn't have an answer to that, so the airwaves fell silent. It wasn't long before there was a crackling in her ear again, though.

'What about Robert, though?'

Ellie frowned. 'What about Rob?'

'Well, he is in love with you.'

'What? No he isn't!'

There was some muttering in Russian and Ellie looked over to see Tanya shaking her head.

'I don't understand,' the woman said when she'd finished her tirade.

'Understand what?'

'How you can be such a brilliant pilot if you are blind!'

There was a click as the Muscovite closed the channel and Ellie was left alone with her thoughts.

If Tanya was right then it would explain a lot, like the way Rob had stormed out after dinner last night, his bad mood at breakfast and how he'd avoided her while they'd been making tea before the briefing.

But she couldn't be right.

Could she?

Surely if Rob liked her he would have said something. Or made it known in some other way. Like Tay had with his smiles and glances.

But he hadn't done any of that, so, naturally, she hadn't been aware of any interest on his part.

Not that she didn't like him. Because she did. A lot. Almost as much as Tay, actually. Enough that, maybe, if *he'd* been the one to ask her out...

Urgh... It was beginning to sound like that ridiculous short story that Sandra had pasted in her scrapbook, the one that Jem and Lottie had swooned over - *A Russian Romance*, she thought it had been called. An overly exaggerated fiction of a love triangle between Lord

Drake, Kitty Wright and Gwen Stone, set during their mission to Muscovy. She had thought it had sounded completely implausible and had told them that there was no way something like that would ever happen in real life, but now it seemed that it might be happening to her.

Things couldn't go on like this. Benedict was already making life difficult for them and they couldn't afford Rob to stop speaking to them as well; they were all supposed to be studying together and there was no way she would be able to get Tay through the officer exams on her own. Also, he was far too good a friend to lose over something so trivial as her.

Something had to be done. She didn't have a clue what at that moment, but she might be able to come up with something if she had some time to think. And maybe Tay would have some ideas. They could try to work something out together.

But that would have to be later, because her growing familiarity with the local landmarks told her that they were approaching their assigned training area.

She put all thoughts of her personal life out of her mind and took a deep breath, clearing her head of everything except the sky and the things that occupied it with her, then reached out with her senses, attuning herself to the aircraft around her, submerging herself in it, making it part of her, an extension of herself...

'Are you with me, Two?'

Tanya's voice came, exactly as expected and Ellie smiled. 'Yes, Leader.'

'Alright, so, dogfighting again! But this time I'm not going to give you an advantage and we're going to start head to head. However, I'm going to be very disappointed if you don't make it more interesting for me today.'

'I'll try to, Leader; I don't want to be stealing biscuits for you forever.'

Tanya laughed. 'No, you don't! Alright, break on my mark, fly twenty seconds, then reverse course and we'll have at it! Mark!'

Ellie pulled a tight ninety degree turn, counted to twenty, then reversed course.

A Spitsteam can fly quite a distance in twenty seconds, even when it's not at full speed and it took her a couple of seconds and judicious use of the magnifying lenses in her lovely new goggles to find Tanya and she adjusted course to meet her.

It was shocking how quickly the tiny dot expanded to become an aircraft and she applied a touch of rudder nervously to make sure she was headed safely to the right of it.

Between one breath and another, the green and brown aircraft had flashed past her and she threw her aircraft onto its wing and pulled hard on the stick. She tilted her head back, straining as it suddenly weighed several times what it normally did, and peered through the top of the canopy, past the rearview mirror, trying to find the other machine. She found it, directly above her, on the other side of the large circle she was describing in the sky, Tanya's face framed in the cockpit, peering back at her, white teeth shining in the sunlight as she grinned widely. Despite the forces that had to have been thrusting her down in her seat, somehow the Muscovite was able to lift her hand and wave. Ellie knew she wouldn't be able to do the same, that if she took her hand off the throttle it would just drop and she wouldn't be able to lift it again until she stopped turning, so she settled for just laughing instead.

With machines that were exactly the same and pilots that were copying each other's every move, the normal thing would have been that they would spend forever locked into the circle until one or other tired or ran out of spring tension. Ellie was well aware that Tanya knew a few tricks to break the stalemate, though; she had used them to great effect during the dogfights they'd had yesterday. The thing was that Ellie had seen her use them and had been busy working out how to do them, when she hadn't been thinking about Tay and kissing, of course.

Alright, Tanya, she thought, *let's see* just *how interesting I can make this for you.*

Ellie smiled wearily as she turned onto final approach. She was covered in sweat and exhausted after just her first flight of the day, but she was satisfied because she had managed to surprise Tanya not once, but twice and had won two of their dogfights. The fact that she had lost the three times after that was neither here nor there, because one of those bouts had been extremely close and Tanya had really been trying by then. The strain on her body had been incredible, though, and she had no idea how she was going to fly properly even once more that day, let alone two or three times. She would never consider asking Tanya to go easy on her in the next flight, though; she was learning too much and, besides, the Prussians wouldn't be going easy on her when she got into combat in a few weeks' time.

She'd be fine, though; the RAC pilots' miracle cure-all - a cup of tea and a few biscuits - would speed her recovery and she'd have at least half an hour to rest while Susie was rewound. Besides, she wasn't going to let a simple matter of some sore muscles keep her from flying with the Muscovite; she'd learned so much already and could only imagine how much the woman still had to teach her.

The airfield was fast approaching now and her hands and feet danced on the controls as she held the slowing aircraft level. The trees were past and then the perimeter fence flashed beneath her and she began to settle to the ground.

A bright flash made her recoil and red smoke blossomed to the front and just off to one side of her.

'What...?'

She stared at the smoke as it passed by her wing, not understanding, but then there was crackling in her ears and an unfamiliar but urgent voice sounded in her ears.

'Goose Two, wave-off, wave-off!'

It took her a moment to realise that she was Goose Two, but then she was pushing the throttle through the stops. The Spitsteam responded quickly, accelerating smoothly, but she had been so committed to landing that she was only just barely able to stop the aircraft from touching the ground.

Only when she was climbing and was sure she wasn't going to fall out of the sky did she press the button on her stick.

'Control, this is Goose Two. What's going on?'

'Goose Two you have a gear malfunction.'

Ellie glanced at her instrument panel. The green landing gear light was on, meaning it was down. 'I'm showing gear down, Control.'

'Roger that, Goose Two, but only one wheel is down fully, the other is stuck half out.'

Ellie blanched. If she'd tried to land like that her wing would have dug into the ground and sent her cartwheeling at more than a hundred and twenty miles an hour down the airfield. The aircraft would have disintegrated around her and she would most likely have been torn apart. She'd been inches from disaster.

'Thank you for the wave-off, then Control,' she said, rather shakily.

'Roger, Goose Two. Orbit at six thousand feet, two miles out on bearing one eight zero and advise on situation, please.'

'Roger, Control. Goose Two out.'

Ellie looked out over her wing as another Spitsteam appeared. Tanya had apparently waved-off with her.

'You look a bit shaken up, Two,' the Muscovite said with a grin, 'anyone would think that you hadn't done any emergency procedures at Gwynedd.'

'It's a bit bloody different when it's real.' Ellie muttered, half to herself.

Still, Tanya had a point. They had simulated a couple of emergencies that were similar to the situation she unfortunately found herself in and she'd been perfectly fine. Things were a bit different in the heat of the moment when your life was on the line, though. Which only made her think how she was going to react when the dogfight was real. When it wasn't Tanya facing her but a Prussian with live ammunition and the very real likelihood that one of them wouldn't survive...

'Retracting gear.' Ellie said, putting the morbid thought out of her mind and pushing the lever on the side bulkhead. She heard the whirr of the small spring that operated the gear and felt the aircraft tremble slightly as the wheels came up. There was a solid thunk as they locked in place and then silence again - just like it should sound.

Tanya's aircraft dropped slightly below hers. 'They're up. They look fine and snug.'

'Alright, deploying again.'

Ellie pulled the lever back and heard the spring start to operate again. It changed in pitch slightly after a few seconds, though, whining as if it were straining against something, then cut out.

'It's stuck half way down again, Two.'

'Roger,' Ellie said. She glanced at her instrument panel. 'I'm running low on tension. I'll be on reserve soon.'

'I've already switched to reserve, Two, but don't worry about that for now; we have plenty of time.'

Ellie shot a glanced across at the other pilot. The reserve spring was there as a small backup in case of emergencies, but it didn't last long at the best of times and often didn't work, so it couldn't be relied upon. Guseva was taking a not insignificant risk by staying with her so she had no time to waste.

'I'm going to try to lower the gear manually,' she said, bending forwards.

There were two levers on the floor, one on either side of the cockpit, that could be used to lower the wheels individually in an emergency or when under maintenance. It was a time-consuming process, as the large and heavy gear was forced down by what amounted to a bicycle pump, and dangerous, because the awkward positioning of the lever meant that you had to duck below the rim of the cockpit to reach them, but if she wanted to land properly it was her only option.

She started pumping the lever, pulling it up and pushing it down over and over.

If she wasn't tired before, she was exhausted now and her arm was burning after only a couple of dozen pumps. She kept at it, though, gritting her teeth and using her whole body to jerk at the lever.

'Level off, Two!' Guseva's calm but urgent voice came over the radio.

Ellie lifted her head to peer out the cockpit and found to her alarm that she had entered a spiralling dive without her realising it, the nose of the aircraft pointed down at an almost forty-five degree angle and the left wing well below the horizon. She had already lost more than a thousand feet and was in real danger of going into a spin too low to recover comfortably. She regained control quickly and put herself into a slight climb, converting the speed she'd gained back into height.

'Turn to zero one zero, Ellie, and let's head back towards the airfield - I have to land.'

'Roger, Leader.' Ellie turned the aircraft gently, but then froze as it lurched and started to drop. She realised what had happened after a split second, though, and reached between her legs to switch to the auxiliary spring. For a moment nothing happened and she held her breath, thinking that it might have failed, but then the aircraft surged as the airscrew regained power. 'I'm on emergency power, Leader.'

'Roger that.' Tanya said. 'Give that lever a few more pumps, the wheel is almost down and I want to check it visually before I leave you.'

Ellie bent down to the lever and started pumping it up and down again. This time she kept half her awareness on the aircraft, feeling how it was, fully aware that neither she nor Guseva could afford any more upsets. Thankfully, after only twenty or so seconds it became impossible to pull the lever any more, which theoretically meant that the wheel was down.

'That should do it, Leader. How does it look?'

'Looks down, Two, but there's no way for me to tell if it's locked.'

Ellie grinned at her as she came back up level with her. 'I'm just going to have to risk it. I don't particularly feel like abandoning her; my fitters would never forgive me.'

Tanya laughed, but Ellie could tell she was nervous, which was far more unnerving than the situation itself, if she had to be honest.

'Let's do this, then.' Tanya said. 'Control, this is Goose Leader. Goose Two is gear down, but may still have problems and I am at zero tension. Requesting priority landing.'

'Roger, Goose Leader. The circuit is clear. Come straight in and land normally.'

'Thank you, Control.'

'Goose Two, you are also clear to land, but please do so as far from the hangars as possible and do not taxi. Shut down in place, evacuate your aircraft and wait for pickup.'

'Roger, Control.'

Ellie swallowed nervously; they weren't taking any chances with her - telling her to land away from the hangars and away from the middle of the airfield meant that if anything happened she wouldn't stop operations.

Tanya looked across at her. 'I'll have the tea ready for you.'

'I like the chocolate biscuits.' Ellie answered with a smile, but then turned to face forwards.

The airfield was fast approaching again and she went about making her final preparations, lowering the flaps, reducing throttle and opening the canopy. She slid sideways, aiming for the side of the airfield rather than the middle, opening up the gap between the two Spitsteams.

She felt very alone all of a sudden. Nobody could help her now, there was no instructor in the back seat to take the controls from her if she did something wrong. It was up to her. She just had to trust her training and instincts and get Susie down as carefully as possible.

As the perimeter fence passed below her she throttled right back, sinking as low to the ground as she could without actually touching down and holding the aircraft there as it lost speed. The Spitsteam was such a good flyer, so aerodynamic, that it barely had any wind resistance and for a moment she thought that it would just keep going and she would crash into the far fence, making the question of whether the gear held or not a moot one, but eventually she felt the aircraft tremble as it approached a stall. She held it, though, fighting with the stick and rudders, bringing the nose up higher and higher to keep the aircraft aloft far longer than it would have liked.

It was a risky thing to do, but she wanted to be going as slowly as possible just in case the worst happened and the wheel collapsed beneath her.

The buffeting worsened as the aircraft slowed further and she began to have trouble controlling it, but then the wings lost all their remaining purchase on the air and sank. The wheels touched softly and the aircraft settled on the grass.

She held her breath as Susie went over a couple of small bumps, but the undercarriage held and Ellie applied just a touch of brakes so as not to run out of room and slowly brought her to a halt.

She exhaled, her chin dropping to her chest, but then sirens brought her back to her senses and she looked up to see several vehicles, including an ambulance, screaming towards her at full tilt. She belted the quick release catch on her chest harder than she needed to do, almost winding herself, then stood and climbed out of the cockpit. Not trusting her legs she sat and slid on her bum down the wing, then dropped to the ground. She landed heavily on all fours, then crawled a couple of yards away before finally allowing herself to collapse. She rolled on her back, closed her eyes and tried very hard not to break down.

'You alright, ma'am?'

Ellie opened her eyes to find an old gentleman in a white smock looking down at her in concern.

'Yes, thank you,' she croaked after a few seconds of summoning enough moisture in her mouth to speak, 'I'm just taking a moment.'

'Right you are, ma'am.' He gestured to the side. 'We'll give you a lift to the base when you're ready.'

'Thank you.'

The man nodded and disappeared from her sight, leaving just empty blue sky. However, her view was obstructed again in just a few seconds by Sergeant McIlroy.

'You alright, ma'am?'

Ellie laughed as the fitter asked the same question the man had with exactly the same tone and inflection. 'Yes, thank you.'

She sat up and looked over at the Spitsteam. A team of about twenty fitters were busy propping it up on a wooden frame so that it wouldn't fall and get damaged if the undercarriage gave way suddenly.

'What happened, do you think?' Ellie asked.

McIlroy scratched her head and pursed her lips. 'Well, I'm thinking some kind of obstruction, but...'

'But... *the curse*.' Ellie said in a dramatic voice, before waving her hand dismissively. 'If Susie was really cursed I wouldn't have gotten down. Instead I've had my first real fright of the war and survived.' She considered a moment then smiled. 'Actually, I've probably learnt more about myself during this emergency than I ever have before.'

She stood up and brushed herself down before looking at the aircraft again. 'Will she be ready to fly again next time I go up?'

McIlroy looked at her in surprise. 'You still want her after what just happened?'

'Of course!'

The woman smiled. 'We'll see what we can do, ma'am!'

24

Tay and Rob made a big deal of Ellie's mishap after the ambulance had dropped her off at the ready room, rushing out to meet her, then making her tell them all about it over the tea and biscuits they plied her with. Even Benedict listened with interest, becoming thoughtful when she finished.

Rob was his old self throughout. It seemed that either he had put aside his feelings at her and Tay going out, or else Tanya had been wrong about him and he'd been annoyed about something else. Whatever the case, it was one less thing to worry about and Ellie was almost as relieved at that as she had been to survive her emergency.

It was good that everything was back to normal, Rob thought as he went to get Ellie a second cup of tea. He'd missed his chance and that was that. Yes, he was desperately disappointed, but it wasn't worth becoming bitter and losing the two best friends he'd ever had.

He put a pile of biscuits on a plate and took everything back to the table, pretending not to notice when Tay and Ellie pulled back from each other slightly at his approach and smiling, even as he pushed the hurt away.

Aside from a single, very brief, assessing look, Drake made no mention of the incident and just proceeded with the briefing for the next flight as if nothing had happened.

'Sounds like you all had a lot of fun dogfighting, but we're going to step away from that for the next flight. Don't worry, we'll be going back to it later this week if the weather holds, but I like to give new arrivals a taste of most, if not all of what they have to expect on their first proper day of flying.' He smiled at them. 'So now we're going to go and have a look at those mountains I showed you yesterday. A much closer look.'

He pointed to the wall on one side of him. It was covered in maps of all types and all scales. There were ones of Europe which were updated every so often to show the current tactical situation of the war, there were several showing the Kingdom of Great Britain, marked up with things like RAC bases and Prussian targets, and there were a couple of Wales and the local area, one of which had a thin red line marked on it, describing a rough circle. It was to this one he was pointing.

'I'm sure you've all had a look at that, but you're not going to learn the Loop by looking at a map. You'll learn it by flying it. You'll go through twice this morning - it's only twenty miles or so, so you'll have plenty of tension for that. The first time you'll do it fairly sedately and at about five hundred feet, but the second time you'll do it a bit quicker and lower. Nothing too strenuous today, though, so that you can get used to the route rather than worry about the rocks. Once you've done the Loop a few more times, then we can start pushing things a bit, but *not today*.'

He emphasised the last couple of words and looked directly at Tanya, who gave him an innocent smile.

'A button.' Ellie said, holding up the offending item between her thumb and forefinger. It was scratched and chipped, with a piece missing, by it was still recognisably from an RAC coverall. It even had a few blue threads still hanging from it. 'That's what caused all that trouble?'

'Yes, ma'am. It got caught in the gear mechanism and the spring didn't have enough power to dislodge it. The manual release works on pneumatic pressure and was able to force it out into the wheel well.'

'And that's it? Susie is airworthy again?'

'Yes, ma'am. Unless you'd like us to give her a full service to make sure?'

'No, no, no!' Ellie said, shaking her head. 'That's not necessary.' She smiled. 'Thank you for offering, though.'

'Ma'am.' McIlroy nodded and went off to join her team, who were still fussing over the Spitsteam, even though everything necessary had already been done.

Tanya had been hovering nearby, waiting for Ellie to finish with McIlroy and she wandered over now and looked her up and down. 'You look different. More confident.' She nodded appreciatively. 'Good for you. So,' she asked, after making sure that Drake wasn't anywhere near. 'Would you like to take it easy this flight?'

Ellie smiled at her. 'What do you think?'

Drake caught the look between the two women and shook his head. He sighed; a part of him desperately wanted to separate them, to stop them from doing stupidly dangerous things every time they went up into the air, but that was only a very small part of him. The rest of him understood that flying was risky, that flying during wartime was even riskier, that to coddle the pilots now would only mean they would die faster later and that the only way to allow a pilot as brilliant as Eleanor Perkins reach her full potential was to take her to her limits and let her carry herself beyond.

That didn't make it any easier, though, and every time he watched her go up he knew he faced the very real possibility that she wouldn't come back. That *neither* of the two women would come back.

Perkins was a special case, though. A one in a million talent. The vast majority of trainee pilots needed a very different approach.

He looked up and down the line of Spitsteams, where his instructors and their students were starting their preflight checks.

This lot was coming along rather nicely.

His eyes settled on Sherborne, who was very thoroughly checking his aircraft, trailing his fingertips over the glossy paintwork on the smooth Duralumin panels with a faint smile on his face.

Very nicely indeed, actually.

Tayler rushed through his checks as quickly as he could and signed off for the aircraft, but when he looked over at Aviator Lieutenant Brunel the frustrating woman hadn't even finished walking around her Spit yet.

It wasn't that she wasn't a good pilot, because she was, amazing in fact - she was an ace a couple of times over and had survived some of the toughest air battles of the war - it was just that she didn't show it, didn't teach him how to do what she could and didn't even allow him to try anything new. To cap it all off they were always the last up.

He couldn't see how the woman could possibly be the right instructor for him, but there was nothing he could do about it. He was stuck with her, unless he complained to Drake.

He kept hoping that things would change, that she would loosen up, but no such luck, at least not that flight, because once again they were the last up. As a consequence they were the last to arrive at the mountains and had had to circle, waiting until the pair before, Benedict and Squadron Leader Niven, were a safe distance into the Loop. Wasting precious spring tension.

'Alright, Two,' Brunel said eventually, 'our turn. Follow half a mile behind me and do what I do.'

'Roger, Leader,' Tayler replied, eyeing the gap in the mountains he'd seen the others fly through with anticipation. This was something that Brunel wouldn't be able to take the fun out of.

He was wrong and his frustration only grew as he followed her through the Loop at precisely the stipulated two hundred and fifty miles per hour and five hundred feet. It was as good as flying in an empty sky, with the valley walls so far away that he wouldn't be in any danger even if he closed his eyes and had a nap.

If he'd stayed this safe when he was crop spraying the liquid would have gone everywhere - he'd had to get right down on the ground, close enough to clip the leaves off hedges and trees as he went past. No matter what Drake had said, how would this ever make him a better pilot?

Just as well he had something, or rather someone, to look forward to when he got down, because at that moment flying wasn't something to look forward to.

Derek kept his eye on the other Spitsteam in the mirror over his head as they started on their second circuit around the Loop, but he didn't expect anything untoward, especially not with how easy they were taking things. Especially not with how good the boy was. And the boy *was* a good pilot. A *very* good one. There was no doubting that. But he still wasn't sure whether that was because the boy had talent or was just more experienced than the other new pilots he'd had under his wing recently and therefore more comfortable in a cockpit.

It was too soon to tell, especially with how Rudy had asked him to handle the first few days of training, but he had a good feeling and at the very least the boy would make a valuable addition to a fighter squadron.

They were half an hour into their lunch break, eating their main course in the busy officers' mess, and Ellie's legs were still shaking.

The flight through the mountains hadn't been nearly as stressful on her body as the dogfighting had been, but it had been far more nerve-racking. She had been on edge the whole time, rolling from wingtip to wingtip to get around a few tight corners, watching the walls of the valleys race past her wings, seemingly only inches away, all while at the same time having to worry about not ploughing into the ground, which had only been a few dozen feet below her at times. It was just as well Tanya was leading the way and showing her where the turns were, because if she'd had to worry about that as well she might have been in real trouble.

However, even though she was exhausted, both mentally and physically, she was very happy with how the morning had gone and it looked like Benedict and Rob were too - Benedict was at a table on his own across the room, flicking through a manual as he shovelled food enthusiastically into his mouth, while Rob was stuffing his face while speaking animatedly with Squadron Leader Drake. Tay, on the other hand, looked anything but happy; despite the fact that they had managed to get a table for two and had a modicum of time to themselves he was just slouching in his seat, sulking, picking at his food and barely even looking at her. She'd made a couple of attempts to speak to him, but beyond a few mumbled answers to her questions he'd remained silent.

There was probably something she could say or do to cheer him up, but she just didn't have the energy to think of anything, so she was just trying to get through the meal as best as possible, force down and keep down as much food as she could in a stomach that seemed to be rebelling against the idea, and get back up into the air. Perhaps the afternoon's flights would lighten Tay's mood and they might both be better company over a good dinner.

'Ellie!' A hand came down on Ellie's shoulder, startling her, and she looked up to find Tanya smiling down at her. 'Excellent work this morning. I hope you had fun, because I certainly did! Keep it up!'

Ellie watched her bouncing over to Drake's table, full of energy and unaffected by the strenuous activity of the last few hours and found a smile on her face. That morning *had* been fun. Extremely hard work, but *such* a lot of fun and well worth a few aching muscles.

That was something she could say to cheer Tay up, actually. That no matter what was happening now, no matter how hard or boring or frustrating or dangerous it was, it was worth it because they were flying bloody *Spitsteams*!

She leaned across the table, put her hand on Tay's and gave him the biggest smile she could when he looked up at her.

25

Rob peered up into the sky for what seemed like the thousandth time that flight. The enemy were up there somewhere, they had to be. The trouble was he couldn't see them. Who would have thought that it would be so hard to see something as big as a fighter aircraft in an empty sky without even a cloud to hide in?

'Keep up your scanning Two.'

'Roger, Leader,' Rob replied, grimacing as he realised that he'd just been staring up at nothing instead of scanning the whole sky around him - the enemy could have been flying right next to him and he would never have known it. Or anything else ever again.

He went back to his scan, taking in the horizon before tilting his head back to scan above him, finishing the circle, then starting again. Drake had said it would become automatic eventually, but for now it was just giving him a headache.

So far you've just been swanning around, having fun, but now we're going to act like there might be an enemy in the sky with you. And I'm going to put one there!

It had sounded like fun in the briefing.

Two pairs of instructors and students would go up together and they would take it in turns to run interceptions on the other pair, who would keep a look out, but otherwise act dumb and fly straight and level, like bombers. The aim was to practice not just the interception itself, but deflection shooting as well, under the practised eye of the instructor, before they starting using live ammunition against towed targets later on in the week.

In reality, though, it was anything but fun. At least, not playing the victim, anyway. He was hoping it would be different when they changed roles. At least then...

There!

'Bandits at three o'clock high!' he called excitedly.

'Well done.' Drake drawled. 'Would you like me to tell you how long ago I spotted them?'

Rob winced, then grinned across the gap at Drake, who was acting as his wingman for the exercise. 'It's not a competition, sir!'

'Right, so we'll be attacking almost completely side on, which means you're going to have to lead the target by a lot, not just when you shoot, but also when you begin your dive, otherwise they're going to get ahead of you and you'll end up having to chase after them.'

Tay rolled his eyes, but made sure to hide his exasperation when he answered. 'Yes, ma'am.'

They'd covered deflection shooting in training, watching specially filmed movies demonstrating it and going through the motions using models. Just because he'd never actually done it in real life, didn't mean he didn't know how.

'Alright, then. Dive when ready.'

'Roger, Leader. Tally ho!'

Tay grinned and stood the Spitsteam on its wing, pulling hard to swing the nose round towards his prey.

He was running the show for this flight and that meant he finally had the chance to show Brunel that she didn't need to keep mollycoddling him.

'Bandits. Eight o'clock.'

'What? I don't...' Squadron Leader Niven started. 'Wait, got them. Good eyes, Two.'

'Thank you, Leader.' Benedict smiled smugly. His instructors had had him scanning the sky for the last couple of years, even though they'd known there was nothing there to see. "Good practice" they'd called it and he'd agreed, knowing that it was a skill that would come in handy later and could very well keep him alive.

He hadn't spotted the bandits because he had good eyes, he'd spotted them because he wasn't an ordinary novice pilot. And sooner or later they'd see that and give him the credit he deserved.

'Ratatatata!' Rob transmitted, as he'd been instructed, letting Drake know when he'd be shooting. He pulled up as soon as he'd finished loosing a three second burst, losing sight of Benedict's Spitsteam as it flashed under his nose at almost four hundred miles per hour.

'Not bad, Two,' Drake said, 'pretty good direction as far as I could see, but you're still opening fire a tad too soon. Don't worry, though; it's an incredibly hard thing to judge and with the cannons on these new models you'll probably still get a kill. But if you judge it right that means you need less shots to do the job, which means you'll have more ammunition left over to shoot more Prussians. Which is why we're here, in the end!'

Rob nodded. 'Understood, Leader.'

He did understand. Completely. When he'd "opened fire" he'd somehow known that he was doing so too soon again, but he had done so anyway, because he hadn't wanted to risk a collision, and had had plenty of time to pull up in the end, even going so fast.

Even in failure, no, *especially* in failure, he could learn and next time he'd do better.

'Wait... wait... wait... Open fire now! Bring the stick back slowly... keep firing... and... pull up, pull up, pull up!'

Ellie brought the stick back into her lap at Tanya's command and was crushed into her seat as Susie pulled out of her death dive. Only when the ground was no longer filling her vision and she was absolutely positive that she wasn't going to hit it did she take a breath.

She shuddered. For the first time ever she was not enjoying herself in the cockpit. Quite the opposite in fact.

Going through the Loop had been frightening, but at the same time it had been dreadfully exciting. Running interceptions on Tay had been an exercise in judgement and had felt more like work than play, but had ultimately been an enjoyable challenge.

This... This was just plain terrifying.

Alright, Drake had said in the briefing before this, their fourth flight of the day, *ground attack. This is one of the least enjoyable and most dangerous of all the activities you might be called upon to carry out as a fighter pilot. It is very much a learned ability, it won't come naturally to most of you, so don't worry if you don't get it right the first time. Or the second...*

'Come on, Ellie!' Guseva said wearily as she slotted in on her wing, a disappointed note in her voice. 'This is *very* basic stuff! The easy version! But if you can't get it right we can't move on to doing it properly...' she sighed. 'Alright, let's go around again.'

'Yes, ma'am.' Ellie cringed at the thought of doing the exercise again, but nonetheless swung her aircraft into a gentle loop in order to approach the firing range again for another strafing run.

Tay's grin widened as he pushed the nose over and dived, beginning his run. He pulled up only feet from the ground where the people in the airbase wouldn't be able to see him and the anti-aircraft guns defending it couldn't aim at him. A small hop and he was over the fence and lined up on the wooden targets simulating a row of parked aircraft.

'Bang bang bang!' He kept firing, gently lifted the nose of his spit to rake the entire line before hurtling over them and leaving them behind. He flashed over the fence on the other side of the airfield and swerved from side to side a few times, making sure that any random small arms fire wouldn't find him before the surrounding trees covered him, then finally allowed himself to relax.

'Excellent work, Oakley!'

'Damn right!' He shouted, after first making sure the radio channel was closed. Now *this* was more like it!

'Alright!' Drake said as he slid into a chair at the big table with them while they were filling out their log books, 'that was your introduction to DARTS. Over the next couple of weeks you'll expand on what we've only really touched on yesterday and today. You'll spend time perfecting your aerobatics and getting to know your aircraft. You'll do plenty more dogfighting to develop the instincts you're going to need. You'll continue to run interceptions, working up to using live ammunition against towed targets. You'll do more strafing runs and start to use live ammunition on the range. And you'll run the Loop a good few more times until you can do it at full speed in your sleep. You'll work with your instructors to start with, like you've done up until now, but when they are happy with your progress you'll pair up for exercises. You'll work together as wingmates and start to develop those skills you'll need in combat to support each other and keep each other alive.' He grinned at them. 'It's not going to be all fun and games, though, because there's that little matter of your officer exams. I've scheduled them for Monday, so you'll have all of your day off on Sunday to swot up for them, but I'm sure they will just be a formality.'

He chuckled at the dismay on their faces, but then turned serious. 'I'm not going to sugar coat it for you - we are going to push you and we're going to push you *hard,* but ultimately it's going to be up to *you* whether you reach your full potential or not. You all have more than enough talent to become truly excellent fighter pilots, but you won't. Not unless you push yourselves *just* as hard.'

He stood up. 'That is all. See you at dinner.'

He gave them a nod, then made his way out, accompanied by Tanya and followed closely by Niven and Brunel. The pilots looked at each other, then by unspoken agreement bent back over their logbooks.

There was a new bounce in Tay's step as he, Rob and Ellie went back to their rooms together and Ellie patted him on the arm, a gesture she thought would satisfy her need for physical contact while not making it too obvious that she needed it. 'You look a lot happier!'

'Of course I bloody am! Ground attack! Haven't I always said that's what I want to do?' he winked at her. 'It's not just me, though; everyone looks a lot happier. Even Rob!'

Tay put his arm around Rob's shoulder, but he slipped away and ran forwards a couple of paces, then turned, walking backwards in front of them.

'Don't forget to wear your dress uniform!' he said. 'We don't want Sergeant Hughes staring and huffing at us in disapproval all evening again.'

Tay chuckled. 'No. We do not!'

They had arrived at their barracks building by now and Rob hurried ahead of them along the corridor and shut himself in his room. Ellie and Tay held back, though. They stopped outside Ellie's door and Tay turned to smile at her.

'See you soon.'

Ellie smiled back. 'See you soon.'

She reached out to him and he took her hand gently in his. She could have held it forever, but there was too much to do, so she just gave it a slight squeeze, then turned and went into her room.

She shut the door, then leaned back against it, smiling.

She couldn't be more happy or excited to be at the start of something with Tay. She had no idea what to expect, no idea what she should really be doing, but it was fun to learn and work it out as she went along. Almost as fun as it had been learning to fly and as it was to work out new things with Tanya.

She had already worked out her next move for that night, for instance, and she hurried to her wardrobe and started setting out her dress uniform, making sure that it was pressed properly - even though they now had servicemen and women who did it for them, she still liked to make sure her clothes were up to her own standards. Then she stood on tiptoes and rooted around on the shelf at the top of the wardrobe where she'd put her personal items, finally finding the small canvas bag she'd been looking for hiding right at the back.

Finally she had the opportunity to wear some of the makeup she'd bought in the NAACI shop at Gwynedd. She just hoped she remembered what Sandra had taught her and didn't make a mess of putting it on; she wanted to look her best for Tay and for the first time she wore her dress uniform as an officer in the Royal Aviator Corps.

26

Over the next few days the weather held, for the most part anyway. There were a couple of days when there was rain and mist in the mountains and they couldn't use the Loop, but otherwise, aside from some early morning mist, visibility was good enough to fly and they began to use live rounds both on a towed drone and on the ground attack range. Predictably, Tayler got the best scores in ground attack, but Ellie was not far behind, having gotten over her early fears through sheer bloody-mindedness. She also got top marks against the drone, but it was Rob who was close behind her in that.

They were worked just as hard as Drake had said they would be and they finished each day absolutely exhausted, with barely enough energy even to dress and get themselves to dinner, and once they'd eaten all they could do was stagger back to their rooms and collapse in their beds. Tay and Ellie had no chance to be alone and do anything to develop their relationship further beyond snatch a few more kisses and hold hands when nobody was looking.

But then it was Sunday and the air base in its entirety closed down for operations. They were advised by Drake to have a lie in and a late breakfast, something they were now allowed to do on Sunday, duties permitting, and that was what they did, wandering into the mess at about nine to partake of the remains of the buffet.

Benedict took his usual seat at one of the small tables against the far wall meant for those dining alone or desiring to be left alone.

The night that he'd been snubbed by Lord Drake he'd made the decision to stop trying to play nice with his classmates. It had made sense when they were so dependent on each other during basic training and he'd made an effort afterwards because of Sandra, but now that they were once again working on their own it didn't. He much preferred to study rather than waste time with idle chit-chat anyway and it would serve him far better in the long run.

He opened his book - the officers' manual that morning, of course - at the place kept by the letter he'd received from Sandra a couple of days before, feeling slightly guilty that he hadn't gotten around to writing a reply yet. He propped it up on a rolled up napkin and held it open with one hand while he ate with the other.

He dipped a soldier in his soft boiled egg, taking care to push it down slowly so that it didn't make the yellow liquid within spill over the edge before the bread had had time to absorb it and lower the level. Satisfied with the payload it had on board, he bent over it to put it into his mouth, not wanting to have to carry it too far and risk accidentally dropping anything before it got to the target. The mission was a success and he chewed contentedly as he straightened back up, but then started, jerking backwards in his seat and almost choking when he found Aviator Lieutenant Guseva's face about six inches from his.

'I don't like you,' the woman started without any preamble, 'but that is alright. Not many people like me and that is alright as well. Respect, though, respect is very important. *I* am respected, but you...' She picked up one of his soldiers and thrust it into his second egg, making him wince as the yolk cascaded down the side of the egg cup. 'You are not respected and you will not *be* respected if you continue to act like this.' She stuffed the bread in her mouth and spoke around it as she chewed. 'Without respect orders get questioned, there is hesitation in carrying them out and then people die.' She picked up another piece of bread and waved it around vaguely. 'This is not how to gain respect.'

She dipped the bread, then stood and wandered away without saying another word.

Benedict watched her steal food from a few more people's plates as she worked her way to the buffet. Despite her youth, Tatiana Guseva had been through a lot, even if you only believed half of the things that were said about her in the papers and magazines, and her opinions and advice was not to be taken lightly. The problem was she hadn't been very specific, but he was fairly sure that when she said this wasn't the way to gain respect she wasn't only talking about him having breakfast alone.

He looked over to where Tayler, Rob and Ellie were having breakfast together. It pained him to have to not just be civil, but friendly with the others, but perhaps he should make another effort. One smart remark from Tayler and he couldn't be held accountable for his response, though.

However... He smiled and looked down at his book. Perhaps he didn't have to be nice or friendly, perhaps an offer to help with material he had known back to front for years might garner some gratitude and earn him just a little bit of that respect that Guseva said he needed.

He gave the remains of his eggs, one gone cold and the other desecrated, a wistful look, then closed his book and stood. If he wasn't going to be able to enjoy his breakfast in peace he might as well make a start.

'So, you've got chapters one, two, five, eight, nine, ten, fifteen and sixteen,' Benedict said, reading from his notes, 'those are the bits you need to really know. The rest you can just skim through and have a notion of, just in case one of the examiners in the oral exam wants to try to trick you, but apart from a few rules and regulations specifically for officers...'

'Like wearing dress uniforms for the evening meal?' Ellie asked dryly.

'Yes,' Benedict said, blushing slightly, but not looking up, 'like that. But, as I was saying, apart from those rules, most of the rest is either common sense or an extension of what we had to learn already in Basic.'

'How do you know all this?' Tayler asked sceptically.

'Because my instructors were all RAC officers. My father is an RAC officer.' He held up the officers' manual. 'And I've read the book from cover to cover half a dozen times.'

The four of them were sprawled on the grass at the edge of the field beyond the hangars where they had ridden the springcycles. A cricket game had been going on on the field since earlier that morning and they had decided to sit in the sun and spectate while they studied.

It was extremely pleasant and far more relaxing than watching any of the other activities, like the raucous massed springcycle dogfight that was taking place on the other side of the airfield, or the men and women that were racing the unmodified springcycles over the nearby hills. Trestle tables had been set up with tea and snacks, there were a few deck chairs, mostly taken by senior officers, and the fitters had brought out a wireless and tuned it to the KBC. They'd listened to Princess Elizabeth's morning address, then the news - it didn't seem that much had changed in the world while they'd been essentially cut off from it for a month, the invasion fleet was still parked across the channel for some reason and the Muscovites were still hanging on - and now it was playing music.

Ellie looked down at her book, trying for the fourth time to read the eighth chapter, which was all about codes of conduct and behaviour while in uniform, but she found her attention wandering the whole time. However, while her gaze kept going to the hangars and the tantalising sight of Susie, her nose poking into the sunshine as her team of fitters clambered over her - they had decided to use some of their day off to give her a good check - others were more distracted by things that were closer to hand.

'Rob!' she hissed, poking him in the ribs.

'Eh? What?' Rob mumbled, turning his head towards her, without really taking his eyes off the game.

'You're supposed to be studying!'

'Uhuh.' he said, patting the book on his lap. 'I am,'

The fact that the book was closed gave the lie to his claim and Ellie followed his gaze out onto the cricket field, wondering what had so interested him. He didn't seem to be following the game as a whole, but rather watching someone in particular and she thought that maybe he was interested in a girl. She was just in time to catch the bowler tossing one down the pitch at what seemed like an incredible speed to her. She could barely see the ball, so fast was it going, but the batter had no problem apparently, she just stepped into it and swung, knocking it flying back over the bowler's head and clear off the large field.

'Good shot!' Rob shouted. He applauded enthusiastically, as did the couple of dozen other people who had come to watch and the batter turned to acknowledge the praise, flashing a very familiar grin.

'Tanya plays cricket?' Ellie asked incredulously. 'I didn't know they played cricket in Muscovy.'

'They don't,' Squadron Leader Niven said, coming up to stand next to them. He was dressed in hiking gear, complete with a Tyrolean hat with a blue feather in it. 'She started playing after we got to Wales, less than a month ago.' He shook his head in wonder as she belted another ball through the covers. 'If you think her batting is impressive, then you should see her bowl.' He looked down at them. 'Any of you twitchers?' he asked hopefully.

'Afraid not, sir.' Benedict said, shaking his head, answering for all of them.

'Oh, well, that's not to be helped, I suppose, but do bear in mind there is still some excellent walking in these hills, even if you're not interested in the wildlife. We'll be going out again next week and you're all more than welcome.'

'Thank you, sir.' Ellie smiled up at him.

He nodded, then wandered off.

'Owzat!' A huge shout came from the players and they all looked over as there was a cheer and they started coming off the pitch.

'What happened?' Ellie asked. 'Did they win? Is Tanya out?'

Tay laughed. 'That's just the end of the first innings. And no, Tanya finished the innings forty-three not out. She just ran out of partners.' He began to stand up.

'Where are you going?' Ellie asked.

'It's time for tea. Anyone else fancy one?'

'We've just finished breakfast!'

Tay shrugged. 'You can never have too much tea and I need a break from all this studying.'

'We've only just started! And it's not as if you were doing much anyway.'

He shrugged again and gave her one of his grins, then turned and sauntered away towards where a couple of trestle tables had been set up with food and drink for players and spectators alike, his hands deep in the pockets of his day uniform trousers.

Ellie scowled. Once again Tay wasn't taking things seriously.

'Typical Tay.' Rob said, shaking his head before looking down at his book.

Ellie couldn't help but agree with him. Tay was charming and funny and handsome, but there were things about him that she really didn't like sometimes and his lack of seriousness about his flying and his career was one of them. Especially since they all thought he'd turned over a new leaf at Gwynedd. He'd started drinking again too. Not nearly as much as before and not nearly enough to affect his flying, but still.

Perhaps if he failed his officer's exam and had to retake it that would force him to reassess his situation, but, knowing Tay, he'd end up scraping through as always. She just hoped he'd buck up his ideas again before it came back to bite him.

Tayler didn't buck up his ideas in the slightest. Not that day, anyway. After the cricket ended in a rout for Tanya's team when she destroyed the batting order, taking six wickets for only eleven runs, he swanned around the base, observing the various other activities available and generally doing anything except studying. The others didn't let that bother them too much, beyond a few attempts by Ellie to convince him that he should do something productive, and the day passed by rather pleasantly. They had a nice roast lunch, a decent supper, a couple of drinks to relax, then got an early night.

'Alright, everyone got a dri...?'
Drake trailed off as he watched Tanya tipping her pint glass to the ceiling, the glass that he had only handed to her a few seconds before, filled with the strong beer she liked. She shook it over her mouth, catching the last few drops, before slamming it onto the bar.
'Another pint for Aviator Lieutenant Guseva, please, Corporal Jones,' he said to the woman behind the bar, wincing as Tanya breathed a long belch before sighing contentedly.
The pint was quickly replaced and he gave Tanya a scathing look. '*Now* has everyone got a drink?'
She shrugged. 'For now.'
'Good.'
He led the small group of instructors over to the table Sergeant Hughes prepared for these weekly meetings with a few snacks and the most comfortable chairs. There was a reserved sign on it, but it wasn't needed; it was after nine and at that time of night on a Sunday there was barely anyone in the mess, just four of the older career officers who worked in administration getting their nightcaps.
'Well,' he said, settling back in his chair comfortably and tossing his notebook on the table, 'I have a fairly good idea of how it's going, but I want to hear it from all of you. Who wants to start?'
Tanya was in mid swig, but she grunted and waved her hand, indicating that she did. She didn't lower the glass until she had drained more than half of it, though, and took the time to wipe her mouth on the back of her hand before speaking.
'Ellie is good. Chastity good. Maybe Gwen or Abby good. But she needs experience.'
She licked her lips, then lifted her glass to take another drink.
'In what way...?' Drake began, but she cut him off immediately with another grunt and a lifted hand.

'I haven't finished,' she said bluntly, glaring at him over her drink before pointedly lifting it again.

Drake blinked, mildly surprised; Tanya had never been particularly enthusiastic about any of her students. She had done well by them, that wasn't in any doubt, they always ended the fortnight far better than when they started and usually came out near the top of their class, but she had never gotten particularly caught up in their training, or invested on a personal level. It seemed that Perkins had changed that and changed it considerably.

'She needs more *bad* experiences.' Tanya said as soon as she'd drained her glass. 'She only began flying a month ago and so far it has all been fairy tales and pony rides. All the fun of the fair. She has only ever seen the good side, from the moment she went up. She has not had to struggle with anything, she hasn't ever not been able to do something. She struggled with ground attack for all of two runs, then,' she slammed her hand on the table for emphasis, making the glasses and the old officers across the room jump, 'bang! Perfect runs one after the other.' She shook her head. 'The one time something went wrong, when she had that emergency, did you see her after landing?'

She looked around the group, who shook their heads. 'We've all had close runs, crash landed, been shot up, any number of things and we know how shaken up we were after some of them, but not like she was, she was bad. Very bad. But then she shook it off, took it in, buried it,' she thumped her chest with a fist. 'It is still there, though, and if she doesn't get used to the fact that flying is not just a wonderful dream where she can do what she want, then the first really bad thing that happens she is going to lose her mind. And we will lose her.'

'Are you saying we should sabotage her aircraft?' Derek asked after a moment of stunned silence as the instructors took in what had to have been the longest speech they had ever heard the Muscovite make.

Tanya snorted. 'No. Anything like that she will deal with. Now that she's had one emergency, she'll deal with any others that occur with a smile.' She grimaced. 'I just don't *know* what she needs. And I'm not sure *we* can provide it.'

She looked around the group again, almost pleading with them to have some kind of idea, but when none of them did she just shrugged. 'That is just my opinion, though, my feeling. I might turn out to be wrong.' She waved a hand in dismissal. 'Perkins is one of the best pilots I've ever seen. No problems. I'm very happy. Top marks. Blah blah. I need another drink. Keep talking, I'll be able to hear.'

She stood and stalked away to the bar.

The instructors watched her go, then turned as one to look at Drake, who could only shrug.

'Who's next?'

'How are we supposed to follow that?' Lieutenant Brunel muttered under her breath to quiet chuckles from the rest.

'Derek,' Drake said. 'Why don't you give it a try?'

Derek took a sip of his wine, considering his words carefully before beginning. 'Aside from none of them being birdwatchers or having any taste in wine, I quite like this group. They are certainly not as obnoxious as some we've had and we've only had a few mild ego problems, which bodes well for their survival when they finally get into combat.'

There were nods of agreement and he smiled and used the opportunity to take another sip of his wine.

'As for Officer Wilberforce. According to Jocelyn Green, he came to her one of those most dangerous of breeds - a pilot who thought he knew everything and had nothing to learn. Once she managed to disavow him of that, his morale was almost completely destroyed, but she and one of the pilots they left behind in Gwynedd managed to build him up again. However, in the absence of that influence, the pilot's, not Jocelyn's, he has been in real danger of regression, only kept in check by the methods that Squadron Leader Drake and I devised. The arrogance is lurking inside him, though, as, I suspect, it is within all members of the aristocracy, with their feelings of entitlement. However well they might hide it.'

'Too true,' muttered Tanya around her third pint, drinking it even as she walked back to her chair.

'What? What?' Lord Drake blustered in a gruff voice, frowning exaggeratedly and pouting comically. 'I'll have you whipped for that, you blighter!'

'Exactly,' Derek said, smiling over his wine. 'Bloody toff.'

He took another sip, then put his glass down. 'Anyway. When Wilberforce forgets everything and just flies he is extremely good, but as soon as he starts thinking he becomes only ordinary. It really is remarkable how easy it is to spot what kind of mood he is in, like watching some kind of aerial production of Jekyll and Hyde. The trick will be to keep him in the right mood and I have no idea how to do that without bringing his girlfriend up and sticking her on his lap every flight.'

'I'm sure he wouldn't object,' Drake said, 'but it's hardly practical or a long-term solution.' He made some notes. 'I'll have a think.' He looked at Brunel. 'Vicky, how are you handling Officer Oakley?'

'The short answer is that I'm not, I'm afraid. He has moments of brilliance, interspersed with moments of what I can only describe as sheer idiocy as he throws himself headlong into whatever he does without thinking first. I haven't been able to instil any discipline in him and at this stage I don't think I'll ever be able to. The last time it apparently took an ultimatum from Sherborne to buck him up, but the two of them don't seem to be on the best of terms at the moment, so I'm not sure that's going to be on the cards this time. Maybe Perkins will be able to provide a steadying influence, but the two of them look rather besotted at the moment and we all know how that tends to make people even bigger idiots than they already are.'

'Quite,' Drake said. He tapped his notebook thoughtfully with his pencil. 'Hopefully he'll settle down eventually, otherwise he'll never not need to be kept an eye on and he'll never lead a flight, no matter how talented and he won't ever be fully trusted by a wingmate. Perhaps after today's performance on the range he might be better suited, and indeed more comfortable, in a ground attack role anyway, but we shall have to see.'

He made a note then looked up. 'And last, but not least - Officer Sherborne is a truly excellent pilot, maybe not quite as good as Chastity, Gwen, or Abby...'

'Or me,' Tanya muttered without lifting her head from a fresh pint that had appeared somehow.

'Or Tanya,' Drake conceded with a smile, 'but he's certainly as good as me. The trouble is he doesn't believe it, so his performance is worse than it should be. He is an intelligent man, though, and I'm sure he'll figure it out on his own soon enough, especially if we give him the chance and a few hints.'

Drake looked around the group, smiling wryly. 'What a fine bunch we have here. Every single one of them has the potential to be a brilliant pilot, but every single one of them also has a fatal flaw that may or may not prevent them from being one.'

'Sounds rather familiar, actually.' Derek said.

Drake chuckled. 'Yes, it's almost as if ordinary, sane people don't make good fighter pilots.'

There was gentle laughter at that and he tapped his pencil on his notebook thoughtfully while he waited for the inevitable joking to die down.

'Alright. It sounds to me that we've gone just about as far as we can, one on one, so, we'll have a last flight or two tomorrow afternoon to work on a few last things, but, starting Tuesday, I'd like to start pairing them up. If Perkins needs bringing down to earth then I'll stick her with Oakley, that should do the trick, and hopefully she'll provide him with a good example to aspire to. Wilberforce...' he chuckled and made a note, 'I have a plan for, and as for Sherborne, I'm sure he'll catch on to how good he is eventually, especially once he's been in the air with Wilberforce a few days.' He looked around again. 'Any objections?' When nobody said anything he nodded. 'That is all, then, thank you everyone. Have a good night.'

He stood and leaned down to kiss Tanya on the top of the head. 'I'll be back soon. I have a call to make.'

She smiled up at him and nodded, but he frowned when she went straight back to her drink and didn't say anything.

He was fairly sure that all she needed was a little bit of reassurance that he would take care of Perkins, but it would have to wait; a commander had to put their job and the people under him first. Personal life always had to come later.

Drake held Tanya's hand under cover of the darkness as they went for their usual stroll around the perimeter track to wind down before bed. They never usually talked very much during their walk unless they were planning something for their time off, instead just using the time to be with each other as far away from everything as they could get. With the blackout in force they couldn't even see the base and they could almost put the war and their jobs out of their minds for a while.

That was impossible tonight, though.

Tanya had been all smiles when he'd returned to the mess, but it had been obvious that it was just for show and there was an unusual stiffness to her now as she walked beside him, a tension in her hand.

He was worried. Not about the amount she was drinking, because as a Muscovite she had been weaned on vodka so beer was as good as water to her, no, he was concerned because she never drank like this unless there was something really bothering her. And there hadn't been anything that had bothered her this much since Malta and the Misfits had started dying.

'What happens to Perkins means that much to you?' he asked softly into the silence.

She grunted her "yes" grunt.

'Why? What makes her different from all the other pilots who've passed through here?'

Tanya grunted again.

She hadn't needed to see the scars, the remnants of the past injuries, that none of the others had noticed to know everything she needed to know about Ellie's past. She wasn't like Sausage Boy, she didn't come from a childhood of princesses and palaces and ponies and would melt if she ever came face to face with the harsh reality of life, she came from hardship and pain and loneliness. You could see it in her posture, in the way she flinched sometimes at a sudden noise without even realising, in the way her nails were bitten completely down - she was prey and they were asking her to act like a predator. It was getting easier for her every day - the further she got from the past and the more she built up herself up the more this version of her became real. But at the moment she was perched on a tower of cards, not the solid foundation she would have someday, and she would fall a long way if the cold wind came too soon.

'Because she is different,' she said, in a low voice that was almost a growl.

'Alright, then, I'll assign you to watch over her and Oakley.'

'Thank you.'

27

They took their officer exams on Monday morning, doing the written part after breakfast and then being called in one by one for the oral part after midmorning tea. Unsurprisingly, they all passed, although Drake admitted later that Tayler had only scraped through by the skin of his teeth.

Flying resumed that afternoon and they were paired up with the instructors as usual, but they had a feeling that things were about to change when Drake called them to the ready room that evening.

'First off, congratulations, Aerial Officers. It's official now and no doubt you'll be very pleased to hear that your salary is now confirmed and won't need to be docked to its previous level.'

There was some chuckling from the instructors, but Tayler frowned; he hadn't thought that one of the consequences of not passing would be losing the rather generous pay rise from cadet to officer.

'You'll now be taking on the full duties and responsibilities of an officer in the Royal Aviator Corps, including serving as duty officer when it's your turn, but nothing much will actually change in your day to day life. What will be changing, though, is your training, because, starting tomorrow morning, you'll be flying in pairs - Sherborne as flight leader with Wilberforce and Perkins leading the other flight with Oakley. You will still be under the supervision of an instructor, but they will only shadow you, they will not interfere unless they deem it necessary. You will be given your assignments for each flight beforehand and it will be up to you to carry them out as you have done up until now with your instructor, but with one added complication - the instructors who aren't assigned to observe will be pairing up as well and they are going to bounce you every so often. They can do so whenever they want, with the only exceptions being on takeoff and landing, while you are running the Loop, or when you are on the ground attack range. Any other time, including when you are transiting to and from those areas, you are fair game. Once the initial attack has been made you will then have to fight them off, just as if they were Fleas.'

He grinned. 'And to make this even more interesting than it already is we will be running a competition. If you spot and avoid the initial attack you will get two points. If you lose the subsequent fight then that's alright, you won't be docked any points, but if you win you get a further four points. However, anyone who fails to spot their attackers until it's too late will be penalised a whole ten points. The winner will get a prize, but anyone ending in negative numbers will be penalised. Of course, if you all end up with negative points at the end of the week then nobody gets the prize.'

He looked at Squadron Leader Niven. 'This will be, what, the fourth time, fifth time we do this?'

'Fourth.'

Drake turned back to the group. 'The fourth time we run this competition and nobody has ever won the prize.'

'They all failed dismally.' Tanya put in, a rather bloodthirsty grin on her face. 'The Fleas got every. Single. One of them.'

'Quite.' Drake said, rolling his eyes and shaking his head. 'And on that note, dismissed!' He waited for everybody to stand and start making their way out, then called out. 'Perkins, a word, please.'

'Yes, sir!' Ellie had made it most of the way to the door and was just about to leave with Tay and Rob, but she stopped, gave Tay's arm a squeeze, then moved out of the way to let everyone pass.

Once they were alone, Drake made his way to the window and looked out to watch the other pilots go. Only when the sound of their voices had faded completely did he turn to smile at her.

'I wanted to talk to you about the pairings.'

'Yes, sir?'

'I'm sorry, but I couldn't help but notice that you and Oakley are involved. Now, ordinarily I wouldn't put you together, but I haven't had much of a choice. Both he and Wilberforce need stabilising influences at the moment and if Sherborne was going to be a stabilising influence on him he probably would have been one years ago. So, that leaves you, I'm afraid. I hope it won't be a problem.'

'I don't think it will be, sir.'

'Good. Good.' He smiled. 'Thank you. See you at dinner.'

Drake waited for the door to close behind Perkins before lifting his head and speaking to the room at large. 'What do you think?'

'I think you're learning. Finally.' Tanya said from behind him.

He turned and she stepped into his arms and sighed contentedly as she lay her cheek on his shoulder. After a moment she pulled back slightly.

'I think that you are a good person and a good teacher and that you are giving them the best chance to survive this war that they could possibly be given under the circumstances.'

'I just wish...'

'Shhh...' Tanya reached up to stroke his face, but said nothing more; they'd said everything that could be said so many times before and it did no good to lament the past, only to hope for a better future.

Officers who wanted to have a romantic assignation had the luxury of private quarters, but the go-to place for those who didn't was the field where they'd ridden the springcycles and where the cricket game had been held.

For such a small base it was remarkable just how many romances were going on, even just among the NCOs and lower ranks, and when Ellie and Tay wandered over they could make out at least a dozen shadowy clumps of figures spread out around the field. They went to the far right, to the shed where the springcycles were stored and spread their blanket on the grass and lay down. Ellie snuggled up to him and they looked up at the stars together in silence, listening to the sounds of the night, the calling of nocturnal birds, the occasional fox and the murmur of the other people around them.

Even though they were officers and had their own rooms, Ellie had insisted they come out there, not so much because the walls of their barracks block were quite thin, or that they didn't want to be seen by Rob going in and out of each other's room, but because she wasn't ready for Tay to see her scars, not in that way. Not that they'd done anything that had put her in any danger of him seeing them; he'd been very reserved, very gentlemanly, frustratingly so, actually, as she was more than ready to take things a step further. And there didn't seem to be much chance of anything happening that night either, because he seemed to be sulking. That wasn't anything new with Tay - he was up and down as much as a Sapworth Sprite in turbulence - but it was new that he didn't buck up as soon as he was alone with her. Which made her think she knew what was wrong.

'You're upset.'

'Mmm, what? No. What makes you say that?'

'Because I know you.'

Tay didn't say anything for a while, he just lay there, gently stroking her arm, but then he stiffened. 'Alright, yes. I am upset.'

'That I've been made your flight leader.'

'I wouldn't put it like that...'

'Would you have preferred Benedict?'

'No! Of course not! That would have been much worse!' he said, raising his voice uncomfortably in the quiet, before dropping it back to a whisper. 'I just don't want to have *anyone* as my flight leader.'

'Ah! The great Tayler Ian Oakley, crop duster extraordinaire, scourge of insect life, answers to no man or woman!'

He chuckled. 'No, it's not like that it's just... I'm getting tired of being told what to do. I want to be able to do what I want.'

'Did you not realise that there were such a thing as ranks when you joined the RAC? Of course you're going to get told what to do!'

She felt him shrug. 'I kind of thought that would just be on the ground. I thought I'd get to do what I wanted in the air...' he trailed off when he realised what he was saying. 'I'm being silly, aren't I?'

'Just a bit, but don't worry about it.' She reached up to stroke his face. 'It's one of the things I like about you. Now, shut up and kiss me.'

He groaned theatrically. 'You're giving me orders already!'

'Yes, I am. Any problem with that?'

'No, ma'am!'

28

Benedict received his chief fitter's salute with a nod. 'Good morning, aviator sergeant.'

'Good morning, sir.'

'Anything to report?'

'No, sir, everything is in tip-top shape. And congratulations on passing your officer exams, sir.'

'Thank you.'

Benedict frowned. The man was smiling far more than usual, his whole team was, for that matter. It was almost as if they were drunk, but the fitters at Galath were far too professional for that and wouldn't last a minute if they were found to have been drinking on duty. He looked down at his flightsuit, thinking maybe a bird had passed over and done its business without him noticing, but as far as he could tell he was as smartly turned out as always. It had to be something else. He couldn't for the life of himself figure out what, though.

'Is there something wrong, sergeant?'

'No, sir, nothing, sir.'

The man didn't stop smiling, though, and eventually Benedict just turned to his machine and started his checks, keeping an eye out for any surprises.

The mystery of the inane grins on his fitters wasn't solved, however, until he got to the cockpit and was brought up short, with one foot in and one foot out, by the sight of a new addition to his instrument panel.

'Sergeant!' he called, then almost toppled into the cockpit when he turned to find the man standing less than a foot away. 'What is this?' he asked, grabbing at the aircraft to steady himself.

'Squadron Leader's orders, sir.' He tilted his head towards the back of the aircraft and Benedict looked and saw Drake standing next to the rest of the fitters, grinning just as widely and stupidly as they were.

'Complements of Jocelyn Green and Miss Orpwood, Wilberforce! Enjoy!'

Drake waved and, laughing gently to himself, wandered off down the line of aircraft, leaving Benedict to flop down in his seat and contemplate his instrument panel, to which was now attached a small portrait of Sandra in a metal frame.

Far from being miffed about everyone going behind his back and playing a joke on him, he actually found himself quite pleased and, after the sergeant had strapped him in and stepped away, he reached out and stroked two fingers gently down the picture.

'Bandits!' Tay called out. 'Five o'clock high!'

Ellie squinted up into the sky over her right shoulder. They'd been watching out continuously, expecting to be bounced at any time, but there had been no sign of anyone on the way to the range and they were half way home now and had begun to think that it wasn't going to happen.

'Where? I don't... Alright, I've got them, Two. Well done. Keep an eye on them.'

'Roger. Shall we give them a call, let them know we've seen them?'

'That would certainly be funny, Two, however, I don't know about you, but I want to win that competition. Let's just keep going as if we haven't. We'll give them a little surprise of our own.'

Tay laughed. 'Roger that!'

'Here's the plan. Break when I say, but don't turn away, just finish the roll, push the throttle through the stops and chase after them. If they stay together so do we, if they split so do we. Got it?'

'Roger! Er... they're turning... they're coming down!'

Ellie craned her neck to peer up at the two aircraft plunging towards them. This was the delicate bit; if they broke too soon then the instructors would be able to adjust course and keep targeting them, but it they broke too late they would be able to "fire" on them and would fairly legitimately be able to claim they hadn't been seen until it was too late.

The steadily aircraft grew in size and her rational mind screamed at her to turn or it would be too late, but she suppressed it and instead used the instincts she'd developed with Tanya to judge the moment.

'Ready... Break!'

She jerked the stick diagonally backwards and the Spitsteam obeyed eagerly, thrusting her down hard in her seat as it corkscrewed around the sky. She kept rolling until she saw the enemy aircraft flash past, then she rightened herself and dived after them.

'Nicely done, Echo Leader,' Squadron Leader Niven's voice came over the radio, 'but can you finish the job?'

Tay completed the roll and pulled back onto Ellie's wing as they dived after the two Spits. He grinned; the manoeuvre had taken them by surprise and they weren't getting away as fast as they would otherwise been able to, which meant they wouldn't be able to just turn back whenever they wanted. They might even be close enough to get in a long range shot when they eventually did so.

He still wasn't quite over the fact that it was Ellie giving the orders and not him. After all, he had so much more experience than her. But at least she wasn't bossing him around all the time like Sandra had bossed Benedict around - now that had been funny! It was also just a bit galling that Ellie's idea had been so good and worked so well. He would never have thought to take such a risk.

He just hoped the enemy split up when they finally decided to do something, so he could get out of Ellie's shadow and win some points, and respect, for himself.

The Spitsteams were slowly drifting apart.

A clear challenge.

They had covered this eventuality in the tactical talks they'd had during dogfighting training. The enemy was presenting them with a choice - either stay together and go after one of them in the hope of taking them down before the other one came around behind them, or tackle one enemy each, trusting in their individual abilities to bring them through. That was oversimplifying the matter somewhat because so many other things needed taking into consideration when making a decision - the experience of the pilots, the damage they'd sustained, the possibility of allies or other enemies interfering, how much spring tension and ammunition they had left and so on - but that was the choice they would be faced with if this was a real life situation.

However, the most important thing to take into consideration at that moment, though, was that this was just an exercise and where would the fun be in staying together and going after them one at a time?

'Looks like we're splitting up, Two. Happy hunting!'

'Roger that, Leader. Tally ho!' Tay laughed gleefully. 'I've really been looking forward to saying that!'

Ellie gave him a last grin across the steadily widening gap, but then turned to concentrate on her enemy. It was impossible to know who it was. She knew that Squadron Leader Niven was one of the pilots, but not which aircraft he was in because she hadn't caught the registrations as they'd gone past, so it could just as well be any of the instructors. Including Tanya, for that matter; the Muscovite was supposed to have been keeping an eye on them, but they hadn't seen a single sign of her since takeoff. She'd know if it was her soon enough, though, because she'd seen her fly too many times not to recognise her style.

The gap between her and her opponent was no longer widening as they both had reached top speed in their identical machines. There was no reason to delay and whoever it was would undoubtedly do something soon, especially because if they didn't they'd have to call off the fight before it began because both she and Tay were beginning to run low on tension.

Even as she thought it, the aspect of the aircraft in front changed as it pulled up into a slight climb. She followed suit, pointing her nose above it in order to head it off, but only seconds later the aircraft pulled up again, this time incredibly sharply. As she watched in amazement, it almost instantly passed through the vertical and looped over to face back at her, rolling smartly to finish off the right way up.

It was a manoeuvre called an Immelmann, which she knew how to do very well. She just didn't know how to do it as fast as the enemy pilot had done it. Or even that it was even *possible* to do it that fast. The slight climb the pilot had done had bled off a little speed before they'd done it, but even so it must have had a huge effect on their body.

As she lined up for a proper head-on pass, not the practice ones she'd first done with Tanya, pointing her nose and guns straight at the enemy aircraft, she grinned. Whoever the pilot was and no matter whether she win or lost, she would learn something from this fight. And that was all that really mattered.

Although it would be nice to think she'd be able to teach the pilot a thing or too as well.

Tayler lost his dogfight, but Ellie's bout finished in a draw when she fought the pilot, who turned out to be Squadron Leader Niven, to a standstill before finally having to declare that she was too low on tension to continue.

As soon as Niven had ordered Ellie and Tayler home, Tanya finally appeared, screaming down out of the sky at what must have been close to six hundred miles per hour. As she flashed past, she crowed "got you Derek!" to which he answered "no you bloody didn't, I saw you coming a mile off!" before diving after her.

Rob and Benedict had arrived a few minutes before them and they convened in the pilot's ready room to compare their experiences over tea. The two were looking very glum, having both lost their dogfights handily, but perked up when Ellie and Tay told them that neither of them had won either.

Ten minutes later they heard Spitsteams arriving and a couple of minutes after that Tanya and Niven bounced in, talking animatedly about their fight, but they quietened down immediately when Drake whistled and beckoned them over to the sofa he'd claimed at the far end of the room. After a short whispered conference they stood and joined their students at the large table. Drake didn't sit down, though, instead he went to the wall at the side of the room where the maps and notices were pinned. There was a chalkboard there where temporary orders and messages and such were written. He wiped it off, then wrote their names along the top before turning to face them.

'It hasn't been as disastrous a start to our little competition as it has been for previous groups,' he said, smiling broadly, 'none of you has been killed without realising it, which is always a good thing, however,' he turned and chalked twos beneath the names of Benedict, Rob and Tay as he spoke, 'none of you have particularly distinguished yourselves either, which isn't exactly unexpected,' he paused, holding his chalk against the board under Ellie's name, 'except for Officer Perkins,' he painstakingly wrote the number four, 'who is awarded half a kill for a draw.'

He put the chalk in its holder and brushed his hands off as he came to the table and flopped into a chair.

'However,' he said, 'don't start getting complacent and thinking you've beaten the game. This was only the first round of many and our Fleas made it extremely easy for you this time round. The real Fleas don't and neither will ours from now on. The only advice I can give you is to expect the unexpected, but don't let it affect your training.' He nodded. 'Keep up the good work.'

The four pilots wandered out to their aircraft together, out of earshot of the instructors.

'"Expect the unexpected" he says,' Tay said with a grin. 'We've covered everything in the books and we've got better eyes than these old-timers. There's no way they're going to surprise us.'

Benedict nodded. 'Watch the sun and watch your six.'

'And don't fly past any really big clouds.' Tay said with a laugh.

'Break! Break!' Rob shouted into the radio, but the enemy aircraft were streaking past even as he did so.

'You're dead, gentlemen,' Niven's calm voice came over their headsets. 'But let's see if you can make some of those points back. Prepared for a head on pass.'

'Roger.' Rob said, before making sure his channel was closed and swearing like he'd never sworn before. *Where had they even come from?*

Ellie held her hand above her head, trying to block some of the sun so that she could scan as close to it as possible.

The middle of the day was when it was most dangerous for fighter pilots. The enemy, who liked to pounce with the advantage of height, could hide in the sun - approaching from an angle that put the sun behind them in relation to their prey. In the early morning or late evening they couldn't get such a clear advantage and it wasn't quite as useful a tactic, but for the rest of the day...

She'd thought she'd seen something a moment before. A dark spot against the bright blue. The suggestion of something that shouldn't have been there. She couldn't be sure, though, and now, because she'd been looking up into the glare for so long, she could barely see anything, let alone spot something as tiny as a fighter aircraft.

She brought her eyes down, blinked away tears as black splotches obscuring her vision. 'Your turn, Tay, I'll take over scanning, you see what...'

'RATATATATA!!!'

They stood in the ready room, staring sourly at the chalkboard.

'It's only the first day,' Ellie said. 'There's plenty of time to make up the score.'

Rob huffed. 'That's easy for you to say; one win, one draw and you've only been bounced once, so you're only at minus four. We're a bit further in the hole.'

'Minus sixteen!' Tay said, wincing exaggeratedly. 'Ouch!'

Benedict snarled at him, then stomped off.

Ellie watched him go. 'You know, I'm not sure this is exactly very good for morale.'

'What do you mean?' Tay asked, smirking at Benedict's back. 'I'm having a great laugh!' He clapped hands on her and Rob's shoulders. 'Come on, dinner time. I'm starving!'

'When are you not?' Rob countered, but nonetheless let Tay propel him in the direction of the barracks buildings.

29

'Are you sure you don't mind coming out here again?' Ellie asked as she helped Tay to lay out the blanket in front of the springcycle shed.

Of course I bloody do, Tay thought. He knew enough not to say so, though. 'Of course not!' he said, forcing a smile, even though it was so dark she would almost certainly not be able to see it.

Four nights they'd been coming to this crummy field. Granted, each night she let him go just that little bit further, but still, he was used to better results with girls after four minutes. Some of them after four seconds...

There were only so many cold showers he could take!

Worse than that, though, it was three days now that he'd been flying on her wing. Yes, she had some good ideas and good advice when he did something wrong and yes, he was second in the competition behind her, far ahead of Rob and Benedict and close to getting back into positive numbers, but he had no freedom. He was no closer to being able to fly how he wanted than he had been with Brunel. Further away in fact, now that he was stuck on her wing and had to do everything little thing how she wanted.

Maybe she'd loosen up if he showed her that there were other ways of doing things. Better ways.

He grinned. Yes, and maybe if he impressed her enough she might finally let him take her back to his room and he could show her that some things could *definitely* be a lot better than the way they were doing them.

'Approaching the entrance to the Loop, Two. Prepare to dive.'
'Roger, Leader.'

Ellie rolled her shoulders and rubbed her eyes gently, trying to get rid of the tension and some of the strain. It was extremely hard work constantly looking out for the enemy and small comfort that this was as hard as it would get, that things would be easier in a squadron or even a flight of four, when there would be more people looking out and the job could be shared.

Only four days into the week and she was already exhausted. She couldn't imagine how tiring it would be to be in a front line squadron, flying just as often, but with the added fatigue brought on by combat and the added strain due to losing friends. She needed to relax. Not necessarily sleep more, because she was getting plenty of that, but have some fun.

She huffed and smiled slowly; it was just as well her idea of fun usually coincided quite well with her job.

'Two?'
'Yes, Leader?'
'How about we push ourselves a bit today?'
'No complaints from me, Leader!'

Ellie grinned, then rolled Susie onto her back and pulled into a fairly steep dive, allowing her to pick up speed. She pointed her nose at the gap in the mountains as she rolled upright, but didn't throttle back like she normally would.

'Alright,' she said to herself. 'Three hundred and fifty miles per hour. That should make things a bit more interesting.'

They flew into the Loop, banking hard to come around the first mountain on the entrance and dropping down so they were fifty feet from the valley floor. The fastest she'd done the run so far was three hundred and twenty miles per hour, which was only thirty less, but it was amazing the difference those thirty miles per hour made. The mountainsides seemed to flash by so much faster, the turns came sooner and the ground looked suddenly perilously close.

It was exhilarating.

Tay groaned as Ellie led them through the first valleys. When she'd said they were going to push themselves he'd been elated, but this wasn't pushing things; they were barely going any faster than they usually did and weren't any lower.

He smiled slowly. Maybe this was his chance to show her how it could be done.

He pushed the nose down and the throttle forward a touch.

'I'm coming to get you, Ellie!' he said to himself as his aircraft slowly began to close the half mile gap with hers.

Ellie pulled hard around the hill and levelled off onto the long straight that marked the half-way point of the Loop. She used the breathing room it afforded her to take her eyes off the terrain and look up at the mirror above her head to check on Tay's progress. She didn't see him, though, and she used the rudder to move Susie's tail back and forth to look into the blind spot directly behind her, but he wasn't there either.

'Two? Still with me?'

'Roger, Leader. On your seven o'clock.'

Ellie craned her head to look back over her wing and eventually found Tay's aircraft, lower than hers and far closer than he was supposed to be.

'What are you doing, Tay? Pull up and get back into place!'

'Negative, Leader, I like the view much better down here. And unless you want me to overtake you, you should get a bit of a move on!'

Ellie gritted her teeth, but nonetheless pushed her throttle forward a touch to keep her distance from him, not wanting any risk of a collision while she made up her mind what to do.

She had three choices: pull up and abort the run, leaving him to follow her or not; let him overtake her and lead; or accelerate and play his game.

She had to admit, it was extremely tempting to push the throttle forwards and see how fast they could do the Loop, but she wasn't going to descend; he could play the daredevil if he wanted, she wasn't going to.

Whatever she decided, she had to do so quickly; the next turn was fast approaching.

She took a deep breath and smiled as she pushed the throttle forward.

Even as she did so she saw the birds.

Startled by the approaching aircraft, a flock of birds, big ones, ducks or geese or something, were lifting up into the air dead ahead of her. She was far too high for them to be any kind of danger to her but...

'Two! Watch out for the birds!'

The turn was there now and she put the Spit onto its wing and pulled around it, somehow finding the opportunity to look up and back as she did so, but the sheer rock face cut off her view of Tayler even as she found him.

She levelled off and went into the next short straight, her eyes glued to the mirror.

'Two! Come in, Two!'

Her eyes flicked to the sheer wall looming ever closer in front of her and, instead of making the next turn, she pulled up sharply, exiting the Loop and climbing into clear skies. She craned her neck and peered behind her, searching for some sign. 'Tay! Where are you? Tay!'

There was a crackle as the radio channel opened and she sighed in relief and slumped down in her seat, but it wasn't Tay's voice that came, it was Tanya's.

'Return to base, Echo Leader.'

'What?' she asked, incredulously. 'No! Tay's missing! He might have gone down, I have to...'

'Return to base. That's an order, Echo Leader. Return to base *now*!'

Ellie swallowed the lump that had suddenly appeared in her throat and blinked to clear vision that had clouded equally quickly before replying.

'Roger. Echo Leader returning to base.'

Ellie managed to keep herself together while she flew back to Galath. She managed to keep her voice level while she obtained permission to land and managed to get down off of the aircraft and hand it over to an ashen-faced Aviator Sergeant McIlroy without her legs giving way beneath her. It was only when she'd taken two steps towards the ready room and seen the look on Squadron Leader Drake's face that she allowed herself to sink to her knees and scream her despair at the sky.

30

When Ellie next became aware of anything, she found herself lying in a bed with crisp white sheets in a large white room. She turned her head, saw the rows of identical empty beds and realised she was in the medical centre. She didn't remember getting there, though.

'You're awake.'

Startled, turned her head the other way and found Tanya sitting on the bed next to hers. She struggled upright. 'You saw?'

Tanya nodded.

'Have they sent someone?' she said urgently. 'He might still be alive. They've got to look! He...!'

'Ellie stop.' Tanya said gently, but insistently. 'He hit the birds and went straight into the ground. His aircraft just disintegrated. It was so quick he wouldn't have even known it had happened. They've sent people to look, but there is no way he could have survived.'

Ellie collapsed back onto the bed and stared up at the ceiling.

'He's dead, then. He's really dead.'

'Yes.'

Ellie squeezed her eyes closed and turned her head away from Tanya.

'He is dead, but you are not.'

Ellie didn't answer and when she finally opened her eyes again, Tanya was gone.

Rob appeared soon after. Still dressed in his flightsuit and with his hair plastered to his head, he had obviously come as soon as he'd landed. He didn't seem too upset, though, and just stood at the foot of her bed looking down at her, his hands wringing the iron bars of her bed frame over and over.

'Rob, I'm so sorry.'

Rob shrugged. 'It's alright.'

'How is it alright?' Ellie asked, incredulously, pushing herself up on her elbows. 'Your best friend just...' her voice caught and she swallowed before forcing herself to continue. 'Just died!'

Rob lifted his eyes and stared out of the window over her bed. 'I always knew something like this would happen. That's why it's alright.' He shifted and brought his eyes back down to look at his white knuckles on the iron frame of the foot of her bed. 'I didn't think it would happen so soon, but a big part of me was also expecting it to happen years ago.' He sighed. 'He was always too reckless, too careless with what he did in the pursuit of excitement. In the air *and* on the ground.' He looked at her and smiled wryly. 'And you know what? I never ever thought it would be the Prussians who'd get him. I always knew it would be down to him. That it would be something he did. I can't tell you how many times over the last six years I must have pictured him ploughing into the ground crop dusting, or clipping a tree as he went past just a little too close. And since we joined up it's the same - holding on to a head-on pass too long, getting too close to the ground or the targets on a strafing run... It's always him doing for himself, though, never once did I imagine a Prussian fighter shooting him down; I guess I thought he was too good for that.'

He sighed and looked at her finally. 'What I'm trying to say is that it wasn't your fault, or my fault, or Drake's for putting him with you, or anyone else's. This was all Tay. And it was always going to happen. Sooner or later. At least he went doing what he loved; he wouldn't have wanted it any other way.'

He smiled weakly. 'Drake's let us off flying for the rest of the day so I thought I'd spend it drinking. Do you want to come?'

Ellie shook her head mutely, not trusting her voice.

Rob shrugged. 'Well, you know where I am if you change your mind.' He patted the iron frame decisively. 'See you, Ellie.' He turned and stomped away without looking back.

After Rob left, Ellie curled up and just lay there, staring at nothing, but it wasn't long before the door opened and Squadron Leader Drake came in. She struggled to sit up again, but he waved her back down and sat on the adjacent bed in exactly the same place Tanya had sat.

'How are you feeling?' he asked quietly.

Ellie had to think for a moment. She hadn't really taken any notice of her body. Or of her own basic needs for that matter. 'Numb, sir. Like it's not real.'

Drake nodded. 'It's my job to tell you that we are at war and people die all the time and that you should get back into the air, just like hundreds of other men and women have done before you. But I'm not going to do that; that is a good way of making uncaring, unfeeling machines who don't care about their own lives or anyone else's. We've lost too many people like that. We almost lost one of our best like that, in fact, and if we had that might actually have lost us the entire war.'

He looked away for a moment, composing himself, containing emotions that he hadn't let himself feel for a while.

'So, I'm not going to make you go back up until you feel you're ready. Take whatever time you need, even if that means not flying again for what remains of the course. It's not as if you'll be missing much, anyway; the meteo people say that there's a front moving in and it's probably going to be raining for a few days.'

'That's kind of you, sir. Thank you.' Ellie smiled weakly. Right at that moment she couldn't move, couldn't think, couldn't dream of getting back into a cockpit and facing... She balled her hands into fists and pressed them against her eyes as her mind suddenly began conjuring images of Tay's aircraft being ripped apart against the mountains. She struggled to draw in air, gasping and moaning as she relived the moment over and over, and shadows began to crowd around her, as if she were turning tightly.

'Just breathe, Ellie.'

Tanya's voice came from right beside her and Ellie would have jumped if she could have moved.

'Breathe.'

Strong, wiry arms wrapped around her and pulled her against an equally hard body as soft singing in a language she didn't know reached out to envelop and surround her, pushing back the visions. Ellie let herself melt into the embrace as she was rocked back and forth and slowly her breath started to come easier, the darkness fading.

Tanya held her for a moment more, then gave her a squeeze. 'Alright?'

'Yes. Thank you.'

The Muscovite released her and she rubbed her eyes then looked up into the concerned face of Drake.

'Sorry, sir. I'm not exactly in control of myself at the moment.'

'No need to worry.' Drake said. 'As I was saying, you have some time. Perhaps you'd like to go home? I could arrange a... Perkins? What's wrong?'

Ellie barely heard him; a wave of cold, like she'd stepped out into rain on a winter's day, had struck her at the possibility that she might be sent home.

It had been a while since she'd thought about her father and the life she'd left behind. She'd buried her past as deeply as she could in the last few weeks, refusing to acknowledge it to herself, or talk about it on those occasions when the subject had come up in conversation, even going so far as to rid herself of everything that reminded her of it until all she'd had left were scars and the few keepsakes of better times that she'd held onto, but the mere mention of it had brought all the pain, all the fear, all the despair that she'd lived through rushing back all at once.

The feeling drained away as quickly as it had come, though, leaving her calmer than she had been since Tay's death, and she slowly came to the realisation that her old life no longer had any kind of hold on her. But it wasn't because the memories weren't still painful or that she could ever contemplate going back - because they were and she couldn't - it was because that life was the reason why she was where she was. It was the reason why she had started flying. And for that she was grateful to it, in a strange way.

And she *would* continue to fly. Not because there was a war on, or because she wanted to stay with her friends, or because it was what Tay would want her to do, but for her. Because flying was her life now and it was the future she saw stretching out in front of her. For as long as her life lasted, at least.

She smiled.

'I'm fine, sir. Just fine.'

The meteo people had gotten it right and the rain came that night and closed operations down completely.

Rob, Benedict, Ellie and the instructors got on a bus after breakfast and were driven to RAC Gwynedd, where they were met by Group Captain Wyvern and Squadron Leader Trevillian who took them to the officer's mess for refreshments. Sandra, Lottie, Jemima and Franklin joined them there for a bittersweet reunion and they caught up on all their news over tea.

There would be a proper funeral for Tayler back in his home village at a later date, but the RAC had its own traditions and after a suitable time Group Captain Wyvern led a silent procession to the entrance hall of the main building. A piece of Duralumin, taken from a downed aircraft, had been shaped and engraved with Tayler's name and Wyvern brought forward Ellie, as Tayler's last wingmate, to stand on a stepladder and hammer it onto the wall, where it joined the dozens of plaques with the names of all those who had died during flight training at the various schools of the Officer Orientation College.

Nothing was said, even when the last echoes of the hammer's strikes had faded, the people there just took their time to remember Tayler in their own way before drifting away.

Eventually, only the seven of them remained, but then Benedict wandered off with Sandra, followed shortly by Lottie, Franklin and Jemima, leaving only Rob and Ellie.

Ellie reached out and fumbled her hand into Rob's and they held onto each other for comfort as they stared up at Tay's name.

'See you, Tay.' Rob whispered after an eternity. He gave her hand a squeeze, then peeled off and walked out with his head down and his hands in his pockets.

'Bye, Tay.' Ellie said, wiping away tears as she turned away and went after him.

Lunch was immediately afterwards in the officers' mess. As was the way of fighter pilots at war, once the goodbyes had been said it was time to move on. That didn't mean that people weren't still sad or affected by the loss, so lunch wasn't the jovial affair it usually was, but the conversation was at least more lively than it had been earlier. Ellie was sat between Tanya and Trevillian and the two pilots regaled each other with tales of her exploits, including her most embarrassing moments as a trainee pilot. Ellie wasn't bothered one bit, though; if two of the pilots she most admired in the world cared enough to talk about her for almost half an hour, who was she to complain?

As soon as the table was cleared, they moved to the bar, but they hadn't had time to order more than one drink before Squadron Leader Drake called for everyone's attention.

'Since the weather seems like it is going to be bad for a good few days, I have decided, in my great wisdom,' he paused because there were raspberries and laughter at that, 'and ultimate authority as the commander and creator of the Dogfight and Risk Training School to declare the current class's training as completed successfully and their operational status as active!'

There were cheers and the three pilots were thumped on the back and toasted.

When the noise died down Drake continued. 'As a result, I am kicking you off the base! As soon as we get back, I want you to pack your things and say your goodbyes because you won't ever be coming back.' He held up a piece of paper.

'I've just got off the blower with a good friend of mine in London and I've booked you three rooms in his little hotel, The Dorchester, overlooking Hyde Airstrip. Today is the sixteenth. You'll take the sleeper from Liverpool to London tonight and have three days leave. Have a dance, take in the sights, see a show, drink yourselves silly if you want to, just try not to get yourselves arrested. Tickets and travel orders will be left for you and on the twentieth you'll take the express train to Scotland for final operational training before joining a squadron.'

He grinned at them. 'Congratulations. As of now you are no longer trainees, but fully-fledged RAC pilots on active duty. And I'm going to be the first to buy you a drink.'

EPILOGUE

'This way *please*, ladies and gentlemen!' the aviator sergeant called out, struggling to make himself heard over the surprisingly loud noise the five men and women were making. Recent graduates of the full eight-month course at Gwynedd, they had boarded the bus with Ellie, Rob and Benedict in Glasgow. Still celebrating the fact that they were the few members of their class who had qualified to become fighter pilots, they had already been in various stages of inebriation and had proceeded to drink, sing and generally make far too much noise during the entire two hour journey.

One of the airmen helping the new arrivals with their bags stopped in front of them and saluted. 'The commander would like you to wait here a moment, if you wouldn't mind?'

He didn't wait for an answer, but just hurried off to grab a kitbag.

Once the rowdy mob had been escorted into a nearby building, the three of them sighed in relief, glad to see them go for at least a while, and turned to look at the base which would be their home for the next couple of weeks.

'Well, it's not The Dorchester,' Benedict said with a wry smile.

The best word to describe the base would be *bleak*. The next best *uninviting*.

The scenery on the journey north from Glasgow had been just as spectacular as it had been on their various journeys through Wales, but far less pastoral and far more rugged, with grey being the predominant colour rather than green. The base was the same. The buildings weren't purpose built, like the other bases they'd been on, but were made of dull grey stone and looked old and worn, like they'd been there for some time. They looked like they'd be very cold in the winter.

'Sorry to disappoint you.'

A woman was stomping towards them from the biggest building and they drew themselves up straight at the sight of the stripes on her sleeves.

'Bloody hell,' Rob muttered under his breath even as he saluted.

'No, it's not The Dorchester, but it serves its purpose.' The woman came to a halt in front of them and peered at them thoughtfully. 'Rudy said you were young, but...' she shook her head, smiling wryly as she returned their salute. 'Welcome to RAC Taymouth. I'm Squadron Leader Bagshot, commanding officer.'

So that's why Rob was so surprised, Ellie thought, her eyes straying down to the woman's legs before she could stop them. She lifted them in a hurry and found Bagshot, *Lady* Bagshot, she corrected herself, looking directly at her.

'Don't worry, Officer Perkins, they don't bite. And I don't often kick.' She winked. 'Now, before we get you settled in, a friend of mine would like to have a quick word.'

She looked over her shoulder and they noticed that there were two more officers behind her, standing in front of the building.

'Bloody hell!' Rob hissed.

Even Ellie knew who these women were; it would be hard not to, as they were two of the most famous women in the country.

While the face of Abby Lennox, the commander of the Misfits, had seemingly been plastered over more newspapers and magazines than the king's, the second woman was more recognisable by her physical appearance; the combination of red hair, short stature and tight flightsuit could only add up to one person - Ophelia "Scarlet" Flynn, also one of the Misfits.

'Good afternoon.' Lennox said, smiling at them. 'I can see that you all know who I am, but what you don't know is why I'm here. It's very simple - as of yesterday, Misfit Squadron has been ordered to reform and I find myself in need of a few pilots. Squadron Leader Drake recommended that I come and look at the three of you and I have. You will have all day tomorrow to impress me in the air. And I sincerely hope that you do.'

She looked at them earnestly, meeting their eyes one by one. 'This is your chance to really make a difference in this war. Don't waste it.' She nodded at Squadron Leader Bagshot. 'They're all yours.'

Lennox spun on her heel and marched away, but the other Misfit, Scarlet, took the time to wink at them, before sauntering after her.

'Bloody hell!' Rob said again.

This time Ellie couldn't help but agree with the sentiment.

ABOUT THE AUTHOR

Simon Brading's interest in aviation began when he was very young and at thirteen he joined the RAF section of the Combined Cadet Forces of Dulwich College with the aim of becoming a pilot. However, when he was 18, had reached the rank of Flight Sergeant in the CCF and was trying to get into a University Air Squadron, he was told that his eyesight wasn't good enough to be a pilot, so he had to move onto plan B... something else.

He tried his hand at many things before it occurred to him that he might have a few stories to tell. He never lost his interest in flight, though, and hopes to add a PPL to his very basic and probably extremely expired glider license.

www.simonbrading.co.uk

For news of special offers, upcoming releases, exclusive content, competitions and events, please follow me on social media.

Instagram - @sibrading
Facebook - Simon Brading Author
Tiktok - @SimonBradingAuthor

In addition, souvenirs and merchandise, including T-shirts, badges, stickers and more, are available from the Misfit Squadron store on REDBUBBLE at -
https://www.redbubble.com/people/misfitsquadron/shop

ALSO BY SIMON BRADING

The "Displacers" series - a time travel adventure series for all ages.
The Pirate's Heir
The Secret of the Ancients
The Whitechapel Plot
The Price of Greed
The Time for Vengeance

The "Misfit Squadron" Series - a Steampunk series set in an alternate World War 2.
The Battle Over Britain
The Russian Resistance
A Misfit Midwinter
The Lion and the Baron
The Maltese Defence
Tales from the Second Great War
The Siege of Gibraltar
The King's Mission
The Home Front
Taking to the Skies

The Dismal Futures books - stand-alone science fiction tales suitable for adults.
Empath
The Lifeboat at the End of the Universe

The "Twin Ambitions" series - ballet books for children ages 7 and up.
Fight to Dance
Back to Basics

The "Ni Hon - The Two Books" Series - a young adult series set in a dystopian future Japan.
The Black Book

Others
Public Enemy

www.ingramcontent.com/pod-product-compliance
Lightning Source LLC
Chambersburg PA
CBHW030615170726
48283CB00002B/609